Duncan Falconer is a former member of Britain's elite Special Boat Service and 14 Int., Northern Ireland's top-secret SAS undercover detachment. After more than a decade of operational service he left the SBS and went into the private security 'circuit'. His first book, the best-seller *First Into Action,* documented the real-life exploits of the SBS. His three subsequent books, *The Hostage, The Hijack* and *The Operative,* follow the fictional exploits of SBS operative Stratton. *The Protector* is his fourth novel.

In the last few years Falconer has operated at length and often alone in places such as Afghanistan, Palestine, Liberia and throughout Iraq. He now lives anywhere between his three bases in England, North America and South Africa.

'A gripping and authentic view of life and death in the dangerous world of private protection by someone who has been there and worn the T-shirt'

Soldier Magazine

The Protector

Duncan Falconer

sphere

SPHERE

First published in Great Britain in 2007 by Sphere
This paperback edition published in 2007 by Sphere

Copyright © Duncan Falconer 2007

The moral right of the author has been asserted.

A CIP catalogue record for this book
is available from the British Library.

ISBN 978-0-7515-3632-4

Papers used by Sphere are natural, recyclable products made from
wood grown in sustainable forests and certified in accordance with
the rules of the Forest Stewardship Council.

Typeset in Bembo
by Palimpsest Book Production Limited,
Grangemouth, Stirlingshire
Printed and bound in Great Britain by Clays Ltd, St Ives plc
Paper supplied by Hellefoss AS, Norway

Sphere
An imprint of
Little, Brown Book Group
100 Victoria Embankment
London EC4Y 0DY

An Hachette Livre UK Company
www.littlebrown.co.uk

To Ricky

1

Mallory's Treasure

The Royal Navy Search and Rescue Sea King helicopter flew low and fast over the flat grubby desert, all eyes in the cockpit focused on a thin trail of black smoke half a mile ahead. Beyond it was a blurred collection of dilapidated dwellings on the other side of a road that marked the northern edge of the town of Fallujah that was a short flight west of Baghdad. Visibility was poor in every direction, a fine dust filling the air like smog and with more trails of carbon smoke dotting the hazy landscape like plumes from the stacks of distant steamships, columns of dark vapour bending gently on a south-easterly breeze. The pilot was tracking a signal that had its focus point a little to the left of the closer, finer plume. It was on an emergency bandwidth emitted by a radio in the hands of a British Tornado pilot whose aircraft had been shot down in the last twenty minutes.

Royal Marine Corporal Bernard Mallory stood beside his Royal Navy partner, Petty Officer Mac Davids, in the narrow doorway that connected the cabin to the cockpit. At thirty, Mac was a couple of years older than Mallory, a head taller and not as strongly built but a hundred yards faster in a mile race. Mallory pushed the inside of his helmet against his ear as he strained to listen to the weak, intermittent radio message from the Tornado pilot who was answering the co-pilot's request for his situation report.

'All I want to know, for Christ's sake, is if the area is hot or not,' the pilot said, a little tense, more to himself than to anyone else. His eyes darted back and forth across the range of his vision, looking for any sign of a threat that he knew was out there somewhere. It would not have been this crew's normal responsibility to carry out the rescue of a downed pilot in hostile territory. That task usually went to Special Forces flights and the rescue crews were normally made up of SAS and SBS operatives. But when the distress call came in none were immediately available and Samuels, the Sea King pilot, a gung-ho type who had missed the first Gulf War by only a couple of months, elected to at least check the level of hostility. The duty watch officer running the operations desk had allowed him to give it a go but only if there was zero enemy ground activity.

Mac and Mallory had exchanged glances when they'd first heard their boss's request to do a recce, knowing his hankering for a bit of the excitement whose lack he had been complaining of. His appetite was more urgent now that the war was fast coming to an end.

The tension in the helicopter increased perceptibly as Samuels took some lift out of the rotors and dropped the heavy beast to a couple of hundred feet above the ground. They were now exposed not only to anti-aircraft guns and rockets but also to small-arms fire.

2

In the back of everyone's mind was the questionable logic of risking the lives of four men to save just one but that was a danger they had accepted before joining the search-and-rescue service. This was the wrong time to dwell on it anyway but the arithmetical reasoning was more acute at this stage of an operation.

Mallory stepped back from the cockpit doorway, pulled his black-tinted sunshade visor down, gripped the heavy handle of the large side door and yanked it across on its runners until it engaged the catch that locked it open. The wind charged in aggressively, ravaging every inch of the cabin and tossing around anything that could not hold firm against it. He held on to the winch above to lean out and get a better look to starboard while Mac went to a port-side window.

Mallory looked down at the arid ground a hundred feet below as it shot past: dirty gold sand with a sprinkling of black giving way to sparsely cultivated patches of bracken-like vegetation, a track with a battered pick-up trundling along it, a line of parched, dust-coated eucalyptus trees, a herd of scattering goats with the shepherd boy twisting in their midst to look up at him. What sounded like far-off explosions were barely discernible above the noise of the engines and rotors chopping the air and except for the handful of distant smoke columns he could see little evidence of the heavy air assault taking place in the southern part of the town.

The Sea King had originally been on its way to an American base – confidently named 'Camp Victory' – at Baghdad International Airport on the west side of the city when they'd picked up the downed pilot's distress call. Soon after diverting from their course and picking up the location of the emergency beacon they heard the Tornado pilot's voice confirming that he was alive. The level of Iraqi resistance in the area was unknown since there were no coalition troops close enough to make that assessment. But it was believed to be light since the main ground-fighting in the sector was concentrated further south on the Baghdad side of Fallujah. The Iraqi military had for the most part disintegrated. Isolated groups of Republican Guard were putting up a token resistance in places but the back of the enemy had been broken and the majority of the army had abandoned their weapons and uniforms. However, a lone helicopter close to the ground was an irresistible target to any Iraqi who still had a gun. One lucky shot could turn the rescue mission into a fight for survival. That danger would only increase when the moment came to hover close to the ground and pick up the downed pilot.

A loud *thwack*, like the noise of a stone striking the helicopter's thin metal fuselage, made everyone start. The pilot banked the lumbering whale of a craft as sharply as it could go, the rotors complaining loudly as he put excessive torque on the engines.

'What was that?!' he shouted.

Mallory instinctively ducked back into the cabin, suspecting that it had been a bullet. Then, gritting his teeth, he leaned back outside to inspect the helicopter's body and saw a small hole only a couple of feet from him, towards the tail. 'Got a strike low on the cabin skin below the numbers,' he shouted into his mike against the wind. He looked inside for the corresponding hole but could not see anything: wrinkled padding and a row of folded hammock seats obscured the inside wall. 'From what I can see we're fine,' he said, guessing while looking at the other side of the cabin for an exit hole. He didn't find one. Mac scanned the roof for any sign of damage, then went back to the port-side window.

The immediate question on everyone's mind was if the attack constituted a high enough level of danger to abort the mission. They all knew that as far as operational procedures were concerned the answer was affirmative – but the important issue was whether Samuels agreed.

Any indecision the Sea King pilot might have had evaporated when the Tornado pilot's voice broke through to say that he could hear them. Samuels reacted by pulling the chopper's nose back around and on track towards the emergency beacon.

Mallory spotted several puffs of smoke above a low wall, giving away the firing position of a machine gun that he could not hear above the helicopter's engine noise. 'Contact starboard! Four o'clock! Four hundred!' he shouted. Samuels responded with another violent turn as a bright-orange tracer flew across the front of his windshield, heading skyward.

Mallory checked the outside of the craft again as best he could, hanging on tightly against the torque, then looked inside for signs of damage before stepping back and going to the cockpit door to see how his crew were doing. 'Everything looks OK,' he said, seeing that they were fine. But Samuels ignored him as he gripped his steerage and power controls while the co-pilot's hands whipped from one instrument button to the next, flicking switches and turning dials.

'Systems functional,' the co-pilot said as he turned off an engine alarm that had been triggered by the violent manoeuvring and tapped a gauge that had gone into the red: he did not seem overly concerned about it. He threw Samuels a couple of anxious glances in between his checks, wondering if his boss still intended to press on. But with no response from the pilot other than a fixed expression of concentration the answer for the moment appeared to remain affirmative.

Mallory was confident in his crew, having been with them for more than three months, and he went back to the external cabin door to maintain his surveillance. He had no say over their actions anyway and he had his own responsibilities. Being the only soldier on board, and a Royal Marine no less, he felt an inherent duty to be the cool-headed bulwark of the team. That was not to say that the others weren't up to the task. But as a Marine he was expected to be a stalwart. There was no doubt in Mallory's heart that he would uphold the pride of the Corps as well as his own if called upon. But this was the first time he had been under direct enemy fire and as the adrenalin coursed through his veins anxiety accompanied it. He was on his guard as he ventured into this level of fear for the first time, not truly knowing how he would react. Crouched in the open doorway of such

6

a large, lumbering and attractive target he felt vulnerable as well as helpless to defend himself. His SA-80 assault rifle was secured in a bracket on the bulkhead behind him but grabbing it to engage an enemy he could not accurately see was pointless. More importantly, his crew would not appreciate him turning the rescue craft into a gunship unless there were clearly no other options.

Mallory had been a bootneck for six years and since graduating from Lympstone Commando Training Centre had spent most of that time in a fighting company of 42 Commando based in Plymouth. But six months after a long-awaited transfer to Recce Troop (42 Commando's reconnaissance team), the most expert fighting group in a commando unit, he tore a ligament in his knee playing rugby. To add to his disappointment he was transferred to the Regimental Sergeant Major's staff in the Company Headquarters to keep him employed during his rehabilitation, not an uncommon post for the walking – or hobbling – wounded. Then, at the outbreak of war, shortly before he was declared fit for duty, his boss read out an e-mail to the office from Naval Command requesting search-and-rescue volunteers. Mallory knew that he would not be able to slip back into his Recce Troop slot within the immediate future. His position had been filled and all he could hope for was to get back on the standby list. Therefore, when he heard the request for search-and-rescue volunteers, a somewhat specialised position, he asked immediately to be considered for the post. Mallory had never previously had aspirations of that nature. Being a part of a helicopter crew had not entered his head before that day. But his decision to volunteer was encouraged by rumours that few if any members of 42 Commando, including the Recce Troop, would join the war, at least the planned early stages of it. Having missed out on the fight in Afghanistan he desperately wanted the opportunity to see action.

The RSM agreed to put Mallory's name forward and within a week he received his acceptance notice. But by the time he had finished the training he had come to doubt the course he had chosen. Rumours abounded that the navy search-and-rescue squadron he was being attached to had little chance of seeing action since only Special Forces rescue teams would be permitted to operate in hostile areas. And for the early stages of the war that had been how it had panned out.

But now that Mallory was heading into the thick of it, having taken a bullet strike already, the old adage 'Be careful what you wish for' sprang to mind.

The Sea King pilot swung the heavy craft in a wide arc away from the source of the gunfire. But once again, as the downed Tornado pilot's voice came over the speakers sounding increasingly desperate as he claimed to have the helicopter in sight, Samuels brought the nose back around.

'I'm showing green smoke,' the downed pilot said, the quality of the communication suddenly better than it had been.

It was now obvious to all that short of a seriously

damaging strike against the Sea King they would not abandon the desperate stranger. The man had fully committed himself by igniting a smoke grenade and would stay close to it, well aware that it could also attract the enemy.

Mallory strained to look through the haze and saw the puff of dark green that was quickly billowing into a substantial cloud in front of a collection of huts several hundred metres from the black smoke that marked the Tornado pilot's crash site. It indicated that the pilot was at least able to move.

Before Mallory could report the sighting he heard Samuels confirm to the downed pilot that he had the smoke visual. They were going in.

Mac joined Mallory in the doorway and both men checked that they had their 9mm pistols in holsters at their sides. The pair contemplated their next move. They glanced at each other, looking for signs of weakness, any talk unnecessary. Mallory forced a grin from which Mac appeared to take little reassurance.

Mac pushed his mike aside and moved his mouth closer to Mallory's ear. 'You ever read "Rendezvous with Death"?' he shouted above the noise.

'What?' Mallory shouted, having heard Mac's question but then unsure if he had done so correctly.

'"Rendezvous with Death." You ever read it?'

'No, but I think I saw the film,' Mallory replied.

Mac rolled his eyes. 'It's a poem.'

'I must've missed that one,' Mallory replied sarcastically. He had never read a poem in his life and suddenly felt a tinge of inferiority. It was not an uncommon feeling for him. Mallory envied servicemen who'd had a good education. It made him want to improve himself in that regard but he had never made the effort. His excuse was the company he kept: fellow bootnecks. A commando unit was not the ideal environment in which to cultivate culture. 'Sounds a bit dramatic,' Mallory shouted, regretting his initial sarcasm.

'First World War,' Mac shouted. 'You should read it.'

Mallory didn't dwell on the matter and concentrated on catching a glimpse of the Tornado pilot.

'Stand by,' Samuels warned over the radio as they drew closer and dropped lower towards the green smoke that was moving along the ground in the breeze before rising and spreading out. Mallory eyeballed the medical pack strapped to the bulkhead near the door as he adjusted his bulletproof jacket. The plates that covered his chest and back were heavy but he had worn them for so long now that they felt like a part of him. He went over the procedure and his responsibilities that they had rehearsed endlessly back in the UK as well as when they'd arrived in Iraq. This was the second live rescue he had taken part in but the other one had not taken place under fire. Although Samuels was bringing the helicopter in as fast as he could it felt as if they were moving through the air like a barrage balloon.

The Sea King suddenly shuddered heavily as Samuels increased the pitch and brought the nose up sharply to slow the massive aircraft. Mallory and Mac reacted by crouching in the doorway, their hands firmly gripping the sides of the opening as they leaned out, hoping that the Tornado pilot would reveal himself.

The ground was close enough for Mallory to pick out fine details such as a goat lying near a bush. The animal must have been dead because the others had scattered. Mallory disconnected the communication cord from his helmet as he got ready to exit the craft.

The down draught of the helicopter's rotor blades hit the ground with tremendous force and just as Mallory caught sight of a man in a grey one-piece flight suit scurrying from behind one of the buildings the dust rose up to mix with the green smoke and obscured his view. Mallory studied the ground as it drew closer, calculating the best moment to jump. It was an exhilarating feeling, getting ready to abandon the safety of the craft to leap into the unknown.

The Sea King jolted as it turned through ninety degrees, its tail majestically sweeping around, its rotors blowing all before them, before dipping a little as it came to a wavering halt. Samuels was positioning his cabin door to face the Tornado pilot, a sign that he too had seen the man and was giving his boys the shortest route and ensuring that they would not have to run around the 'copter's nose or tail.

Mallory estimated that he was a body's length from the ground and jumped out of the doorway, hitting the packed sand hard. He dropped to one knee, his outstretched hands only just stopping him from falling on his face. He cursed himself for not allowing for the added weight of his body armour and equipment. As Mac landed beside him he pushed himself up and, though all he could see ahead was swirling dust and

11

green smoke, he ran on into it, knowing that the downed Tornado pilot was somewhere beyond.

As Mallory emerged a few paces ahead of Mac, his mouth and the back of his throat coated in dust, he saw the pilot on his knees the length of a tennis court ahead and wondered why he was not running towards them. As Mallory closed the distance the pilot wobbled as he got to his feet, one of his legs unable to support him – it was clear the man had an injury.

Mallory glanced left and right for any sign of the enemy as he covered the last few metres. He threw an arm around the pilot's back as Mac grabbed him from the other side.

'You OK?' Mallory shouted.

'Did something to my bloody leg on landing,' the pilot said in a refined English accent, his breathing laboured. 'Just get me going and I'll be fine,' he added, displaying a strength of character as he clung on to both men's shoulders.

Mac and Mallory part-carried, part-dragged him back towards the dust storm as he tried to put his weight on his good leg when he could.

A shot rang out close by, followed by another. The three men kept up their pace as Mallory looked in the direction of the firing, an action made difficult due to the pilot's arm wrapped tightly around his neck. More bullets ripped into the sand in front of them and as the men responded by increasing their speed Mallory was struck by what felt like a hammer blow to his right foot. It was followed by a searing, burning pain. His leg gave way as if the nerves had been severed and he dropped, unable to stop himself.

The pilot released him and Mac slowed to look back for his partner. 'Mallory!' he cried.

'I'm OK,' Mallory shouted as he got to his feet. 'Keep going! Keep going!'

Mac saw him stand and obeyed, taking the pilot's weight onto his hip and pushing on into the swirling dust and smoke.

Mallory took a step but his leg gave way and he dropped to the ground again. The limb seemed to be losing its strength near his hip, as if a major nerve had been severed, even though the wound appeared to be in his foot. He pulled himself up, forcing his wounded leg ahead of him in an effort to kick-start it back into action. But a painful spasm short-circuited the muscles and it buckled again. He looked up from the ground to see Mac and the pilot disappear into the dust storm and with a growling shout intended to inspire a supreme effort he pushed himself up once again. It appeared to have the desired effect but as he moved forward the ground immediately in front of him exploded in a series of bullet strikes from a machine gun close by and a round slammed into the side of his helmet, throwing him over like a rag doll. It was as if he had been kicked in the head by a bull and his vision blurred.

Mallory's animal will to survive took charge and he staggered to his feet once more. But as he lurched towards the helicopter another swarm of bullets spat around him. His subconscious screamed at him to take cover and he dived towards a low wall, misjudging the distance and hitting the top of it. As another volley struck the wall beside him he slipped over the top to fall hard on to his back. The voice in his head continued to cry out for him to move and he crawled as fast as he could, scurrying on his belly like an alligator, every limb pushing and clawing at the dirt, keeping his head and backside low. He reached a small gap in the wall and caught a glimpse of the helicopter inside its shroud of dust – the green smoke had dissipated now that the dispenser was exhausted. The seconds were ticking away and Mallory knew that the Sea King would lift off as soon as Mac and the pilot were on board. They had to. The extraction had turned hot and the chopper pilot had a responsibility to the others.

Mallory braced himself to get up and run towards the craft but as he raised his body and brought his good leg beneath him the Sea King's screaming engines powered up to the max and the rotor-driven sand-storm intensified. The hub of the 'copter's blades then emerged from the top of the dust cloud. The craft followed its nose in a tight turn before straightening up as it continued to rise, gaining speed with every second. The nose dipped as the helicopter moved away from Mallory, the aircraft banking to one side and then the other like a fish trying to avoid a shark snapping at its tail. Mallory was compelled to stare at it, partly in disbelief and partly hoping that it would turn in an arc to come back for him. But deep down he knew that it had gone for ever and a voice inside his head urged him to run . . .

Mallory could hear his own heavy breathing as the sound of the chopper's engines faded. He scanned around, assessing his options, and saw his only way out: the collection of buildings where the Tornado pilot had originally hidden. He dropped to the ground and scrambled as far as he could on his stomach away from the wall, keeping it between him and the original source of the gunfire. But Mallory was moving far too slowly and, unable to bear it, he leaped to his feet, gritted his teeth against the pain in his leg and ran for all he was worth. The nerves in his hip seemed to have rediscovered their connections and he got into his stride. But he had covered barely a dozen metres when he was struck by a fierce blow to his back that punched him forward with the force of a flying sledgehammer and he sprawled in the sand. Mallory did not pause to speculate about what had happened nor about his condition. If he was alive he would keep going and if he was seriously wounded he would not be able to. He pushed himself up and onward and another round whistled past him. He dived over a waist-high wall as several bullets struck it and he rolled ungracefully onto his knees. Then, pushing off like a sprinter starting a race, he propelled himself forward, straightening up as he gained speed, and ran as if the very hounds of hell were snapping at his heels.

Mallory arrived at the first building and skidded around the corner where a dirt street separated two blocks of shacks opposite. Not a soul was about: the only movement that caught his eye was a goat wandering along the street. He sped across the gap, the pain shooting up his leg which he fought to control.

As he ran down the line of dilapidated buildings he reached for his holster, finding the pistol and wrapping his hand around the grip, his thumb pushing aside the Velcro tab that held it in place. He pulled the gun free. His feet lost traction on some slimy garbage as he made a sharp change in direction into an alleyway but hitting the far corner wall helped him to regain his balance. He jumped over a mound of trash and charged on through a long puddle of rancid water, close to slipping several times. But his momentum kept him going. Unable to look back as he ran in case he lost his footing, a strangely euphoric feeling spread through him. Perhaps it was the release of endorphins into his bloodstream, or the buzz of fear itself. Whatever the cause he suddenly felt he had the wings of Mercury on his heels. But the high was not enough to kill the pain in his leg or lighten the reality of his position. Although the shooting appeared to have stopped he had to believe that the bullets could fly his way again at any second.

A woman carrying a bundle suddenly stepped from a doorway and, unable to change direction, Mallory slammed into her with such force she hit the wall of her house and bounced off it to fall flat on her back in the dirt. Mallory hardly felt the impact: his weight, more than twice hers with his body armour, and the kinetic force of his speed must have been like having a horse hit her. Mallory kept on going without a backward glance, every sense concentrated ahead.

The end of the dead-straight alleyway was still some distance away and Mallory's fear of being shot from behind became more intense. Unable to bear it any longer he slammed on the brakes and swerved into the opening of a hut, bouncing off the wall as he fell in and slipping onto his side on the dirt floor. He got to his feet right away, hunched in a stoop because of the low ceiling, and spun in a circle, gun held tight in a two-handed grip, ready to shoot, gulping in air as perspiration flowed, his eyes straining to see into the darkened corners. The room looked like someone's home: rugs, cushions and cooking implements were laid out as if the occupants had recently departed in a hurry. An opening in the opposite wall, looking as if it had been fashioned with a sledgehammer, led to an adjoining room and Mallory moved to look inside. It was another living quarters, with blankets and pillows on the floor, its walls bare but for a jagged hole high up that served as a window.

Mallory was breathing heavily and he removed his helmet, feeling stifled by it. He wiped away the sweat that was flowing into his eyes as he moved into the smaller room where he jumped up and held onto the edges of the opening to take a look outside. It was another narrow alleyway like the one he had just run down but the point was that it was a different one. He tossed his helmet out, pulled himself up, wriggled through like a maggot and dropped hands first without dignity onto the mucky ground outside. As he got to his feet and picked up his helmet the pain shot through his leg again and he part-jogged, part-limped along the cramped passageway. He checked behind him every few paces, anxious to increase the distance from his landing place but at the same time mindful of the risks of remaining out in the open. Moving increased the chance of running into other dangers and the wisest option was to find somewhere to hide. That would also give him time to formulate a plan, sort himself out and, most importantly, open up communications with his people.

A wrecked car blocked the end of the alleyway, as if someone had once tried to drive it through, got stuck between the buildings, given up and left it to rot. Tatty flat-roofed mud huts lined either side of the alley and just before Mallory reached the car a gap appeared on his right as if one of the buildings had collapsed. He slowed as he reached it, his gun held in front of him, and turned the corner into what looked like a small yard surrounded by buildings on three sides. Each had an opening although only one had a door, fragile and battered, which Mallory opted for since it offered concealment. He approached it stealthily with his pistol leading the way and eased it open, helmet in his other hand, and looked inside. It was dark with no windows and he quickly moved into the room, stepping away from the doorway and out of sight in case someone passed. The air was musty, smelling like rotten rags, and the room did not look as if it had been recently used, although there were some signs of a previous occupation: cooking pots, wooden boxes containing what appeared to be rusty electrical fittings, a stripped engine block and an assortment of other junk. A rug covered a large portion of the dirt floor but like everything else in the place it was decomposing and caked in dust.

Mallory closed the door and, feeling overheated, took a moment to get some air. He would have liked to undo his bulletproof jacket to let the air circulate around his sweating body but he knew better than to relax. His injured foot was throbbing and he allowed himself the luxury of squatting on a log for a moment to stretch out his legs and ease the pain. He moved the injured foot into a shaft of sunlight coming in through a crack in the door and inspected it. There was a hole through the instep of the sand-coloured suede boot with a corresponding one on the other side, a dark bloodstain around both. But there was no sign of blood leaking from the wound at that moment. A bullet had passed through the fleshy part of the sole of his foot but it had missed the bone or at worst had only grazed it. An inch higher and the outcome of his escape might have been different, not that it was by any means a done deal at the moment.

The foot grew more painful as blood was allowed to circulate more freely through it and Mallory contemplated removing the boot to put a dressing on it. He had a small medical pack on his belt but the risk was too great. And the boot might be difficult to get back on if his foot swelled. If it had been bleeding he might have taken the chance but no one ever died from pain, he mused, and decided to forget about it. The worst that could happen to it now was infection and that would take days before it showed.

He picked up his helmet which gave no ballistic protection and inspected the entry and exit holes in the top of it. He felt the top of his head in case it had been nicked by the bullet and though it was soaked a check of his fingers revealed only sweat – no blood. He had been lucky there, too – an inch lower and it would have been curtains. He reached around his back to search for the third bullet strike in his body armour, his finger finding the hole in the shock-absorbent powdery material that had done its job. Mallory had used up a lot of luck so far but he was going to need more if he wanted to make it home in one piece. The thought of what he needed to do to get out of this mess was depressing and he considered his options for escape.

The first thing he had to do was set up communications to let his people know he was alive and where he was. He removed his standard-issue SARBE emergency search-and-rescue radio and beacon from its pouch on his belt. It was a waterproof and robust device no bigger than a cigarette pack, and he checked it for damage. He turned it to the radio function long enough for a light to flicker – indicating sufficient power – before turning it off and putting it back in its pouch. This was not the place to send his emergency signal. Mallory needed to be in a secure open area for any rescue craft to land.

He checked his watch. The ideal location for a pick-up was outside the town and that meant waiting until dark. The Tornado pilot had initiated his beacon immediately because he was in dire straits but Mallory had a responsibility to ensure the rescue team's safety as well as his own. That meant he had to find a safe landing site.

Mallory was parched, his mouth dry as a bone, but he had no water. Adding a bottle to his belt kit was something he had considered but decided against, limiting the amount of equipment he carried to enhance his mobility.

Mallory's eyes gradually became accustomed to the dim light and he noticed a dirty sheet that was hanging on a couple of nails on the opposite wall and that appeared to cover a hole. He got to his feet, ignoring a stab of pain from his stiff foot, limped over to the sheet and moved it aside. The roughly hammered hole was an entrance to a smaller, darker room that seemed to be filled with more junk. He removed a small pencil light from a pouch and switched it on. The light revealed a weapons store, an Aladdin's Cave of armaments: dozens of AK47 assault rifles, RPG7 hand-held rocket launchers and an assortment of metal ammunition boxes. Mallory's first thought was to get out of there, imagining that the owners of such an important storage facility might not be far away. But on the other hand a high-velocity rifle would be more useful in a fight than his pistol.

He stepped inside, allowing the sheet to drop back across the opening, and took a closer look at the cache. There were hundreds of AK47 magazines, many of them filled with bullets, and inside an open ammunition box were several pistols. On closer inspection much of the ordnance turned out to be old and rusty, while the wooden stocks and butts on some of the AK47 rifles were badly damaged. Mallory holstered his pistol to inspect an AK47 that looked in better condition than the others and carefully drew back the working parts to check the breech and ejection mechanisms. It didn't look too bad – a touch of oil would do it the world of good. The AK47 was a cheaply manufactured weapon but that was also its advantage. Its low-tolerance moving parts could function even when poorly maintained, one reason why it was the most popular weapon with poorly trained ragtag armies.

Mallory sorted through the ready-filled magazines, all of which were in bad condition. A couple of empty ones were in reasonable shape but he needed some loose ammunition to fill them with. The next ammunition box he inspected contained pistol rounds and the one beneath that was empty. Another ammunition box was filled with spare parts for an 82mm mortar: a rusty tube and base-plate lay on the floor beside it.

A clean, relatively new-looking metal ammunition box sitting alone in a corner under a stack of empty sandbags caught his eye. Mallory squatted on a bundle of dirty Iraqi army uniforms in front of it to take the weight off his throbbing leg. He removed the sandbags and pulled on one of the box's catches but it was tight. He put the end of the flashlight in his mouth, allowing him to use both of his hands, and after a struggle the catch sprang open. He gripped the sides of the lid and raised it. The light bathed the inside of the box and Mallory almost dropped the small torch from his mouth when he saw what was inside.

He pushed the lid back fully and removed the pencil light from his mouth – which stayed open in disbelief. The box was filled with neatly packed rectangular bundles of green-grey printed paper, each sheet of which had the image of Benjamin Franklin in its centre and the figures '100' in each corner.

Mallory took out one of the bundles to examine it more closely, turning it on its side and flicking through the crisp notes with his thumb to find every one identical apart from its serial number. He took out a couple more bundles to reveal that the ones beneath were also all made up of United States of America hundred-dollar bills. Suddenly worried that the owners might appear at any moment he went back to the opening to peer through it.

He stepped into the outer room and crossed to the front door to listen. The only sound was a distant rumble but the urge to get out of the building consumed him.

Mallory hurried back into the small room, grabbed an empty sandbag, shoved several AK47 magazines – loaded and unloaded – into it, picked up the assault rifle he'd selected and his helmet and looked down at the box of money. It suggested to him more than anything else in the room that the owners could return any time. Nobody would leave that amount of money unattended for long, certainly not these people to whom it was worth ten times its western value. At the same time he found it impossible to simply walk away from that amount of cash.

He had at least to satisfy a nagging curiosity. He

put down his hardware booty, sat back down in front of the box, picked up a bundle of notes and riffled swiftly through it. A rough calculation put the bundle at ten thousand dollars and there were ten bundles per stack and eleven stacks. Mallory whistled softly to himself as he realised he was staring at over a million US dollars – worth well over five hundred thousand pounds, more than he could earn in the Marines if he stayed in for the next twenty years.

Mallory got to his feet, his stare fixed on the treasure, and wondered how a person could have the worst and best luck in his life all in one day. That was so typical for him, though, he thought. In this case each sort of cancelled the other out, leaving him with a fat zero and the rest of the day still to go. Even if he were to take the money, and assuming that all went well with the rescue, the first thing he would be asked about would be the contents of the box. And once declared, there was no doubt about how much he would be allowed to take home with him: none of it, since it was war loot and hence illegal.

But on the other hand he *could* take a little if he hid it on his person. So he stuffed one bundle into a thigh pocket, another into a breast pocket which was only barely big enough – and then he stopped himself. Greed simply increased the chance of discovery. After his rescue Mallory would be escorted to the hospital where he would have to discard his clothing. He could probably secure one bundle but more would be pushing it. It all depended on so many things: being left alone for even a few seconds before he was examined; his clothes being taken away once he was in hospital garb; finding somewhere in the examination room to hide the bundle so that he could retrieve it later. He knew he was probably being too paranoid but it worried him nevertheless.

A noise outside startled him and he drew his pistol, grabbed up the bag, AK47 and helmet, carefully pushed the concealing sheet aside and moved stealthily across the room to the door. There was no follow-up to the sound, the source of which was unclear, but it was yet another warning to get out of there as soon as possible.

As Mallory placed a hand on the door to open it he paused and looked back towards the storeroom. There was one possible low-risk solution to keeping the money that was admittedly a long shot but better than simply walking away and eternally regretting that he had not given it a go. He was already succumbing to peer pressure, imagining some of the names he would be called by the lads back home if he told them how he had found a cool million and then just walked away from it.

Mallory reached into a pouch, pulled out his GPS and turned it on. A message window declared it was searching for satellites and he turned it off, satisfied that it was working. He weighed the pros and cons of his hastily thought-out plan and the pros came out on top, no doubt enhanced by thoughts of a fancy new house with a pool, a new car, et cetera. Enough, he told himself. He could daydream later, which was another positive aspect of the plan since it gave him something more to look forward to, not that the prospect of survival wasn't encouraging enough.

He pocketed the GPS, placed his helmet, AK47 and bag on the floor by the door and went back into the storeroom.

He took the bundle poking out of his breast pocket, tossed it back into the box, leaving the one in his thigh pocket, closed the lid and picked it up to test its weight. It was heavy but manageable. The problem was that he would need his hands free to hold his gun. He scanned around the room, found a length of old nylon rope that appeared to have the strength for the job and threaded it through the handles at either end of the box, tying it off to form a loop. He bent forward, placed the line over his head, stood up, moved the box around so that it hung low across his back and tested it. It was not perfect and would annoy the hell out of him but it was worth a try.

The urge to get out of the building was now over-powering. Mallory went back to the front door, took up his Kalashnikov and bag, elected not to wear his helmet at that moment since it impeded his hearing, clipped it around the nylon line by the chin strap, took his pistol from its holster and opened the door.

He crossed the yard and checked inside the opposite building. There was a partially open door at the far side and he crossed the dirt floor towards it.

The door led onto a street and Mallory carefully looked out and checked in both directions. A man was on the road in the distance but far enough away not to be an immediate threat. Otherwise it looked clear.

Mallory focused on the entrance to an alleyway directly opposite and, holding the box in place with the same hand that was holding the bag and AK, his pistol in the other, he moved off.

Mallory wasn't far along the alleyway when the difficulties he had expected to have carrying his load became a reality. He paused long enough to undo the helmet, drop it to the ground, and kick some rubble over it. Then he moved on.

Halfway along the alley he ducked through a gap between the houses, stepping around what looked like an old generator to arrive at a corner where he stopped. In front of him was a large expanse of open ground, marked with the rudimentary boundaries and goal-posts of a football pitch, whose perimeter was lined by brick buildings, many of them two-storey. A few metres away in a corner of the waste ground was a flimsy wooden shed that looked as if it had been built to keep animals. He needed somewhere to wait until dark; he didn't fancy backtracking and since he couldn't risk moving in the open any more it was the only option he felt he had.

Mallory moved towards it at the crouch, eyes checking in every direction while the box swung awkwardly behind him. He ducked inside the rickety construction.

The dirt floor was covered in old palm leaves and the ceiling was not high enough for him to stand upright. He dropped to his knees, quickly removed the line from around his neck and moved to the back of the hut to watch the direction he had come from in case he had been followed. The smell and the absence of any man-made implements suggested that animals had probably been the hut's last occupants. Mallory remained still for several minutes, listening intently to the local sounds, until his breathing returned to normal.

A glance at his wristwatch told him he had at least another hour before the sun began to set and probably an hour more until it was really dark. He couldn't remember if there was a moon or not that night but it didn't matter. He was moving out whatever happened.

Mallory quickly set about his next task and emptied the contents of the sandbag onto the floor. He quietly unloaded two old AK47 magazines and one by one pushed the bullets into the ones that were in better condition. Once they were loaded he firmly pressed a magazine into its housing on the weapon until it clicked home. Then, pulling the working parts to the rear, he controlled the return spring, letting the breech-block slide forward to push a bullet out of the magazine and into the breech. He could not allow the return spring to fly forward as normal because of the noise it would make and so the breech had not seated properly and he spent a couple of minutes working it into place. Once he had the AK47 properly loaded he left the safety catch off and rested the gun across his lap – not normal safe practice as he was taught but this wasn't a normal situation, alone and unsupported.

His ears gradually tuned to the noises that surrounded him, far and near, and he leaned back against the wall that moved a little under his weight but held firm. He stretched out his legs. The pain in his foot had eased and Mallory's thoughts drifted home to Plymouth and to the apartment he had shared with Jenny, his girlfriend, until she'd dumped him for a policeman two days before Mallory left for Iraq. Her reason for leaving after two and a half years together was that she did not want to live with someone who was not home every night. He knew the real reason was that she didn't fancy him any more. If she had loved him she wouldn't have left. But then, the truth was that *he* didn't love *her*. He couldn't have or it would have been more painful than it had been. It made him wonder why he had lived with Jenny in the first place. But there had been some good times − in fact, it had all been quite good for him. Clearly not for her, though. But at that moment she would have been nice to come home to.

Mallory exhaled heavily as he checked his watch, calculating that it was three p.m. back in England. It was also Sunday and the lads would be watching football down the pub. What he wouldn't give to be with them at that moment, having a pint and a fish-and-chip lunch covered in tomato sauce and salt and vinegar. His mouth was dry as paper and thoughts like that only made it worse. He forced himself to think of something else.

A sudden noise took care of that. He pointed the Kalashnikov at the hut opening and his ears focused on the sound. It came again, like a tapping noise but not in any kind of rhythm. It seemed to be coming

29

from the direction he had arrived from and was getting closer.

Mallory placed the butt of the weapon against his shoulder as the noise stopped. When it started again Mallory leaned forward onto one knee, both of his eyes open and looking down the length of the rifle, the pad of his index finger resting lightly on the trigger.

Something came into view below the end of the barrel and he dropped the front sight enough to see the shadowy outline of a goat. The animal continued out of the alley, oblivious to Mallory's presence, and ambled towards the hut where it stopped in the entrance.

Mallory and the goat stared at each other as if each of them was waiting to see who would make the first move. Mallory exhaled slowly in relief and as he lowered the rifle the goat turned on its hooves and trotted away, flustered that its planned rest in the cover of the shed had been thwarted.

Mallory felt suddenly exhausted by yet another shot of adrenalin and he realised that his hands were shaking. The fear of being stuck in a place where anyone who saw him would kill him or alert others who could was getting to him. The million dollars and the comforts it could buy gave him no pleasure at that moment and he wished the damned Tornado pilot had not been shot down.

He leaned back as Mac's last words in the chopper popped into his head – something about a rendezvous with death – and wondered why the man had brought it up at such a moment.

Mallory closed his eyes, let his ears monitor the outside and waited in silence as darkness fell. Eventually he could hardly see the spot where the goat had first appeared.

He crept outside quietly, carrying the box, leaving the empty magazines and the sandbag behind. There were no street lights and only a handful of the houses had lights inside, faint orangey-yellow glows from kerosene lamps. The southern sky was a dull orange, silhouetting the rooftops as if a large fire was burning, but it could also have been the lights of the US military base around Baghdad airport. Mallory considered walking in that direction. It was not more than thirty kilometres away and he could cover the ground by the morning. But that would mean heading through the middle of Fallujah – or going around its perimeter, since he was near the northern edge of the town. Either way, it was not a good idea. He could end up a victim of either side.

Mallory looped the line attached to the box over his head, got to his feet and headed across the waste ground, keeping his distance from the dark, silent, dried-mud dwellings.

His foot throbbed but Mallory ignored it. This was the final phase of his operation, with luck, and he hoped sincerely that the next time he fell asleep would be in the safety of his camp. His basic plan was to make his way out of the town and find a deserted patch of ground large enough for a helicopter to land on and where he could establish communications and activate his beacon. From what he could remember of the terrain, a mile or so should see him well north of the town and in farmland. The moon had not yet shown itself and there was a slight breeze. The temperature had dropped, making conditions as good as he could expect, for which he was thankful. If he needed to run he would have to dump the money but that was part of the deal he had made with himself.

Ten minutes later, moving carefully and then only after frequent pauses to look and listen, Mallory came to a low wall and went to ground as much to rest as to check the route ahead. An inspection over the wall revealed that he was at the boundary of a cemetery. It was difficult to tell how large it was: the awkward, tilted headstones and ragged flags moving gently on poles filled the view.

Mallory lifted the box over the wall and crouched on the other side. The box was a complete pain, not just its weight and awkwardness but the metallic noise it made every time it touched something solid, a sound that carried a long way on the night air.

The cemetery seemed an ideal place to cross as the odds on meeting anyone there at such a late hour were slim. However, there was a risk of being silhouetted due to the lack of background and tall structures: the majority of the graves were bordered by low concrete rectangular frames, and he would have to keep low.

Mallory set off among the graves at a crouch but after several metres he lost his footing and the box scraped loudly against a gravestone. He lay flat and took a moment to listen, worried not only that he had been heard but also that the accident had every chance of being repeated. The graves were close together and it was so dark that stumbling as he walked in such an awkward way was unavoidable.

Then Mallory had a thought. The cemetery could be the ideal location to hide his booty. He had originally planned to bury the box somewhere near his pick-up point simply because if it was quiet enough to serve that purpose it would also be an ideal spot to dig a hole. But the bigger problem at the moment was getting to that location undetected.

He put down the box and sat on the edge of a grave to give the matter some serious thought. Burying the money inside a grave might work – but then, there was a chance that it could be visited in the near future and the freshly turned earth would attract suspicion. Mallory looked down at the narrow path he had been following between the graves and it struck him as actually a highly unlikely place to dig a new grave. Therefore it just might be the perfect place to bury something so that it would not be discovered.

Mallory pushed a finger into the earth. It wasn't too firm. He placed the ammunition box on a grave, set his rifle against it, removed his penknife from its pouch, opened it and shoved the blade into the soil. It sank in easily. He carved out a rectangle slightly larger than the box and began to scrape away the topsoil, placing it in a pile to one side.

Mallory was soon frustrated with the small amount of earth he was shifting and he searched around for a better digging implement. A can with a couple of plastic flowers in it was resting on a nearby headstone. He put the flowers to one side and used the tin as a shovel. Several minutes later he'd dug a substantial hole. He compared its depth with the height of the box. Ideally the top needed to be at least a foot below the surface. After a pause to look around and listen he pressed on.

A minute later Mallory had dug a considerably deeper hole, although now stones began to obstruct his efforts. He discarded the can and pulled the stones out by hand, decided he'd gone deep enough, picked up the box and lowered it inside. It lay at a slant, its highest point nine inches from the top, which Mallory reckoned was good enough. He dragged the loose soil back into the hole with his hands. When he had created a slight mound he got to his feet and, stamping as hard as he dared, used his weight to level it off. Then he spread the remaining soil around, depositing the stones further away.

As a final touch he shuffled up and down the path, trying to obscure any traces of his efforts on the surface for several metres in both directions. It was difficult to tell in the darkness how successful this operation had been and he would never know until the day he came back to retrieve the box. And God only knew when – or if – that day would come.

Mallory put the plastic flowers back in the can, placed it back on the headstone, wiped his hands on his thighs and removed his GPS from its pouch on his belt. As he turned it on he covered the small glowing screen and scanned around while he waited for the device to acquire the local satellites. A screen message eventually indicated this had been achieved and was followed by a display showing his position in latitude and longitude. He hit the 'man overboard' button and went through the menu to select the 'save' option. It asked him to provide a name and he paused to consider the request. He wanted something memorable but not obvious to anyone who might come across it and as he considered several possible names the word *rendezvous* popped into his head. He counted the letters on his fingers, ten being the maximum number of characters he could use, and since the word fitted perfectly he punched them in and saved it to the memory chip before turning off the instrument. He placed it back in its pouch, picked up his weapon and, after a final check around, headed between the graves towards the northern boundary wall, feeling relieved at having rid himself of his main burden.

Mallory saw a tarmac road on the other side of some waste ground beyond the low wall that marked the northern edge of the cemetery and took a moment to watch and listen. The only sounds were distant *booms* from the direction of Baghdad accompanied by flashes of light but ahead was total blackness. He climbed over the wall and moved down a slight incline and onto the waste ground, looking left and right as he dodged across the narrow road before picking up speed on reaching the other side. He carried on without slowing down and covered several hundred metres before he stopped and lay down near what appeared to be a motorway running across his way ahead. He remembered a major artery north of the town, a road that ran from Baghdad to the Jordanian border, and then the sound of a distant vehicle reached his ears and he looked east to see a pair of flickering headlights in the distance.

Mallory's first thought was that it could be a coalition vehicle – but that was not necessarily good news. This was a war zone, at night, and alert and often nervous fingers were constantly poised on triggers, their owners ready to shoot at anything remotely suspicious. A lone figure in the darkness might invite an attack before any recognition was attempted. On the other hand, it would be unusual for a military vehicle to travel alone in a hostile environment and Mallory elected to remain where he was, hugging the ground until it passed.

The dark shape behind the bright headlights gradually took on a form that was distinctly civilian and Mallory watched it as it drove on by and out of sight.

The motorway had two lanes either side of a meridian flanked by crash barriers and it would take Mallory a few seconds to cross. A thought struck him that the road might be watched. Still, the car had driven along unmolested. The other side of the road was in complete darkness and this was, he hoped, the final obstacle. Luck had remained with him so far and he needed it to stick around a little longer.

Mallory got to his feet, moved forward at a crouch and raised his injured foot over the first of the knee-high crash barriers. Pain shot through him as the edge of the tarmac dug into his wound but he did not falter. It then suddenly occurred to him that if troops were watching they would have night-vision aids and the AK47 with its uniquely curved magazine was unlike any weapon carried by coalition forces. They might allow a car to pass but a man with a gun would be an irresistible target. He held the weapon close to his body to remove it from his silhouette, ran to the meridian, climbed the double set of barriers, and hurried across the final stretch of tarmac, over the last barrier and down a sandy bank. Mallory did not slow and ran across a stretch of open ground, still feeling exposed and vulnerable, towards what looked like an earthwork that in the darkness appeared to be further away than it actually was. He was soon upon it, scrambling up a short incline where he dropped over the other side and found himself in a dry ditch. He moved along the earthwork for several metres before crawling back up and looking in the direction he had come from to see if he had been pursued: anyone following would be silhouetted by the glowing horizon beyond Fallujah. But there was no sign of movement and he slid down to the bottom of the ditch, scrambled up the other side and ran on across another flat open space.

A black scar appeared in front of him that did not quite look like a road and as he drew closer it became a railway line that he had forgotten about. Mallory crossed the rails and pressed on into the darkness, his breathing becoming laboured, his dry mouth aching, his foot throbbing wildly. But the promise of freedom pushed him on, with every step making the prospect more of a reality.

Mallory passed through a line of bushes and found himself on the edge of what appeared to be an open area. He dropped to his knees beside a bush, utterly exhausted, and gulped in air through his sandpaper mouth. He could not remember ever being as exhausted: his only truly comparable experience had been during his commando course when he had run with a thirty-foot telegraph pole from Woodbury Common to the Lympstone camp, a six-mile race, sixty men, six poles, ten men on each. With two miles to go and despite his pole being down to just four men they were in the lead by a couple of hundred metres. But then, with under a mile to go, the man beside him dropped out, unable to keep up the pace and Mallory was left with the end of the pole to carry on his own. He began to see stars, almost collapsing under the physical stress and might have done so had he not seen the tops of the rugby posts that were the finishing line beyond some hedgerows a few hundred metres ahead. Those days seemed as far away as his early childhood at that moment.

Mallory decided the location would do and he pulled his SARBE from its pouch, took hold of a bright-orange cord on its side and pulled it, releasing a pin that activated the device. There was no sound and the only indication that the beacon was transmitting was a small flashing LED light. The transmitted signal would include his GPS position as well as his pre-programmed identity. He laid the Kalashnikov on the ground beside him and waited for the voice of the rescue crew informing him that his signal had been received and that they were on their way.

Mallory was supremely confident that he would be picked up some time that night. If there was one thing he had experience of it was the Air Sea Rescue teams. As long as his SARBE was working, and they rarely failed, he was as good as home. Most passing aircraft, or an AWACS if one was in the area, which was likely, would be able to pick up the signal. The information would be passed on to the relevant operations room and the rescue mission would be set in motion.

An hour passed before the voice of a pilot brought Mallory's SARBE to life. He almost jumped when he heard it. He pressed the 'send' button and was horrified when he could not talk. His mouth, without a trace of saliva, could not form an intelligible word. It took what seemed an age before the pilot finally understood and informed him that they would be with him in approximately ten minutes.

Mallory got to his feet and several minutes later heard the distant drone of an aircraft engine. A minute after that he thought he could see a black speck in the sky to the west and although he could not be sure his eyes weren't playing tricks on him his ears were in no doubt. As the sound grew louder the suspicious speck became larger and formed into two separate objects which shortly after became silhouettes that he recognised: Blackhawks.

They flew towards him, one close behind the other and then they suddenly split up, one chopper dropping height while the other moved into a circling pattern above. Mallory knew that the higher craft would have a heavy machine gun mounted in its doorway to provide covering fire if the pick-up point came under attack.

The incoming craft covered the remaining distance in seconds and when the dust kicked up as it came into the hover Mallory ran towards it. Several figures jumped out of its side when it was a couple of feet off the ground and while two knelt in firing positions the others ran forward, took hold of Mallory and unceremoniously guided him back to the craft.

Seconds later they were all aboard and the helicopter lifted off and accelerated away.

'You OK?' one of Mallory's rescuers asked in an American accent.

'Fine, thanks,' Mallory replied in his parched voice. They were US Special Forces – Delta, he suspected – though the Yanks also had guys who trained specifically for hostile extractions. One of them handed Mallory a bottle of water which he practically drained on his first hit. When he sat back, clutching the empty plastic bottle, his hand drifted to his thigh map-pocket and felt the bundle of money inside.

Thirty minutes later they had landed somewhere near Baghdad airport and Mallory was on his way to his accommodation. Worried about the bundle of money he had concealed in his pocket he had not mentioned his injury and expressed a desire to go to his basher where – he said – he badly needed the toilet and to change his clothes before his debrief, hinting that he'd had an accident in his trousers that needed to be taken care of. As soon as he'd secreted the money in his backpack by cutting into the padding and placing the cash inside to be stitched up later he had a shower, got changed and then made his way to the sickbay to have his wound seen to. After a hearty meal Mallory attended a debrief after which he was exonerated of any blame for having been left behind and, since no one had suffered any serious injuries and his crew's Sea King had returned with only minor damage, the affair was quickly forgotten. The war was coming to a speedy end and the powers that be were preoccupied with preparations for the occupation.

Within five days Mallory was on an RAF flight back to the UK and his unit, where he was immediately sent on leave after being congratulated by his RSM for his war efforts.

Mallory arrived at his apartment to discover that most of his furniture, including his television and stereo, had been cleaned out – not by burglars but by his former girlfriend. Under normal circumstances Mallory would have been annoyed enough to go and look for her and demand an explanation since it was his money that had bought everything. But he decided to forget about it as he placed the bundle of dollars on the kitchen table, made a cup of tea, sat down and stared at his money. Chasing after Jenny would have been a hassle anyway and he preferred to focus his efforts on more important matters.

Mallory had checked the exchange rate at the first opportunity and calculated that his dollars were worth just over six thousand pounds sterling. Another calculation revealed that it was more than the Royal Marines had paid him after deductions for the period he had been at war. All he had to do now was find a way of changing it to pounds without drawing any attention to himself and then spend it. The best idea he could come up with, and quite an attractive one at that, was to go on holiday to the United States – Orlando, for instance – have a good time, buy some new technical stuff from the duty-free shop, change the rest to sterling on his way home and then buy a TV and some furniture. There wouldn't be much left after all that and Mallory wished he had stuffed another couple of bundles into his pockets.

Mallory thought about the ammunition box filled with money that he'd buried in the cemetery in Fallujah: a million dollars just waiting for him to dig up and bring home. But the only way he was going to be able to do that was to get over there – and that would require some planning.

The first step would be to find out which commando unit was going next to Iraq, specifically Baghdad, and then explore the chances of it making a trip to Fallujah, something which would probably be difficult if not impossible to find out in advance. He would then need to apply to join that unit, which of course he might not be permitted to do. And there was another even bigger problem. The Yanks were in the centre and north of Iraq and the Brits were in the south, and it didn't take a genius to figure out that those positions were unlikely to change. Even if by some remote chance Mallory could get to Fallujah he would still have to slip away from the rest of his troop without them knowing, dig up the box without being seen, conceal its contents and keep it secure until he was finally moved back to the UK. Each phase was fraught with impossible difficulties and if he was caught at any stage he could end up in jail for his troubles or at best lose the cash.

Mallory gave a long sigh as the possibilities of ever getting his hands on the money shrank – at least while he remained in the Marines.

As soon as the implication of that thought sank home it struck him that the only way he was ever going to get hold of the money was as a civilian. He needed freedom to go where he wanted, when he wanted, to go to Fallujah on his own terms, take as long as he wanted and decide how he was going to get out of the country with the money. The burning question he needed to answer was whether he really wanted to leave the Royal Marines and end a career that he had set his heart on since he was a boy.

Mallory got up and looked out of the window onto the field below where several youngsters were playing football. The thought of quitting the Marines didn't sit comfortably with him. He had planned on doing his full twenty-two years of service up to retirement before seeing what else the world had to offer. But now, out of the blue, here he was contemplating his resignation with only a quarter of his time done. It was a gamble on so many levels, not just on whether the money would still be in Fallujah when he got there but on whether that was more important than quitting his chosen career. But a million dollars was a

43

lot of money, to be sure, enough to buy a damned nice house as well as a damned nice car.

Mallory decided to explore all the pros and cons and only when he was satisfied that he had covered everything would he make a decision. It had to feel right and at that moment the notion of leaving the Marines did not. Perhaps it was just fear of the unknown.

But the period of indecision was not easy for Mallory. He tried at first to forget about the money – which turned out to be impossible – and then took to concentrating on the negative aspects of leaving a fine career in the Royal Marines simply to pursue a pile of cash. But the thought of the box in the grave-yard would not let him go and tormented him endlessly. He didn't take the holiday to Orlando in the end. In the back of his mind he knew that if he did decide to leave the Marines he would need to finance his Fallujah operation.

When Mallory returned to work he was told to report to Recce Troop, the position he had originally longed for. But the satisfaction was no longer there. Finally, a month after his return from Iraq, he made the decision to resign. The money or the adventure of retrieving it dominated his thoughts and he knew that he would remain restless until he did something about it. It was only after he committed himself, when he walked into HQ Company, met with the duty clerk and asked for the necessary papers, that the thought of the cash in the graveyard stopped pestering him and he set about planning his expedition in earnest.

But he was soon to acquire a whole new collection of concerns.

Mallory's initial research had already revealed that his mission was going to be more complicated than simply arriving in Iraq, digging up the box and leaving with it. The struggle between the various religious and political factions in the country as well as the general resistance to the coalition occupation had begun. There was an increase in crime and banditry due to the absence of law and order. Further research revealed that westerners were not permitted visas to enter the country unless they were employed by a certified Iraqi reconstruction contractor. But the Marines were not going to let Mallory go for another ten months anyway, by which time he hoped Iraq would be back to normal. With luck, he could then go there on holiday, hire a car, buy a shovel, dig the money up at his leisure, take a tour of the country, go out by road through Turkey or Jordan and start spending his cash on a relaxing drive back through Europe.

Mallory saw it all as a great adventure and began to feel more relaxed about the whole thing. He started enjoying his work once again and appreciated the company of his colleagues more than ever, knowing that it was all soon to come to an end. And, of course, he spent many hours contemplating the delightful problem of how he was going to spend the money. What finally made everything much more worthwhile was the realisation that whatever happened, even after he'd got the money, he could always rejoin the Marines and pretty much take up where he'd left off. There'd even be an amusing exploit to tell his grandchildren. Mallory would be a winner whatever happened: he looked forward with relish to revisiting Fallujah and concluding the greatest adventure of his life.

2

Abdul's Dilemma

Abdul Rahman stood beside his hand-painted white and blue Iraqi police Toyota pick-up parked near a busy road junction outside one of the north-west entrances to the Green Zone that were heavily guarded by the US military. The elaborate checkpoint, protected by layers of interconnecting sections of concrete blast-walls, was overlooked by the majestic historical monument known as the Assassins' Gate. It was also one of the locations where a year previously jubilant Iraqis had unceremoniously pulled from its plinth a statue of Saddam Hussein in celebration of his defeat by the US-led invasion forces.

The afternoon was a normally busy one despite the thousand-pound vehicle bomb that had gone off the day before directly outside the checkpoint. The death toll eventually totalled more than twenty people after the most severely wounded had failed to survive the night. One man had been killed almost a kilometre away while shopping in an open market after a piece of the artillery shell that had made up part of the bomb landed on his head. Seven of the dead were at the time inside the van which was ferrying workers who lived in the city into the Green Zone. The only person in the vehicle aware of the explosives packed under the seats and in boxes in the back was the driver. As instructed by his religious guide, he had picked up his passengers after explaining to them how the normal taxi had broken down and, since the replacement van belonged to him, he would be taking the driver's place until the other one was fixed. As they arrived at the checkpoint and waited in line to pass through a security inspection he flicked the two arming switches, cried, '*Allah akbar*' – and pushed the final firing button.

The large crater over a foot deep and surrounded by a wide black scorch mark was a few metres in front of Abdul near the centre of the junction. Like most of the other bomb holes in the city it would not be repaired in the foreseeable future, thus adding to the increasing deterioration of road conditions.

Abdul was holding the butt of an old AK47 against his hip, resting the tip of the barrel on the ground. The tattered, knotted shoulder strap attached at either end of the weapon had broken twice since he had been issued with the gun and it was too heavy to carry all day. He wore black trousers and the sky-blue long-sleeved shirt of the Iraqi Police with the letters 'IP' stencilled on a white band tied over his left shoulder. Abdul had been a police officer for three months after completing a six-week training course in Amman, the capital of Jordan, followed by another week at the Stadium School, the former international football arena, near the centre of Baghdad. The training fell short of the Academy's pre-war standards but the necessity to produce high numbers of officers and get them onto the streets as quickly as possible was paramount. But lack of proper skills and discipline among the police was only one of the problems causing Abdul anxiety in his newly chosen profession – which, it had to be said, had never exactly been a vocational ambition for him. In his younger days Abdul's main feature had been his bright, cheerful smile and although he was a quiet-spoken, introverted young man who tended to daydream when he should have been listening, the little he had to say suggested an above-average level of intelligence. But the smile had rarely been seen since the war and probably not at all since he had joined the police.

The main reason for Abdul's glum feelings while at work was the poor quality of some of the other police officers: there had been a marked lack of vetting procedures when they'd been selected. This was no more evident than in the squad of which he was a member. Abdul's immediate colleagues on the force were, to a man, all Ali Babas, crooks and villains, and one or two of them were possibly far worse than that.

Abdul had been brought up as a good Muslim – the word itself meant 'one who submits', a concept which he fully embraced – and by his late teens he was by far the most religious member of his family, the only one who prayed five times a day. But since the war his faith had slipped, at least as far as his regular acts of worship were concerned. This dilution of his belief was also at the core of his distress since, much as he wanted to re-establish a full commitment to

Allah, possibly even in a more active way than before, he felt unable to. For Abdul believed that he was no longer worthy of Allah's attention. He had allowed an obstacle to come between him and God and was too weak to do anything about it. This obstruction on the divine path was a result of allowing himself to be drawn into a perk of the job, for want of a better term, that had seemed innocent enough at first but had developed into something that in his heart he wholly disapproved of, a disapproval shared by the person he admired most in his life, his sister.

Abdul was a dichotomy. He had never been very strong, physically or mentally, but there were occasions when he was painfully contrary and displayed such levels of determination as to cause suspicion among members of his family, his father in particular, that, as a baby, the boy had been exchanged for an impostor. These moments of defiance were seen as uncharacteristic by everyone else but it was his beloved sister, Tasneen, who was always supportive and read them as evidence of Abdul's great potential. He always showed promise when it came to family duties and honour, motivated as he was by his heritage: tribal, ancestral and, of course, religious. He was unaffected by politics. But it was the ordinary pressure of everyday life that revealed Abdul's character flaws and lack of forcefulness and independence of thought. Those were the qualities of Tasneen, the only other surviving member of his immediate family. Abdul cherished her deeply. She was not just his older, wiser sister. After the loss of their parents she took on many of their functions.

But Abdul often resented her for those very reasons. The strengths she possessed only highlighted his own weaknesses, revealing them not only to others but to himself. Still, he loved her and remained guided by her but only until, he assured himself, he broke through to true manhood.

Abdul had been born on 23 September 1980, the day after Iraq invaded Iran, in Baghdad's Yarmuk Hospital, and was brought up in Al Mansour, one of the city's more affluent districts on the west side of the Tigris river. He was a Sunni Muslim, the same religion as that of his country's leader, Saddam Hussein, a factor that gave Abdul's father undeniable advantages in his business dealings at home and abroad. Abdul's full name, a legacy from twelve successive heads of family, was Abdul-Rahman Marwan Ahmed Mussa Akmed Dawood Sulaiman Abdullah Abdul-Kader Abdul-Latef Abdullah Maath Dulaimy Al Aws. 'Dulaimy' was the official tribal name since 'Al Aws' was the name of one of the two main tribes that the Arabs had divided into around the time of Mohamed, the other main tribe being the Al Kharaj. The Dulaimy tribe originated in Saudi Arabia and during Abdul-Latef's reign in the last quarter of the nineteenth century they emigrated to a village called Ana in the open desert region of Al Anbar some four hundred kilometres due west of Baghdad on the Jordan road. Two generations later, Abdul's several-times-great-grandfather Sulaiman fought against the Turks during the great Arab revolt under the leadership of Prince Feisal with the aid of the famed British soldier, Lawrence of Arabia.

The Sunnis were a minority in modern Iraq at around thirty-five per cent of the population. Take away the Sunni Kurds in the north who constituted some twenty per cent and that left the former ruling class in Iraq now holding a considerably smaller percentage.

Abdul had enjoyed a comfortable upbringing and it was not until his early teens that he began to worry about reaching his eighteenth year, when he would be eligible for military conscription. The very thought filled him with dread. Having a well-connected Sunni father might have held some advantages for him when it came to avoiding the draft but unfortunately for Abdul his father believed military service to be an obligation of every young Iraqi. The Sunni – or, to be more precise, Saddam Hussein's family and friends – occupied practically every important position in the government and military. Thinking that it might bolster the rather tenuous advantages of the Dulaimy tribe's somewhat remote connection – Hussein's tribe were the Tekritis from north of Baghdad – Abdul's father also regarded his son's term in the army as a wise and necessary insurance for the boy's future. But Abdul had nightmares about becoming a soldier and the closer that day came the greater grew his desperation to find a way of avoiding it, without attracting scorn from his father. In fact, Abdul was unlikely to be able to avoid his sire's disdain. But he still preferred parental abuse to three years under arms.

His first and most simple plan to delay conscription was to enrol in a university and embark on a long and difficult degree course. He chose computer technology, normally a four-year programme. But, even so, after it he would still have to join the army. His second delaying tactic was to drag out the degree course for as long as he could by failing examinations. There was a limit to how long Abdul could use this technique and by year six his father began to suspect his son's plot. He warned Abdul that if his next results were not a satisfactory pass he would take him out of university and enrol him in the army himself. Abdul did not take his father seriously enough, perhaps, because to do so would have been unthinkable and maybe he hoped that his father would eventually realise how important his studies were to his son. When Abdul failed to make the grade yet again his father was furious and delivered his ultimatum: join the army or leave the house for ever. His father also made it clear that if Abdul chose the latter course he risked losing all claim to his inheritance.

The threat, particularly its disinheritance component, proved to be more painful to Abdul than his hatred for the military and he finally accepted the inevitable. The day he left the university he registered himself as eligible for conscription and within a week he had received his marching orders. He was sent to a training outpost in the western desert not far from his tribal home of Al Anbar, which was not a coincidence. He arrived at the camp along with four hundred other recruits at six a.m. Within a couple of hours they had received an induction speech, followed by a severe haircut, and were then lined up outside the barracks where their training team introduced themselves. The recruits were invited to lie down on their stomachs, whereupon the instructors went around kicking and hitting them with a level of enthusiasm that went far beyond even Abdul's expectations. The beatings were immediately followed by a gruelling run without water in the midday sun where they continued to receive kicks and blows for no apparent reason. After a brief rest and a paltry meal the abuse was resumed. By four p.m. the recruits were ordered to return to their barracks and, expecting more of the same the following day, two dozen of Abdul's fellow conscripts conspired to desert. Abdul needed little encouragement to take part in the mutiny and as soon as darkness fell he joined the others at a hole in the perimeter wall through which they filed. Then they dispersed.

Abdul arrived home late that evening, walked into the house and went directly to his father who was horrified to see him. Abdul attempted to relate his terrible experiences but before he could begin his story his father demanded that he return to the camp immediately. Abdul found the strength to refuse abjectly to obey, pleading to be heard and swearing that no matter what punishment his father inflicted he would not go back. His father responded promptly by ordering him out of the house, never to return. Abdul continued to make his pleas but his father shouted violently for him to leave, even picking up a cane at one point to beat him. In a storm of shouts and screams Abdul ran out of the room, bundled some of his things into a bag and left the house.

But Tasneen was waiting for him in the street, having already made a plan to help her little brother. She led him to a friend's house nearby and arranged for him to stay in a small room there. She personally ensured that he was well fed while she embarked on a subtle crusade to change their father's mind. Abdul's world had turned utterly on its head and he believed that Tasneen's task was an impossible one. He was convinced this was the end of the family for him and so he concentrated on how he was going to manage life on the run from the army while making a living. But he could not come up with anything: he slipped into a deep depression and became absorbed in self-pity.

Four days later Tasneen woke him up with the announcement that she had come to take him home. Abdul could not believe it at first, then quickly wanted to know how and why their father had changed his mind. Tasneen gave her brother no explanation, appearing neither pleased nor disturbed by whatever had happened, and simply told him to come back home with her.

When they walked into the house she stayed by the front door and told him to go into the living room alone. Abdul became nervous, not knowing what to expect. The only encouragement Tasneen gave him was an assurance that it would be all right. Abdul believed her but as he approached the living-room doors his doubts grew and he reached for the door-knob with a shaking hand.

When he entered the room his father was standing at the window, looking through it with the kind of empty gaze that suggested he was not so much looking outside as inside at his own thoughts. To Abdul's surprise, when his father turned to face him there was not a trace of anger in his expression. Instead, there was a deep concern and, unless Abdul was mistaken, a trace of fear.

Abdul's father gave a strange kind of slight smile that unnerved Abdul further, although it disappeared as soon as the man sat down and bid his son to sit in the chair opposite. Abdul did not say a word, unable even to begin to guess what his father was about to say to him.

'Abdul, my son,' his father finally said. He was looking down at his hands at first but then he looked up into his son's eyes. 'Do you still refuse to go back to the military?'

Abdul could feel the heaviness of his father's heart. But despite his inability to find a solution for his own plight during his past few days' seclusion one thing he remained certain of was his future regarding the military. 'I will not go back, Father. I cannot. They are animals. I—'

Abdul's father put up a hand to stop his son from saying anything more. They sat in silence for a moment longer as the older man considered a deeper, much more troubling question. 'It will only be a matter of time before they come to look for you. You know that, don't you?'

'Then I will leave . . . ' Abdul began to say. But his father interrupted him once again, this time with a hint of anger in his eyes.

'Let me talk,' Abdul's father said firmly. 'It is not the army who will come here looking for you. It will be the secret police . . . And if they cannot find you they will take *me* away.' There was no shortage of horror stories about the secret police and what they did to people in their custody, no matter how trivial the reason for their arrest, and Abdul knew the tales as well as anyone.

'But . . .' Abdul began, and again his father stopped him.

'You are a man now, not a boy. The world is a different place for men than it is for boys. There are different rules – rules of survival. It may seem to you, in the protection of this house, with me and your mother here, that there are more choices out there for men, that we have greater freedom than you. But in reality we have much less. There are far more rules for men and the punishments for breaking them are harsh. But I believe these rules to be important. Without them we cannot maintain our values and we will end up living by someone else's rules.'

Abdul listened quietly as his father continued in some detail about the advantages and disadvantages of the decisions, many of them unavoidable, that we all have to make in life and then the consequences of making the wrong decisions, especially in the times in which they lived. It was all so very complicated, intimidating as well, and Abdul could only wish that he had convinced his father not to send him to the army in the first place. There were ways of avoiding conscription but it had to be taken care of well in advance of the call-up date. One solution was to pay a fee, around two thousand dollars, to a certain someone a friend knew in the military who would have annulled Abdul's obligation. But his father would never have done that, partly because the man believed that Abdul would have enjoyed it once he had settled in but mostly because of what he was talking about now: the rules and the penalties for breaking them.

As Abdul watched his father wring his hands while he talked it became apparent that it was his duty, Abdul's, to resolve this most serious dilemma that he had created for his father and the rest of his family. When the older man finally grew silent Abdul stood up, put his hand on his father's shoulder, and with an uncommon resolve in his voice promised, as Allah was his witness, that he would find a solution, and if he failed he would let Allah decide his fate. But Abdul's father took little satisfaction from the declaration and did not look at his son who had always been much more of a talker than a doer. Abdul was aware of that, having been accused of it many times. This time he vowed to be different.

Abdul immediately set about making use of the many friends he had made at university and seeking out those he had heard rumours about in the past, men who had managed to somehow avoid the draft. Within a few days he learned of an army officer who held an influential position in the administrative office that dealt with army deserters and who – for a fee, of course – could have a name removed from the dreaded list. Abdul made contact with the officer through a man who had apparently benefited from his services. At a rendezvous in a coffee shop by the river near the Ishtar Sheraton Hotel the officer confirmed, after the customary ritual exchanges, that he could indeed help Abdul, at a cost of fifteen hundred dollars. Abdul did not want to go to his father for the money, part of his deal with himself and with Allah, and went directly to his mentor and only ally, Tasneen. Together they emptied their own bank accounts and raised the balance from various sources, mostly in the form of loans from other family members. But on the day they were to meet the officer and hand over the cash he called to explain that he was very sorry but Abdul's paperwork had been forwarded to 'other' authorities. Abdul was horrified and immediately asked if it was possible to bribe the new recipient of the paperwork. The officer explained how that would be impossible since the new recipients included the police, the army, the National Guard, the border guards and, of course, the secret police. Abdul's details would remain on file indefinitely or until he turned himself in or was captured.

Abdul had to sit down before his knees gave way. He had failed his father, dishonoured the family, but — far worse — he would be on the run for the rest of his life. The officer had suggested that Abdul's best course of action was to return to the army camp. He could expect imprisonment for a year or so, which would be unpleasant to say the least. There was, of course, a chance that Abdul could be hanged as an example to others, something that Saddam encouraged. But if

Abdul's father made a personal plea it could help his case. If Abdul was captured while on the run his chances of being executed were difficult to judge.

When Abdul's father learned of the news he slipped into a depression as he recounted a recent story of an old friend whose son was wanted for something by the secret police. After failing to find the boy they took the father instead. The son eventually turned up and the police hanged him in front of his father.

Abdul was faced with a serious quandary. If he ran his father might pay the price but it would still mean that Abdul would remain a fugitive. If he gave himself up he could be hanged or at least spend a horrifying time in an Iraqi jail, a period that he did not think he would survive. Abdul told his sister that had he known it would turn out as badly as this he would have done his time as a conscript. But it was too late now.

Abdul's fears were to be short-lived. So too, unfortunately, were his father and mother. A month later the coalition force invaded Iraq and a week after that his parents were killed when their car was crushed by the reckless panic-stricken driver of an Iraqi Army armoured vehicle heading out of the city as the Americans closed in on it.

'Abdul,' a voice growled behind him. He turned to see Hassan, his team sergeant, looking at him, a snarl on his face, an expression that as far as Abdul was concerned seemed to be a permanent fixture. Hassan was a strong, stocky man with a barrel gut that was the result not just of a large appetite but also of a taste for strong drink, a suspicion confirmed most mornings by Hassan's fetid breath. Hassan disapproved of everything about Abdul. But then he disliked everyone, it seemed, except his younger brother Ali. Hassan's animosity towards Abdul was partly due to his resentment of Abdul's more privileged upbringing, something which Hassan often sarcastically referred to. As far as Abdul was concerned the man was a lowlife and rotten to the core. Hassan was one of the thousands of prisoners that Saddam had released from jails all over the country shortly before the war, although he would deny the accusation. But after several men confirmed that they'd known Hassan while in Abu Ghraib prison he took to explaining his incarceration as an administrative error: he'd been inside for nothing more serious than a driving offence. Since most prison records had been lost or destroyed during the war, Hassan's included, it was not possible to disprove his claim. Abdul suspected his team sergeant was lying. To him, Hassan was quite simply a criminal in a police uniform.

The truth was that Hassan had always been a criminal, since childhood, and like his brother and the rest of the squad he had joined the police only to further his unlawful ambitions. They were all Sunni Muslims from the Dora district in southern Baghdad, near the large power station which with its smoking chimneys dominated that part of the city's horizon. It was an area notorious for its criminal element as well as for the insurgents who lurked there. The resistance and the crooks were hard to tell apart: their operational methods overlapped in places, both groups often working hand in hand.

Abdul could not understand why the police hired such men when their backgrounds and motives were so obvious. It seemed bizarre to Abdul and he could not believe his bad luck when, soon after joining the squad, he realised what kind of men the rest of his team were. He had initially assumed that his placement with them had been because he too was Sunni but then he learned that many of the other squads were of mixed faith. A week after joining the team Abdul applied for a transfer to another but his request was not even considered, his bosses having far too many more important things to worry about than a young police recruit's unhappiness with his fellow officers.

Iraqi Sunnis had a reputation for being more aggressive and militant than the Shi'a, and Hassan and his cronies were a perfect example. When it came to murder, for instance, an Iraqi Shi'a was likely to accept a financial payment from the murderer in compensation for the family's loss, as the Koran advised. But a Sunni was more likely to demand blood, an eye for an eye – and immediately, too.

There were two other police officers in the team besides Abdul, Hassan and Hassan's brother Ali. Arras and Karrar were boyhood friends, originally from the Sunni stronghold of Ramadi, west of Fallujah, and they had moved to Dora as teenagers. Ramadi, was notorious for its robbers and highwaymen, skills on which

Arras and Karrar hoped to build in Baghdad. All four officers were strong and determined characters who could see nothing wrong or even un-Islamic in what they did and believed it to be an acceptable way to make a living. The chance to commit crimes while working as legitimate police officers was seen as heaven-sent. It removed practically all the dangers and, better still, their victims had nowhere to turn to complain. They were certainly not the only officers of the law who practised extortion on the general public. Corrupt policemen were an accepted part of daily life in Iraq. Before the war a police officer took his life in his hands if he was corrupt. Saddam once had three officers hanged in public after they were caught demanding the equivalent of three dollars from an errant motorist.

Abdul was the smallest and most frail member of the squad. In fact, he was one of the least substantial men in the entire force. Like the majority of city Iraqis the team all wore their hair short and had well-groomed, closely trimmed facial hair – all except Hassan who wore a beard that he trimmed occasionally when it got too bushy.

'That car,' Hassan barked, indicating a fresh-looking BMW with a well-dressed young man behind the wheel who was waiting to enter the busy junction from the bridge. 'Go!'

Abdul looked at the BMW, knowing what he had to do and hating it. He picked up his Kalashnikov, pushed away from the police vehicle and walked towards the car, reluctant but obedient as always. This was why he loathed being in the police, or at least in Hassan's squad.

Disobeying traffic signals had become a national pastime in Iraq since the end of the war. Not a single electrically operated traffic indicator worked and since many of the major roads were partially or fully blocked off for security reasons drivers drove pretty much any way they wanted to in order to get to their destinations. That included mounting pavements, driving the wrong way down roads – including motorways – and going against the flow on roundabouts. This practice played into the corrupt police officers' hands: they selected their victims like sweets on a tray. When Hassan ordered Abdul to commit his first crime, the extortion of a few thousand dinars, equivalent to a couple of US dollars, from a motorist the peer pressure had been overwhelming and Abdul had not been strong enough to defy it. But since the crime involved little more than a brief conversation with no threat of repercussion, Abdul had slipped into it rather too easily. His excuse was that it was far less hassle to take part in the team's 'extracurricular' activity than to defy it. But if Abdul had examined himself more honestly he would have had to admit that although he did not like doing it he did enjoy the extra spending money it provided. Over a short period of time the battle with his conscience had been lost and at the end of the day all that remained was a general distaste for what he did. But he did it anyway.

Abdul walked to the front of the BMW and held out his hand to stop it. The young driver immediately rolled his eyes as he obeyed and pushed the button that rolled down his window.

'Can I see your registration papers?' Abdul asked.

The young man reached into his inside breast pocket, removed the papers and held them out to Abdul.

Abdul scanned through them quickly with an experienced eye and spotted a discrepancy. 'Where is the court registration?' he asked. The process of registering a new car was not particularly complicated in Iraq but since there was no longer a mail system a new owner had to present himself and the paperwork at the relevant courthouse as well as at his local police station to complete the transaction. It was an inconvenient process for many but a car was technically illegal until the procedure was completed. Although the offence was considered nowhere near serious enough for the car to be confiscated or to have the offender appear in court, technically the vehicle could be temporarily impounded and it therefore left a window of opportunity for corrupt officers to harvest a little bribe.

'Your registration is incomplete,' Abdul said.

'I plan to do it tomorrow,' the driver said, wondering why he was wasting his time debating the subject. But the Arab instinct to haggle was far too strong in him.

'I understand,' Abdul said. 'But do you understand that it is not complete today?'

'Yes, I'm sorry,' the driver said. 'I will take care of it immediately.'

'But you understand,' Abdul said politely, beginning to wonder if indeed the driver *did* understand what he meant without him actually having to say it up front.

The driver sighed as he reached into his pocket and produced several notes.

'I see you do understand,' Abdul acknowledged as he took the money and stepped back from the car to allow it to continue.

Abdul turned away and almost bumped into Hassan who looked down at the cash, took it from Abdul's hand and inspected the amount, maintaining his snarl as he pocketed it. 'Just four thousand? You don't try very hard,' he said.

'I'm not very good at it,' Abdul replied.

'Bullshit,' Hassan said. 'You're weak.'

Hassan walked away, leaving Abdul with the usual bad taste in his mouth. Much as he hated Hassan and the job that he was trapped in, gainful employment was hard to find in Iraq and since Abdul was not the entrepreneurial type it was either the police, the army or the private security sector. The army had been a non-starter since what little experience he'd had of it still haunted him. He did not have the patience and confidence nor the right contacts for a security-guard position, even though a job like that meant better pay if the right employer could be found. Joining the police force was the easiest and most convenient option because it was a simple case of filling in an application form, waiting a few weeks to be vetted cursorily and then completing the brief training course.

At the end of that day's shift, before the team dispersed to their homes or wherever, Hassan divided up the day's takings among the squad. As usual, Abdul received less than the others because, as Hassan put it, he had showed zero initiative and done the least work. But that day's collection meant fifteen dollars to him and, considering his monthly wage was a hundred and fifty dollars, he could get over twice as much in ill-gotten gains for the same period if he maintained that level of take.

Abdul arrived in Al Jeria Street in the Al Kindi block in the southern part of Al Mansour, not far from the old zoo in the centre of Baghdad. He parked his four-year-old Opal in a spot outside the apartment block where he lived and sat for a moment listening to a cassette tape of an Egyptian band, his current favourite. It was a quiet street with little traffic since it was used only by those who lived in the immediate area, although there were more cars than usual this month. They were owned by the men constructing a new house on the corner.

Abdul pulled up the collar of his leather jacket and held the lapels together to ensure that his police uniform was hidden from the gaze of any passer-by. When the track came to an end he ejected the tape and placed it in a plastic bag among a dozen or so others lying in the footwell of the back seat, climbed out of the car, lifted out a couple of shopping bags, checked there was nothing of any value visible inside the car, shut the vehicle's doors and locked them. After making the usual surreptitious glance around for strangers, he crossed the untidily finished concrete side-walk, walked in through the apartment-building entrance and up the stairs that were clean though poorly appointed. He arrived at the third floor, one from the top, a small landing shared by one other apartment, placed his key in the lock and opened the door.

'Tasneen,' he called out as he entered the apartment and closed the door behind him, making sure it was bolted at the top and bottom.

'I'm in my bedroom,' she replied, her voice young and sweet-sounding.

The clean and tidy apartment was simple and inexpensively furnished. There were signs everywhere that the occupants were young and caring: family photographs in ornate frames, a collection of dolls from Tasneen's childhood, a violin that Abdul's father had bought for him when he was a little boy in the vain hope he would one day learn it, a small hi-fi system and a television on a stand in a corner. The couch and matching side chair were made of high-gloss varnished wood with colourful flower-patterned upholstery. Against a window was a polished darkwood dining table with an empty vase in the centre of a delicate white cotton doily. A long varnished wooden shelf fixed high on a wall bore several local ornaments and an ornately bound copy of the Koran. An inexpensive floral-patterned carpet was fitted throughout the flat, except in the bathroom and the small kitchen. The finishing touch was a small, cheap but delicate chandelier that shone brightly in the centre of the ceiling.

Abdul went to the shelf, reached for the Koran,

gave it a kiss, replaced it, walked into the kitchen and put the shopping bags on the counter-top beside the sink. He went back to the door to check if Tasneen had come out of her room yet, heard a tap running in the bathroom and reached for the top of one of the two small wall cabinets. He moved a cooking pot aside and took down a china vase. He quickly stuffed the day's illicit takings inside and as he reached up to replace it he heard Tasneen walk through the living room. He hurriedly slid the cooking pot back in front of the vase and went over to the shopping bags as she walked in.

Tasneen was beautiful. Her classic dark Middle Eastern eyes were large, her olive skin perfect, her dark hair long and slightly curly with a little pink ribbon holding the ends together in the middle of her back. She smiled on seeing Abdul and gave him a kiss on his cheek, her usual greeting for him that never failed to soften his mood.

'How was your day?' she asked as she leaned over the shopping bags to look inside. She was slightly smaller than Abdul but unlike him could not be described as frail.

'Usual,' he said, moving to the window beside the sink.

'How was Hassan today? Your friends still mean to you?'

'That's like asking me if there were traffic jams in the city today,' Abdul replied as he watched Tasneen take items from the bag and place them in their correct places in the cupboards. 'There was a car bomb in Sadoon Street. It went off right across the river from us.'

Tasneen sighed. 'You know I don't like to hear those stories.'

Abdul shrugged. 'You asked how my day went . . . We went to investigate. You know how Hassan likes to drive anywhere that gives him an an excuse to use his siren and flashing lights . . . It wasn't too bad, though. Only three people killed. They think the driver blew himself up by mistake because there wasn't any target that anyone could see . . . As usual, Hassan told anyone who cared to listen that it was an American rocket . . . The man's an idiot as well as everything else.'

Tasneen folded the empty bag, put it into a drawer and started on the second one.

'I was thinking about getting a job as an army interpreter,' Abdul continued.

'You should. Your English is almost good enough,' Tasneen said as she placed a bag of rice on the counter for use later.

'Almost?' he queried.

'Almost, but not quite. But I will help you,' she said as she pulled out a jar of coffee, inspected the label and then turned to face Abdul while holding it up for him to see. 'Turkish Abala?' she asked, a frown spreading across her face.

'Yes,' he said, shrugging. 'So? It's your favourite.'

'It costs seven thousand dinar.'

'I got it because you like it.'

'There are a lot of things I like that we can't afford

70

any more.' Tasneen stared into her brother's eyes, her frown intensifying until he could no longer hold her gaze.

'Why do you always do this?' he said as he walked out of the room.

Tasneen put down the coffee jar and looked into the bag at the rest of the contents. As she picked out a couple of other expensive items her frown was replaced by a look of hopelessness.

She left the kitchen, saw that Abdul was not in the living room and walked across to his bedroom. She stood in the doorway, watching as he removed his jacket.

'You're still taking money, aren't you?' she asked accusingly.

Abdul ignored her as he removed his semi-automatic pistol from its holster and placed it on a dresser. Then he sat down on the bed and started to untie his shoelaces.

'My brother is a thief,' she said resignedly in response to his silence.

'I'm *not* a thief,' he snapped, glaring at her.

'You take money that is not yours under false pretences. That is stealing.'

'They're fines.'

'Fines,' she said, hitting a higher note. 'Fines go to the government. When you put the money in your pocket it's theft.'

'They owe us it, anyway.'

'Who does?'

'The government. You know how little we get paid.'

71

'Is that what you tell yourself? Or is that what your new friend Hassan tells you to get you to do it?'

Abdul held onto his temper as he removed his boots, got up and walked past her. 'What's for supper?' he asked as he sat on the couch and picked up the remote television control.

'I'm not your wife, Abdul. I work too.'

He sighed heavily, struggling to overcome his anger as he repeatedly clicked the remote, unable to get it to respond correctly. 'There is no government anyhow.'

'You're getting more like them every day. You're not in a police force. You're in a gang.'

The television came on too loudly – an Egyptian soap opera – and Tasneen moved briskly across the room to turn it off. 'Abdul? Listen to me. Don't you realise what you are doing?'

'I'm earning us a living, that's what I'm doing,' he said, raising his voice unconvincingly in his effort to dominate her.

Tasneen might have been delicate in stature but the fire in her bright oval eyes showed greater determination than her brother possessed. 'At what price?' she said, placing her hands on her hips. 'Our mother and father would be horrified if they knew.'

'Father left us nothing. The house was practically destroyed and no one will buy it for years.'

Tasneen exhaled heavily, calming herself in an effort to bring down the temperature. 'We earn a good enough living between us. You don't need to steal.'

'This is not a living. You work for an American contractor in the Green Zone. You have to hide

72

yourself each time you go in and come out, every day wondering if a suicide bomber will blow himself up at the checkpoint, always wondering if someone will follow you home and one day kill you for working for the Americans.'

'And what about you?' she snapped. 'It's the same for you, isn't it? You hide your police uniform when you come home for the same reasons. It's how things are, Abdul. It's how we live. But at least I have my self-respect.'

'I'm not a thief! You know that. But you don't know what it's like working with those people. I can't refuse them.'

'Why not?'

Abdul shook his head in frustration at her complete ignorance. 'What do I say to them? That I'm not going to be a part of the squad any more?'

'Yes,' Tasneen said, hitting her high note again.

'I would have to quit the police.'

'And what's wrong with that? It's better than doing what you do.'

'And then how do we live? You don't earn enough money for the both of us.'

'Get another job.'

'Doing what?'

'As a security guard. You can earn maybe four, five hundred dollars a month doing that.'

The first thought that popped into Abdul's head was that he earned more than that with his supplementary income anyway. But he dared not say that to her. 'Then get me a job,' he said.

Tasneen gritted her teeth in irritation as she watched him fold his arms across his chest and stare at the blank television screen. 'We cannot go on like this, Abdul,' she said. 'You know it as well as I do. It can only get worse.'

He didn't move other than to direct his sullen stare down at the floor.

'I hate this bad feeling I have for you,' she said. 'I hate it when we talk like this to each other . . . You don't even seem to want to try to change the way you are living . . . What happened to you, Abdul? You were always a good boy. You and I were always happy together.'

'*You* were always happy,' he snapped. 'But you're a girl. It's easy for you. I'm a man.'

'Are you?' she said softly.

Abdul glared at his sister and for the first time in his adulthood he wanted to hit her.

'I still only see the little boy in you,' she went on. 'I love you, Abdul, my little brother, but I have never seen the man in you yet.'

He jumped to his feet and took a step towards her, his fists clenched, one of them slightly raised as if he was about to strike. But she did not waver, her eyes staring into his.

Tasneen had not seen this coming and she was shocked. She did not flinch or try to avoid his threatened blow, mainly because Abdul's aggression had taken her completely by surprise – not that she would have moved to avoid it, anyway.

But, after all, Abdul could not hit her and was

immediately filled with remorse at the thought of it. He lowered his hand and went back into his room, closing the door behind him.

Although he had not struck her, Tasneen had felt a sting of a kind. She had not been aware of the level of stress that Abdul was experiencing and instead of remaining horrified she was suddenly filled with pity for her brother. She always listened to his daily stories about his work with interest, except when he talked about death and explosions. But she realised that she was listening without really hearing, especially what he was saying between the lines. Abdul had always been highly strung and talkative about his woes, often painting an exaggerated picture – as far as she could tell, anyway. She knew he was different from her: weaker, or more sensitive, to put it kindly, but she never made allowance for that when she heard how he reacted to events. He always laughed at things that didn't amuse her, trivial things like children's cartoons, for instance. But then he became stressed over things that she hardly took seriously. Money was one example. But then, Abdul was more materialistic than she was.

Tasneen was a strong-willed self-sufficient woman. She was modern by Arab standards – far too modern for Abdul's liking, despite his attraction to western trappings such as cars, digital watches and electronic gadgets. He was technically head of the household and was strongly drawn to the family's ancient tribal doctrines, ethics and religion, things that his sister had little time for even though she was in effect its driving force and the guardian of its principles. She liked equality of the sexes and was interested in other cultures, though she had never been outside Iraq. The idea of one day going to London or New York would set her daydreaming. She could gaze for hours at pictures of the Alps and she loved modern movies, especially those filmed in places like Florence or Paris, and not always only because of the story. It was the views of the lives of others she liked, specifically those of Americans and Europeans. The attraction was the freedom that she felt those countries offered.

As a woman Tasneen was stifled in Iraq and since the end of the war, or more specifically since working in the Green Zone among Americans and Europeans, the kind of people whose company she had never experienced before, she had begun to believe that she might have a chance to live her dream. She hated every aspect of the war but the end of the dictatorship, despite its violent circumstances, had given her a hope that she'd never had before. She had no real plans to travel across Iraq's borders in the immediate future, but one day she hoped to. She was relying on fate to turn her dreams into reality and hoped that it would one day free her to fly away and explore all the places and experiences she had so often imagined.

She faced Abdul's door, wanting to speak to him, to apologise for not understanding him. But she decided to let it go for the time being. He was clearly deeply troubled and the best thing she could do, she felt, was what she always did at times like this: to simply be there for him if he needed her. The fact that she had no real solutions for him either sometimes made

76

her feel like a hypocrite anyway. Perhaps one day fate might be good to him too. She knew he would never have deliberately chosen to be a thief and Tasneen could only hope that he would find a way out of his dilemma.

'I'll make us some supper, Abdul,' she said softly.

He did not answer. She raised a hand to touch the door, changed her mind and walked away into the kitchen.

Abdul lay on his bed, staring up at the ceiling. He had heard his sister but had chosen to stay silent. His anger was already receding. She was right, as always. But then, it didn't take a genius to figure out how wrong his position was. It might take one to figure out what he was going to do with his life, though, for he could see no hope or opportunities on the horizon. He felt as if he was wasting his existence on this earth. So many people he knew were making a fortune out of the war and there were so many stories of success. The truth was that he had no idea what 'success' really meant to him. It wasn't money. Not really. Abdul appreciated it but it was not what drove him. His problem was that he didn't know what did. That was Allah's job, to direct him, guide him, show him what to do. Perhaps Allah was unable to do this while Abdul conducted himself as he did, stealing from drivers. It was an impossible dilemma.

Another thing that was starting to bother Abdul was his marital status. He needed to find a partner and get married, and soon. It was important for a young Arab man and an essential religious as well as social step. But there were two important obstacles he needed to overcome. The first was that he didn't know a girl whom he wanted to marry and the second, which he needed to solve before he could deal with the first, was his income. A police officer's pay was far too low to attract the kind of woman he wanted or, more to the point, impress the *parents* of the kind of woman he would like to wed. Good families expected suitors at least to provide a home for their daughters, preferably one they owned and did not share with other members of the suitor's family. He needed a higher income and therefore a better job. And as for sharing the apartment, the only way around that was for Tasneen to get married to a man who had his own house so that she could move out. But that was not going to be easy either since Tasneen was not a normal girl.

Abdul's sister was eligible, beautiful and intelligent, not that any of those factors mattered except the first while the last one was valued least of all. The biggest problem was Tasneen herself. She didn't seem to like any man, not enough to marry him, anyway. The disadvantage of her having no parents was that there was no one pressuring her into marriage other than Abdul who had about as much influence over her on that subject as the Pope. Tasneen was far too western in her outlook and attitude. She was too free a thinker, too liberated and most un-Islamic. Considering the concern that she endlessly expressed for him Abdul found it irritating how Tasneen could not see that his advancement was directly related to her getting married as soon as possible.

It was all an impossible situation and one over which he seemed to have little or no control. Abdul decided that the best thing he could do was concentrate on the main issue of the moment which was his job with the police or, to use Tasneen's admittedly accurate description, with his gang of thieves. Since he could not get a transfer he would simply have to tell them that he could no longer take part in their corrupt activities. But the thought of actually telling them filled Abdul with dread. Everyone in the team had to be in on the game. Even Abdul could see the reasoning behind that. Hassan would not allow it to be any other way. There was only one other thing Abdul could do and that was to quit. Deep down, he knew that was the only way out.

Abdul's phone began to chirp a cheerful Arab tune that got louder the longer it remained unanswered. He dug it out of his pocket and looked at the screen to read the number. It was Hassan.

Abdul did not answer it right away, wondering what the man could be wanting. Perhaps God had made Hassan call so that Abdul could tell him he was quitting. Abdul immediately erased that thought out of fear of Hassan's reaction.

He took a grip of himself. There was nothing to be afraid of in the long run. Hassan couldn't kill him just for quitting the police. It was possible that Hassan might even find the prospect acceptable since he did not like Abdul in any case.

Abdul hit a button on the phone and put it to his ear. '*Salom alycom*, Hassan,' he said.

'Shut up,' Hassan growled. 'We are meeting at the police academy tonight at ten.'

'But I am not working tonight—'

'Shut up, I said. You *are* working tonight. There is an operation and we are a part of it. We will meet at the rear entrance to the academy on Palestine Street. Don't be late.'

It was pointless to argue with the man. He was the sergeant and an order was an order. It was not unusual to be called at home to take part in an operation even when you'd just come off duty. There was a shortage of police officers and the bosses usually called in as many men as they could if the job was anything to do with capturing insurgents. This was only the second time Abdul had been called out for a night operation and although he had been looking forward to an evening in front of the television and a good night's sleep, duty called. At least he would not have to stop cars and ask for bribes.

'I'll be there,' Abdul said and the phone went dead.

He tossed it onto the bed and massaged his hands. Hassan always made him tense.

Abdul got to his feet and exhaled deeply as he rolled his shoulders in an effort to relax and compose himself. His thoughts went back to his sister as he heard a noise from the kitchen. He would go and be nice to her and even help prepare the meal. She did far more than he did in the home, all the cleaning and laundry as well as making most of the meals. Abdul often washed up the dishes afterwards but he did little more than that. That was OK for ordinary Arab girls but

Tasneen was different and she meant more to him than their sisters did to other Arab boys.

Abdul decided not to tell her about his plan to quit the force. He would break the news to her once he had told Hassan. And for the rest of the evening until he left he would be his old cheerful self.

Abdul opened the door, stepped into the living room and was about to cross it towards the kitchen when he stopped and looked up at the Koran on its shelf. He reached for it, took it down and held it to his heart as he begged Allah to watch over him and help him with his plans. Then he kissed the book, put it back on the shelf and, suddenly feeling a lot better about everything, headed for the kitchen, a broad smile on his face.

3

Abdul's Miscalculation

Abdul drove along Palestine Street, a dual carriageway that ran into the southern corner of the infamous Sada City in the north-east quadrant of Baghdad. He glanced over his left shoulder at the rear entrance of the police academy as he passed it, a narrow opening in a high wall that looked like it led into a long alleyway with a heavy steel security gate at the end. It was a dark, chilly night. There were no street lights and, due to the nightly curfew, traffic was light, one of the few benefits of being a policeman and driving at night in Baghdad.

Abdul caught sight of several vehicles parked off the road against the perimeter wall near the entrance, one of which looked like Hassan's sparkling new red Opal.

A couple of hundred metres further on Abdul reached a wide junction beneath a motorway under-pass where he made a tight U-turn into the oncoming lanes and headed back towards the academy entrance.

He pulled off the road and onto the rubble-strewn ground, stopped behind the group of cars he recog-nised as belonging to Arras, Karrar and Ali, killed the engine and climbed out. There were several groups of men huddled together along the perimeter wall, and Abdul saw his squad standing in front of Hassan's car, all of them smoking. Abdul locked his car doors, pulled his leather jacket tight against the chilly air and walked over to join them.

None of the men greeted Abdul as he stepped in among them. He was used to their coldness towards him and bid them hello despite it, determined to remain positive for his planned conversation with Hassan. The only thing Abdul had not decided on was the ideal moment to broach the subject. But as soon as he saw the faces of the others he suspected that something was not quite right with them, as if they had heard some bad news and were unable to look at him squarely. Another oddity was that he could always expect a rude or insulting comment from at least one of them but tonight they appeared to be too distracted even for that. Perhaps they were unhappy about being dragged out to work at a time when they all would have preferred to be at home.

'What's the job, then?' Abdul asked, deliberately acting perky as proof that he did not mind being out at that time.

Ali took a last draw on his cigarette, dropped it between his feet and ground it into the soil with the toe of his boot. As if it was a signal to the others, Arras and Karrar also tossed their cigarette butts away.

'You have a balaclava?' Hassan asked Abdul.

'No,' Abdul replied. Many officers carried some kind of headwear that they could cover their faces with, often wearing them while on the job. Police officers were perceived by many Iraqis as lackeys of the Americans and there were considerable dangers in being recognised. Depending on where a man lived or where a task took him there was a risk of retribution. A high number of officers had been killed while off duty, although no one knew the exact figure because the authorities did not like to publicise it. Many policemen had simply disappeared, never to be heard from again, while the corpses of others had been found in one of the several popular places to dump bodies. There was a large piece of open ground to the east of Sadar City for Shi'a victims, another east of Dora for Sunni. Or there was always the Tigris river. Mothers, wives and children often turned up at police headquarters looking for their loved ones, having seen or heard nothing of them for days. Abdul never bothered to disguise himself, mainly because none of the others in the squad did. He also lived in a relatively safe neighbourhood and considered the precautions he took to be adequate.

Hassan reached into a pocket, removed a balaclava and tossed it to Abdul. It hit his chest and dropped to the ground. Abdul picked it up and shook the dust off it.

'Button your jacket up to the top,' Hassan growled at Abdul. 'Hide your uniform.'

Abdul obeyed. 'What is the operation?' he asked again, hoping for a reply.

'A raid,' Hassan said.

'A raid?' Abdul asked. 'Where?' No one replied but

Abdul had the feeling they knew more about it. 'Who are we raiding?' Abdul persisted, finding the courage to push them a little.

'You ask too many questions,' Hassan growled. 'We'll take two cars,' he said to the others, disconnecting from Abdul. 'Yours and mine,' he said to his brother.

Several cars appeared in the alley heading out of the police academy towards Palestine Street.

'That's the chief,' Hassan said. 'Let's get in the cars.'

The other police squads dispersed to their vehicles and Abdul followed Hassan. He had been on one previous night raid and had been told nothing about it beforehand either, which was understandable. It was no secret that the police had been infiltrated by supporters of the insurgency and in the past warnings had been communicated to evacuate targeted premises before the police squads arrived. Abdul wondered if Hassan actually knew the location himself but that did not explain the strange atmosphere within the group.

'What are you waiting for?' Hassan shouted at him. 'Get in with Ali.'

Abdul climbed into the back of Ali's BMW while Arras occupied the front passenger seat. The cars started up, their headlights flashed on and Hassan followed the last of the other squad vehicles onto the road with Ali moving in behind.

Abdul thought he could sense a level of tension among the members of his team which was unusual, especially if they didn't know where they were going or what they were doing. Abdul thought he was imagining it until both men lit up cigarettes having only just put one out.

'Do you think this will be a short raid or an all-night one?' Abdul asked. He didn't receive an answer and sighed audibly. 'Why do you people always treat me like an idiot?'

'Because you *are* one,' Arras snapped, looking around at him, his eyes cold.

'There are several raids tonight,' Ali eventually said.

Ali was the most intelligent of the bunch. But it was a sly intelligence, like that of a desert fox. He was the least abrasive towards Abdul but for no other reason than it was his nature to be more controlled. Karrar, driving with Hassan, was generally mute most of the time but that was because he was as thick as a tombstone and incapable of independent thought. Abdul judged Arras to be the most lethal of the bunch. He was utterly ruthless, had a short fuse, and without Hassan to control him Abdul suspected that he could be very dangerous if upset.

'Several raids?' Abdul asked, surprised.

Arras glanced at Ali as if wondering why he had revealed so much. But Ali was as confident as always. 'They are taking place concurrently,' Ali said.

'Why did Hassan not say?' Abdul asked.

'There's no secrecy,' Ali said smoothly. 'It's only security. Why do you need to know? Why do any of us, other than Hassan, need to know, for that matter? He is the only one who needs to know where we are going. When you see the place and are doing the job you will know everything.'

'Why don't you just shut up and relax, eh?' Arras said, glancing back briefly at Abdul.

They passed the old sports stadium, crossed the motorway flyover and headed into the Karada district. Traffic was light but as they turned around the Ali Baba roundabout – where there was a statue of Kahramana filling the fabled forty pots – a combined US Army and Iraqi police checkpoint came into view ahead. The other squad cars were passing through it and Hassan looked as if he was about to follow when he suddenly swerved past the turning and took the next roundabout exit.

Ali followed Hassan and Abdul sat forward in his seat, looking at the road ahead and wondering why they had left the other police vehicles.

'We are going to do our part of the job,' Ali said, as if he had noticed Abdul's concern.

Abdul sat back again and looked out of his window, Ali's suggestion that he would know soon enough echoing in his head. The car's heater was on too high for Abdul and he undid the buttons on his leather jacket to let in some air.

Hassan pulled off the main road and slowed as they entered a quiet residential street. There was no street lighting and no moving traffic. Parked cars were drawn up on both sides of the road. Most of the houses were in darkness, indicating a power cut in the neighbour-hood which was normal for this time of night. Those that had lights obviously had their own generators or benzene lamps but with the current fuel shortage only those who could afford the black-market prices enjoyed the luxury of power at night.

Hassan turned his vehicle along another narrow street, pulled over and parked against the kerb. Ali tucked in behind him and both cars fell silent as their engines and lights went off.

Abdul was expecting everyone to climb out right away but they sat still in the darkness without even communicating. This seemed like further evidence of a pre-raid plan to which he was not privy.

After a couple of minutes, Hassan climbed out of his car and, leaving Karrar in the passenger seat, walked down the road looking at the houses on both sides as if searching for a particular one.

Hassan walked out of sight into the darkness and was gone for several minutes before Abdul saw his silhouette walking back on the other side of the street. He crossed back to his car, leaned in through the open window to say something to Karrar, then headed for his brother's car as Karrar climbed out.

Ali opened the door and Hassan looked in at the men. 'Everyone out and follow me,' Hassan said.

Ali and Arras obeyed. Abdul followed, but the sudden palpable rise in tension infected him and he began to feel uneasy.

Hassan walked down the pavement a short distance before stepping sideways into a large doorway and out of what little light there was. The others followed him, Abdul bringing up the rear. He stayed just outside the small recess.

'Get in here,' Hassan hissed.

Abdul moved in closer, aware of a distinct rise in Hassan's anxiety as his stare flicked in all directions.

Hassan removed his balaclava from his jacket pocket, put it on his head and pulled it fully down over his face, adjusting it so that his eyes were centred in the oval slits. The others followed his example.

Abdul took his balaclava out of his pocket and paused before putting it on. 'What is my part in this?' he asked in a low voice.

'Just put on your balaclava,' Hassan growled.

'When will you tell me?' Abdul asked.

Hassan gritted his teeth and clenched his fists as if he was about to thump Abdul.

'Do what you are told, you prick,' Arras snarled.

Abdul stepped back from the men in their black balaclavas, their white eyes glaring at him. They looked like a pack of satanic beasts. There was something unholy about whatever they were up to, Abdul was certain of it. The mistake he had made with this evil partnership was getting involved in the first place. Whatever these men were about to do was worse than taking petty bribes from drivers, he was sure of it. 'I don't want to do this,' Abdul suddenly blurted out.

The others looked between Hassan and Abdul, wondering what the boss was going to do about this untimely and wholly inconvenient outburst.

'I don't want to be in this team any more. I wanted to tell you earlier but you never gave me the chance,' Abdul added quickly. 'You don't like me. You treat me like a leper. Why don't you just let me go?' he demanded.

Hassan was staring at him, weighing his response,

barely controlling a gut instinct to pound Abdul into the ground.

Arras had no doubts about what he wanted to do with Abdul but he would have to wait for Hassan to give the word.

'I've made my mind up,' Abdul said. 'I'm going to go back to the car and wait for you there.'

But as Abdul started to turn away Hassan grabbed his arm with one hand and gave him such a brutal swipe around the side of his face with the other that Abdul would have fallen to the ground had Hassan released his grip. Abdul raised his hands to protect himself against another blow which Hassan was about to deliver when Ali caught his hand.

'Hassan,' Ali said in a loud whisper. 'This is not the place for this.'

Hassan glared like a maniac at his brother for a few seconds before the words filtered through his rage. He lowered his hand and faced Abdul, pulling him close and holding him firmly so that their noses were inches apart.

'Listen to me, you little turd,' Hassan said with intense malice. 'You will do as you are ordered. One more word out of you and I'll break your neck. Do you understand me?'

Abdul had seen Hassan this angry once before. On that occasion the recipient of his ire, an errant driver who had made the mistake of telling Hassan to go screw his mother, apparently did not regain consciousness for several days. Abdul nodded.

'Tell me,' Hassan hissed, tightening his grip around Abdul's neck until his windpipe started to hurt.

'I understand,' Abdul croaked.

'Put on your balaclava,' Hassan said again, releasing Abdul but staying threateningly close.

Abdul took a few seconds to regain his breath before pulling his balaclava onto his head and over his face.

Hassan pulled his weapon out of its holster and moved out of the doorway. 'You,' he said, looking back at Abdul. 'With me.'

Abdul moved alongside Hassan who grabbed his arm and pushed him ahead. 'Take the lead,' Hassan said.

Abdul walked slowly up the pavement for a short distance before looking back to see the others following in a line. Fear and anxiety began to course through his body as he wondered what Hassan was going to do with him – and what was going to happen on this raid that he was now leading.

Abdul walked on a little further and when he slowed to look behind him again Hassan urged him on with a stiff shove.

Halfway down the street Hassan grabbed the back of Abdul's jacket to halt him. When Abdul turned to see why, Hassan was looking at a car parked against the pavement beside him. It was an old dark-blue BMW and Hassan looked back at his brother who nodded in confirmation.

Hassan pushed Abdul forward again. 'Keep going,' he whispered.

They reached a house where a light glowed dimly on the second floor. Hassan moved nimbly past Abdul and went to the front door. He paused to look around before moving closer and pressing his ear against it.

A moment later he beckoned Abdul to join him. Abdul stepped beside Hassan who suddenly grabbed him roughly. 'Keep your ear to the door and listen,' Hassan whispered. 'You hear a sound, you let me know.' Hassan did not wait for a response from Abdul and moved to join his men who had gathered in a tight group in the shadows of the building.

Abdul watched the devilish quartet whispering together and kept his ear to the door as he'd been ordered. He thought he heard a sound from inside and as he focused his attention on it he was suddenly yanked unceremoniously back. Arras moved to take his place, opened his jacket and removed a hefty crowbar as he pressed his ear to the door.

The others stood close by, Abdul a head shorter than any of them and hemmed in tightly, unable to escape even if he had dared to try.

Arras stepped back from the door and worked the crowbar into the frame. As he slowly levered it to one side the wood began to split but the lock held. He wiggled the bar further in and then levered it back once again. There was a loud crack and the door popped open.

Hassan did not waste a second and pushed past Arras and into the house with anxious haste. Ali and Arras followed quickly while Abdul was shoved inside by Karrar who brought up the rear.

Karrar closed the door behind him and the five men stood like black sentinels in the hallway as if waiting for a signal to move. Halfway along the dark narrow hallway a flight of stairs led to the floor above and Hassan moved to the foot, his pistol in his hand. Without looking back he signalled for the others to move and they obeyed stealthily.

Arras and Ali passed Hassan and continued along the hall to the first door, which was partly open. The room was dark inside. The two men went inside and a few seconds later reappeared and moved further down the dark passageway to the next door.

A few seconds later they came out and went further back into the house, disappearing into the darkness.

Abdul hardly moved, watching Hassan who kept his pistol aimed up the stairs. Karrar breathed deeply behind him. Judging by Hassan's air of intensity and his cautious stance, the man was expecting resistance. Abdul hoped it would end soon but then he realised that he would still be left to deal with Hassan and the matter of his resignation. Abdul was no longer confident that the issue was going to be resolved quite as easily as he had hoped.

Ali and Arras returned from the dark hallway and Ali shook his head at his brother.

Hassan directed his full attention to the top of the stairs. As he placed his foot on the first step it creaked. He paused before applying his full weight but the step creaked again as he raised his other foot and placed it on the next one. That creaked too but the third did not and Hassan continued slowly towards the top, the business end of his pistol leading the way.

The others mounted the stairs behind him. Ali and Arras avoided the first two steps. Karrar nudged Abdul forward: he placed his foot on the first step that once

93

again creaked loudly. Arras stopped to look back with a scowl and Karrar jabbed Abdul viciously in his side.

Abdul winced at the blow and placed his other foot higher up. Arras maintained his warning glare for a moment longer before looking back towards the top of the stairs and taking another step up.

Hassan reached the final step where a closed door blocked access to the floor. The others closed in behind him.

Hassan looked back at his pack to ensure that they were ready. Every white eye, encircled by its black woollen slit, was wide and alert – except Abdul's. His eyes flickered with frightened uncertainty. He was jammed tightly between Arras and Karrar, both of them holding their pistols at the ready.

Hassan faced the door which was painted dull brown, leaned forward and pressed his ear to it. His free hand reached for the doorknob and slowly turned it. He gave it a slight push but the door did not move. Hassan exhaled through his nose – the sound was quite loud in the still air – and stepped back until his arm holding the doorknob was at full stretch. The others leaned back to give him room. With a sudden sharp intake of breath, Hassan shoved his full weight forward. His shoulder struck the wooden door, the bolt inside sprang free and it flew open.

Hassan moved forward with his own momentum and his men followed. Abdul was caught up in the press of bodies as Karrar shoved him hard and they spilled into a room that was bathed in a dull golden glow from a benzene lamp.

The room was not very big and was sparsely furnished with a couch and a dining table. A kitchenette took up one corner. Abdul saw two people lying on mattresses, one a man in his fifties, his eyes wide in shock and holding a book next to the lamp. Ali and Arras were upon the two figures like hyenas, Ali grabbing the man by his neck and jamming a gun into his face. The other figure, a woman as old as the man, awoke and sat up as her eyes tried to focus, her mouth opening in fear. Arras threw his weight onto her while shoving his hand over her face, brutally pushing her head back onto the mattress.

Meanwhile, Hassan continued through the room to its only other door. He raised his leg and kicked open this latest obstruction. Karrar shoved Abdul across the room to the doorway where he left him. In the second room a man and woman were in bed under a sheet. Karrar joined Hassan as they sat up. Hassan pulled back the sheet to reveal that they were both naked and, grabbing the woman by her hair, dragged her off the bed as she screamed. Karrar took hold of the man by his throat and shoved his pistol in his face.

Abdul watched in confused horror. These pathetic-looking people were not the hardened desperados he had been expecting.

'Bring him,' Hassan shouted. Karrar obeyed, brusquely turning the frightened man over, twisting his arm halfway up his back and pulling him off the bed. The man yelped at the pain while complying as best he could with Karrar's efforts to get him to his feet, around the bed and to the door.

The slender woman was in her early thirties and Hassan kept a firm hold of her thick long dark hair as he pulled her past Abdul and into the main room. The naked man followed, grimacing while balancing on tiptoe as he struggled to reduce the pressure on his arm. The man's skin was white and his hair was light, neither feature uncommon in the western reaches of Iraq, but his overall look was distinctly Anglo-Saxon.

The naked woman yelped at every tug on her hair while the Anglo-looking man groaned in response to Karrar's brutal grip. Abdul was conscious of the bala-clava over his face and felt distinctly weird as he looked through the narrow eyelets at the unfolding scene.

The older couple were forced to their feet by Ali and Arras who shoved them against the wall. Hassan pushed the naked woman beside them and released her. She held her hands over her breasts and genital area as she cried out. 'Please, please don't hurt us,' she kept begging.

'Shut up!' Hassan shouted as he aimed his gun at her face, his eyes intense. She immediately stopped speaking, although she could not control her whim-pering. Karrar kept hold of the male westerner as Ali and Arras stepped back, their pistols levelled at the terrified older couple.

Then Hassan seemed to calm down a little as everyone in the room came under his control. He turned his attention to the naked man. Karrar pulled the man's head back by his hair so that he was forced to face the boss.

'What's your name?' Hassan demanded. The man did

not answer as he looked fearfully at Hassan and then at the naked woman. 'Abdul,' Hassan growled. 'Ask him his name.'

Abdul was almost as frightened as the man and did not understand what Hassan had asked him. 'W–what?' he stammered.

'I said ask him his name,' Hassan repeated.

Abdul looked at the frightened man who was only slightly bigger than himself. 'What is your name?' he said.

'In English, you idiot!' Hassan shouted. 'He is not Arab.'

Abdul made an extreme effort to compose himself as his mouth suddenly went dry. 'What your name?' he asked in broken English.

The naked man glanced at Abdul with pleading eyes when he recognised his language, perhaps sensing in the tone of his voice that this Arab might have some sympathy in his heart. 'J–Jeffrey Lamont,' the man stammered, his face a picture of utter fear. 'You will be paid a lot of money if you—'

'Who does he work for?' Hassan snapped.

'What you company work for?' Abdul asked in heavily accented English as he struggled to get his lips and tongue around the language that he had learned in school. He had only spoken it very occasionally with his sister in the last few years.

'Detron Communications,' the man said.

'A communications company,' Abdul relayed to Hassan.

'What kind of communications?' Hassan asked.

'I don't know,' Abdul said.

'Ask him, you idiot!' Hassan shouted, his temper going up and down with his blood pressure.

Abdul took a moment to form the words but he was not quick enough for Hassan. 'You said you could speak English,' Hassan said accusingly.

'It's been a while,' Abdul said nervously.

'Ask him!' Hassan shouted again.

Abdul swallowed hard and made an effort to concentrate. 'What you communications?' he asked.

'I . . . I don't know what you mean,' the man said, desperately wanting to comply but too confused.

'What . . . kind . . . of communication you work for? What communications?' Abdul asked.

'Phones. We put up mobile phone masts. We're bringing communications to your country,' Lamont said, pleading. 'Please don't hurt us.'

Abdul felt desperately sorry for the man but tried not to let it show as he spoke to Hassan. 'He builds mobile phone masts.'

The man's stare dropped to Abdul's jacket that had opened and he caught a glimpse of his chest badge on his blue shirt. 'You're police,' the man said.

Hassan looked at Abdul's open jacket, then at the naked woman and the old couple who were staring at the badge.

'I have a DoD pass,' the man said. 'In my pocket,' he added, suddenly hopeful that this could be resolved. 'In my trousers. In the room,' he went on.

Hassan looked at the man. He knew what a DoD pass was. It was an identification badge that all foreign reconstruction contractors carried. Issued by the US Army, it allowed them into the Green Zone as well as into coalition camps anywhere in the country. As a police officer, often running checkpoints, Hassan had seen hundreds of them. 'Where's his DoD?' he asked Abdul.

'In his trouser pocket in the bedroom,' Abdul answered.

Hassan went into the bedroom.

'And my passport,' Lamont said. 'I'm an American citizen,' he added, clarifying his legitimacy.

Hassan returned with the man's DoD, passport and wallet. He checked the documents and then the wallet: it contained a few hundred dollars which he pocketed. Then he turned his attention to the woman.

She had calmed down a little on realising that the intruders were police but she was still frightened.

'Are you a whore?' Hassan asked her coldly.

'No. I am not a whore,' the woman said in a defiant tone.

'Are you Muslim?' Hassan asked her.

'Yes,' she replied.

'Then why are you sleeping with this infidel?' Hassan asked as he looked down at her naked body, his gaze resting for a moment on her hand cupped protectively over her vagina.

'Because I love him,' she declared.

Hassan removed his balaclava and looked at her, a grimace of disgust on his face. He raised his gun, aimed it at her eyes, and squeezed the trigger. The pistol fired. Blood shot from the back of the woman's head and splashed the wall behind her as she dropped to the floor, the life instantly gone from her.

'NO!' the naked man yelled, struggling in Karrar's grip. The other woman screamed. Hassan gave Ali and Arras a cold look and the men fired their guns into the heads of the older couple who dropped instantly to the floor, their corpses sprawling next to each other.

Arras took a step forward and fired a bullet into each of their heads and another into the naked woman's for good measure.

Lamont howled despondently, his face contorted with grief, his mouth wide open as his eyes filled with tears.

'Take him,' Hassan said as he stepped over the bodies towards the door.

Karrar pulled the westerner towards the door but the man wrenched himself out of his grasp and threw himself at the dead naked woman. 'Fatima!' he shouted, the pain in his voice startling in its intensity.

Arras moved quickly to help Karrar control Lamont who fought strongly to resist them. Arras had a simple solution to the problem and slammed the butt of his pistol down onto the top of the man's head, following it up with a savage punch to his kidney. The man went limp but remained conscious and Karrar lifted him to his feet and steered him to the door.

Hassan let Ali lead the way out of the room, followed by Karrar and the American. He was about to follow when he realised that Abdul had not moved and was staring down at the bodies.

'Abdul!' Hassan called out. 'Move!'

But Abdul could not hear him through the dreadful mist of revulsion that filled his mind.

'Get him,' Hassan growled. Arras responded, grabbing Abdul by his lapel and pulling him to the door. Abdul did not resist, as if he had lost control over all his motor functions other than his breathing and the beating of his heart. He stumbled over the legs of the dead couple and the near-fall brought him back to life: as he reached the doorway he grabbed the door frame to stop himself.

Abdul looked back at the corpses of the old couple and the naked woman. Then he peered at Hassan who was staring at him.

'You want to join them?' Hassan asked.

The words were as sincere as any that Abdul had heard in his life. He shook his head.

'Get going, then,' Hassan said, his voice soft.

Arras pushed Abdul through the doorway and he clambered down the stairs, hanging on to the banister to stop himself from rolling down into the darkness.

Arras followed closely and as Abdul reached the bottom he was shoved along the corridor and out through the front door. Arras did not let up – he took hold of Abdul's lapel again and pulled him along the pavement, following Karrar and Ali as they man-handled the naked Lamont towards the cars. Hassan was in the rear, his gun held by his side, ready in case they should be challenged.

Karrar and Ali speeded up as they reached Hassan's red Opal and bundled the American into the back.

Arras shoved Abdul into the back of Ali's car where he joined him. Ali climbed in behind the wheel.

Both cars came to life and seconds later were turning out of the side street and onto the main road.

Arras and Ali removed their balaclavas and Arras pulled off Abdul's, giving him a hard shove in the process. 'What's your problem?' Arras shouted. 'Why are you so pathetic?'

'Leave him,' Ali said, still on full alert, his stare darting everywhere.

But Arras's blood was up and he could not back down easily. 'Why is he in this team?' he demanded.

'Because he is, that's all,' Ali said.

'But why? Why do we keep him? Why don't we get rid of him?'

'Because we can't,' Ali stated.

'I mean as in get *rid* of him,' Arras said, putting his gun at Abdul's head, itching to pull the trigger.

Ali grinned as he looked in the rear-view mirror at the pair, Arras with murder in his eyes and Abdul with total fear in his. 'We'd have to make a report. We don't want to draw attention to ourselves. Don't you think Hassan would have thrown him into the river ages ago if he'd wanted to? He's been given to us by God and we must look after him.'

'But he's useless,' Arras said, exasperated. 'He's a liability.'

'He won't be. Isn't that right, Abdul? You're a good little boy who does what he's told.'

Abdul had hardly heard a word. His head was filled with the images of those people being shot, replaying the scene over and over.

'He's a hypocrite,' Arras spat. 'He takes money but he disapproves of how we get it. What kind of a person is that?'

'Be fair, Arras. He gives us legitimacy,' Ali said.

'Legitimacy!' Arras exclaimed.

'Of course. Anyone who looks at our squad sees that pathetic individual and thinks, they may be rough-looking guys but they can't be all that bad.' Ali chuckled, amused by his own wit.

Arras took his gun away from Abdul's head and looked out of the opposite window, unconvinced. Then a thought struck him and he looked back at Abdul. 'Give me your gun,' he growled.

Abdul didn't respond and Arras hit him in the chest. 'Give me your *gun*!'

Abdul looked startled as Arras pulled his jacket aside, found the pistol in its holster and snatched it out. 'I don't trust him,' Arras said. He moved his face closer to Abdul's and spoke softly. 'You ever tell a soul about this, about anything, one word to anyone, I don't care who, and I'll kill you – and that sister of yours. You understand me?'

Abdul did not respond outwardly but he felt a rush of fear flooding through his system. He believed the threat wholeheartedly.

Arras dug his elbow viciously into Abdul's ribs, either to get an answer or out of sheer malice. Abdul pulled his jacket closed and moved as far away from Arras as he could, cowering against his door.

'Pathetic little animal,' Arras said, turning away as if he had done with him.

The cars headed south, using backstreets to avoid any checkpoints, and reached the southernmost Tigris river bridge in the city. After crossing it they continued towards Baghdad's largest power station, its slender smoking chimney stacks towering into the night sky. The cars turned off onto a minor road well before they reached the power station and slowed to a crawl as the road surface deteriorated drastically, with numerous water-filled potholes close to each other.

Abdul had been so preoccupied with the night's events that he had not been paying attention to where they were going. Only when the car went over a large bump, jolting him out of his trance, did he realise they had not headed back towards the academy. Then he realised how unlikely it would be if they did: they were carrying a westerner whom they had kidnapped, clearly without the blessing of the authorities. Abdul wondered why on earth they had kidnapped the man anyway. It had obviously been the aim of the operation. He could not imagine why they had killed everyone else in the room – until it suddenly struck him that it was because his police uniform had been exposed. If that was true then *he* was responsible for their deaths. Abdul suddenly felt sick at the thought. He could hear the woman declaring her love for the westerner and then he saw Hassan shoot her in the eye. The horrific images made Abdul feel more nauseous. Hassan and the others were even lower forms of humanity than he had originally thought. And they called themselves Muslims. Hassan had even accused that woman of not being true to Islam and then had executed her as if it was his right to do so. The cold way in which the team had murdered those people was like nothing Abdul could ever have imagined. He was sharing a car with genuine servants of hell – and he was one of them.

Abdul looked out of his side window at the power station. Its proximity meant they were in Dora, a notoriously bad part of the city. The Americans did not venture into it unless they were looking for a fight and the police were just as unwelcome with the locals. The area was home to insurgents and criminals but Hassan was not here on police business.

Abdul watched the back of Hassan's car bathed in the beams of Ali's headlights as it lurched from one side of the road to the other, weaving between the potholes in an effort to avoid the worst of them.

It seemed an age before they finally came to a stop. Abdul looked out the other side of the car to see that they were outside a run-down two-storey house, the glow of benzene lights inside seeping through gaps in tatty curtains.

Ali followed Hassan's lead and turned off his engine and lights. The area around them plunged into blackness, except for the glow from the house.

Everyone sat in silence. As Abdul's eyes gradually grew accustomed to the dark he thought he could make out Hassan's silhouette, his phone to his ear, inside the car.

A few minutes later the door of the house opened, allowing a shaft of orange light to illuminate the cars. Several men stepped outside. They wore *dishdashes*, shirts that reached to the ground, and a variety of *shamag* headdresses. They sported untrimmed beards, several of them long. These men looked very serious. And dangerous.

Hassan got out of his car.

Ali opened his door. 'Stay here,' he said to Arras as he climbed out. He closed the car door and joined his brother who was already greeting the men. Hassan's demeanour towards them was visibly respectful.

Abdul watched the meeting with interest until a movement at the side of the house caught his attention. He looked into the shadows to see several tough-looking men carrying AK47 assault rifles. One of them stepped into the light to take a closer look at the cars and stared at Ali's car as if he was looking directly at Abdul. Then he crossed the muddy track to Hassan's car and looked in through the windows. Moving across to Ali's car, he bent down to peer inside.

Abdul looked at the man's face which bore as demonic a look as he had ever seen on a human being: rugged, gaunt features and unsmiling eyes with pure murder in them. He stared at Abdul like a wild beast contemplating its helpless prey, his black pupils large and empty. He then stood upright to display a full bandolier across his chest and a belt with a Russian pistol tucked into it. Another belt of full AK magazines and a long knife in a sheath completed his personal arsenal. He walked around the rear of the car before crossing the track back to the house.

The group of men with Hassan went to his car and Hassan opened the rear door. The naked American, now wearing a balaclava but backwards so that he could not see, was unceremoniously pulled out. The group continued their discussion while Hassan handed over the man's documentation and the American was then taken across to the house and inside. The door closed and the street went dark once again.

Hassan and Ali waited alone in the street, talking quietly, all the time being watched by the demonic-looking fighter standing at the corner of the house. He looked like a leashed attack beast waiting for its master to snap his fingers before it struck.

Abdul could tell from the brothers' body language that they were uneasy about something. The pigs had kidnapped a westerner for a bunch of insurgents, that much was obvious. And three innocent people had been killed because they'd happened to be in the way. It was diabolical.

The door to the house opened once again and two Arabs stepped out and walked over to the brothers. A small bundle was handed to Hassan who thanked the men profusely while bowing with great servility. The men withdrew from Hassan, their contempt for him clearly apparent, and went back inside the house, closing the door behind them.

Hassan and Ali went back to their cars and climbed in.

Ali looked nervous though he tried to conceal it.

'Everything go OK?' Arras asked anxiously.

Ali reached for his cigarettes on the dash, took one and lit it with a lighter. His hands were shaking slightly. 'For a moment there I thought the pigs were going to kill us . . . Hassan asked about the money and one of them said we should be doing this for Islam, not for cash. It's the first time I have seen my brother lost for words,' Ali said as he took a deep drag and then exhaled noisily. The air was cold but the beads of sweat on Ali's forehead joined to trickle down his face.

'So it went all right?' Arras asked, impatient to know.

Ali nodded. 'Yes,' he confirmed.

Hassan's headlights came on. Ali started his car and switched on his own beams. They pulled away, tyres crunching on the loose soil, and headed down the road. Arras turned to look back through the rear window and saw the evil-featured gunman step into the dim glow coming from the house's windows to watch the cars move away.

When the house was out of sight Arras became visibly relieved. 'What did Hassan say?' he asked.

Ali was concentrating on his rear-view mirror. 'What?' he asked.

'What did Hassan say when they told him he should be doing this for Islam?' Arras asked.

'Hassan asked if they did not reward their followers too. That's when I thought they were going to kill us. They didn't answer and walked back into the house. But then they came back with the money . . . I thought we were for it, I tell you,' Ali added, a nervous smirk appearing on his face as he began to loosen up.

'How much did they pay?' Arras asked.

'We didn't stop to count it,' Ali said. 'We didn't want to push our luck . . . But now they know that if they want to do business with us again they have to pay.

If word got out that they had killed us no other police would do business with them.'

'How much do you think they paid us?' Arras pressed.

'Be patient. You'll find out soon enough,' Ali said.

Abdul was feeling sick to his stomach as he listened to them. All they could talk about was the money and not once did they mention the poor fool whose life they had sold as if he was a piece of meat. Abdul could not believe that he was with such people. It was utter madness. He couldn't even use the excuse that he was an innocent bystander. He had been the group's official translator, and it was his police uniform that had caused the deaths of the others.

Abdul fought to drive the voices from his head. They were threatening to send him mad. Tasneen's face suddenly appeared in his mind's eye and he wondered what she would have done. He wondered what she would say if she knew and in his imagination the horror in her face was immediate. He did not need Arras's threat to stop him from telling her.

The vehicle swerved suddenly and Abdul looked up to see that they were on Palestine Street and approaching their other cars. His nervousness increased: he knew that some kind of closure to the evening was inevitable and would no doubt include more threats. All he wanted to do was to go home without talking to anyone. Tasneen would be asleep, thankfully, and he would remain in bed in the morning until she went to work. That way he could avoid her for the rest of the day. He would need the time to compose himself so that he would be as calm as possible by the time she returned. But his sister would still suspect something was wrong even then. He couldn't hide such an emotional trauma from her. The trick would be to replace the truth with a lie. But any untruth he told would have to be about something serious, otherwise she would not believe him and would keep on digging. Quitting the squad would be a positive element to throw in the mix and would help to throw her off the scent. He could say that Hassan had threatened to kill him, which was why he was frightened. It was the truth, anyway. He could not remain with the team now. Not after tonight. He hoped never to see any of them ever again. But if they did threaten him he might have to run away and and take Tasneen with him. They would have to leave the apartment, perhaps even Baghdad. If that happened Tasneen would want to confront the chief of police. Abdul's head began to spin with the pressure.

The car came to a stop and Ali and Arras climbed out.

Abdul remained where he was as Hassan and Karrar walked over to the others. They gathered in a tight group to have a discussion. Hassan took a bundle from his pocket, the one the terrorists had given him, opened it up and handed portions of it to the others. He looked over towards Ali's car and the others followed his gaze.

Abdul went numb and stared back at them, feeling pathetic.

Hassan said something to Arras who left the group,

came around to Abdul's door and opened it. 'Get out,' Arras said.

Abdul wanted to stay in the safety of the car but that was ridiculous. Arras stood back as Abdul climbed out and then he pushed him towards the group.

Abdul stopped a few feet away. Hassan looked at him with displeasure.

'Here,' Hassan said, holding out a bundle of US dollars. 'Two thousand is your cut . . . I should give you nothing, because of the way you acted. But, whether I like it or not, you are part of the squad . . . Take it,' Hassan said, thrusting it at him.

Abdul shook his head.

'Take it,' Hassan growled.

'I don't want it,' Abdul said quietly.

'What?' Hassan asked.

'I don't want it,' Abdul repeated, louder this time.

The others looked from Hassan to Abdul, aware of the serious implications of such a refusal. They were waiting for Hassan's response.

'I don't want to be with this squad any more,' Abdul continued. 'I quit.'

Another nail had just slammed into Abdul's coffin. But still he could not see the real significance of it, even though it was written on the faces of everyone who was looking at him.

Arras leaned close to Hassan and whispered something in his ear that Hassan appeared neither to agree with nor disapprove of. But as Arras looked back at Abdul the young Arab saw something in the man's eyes that he recognised. He saw a similar look in the eyes of the others and suddenly felt like a wounded animal facing a pack of salivating hyenas. He wanted to run. But trying to escape would not help. He wouldn't get far – Arras and Karrar would run him down in seconds. And even if he did manage to escape it would only be temporary. They would come after him and would probably go straight to his apartment.

The group was suddenly bathed in the headlights of several cars as they turned off the main road into the entrance to the academy. The lead car stopped and the rear passenger window opened. It was their police captain.

'Where have you lot been?' the captain asked, none too politely. He did not like Hassan or his squad and knew exactly the kind of people they were. But like everyone else he had to accept that scum like Hassan were a part of the system until things improved and they could be replaced. 'You were not in your position tonight. What happened to you?'

Hassan and the others had hidden their money as soon as the other cars had turned off the road. 'We got split up from the others and ended up in the wrong location, chief,' Hassan said, smiling. 'Maybe it was my fault or maybe not. We came back here, hoping someone would come and tell us where to go but no one turned up. How did it go?' Hassan asked with feigned interest.

The captain looked at Hassan and his men with contempt.

Abdul wanted to say something, anything that might extricate him from the mess he was in. But the end result would be the same, he realised. He and Tasneen would remain in danger. Perhaps the captain's timely appearance and Abdul's silence might have a calming effect on Hassan.

'Get to your homes,' the captain said.

'We're on our way, captain,' Hassan said. 'Good night to you.'

As the captain's car lurched forward between the heavy blast walls and drove away Abdul felt as if a safety net had been removed. The other cars followed and seconds later the group was once more on its own in near-darkness, with all eyes again on Abdul.

Arras whispered again to Hassan and after some thought this time the squad leader nodded in agreement. 'Go home,' Hassan finally said, breaking the silence.

Abdul did not move. Fear and suspicion kept him fixed to the spot.

'Karrar. Put him in his car,' Hassan said.

Karrar took Abdul by the arm and pulled him towards his car.

Abdul glanced over his shoulder to see Arras following them. His fear escalated but he had to believe that they were really letting him go.

'Your keys,' Karrar said as they stopped outside Abdul's car.

Abdul nervously reached into his trouser pocket and pulled out his keys.

'Open the door,' Karrar said.

Abdul fumbled the car-door key into the lock with a shaking hand. When the key finally slipped in and he turned it to release the central locking Karrar grabbed Abdul around the neck in a vice-like choke hold that almost crushed his windpipe. Arras joined them in a second to open the rear door and help restrain Abdul. Abdul tried to cry out but was barely able to breathe. Karrar moved backwards onto the rear seat, dragging Abdul in with him while Abdul fought to prise the man's arm from around his throat. Karrar manoeuvred himself out from beneath Abdul until he was on top and applied his full weight, his arm releasing its hold around Abdul's neck but his hand clamping down on to his face.

The other door opened and Arras leaned in to lend his weight until Abdul was pinned down as solidly as if he'd been set in concrete.

Hassan's head loomed over Abdul as the squad sergeant glared down at him. 'Arras wants to kill you but Ali is right. The captain has seen you tonight and if you disappeared it would look bad for us. Besides, I don't think we need to go that far, do you?'

Abdul could only stare up at Hassan's evil eyes while he did his best to draw a breath.

'So you want to get out of the police?' Hassan continued. 'I agree. If you can't be in our squad you should leave the police completely. We can't have you joining another squad now, can we? You might become chief of police one day and then where would that leave us?' He smiled. 'Of course, there's only one way to ensure that you really do leave,' Hassan said. He looked at Arras and nodded.

Arras grabbed Abdul's right arm, straightened it so

that it was sticking out of the car and knelt on it with his full weight.

'The police don't allow invalids on the force. Did you know that?' Hassan asked.

Arras took a length of cloth from his pocket and wound it tightly around Abdul's wrist. With each turn it got tighter and tighter until the pain became excruciating. Abdul's scream was muffled by Karrar's fingers clamped across his mouth.

Arras tied off the line and Abdul could feel his hand swelling as the blood built up in his arm. Arras produced a large hunting knife from a sheath in his jacket. Abdul struggled with intense desperation, making a Herculean effort to throw his captors off, but he might as well have tried to lift the car itself. Arras lowered the blade to his wrist.

Abdul went rigid as he felt a burning sensation which his senses could not fully explain although logic told him what was happening. The burning intensified as Arras sawed at Abdul's wrist with some effort, cutting through the sinews and arteries, working the blade into the joint to sever the tendons. There was not a great deal of blood due to the tourniquet and as Arras cut through the last strip of flesh Abdul fainted and went limp.

Arras held up Abdul's severed hand for the others to see, grinning as he pushed himself out of the car. 'The dogs can have that,' he said as he tossed the blood-dripping thing away, wiped the blade on Abdul's jacket and replaced the knife in its sheath.

Hassan looked down on Abdul who remained

unconscious as Karrar removed his weight from him and climbed out of the car.

'Drive him to his apartment,' Hassan said to Karrar. 'You follow and take Karrar home,' he ordered Arras. 'Leave Abdul in the car when you get there.'

Karrar climbed off the unconscious body, pushed Abdul's legs inside and closed the doors. He took the car keys, climbed into the driver's seat, started the engine, manoeuvred the car onto the road and waited until Arras was behind him in his own car before driving off down the road.

'I'm wondering if we should have just killed him, after all,' Ali said.

'He'll keep his mouth shut,' Hassan replied. 'He's not stupid . . . I need a drink,' he grunted as he headed for his car.

As Abdul opened his eyes a bright light pierced them. He squeezed them shut and rolled onto his side. He took a moment before he reopened his eyes to discover the morning sun shining in through the front window of his car. A fierce pain shot up his arm and he looked for the source of the stinging sensation. As he focused on the bloody stump the memories of the night before came flooding back – it was like a dam bursting inside his head. In his delirious half-asleep state he thought it had all been an awful nightmare. But it was now horribly clear that it had not been.

Abdul struggled to sit up and raised his stump in front of his face. As he focused on the bloody end, seeing the torn flesh, ripped tendons and scabby holes where the arteries had dried and shrunk, he burst into tears.

Abdul sat there for some time, crying deeply at first and then whimpering like a child, except when a spasm of intense pain burned up through his arm. Then he would let out a loud moan as he rocked forward and backwards.

He felt incredibly thirsty and it was the desperate need for water that eventually forced him to slide over to the car door, carefully protecting his highly sensitive stump in case it should brush against anything. He looked around outside, recognising the road he lived in. The urge to get upstairs to Tasneen was overwhelming. The tourniquet had saved him from bleeding to death but he had to get to a doctor as soon as he could. The sight of the wound made him grimace, the ugly finality of it, and soon he could not bear to look at it any more. Suddenly he began to retch uncontrollably but all he brought up was bile that hung from his mouth in sticky strings. Abdul began to cry again as self-pity welled up in him and he held the stump close to him.

He had to get out of there and do something about it. Gritting his teeth, he made a supreme effort to bring himself under control. The task was simple enough. All he had to do was get out of the car and walk upstairs.

He reached for the door latch and pulled it open, his hand going straight back to the stump to protect it. He barged open the door, shuffled to the edge of the seat and let his feet find the road. He took a moment to gather himself before leaning forward and as he stood up his knees almost gave way. He had to release his stump to grab hold of the door and steady himself.

Abdul straightened up and took a quick look around, worried that someone might see him. The street was empty and he shut the door, leaned back against the car to take another breather, then set off on the last stage of his painful journey home.

He stumbled as he mounted the pavement but kept on his feet and headed towards the entrance of his apartment building, leaning forward like a hunchback unable to stand fully upright. A sudden dizziness came over him and he staggered forward, lurching uncontrollably from side to side as he focused on the entrance. His knees gave way and he instinctively put his hands out to stop himself. The end of the stump slammed into the ground and the pain was so intense that he almost lost consciousness.

Abdul gave a long, deep moan as he rolled onto his back, his entire body shaking. But he fought to regain control and continue with his mission, pushing himself up with his good hand until he could move forward into the sanctuary of the apartment-block entranceway.

Abdul leaned against a wall to support himself while he fought to control the pain. This was almost too much. All he wanted to do was drop to the floor and curl up into a tight ball.

Abdul forced himself away from the wall towards the stairs and began the long march upwards. He got himself into a rhythm, bent over like an old man, raising one leg after the other and moving as if he was not so much climbing as falling up the steps.

He turned the last corner to his landing, clasping his stump, shoulder against the wall, his mouth drooling like a child's. When he reached his front door he leaned heavily against it. It was the final obstacle and he reached with his stump for his right-hand pocket where he always put his keys, momentarily forgetting that he had no hand to retrieve them. He gritted his teeth against the pain as he moved his good hand around to the pocket. But there was nothing inside it. Where were his keys? he asked himself. Then, in a surprisingly lucid moment, he wondered if they were still in the car. If so, who had driven him home?

Nothing could make him go back down and look for them, not even the threat of death, and he slid down the door and slumped on the floor. The need to cry welled up in him once again but this time he fought to control it. He banged his head lightly on the door and then repeated the action again and again, not so hard that it hurt but enough to distract him from the agony of his throbbing stump.

It was early but Tasneen was in the kitchen, making some tea. She had been unable to sleep properly, worrying about Abdul being out so late as she usually did the rare times when he worked nights. She had checked his room several times in case he had sneaked in during one of her fitful sleeping spells. When the sun had come up and he was not home she got dressed to wait for him.

When Tanseen first heard the thumping against the door she was afraid, unable to think what it might be.

As she got to the door the thumping stopped. But it started again as she reached for the lock.

'Hello?' she called out. 'Who's there?'

Another sound came from beyond the door. It sounded like a moan. Then she thought she heard her name and knew immediately that it was her brother outside the apartment.

Tasneen unbolted the door as quickly as she could. When she opened it she froze in horror for a second at the sight of Abdul looking up at her, his face white, his eyes red and with a horrendously painful expression in them. Only then did she realise that he was gripping his truncated wrist. She stifled a scream and dropped to her knees to take hold of him, unsure what to do. She wrapped her hands around his head and Abdul buried his head between her breasts. He burst into tears, sobbing uncontrollably.

'Help me,' he whimpered.

'I'm here,' Tasneen said. Then the tears streamed down her cheeks.

4

Stanza's Dilemma

Jake Stanza walked down the steps of the Royal Jordanian F28 passenger jet and onto the tarmac of Baghdad International Airport. He slung his laptop bag's strap over his shoulder and, along with sixty other passengers, headed towards the modern terminal building. The air was not as hot and sticky as he had expected. He had read that temperatures in Iraq could be blistering, especially in August, but by then he hoped to be long gone. The reputation of the place was bad enough but the excessive heat would only add to the discomfort.

He studied the enormous terminal building that stretched for several hundred yards in front of him, expecting to see evidence of the war that had ended less than a year before. But it appeared to be unscathed. He had taken little notice of news reports about Iraq from day one. It wasn't a war or a place that interested him greatly and besides, he'd never expected ever to come to the country in a professional capacity, not the way his career was going. But on receiving the assignment he'd researched as much as he could in the little time he'd had before leaving home. He'd read more than one report of mortar attacks against the airport and was expecting to see evidence of the brutal fighting as soon as he got off the plane. But the facility looked quite normal apart from a couple of uniformed Nepalese-looking security guards nearby who were carrying rifles. There'd been the unusual approach and landing, of course. Instead of the aircraft gradually descending on a long approach path as one might expect, it remained at fifteen thousand feet until it was directly above the airfield before spiralling down in tight turns and pulling up at the last moment to touch down – a defensive procedure against terrorist anti-aircraft missiles, he was told.

After conducting his initial research, Stanza had originally planned to drive into the country. There were three main land routes into Baghdad: from Turkey in the north, from Kuwait in the south, and from Amman, the capital of Jordan, in the west. According to reports each route had its security-related pros and cons and acting on advice from a so-called experi-enced source Stanza chose the Amman road. It was the longest route: four hours from Amman to the Iraqi border, an hour or so's wait at immigration and then another four and a half hours to Baghdad itself. It wasn't until Stanza arrived in Amman and hired a local driver that he learned from a security expert at the bar in the hotel how utterly out of date his advice was and that to attempt that way into Iraq was now considered suicide. From the Jordanian border to Baghdad was considered one of the most dangerous stretches of motorway for banditry in the country, especially the section that passed north of the towns Ramadi and Fallujah. It was possible, at considerable cost, to hitch a ride with a PSD (Private Security Detail) convoy that offered armed protection. But even then safety from attack was not guaranteed and there were those who reckoned that the openly aggressive teams only attracted trouble. When Stanza heard of four Japanese journalists who had travelled that route the week before and were now awaiting their fate at the hands of insurgents who had taken them hostage there was no longer any question in his mind of how he was going to arrive in Iraq.

In the early days of the conflict journalists had enjoyed, for the most part, their customary status as impartial observers. But a year into the conflict they were simply seen as westerners – and as spies by many – as much a commodity for economic or political kidnappers as any other foreigner.

Stanza entered the terminal that was a few degrees cooler than the tarmac and joined the line of people waiting to be processed by Iraqi immigration officers. When his turn came he presented his passport, visa and press card and after a brief scrutiny by an officer he was allowed through into the cavernous baggage-reclaim hall.

Twenty minutes later, after his bags had been searched by a Customs officer, he walked through a pair of automatic glass doors into the arrivals lounge and looked around for the security officer employed by his office who was supposed to be waiting to meet him. Stanza had not been given any details of who he was meant to meet, where they were staying in Baghdad or what to do if the rendezvous failed to take place. Like most journalists he arrived with a prima donna attitude, expecting all his needs to be taken care of. Pretty much anywhere else in the world Stanza would have made his own way to a hotel but he suspected this was not the case in Baghdad and that he was going to have to wait. He did wonder briefly about what he might do if his security officer failed to turn up but since he did not have a clue he put the question aside.

Iraq had changed a great deal in the year since the end of the war, with violence increasing tenfold after the initial post-war celebrations. Insurgents were infiltrating every area of civilian life and kidnappings and suicide bombings were commonplace. In the early days after the overthrow of Saddam Hussein journalists were able to tour the country relatively freely in search of stories, from Basra in the south to the Turkish border in the north, from Iran in the east to Syria and Jordan in the west. There were few serious threats, the greatest danger being on the bad roads where horrendous Iraqi driving skills made perilous situations actually lethal. Stanza had been warned in Amman not to expect much freedom of movement these days and that he would probably spend most of his time confined to Baghdad unless he chose to embed with a military unit. More paranoid advice that he received was to stay in his hotel and limit his trips to the convention centre in the Green Zone for press conferences and meetings with political and military figures.

The picture was very [...]
by Patterson, his foreign [...]
been to Iraq. Stanza wond [...]
erately lied to him about th [...]
him to go – there was no on [...]
would even consider it any mo [...]
left Amman he had developed an u [...]
the trip.

But no one knew better than Stanz[...]
foreign editor and the other senior mar [...]
paper, that he had little choice if he wan[...]
on to his job as a journalist, or even actually [...]
in the media business in any capacity. Ironical[...]
had once been a time when Stanza would have l[...]
at the chance to report from a war zone to fur[...]
his career. Then, after a long period when he was n[...]
allowed to go anywhere, he suddenly found himself
on a dangerous assignment to save what was left of it.
But that was because no one else would do it and to
cap it all ultimately there were no guarantees that he
would have a job afterwards. If anything, Stanza believed
this could well be his swansong – and he was only
forty-two years old.

Stanza was a fallen star on the verge of plummeting
right out of sight due to a serious incident a year
earlier. With sixteen years in the news business behind
him he had long since come to accept that he had
seen the best of his job opportunities and there was
no way a two-month assignment in Iraq, regardless of
all that was going on in the country, was going to
revitalise his career or even prevent its premature end.

ould muster
if he had
uld admit
had he
to fall,
imself
voca-
ever

different from the one painted
editor, who in fact had never
...ered if the man had delib-
...e dangers in order to get
...e else at the paper who
...e. Even before Stanza
...neasy feeling about
..., except for his
...darins at the
...d to hang
...remain
..., there
...aped
...her

more ...on from them. ...nigh school he made ...set his sights on a career in ...ss. But his first significant effort in that ...was shot down in flames, something that was ...become a frequent feature of his working life.

Stanza was the only son of an Italian-American middle-class family and had been brought up in a strongly Irish working-class neighbourhood in the Bridgeport section of Chicago. He was described as a generally quiet boy with a pleasant temperament, unnoticed either on the sports field or in the classroom for the same reasons – he was not outstanding but neither was he an embarrassment. He was more attracted to the idea of academic pursuits and never once appeared on the principal's punishment list, avoiding relationships with any thuggish, rebellious or ostentatiously cool fellow students. From an early age he was attracted to all things classy and sophisticated but unfortunately class and sophistication were not attracted to him. Even though many of his so-called best friends during high school came from wealthy families it was an exclusive club whose doors he could not pass through. Had he been noticeably talented he might have broken down more of those barriers than he did. When the time came for him and his friends to leave high school and apply for admission to the Medill School of Journalism at Northwestern University in Chicago, one of the finest schools for journalism in the country, he was denied entry because he had neither the grades, a letter of recommendation nor the money to buy his way in. One journalistic virtue that Stanza did have, though, was tenacity and, determined to pursue his chosen career, he enrolled in community college. Two years later, after leaving the college with an associate of arts diploma, he applied for entry into Northwestern but was again denied. He was, however, accepted into the University of Illinois, Chicago and its college of journalism, and after flunking a couple of semesters he eventually graduated at the age of twenty-six with a Bachelor's degree.

Undeterred by his non-Ivy League education, and still displaying more naivety than courage, Stanza set about applying for internships with such newspapers as the *Chicago Tribune* and the *Washington Post*. After being rejected by all of them, something he was learning to deal with, he pressed on with other notable papers such as the *Sun-Times* and the *Reader*. After months of disappointment and on reaching the bottom of his wish list without a single bite he compiled another list of lesser newspapers, and then another of even lesser journals to apply to. Four months after leaving university Stanza was finally offered a position at the *Champagne Regatta* in southern Illinois, a rag that was second from the bottom of his final list.

Stanza spent four years with the *Regatta* before moving to Gary, Indiana and joining the *Gary Gazette*, a move that was not entirely in defiance of gravity. Gary was a depressing steel town where he was tasked with covering mostly public works and social drama. Undiscouraged, Stanza applied himself to the work and was rewarded four years later with a position at the *Herald* in Milwaukee, which was without doubt several steps up the ladder. The editor had been impressed with Stanza's sensitivity when it came to writing about certain social problems and gave him a post at the metro desk covering urban conflict: crime, mayhem, riots and all things grim and disturbing. In Stanza's case it turned out to be the inspiration he needed.

On his thirty-sixth birthday he received a reward for his hard work in the form of a significant pay rise, along with a hint that he was to be considered for a post on the foreign desk. Stanza had discovered within himself an affinity for the dark side of news gathering – homicides, domestic atrocities and disasters – and so he focused his reporting talent on human conflict of the more brutal variety. Stanza's breakthrough came during a period of violent race riots that seemed to be spreading across the country. At this time he could most often be found in the forefront of the worst clashes between demonstrators and police. His first experience was in New Jersey in 2000, the scene of a clash between blacks and Latinos where he learned some serious lessons in self-preservation that included the proper clothing to wear, defence against various uses of pepper spray and CS gas, and where or – more to the point – where *not* to position oneself in a riot. In February 2001 he covered the violent Mardi Gras disturbances in Seattle and a couple of months later he was in Cincinnati for another round of more of the same until a little too much complacency was almost his undoing. Wearing a balaclava and gloves to disguise his skin colour Stanza found himself in a cauldron of rock- and Molotov cocktail-throwing, where he was first battered by the police and then barely escaped serious injury when a black rioter discovered that he was white and, believing he was a police spy, kicked him almost senseless. Ironically, Stanza was rescued by police who also thought he was an undercover cop.

When asked by his editor one day why he took such risks Stanza couldn't think of a satisfactory answer. He didn't bother to examine this apparent lack of purpose too closely, suspecting that it might turn out to be nothing more than a desperation to succeed. But not wishing to look a gift horse in the mouth, Stanza looked ahead and enjoyed his reputation for daring reporting, finally confident that he could make something of a name for himself. When an editor at the *Chicago Tribune* hinted to him at a cocktail party one evening that there was possibly a position for him at the renowned newspaper Stanza knew he was finally on his way. Then, shortly afterwards, he made the most catastrophic mistake of his career.

Around the time when Stanza was joining the *Herald* in Milwaukee the newspaper industry was suffering numerous blows to its reputation because of the exposure of various hoaxes, gross exaggerations and entirely untrue stories that had appeared in various prestigious journals, many of them written by well-known reporters. On one occasion a Pulitzer Prize had to be returned. Heads, some of them very senior, rolled within the various organisations responsible. Safety measures were introduced across the industry in an attempt to ensure that such scandals could never occur again. However, to vet for authenticity every quote and observation produced by a journalist was impossible. In many cases the problem lay as much with the editors and publishers as it did with the reporters themselves. Competition for readers was fierce and the pressure placed on hacks of all kinds to produce popular stories was intense.

Stanza needed a series of notable stories to propel him into the limelight where the biggest publishers in the country would notice him. His crime, when he eventually committed it, was nowhere near as heinous as those committed by many others – at least, not to those outside the business. But for those within the industry it was precisely the kind of corrupt reporting practice that needed to be stamped out.

Stanza had been searching for an attractive heading

for a political piece about the state's governance that he was developing. He found exactly what he was looking for in an enticing quote made by a local politician that he read on the wires. But the quote came from an interview that the politician had given to another journalist and Stanza needed it to sound as if it had been given to him. So he came up with what he thought was a simple way of making it appear as if that was what had happened.

Stanza telephoned the politician and requested a brief phone interview since he did not have the time to meet him personally. When the man came on the line Stanza asked him if he had indeed given the quote concerned. The politician acknowledged that he had. Stanza thanked him, ended the conversation and finished off his piece in a way that clearly conveyed to the reader that the quote had been made directly to him.

Two days after the piece was printed the *Herald*'s managing editor called Stanza into his office. Also at the meeting were the managing editor's boss, the executive editor, and *his* boss, the publisher himself. Stanza was dragged over the coals for his 'lie' and the only reason he left the office with his job intact was because the publisher wanted to bury any scandal and preserve the paper's reputation. But Stanza took with him a warning – delivered in no uncertain terms – that he did not have a future with the *Herald*, nor with any other paper for that matter. The management strategy was to keep Stanza at the *Herald* until the incident became ancient history and then dump him.

A year later Stanza was called into the office of Patterson, the paper's foreign editor. Due to the notably unimproved attitude of his bosses towards him, Stanza suspected that the time had come for him to be handed his cards. But to his surprise he was offered an assignment to Iraq. Patterson did not hesitate to tell Stanza that he had in fact been due to be 'let go' that week. But as matters stood the paper had a problem and Stanza was the only solution. Patterson's dilemma was that no one else at the newspaper wanted to take the risk of going to a war zone that had already claimed the lives of more journalists than any other in history. Patterson hinted that if Stanza did an outstanding job – and it would need to be exactly that – the paper *might* not be in such a rush to get rid of him. The way Stanza saw it was that if he did an outstanding job he could make Iraq his reporting home. He thanked Patterson before leaving the office but when he closed the door behind him he wondered why he'd bothered.

Stanza carried his two heavy bags and a laptop across the arrivals lounge towards a large set of double doors beyond which bright daylight shone. He stepped through them onto a covered concourse where a dozen or so hardened and grizzly-looking Caucasian men were standing around. They looked like mercenaries or ex-Foreign Legionnaires, unshaven, their hair cropped, obviously waiting for people to exit the terminal. Many had pistols strapped to their thighs and wore bulging khaki waist jackets containing radios, spare magazines and God only knew what other military-style gadgetry in the multitude of pockets and pouches. As Stanza passed between them he noticed that the English some of them spoke came in various accents while others appeared to speak a range of Eastern European languages.

Stanza emerged from this collection of ruffians and dropped his bags at the side of a road that ran along the front of the vast terminal building. A handful of vehicles were parked against the kerb and directly across the road was an immense three-storey concrete car park, the lower floor filled with vehicles.

'Jake?' a voice called out from behind him.

Stanza turned to see a fit-looking younger man heading towards him. The fellow had short neat hair and a closely cropped beard and was wearing a short-sleeved check shirt. He could have mingled easily with the other mercenary types, although his look was not as menacing. He wasn't sporting a combat-ready waist-coat, for one thing, and he carried no visible weapons. However, there was an air of controlled, efficient tough-ness about him and Stanza suddenly felt like a tourist who had arrived in the wrong country.

'Jake Stanza?' the man asked again, with a friendly smile.

'That's me,' Stanza said dryly, doing his best to appear self-assured and cool about being in the most dangerous place in the world.

'Bernie Mallory,' the man said as he held out his hand.

Stanza shook it, suspecting that the man was English

– although he would have to hear him talk a little more before he could be certain.

'I'm your security adviser,' Mallory said.

'I guessed that much,' Stanza said light-heartedly.

'How was the flight?'

'Great,' Stanza replied, looking around and wondering where the transport was. Several people in suits walked out of the arrivals lounge and were ushered into a couple of heavy-duty 4X4 vehicles by some of the armed thuggish-looking types.

'Our transport is in the car park,' Mallory said, pointing across the road. 'Those are VIPs,' he added, suspecting that Stanza was wondering why he had to walk to the car whereas the suits had been met at the terminal. 'Let's try and beat the rush,' Mallory said, stepping past Stanza onto the road. 'We don't want to be hitting the BIAP road with the rest of these targets,' he said, ignoring Stanza's bags.

Stanza picked up his bags and followed. 'What do you mean?' he asked Mallory who was a few feet ahead of him and heading towards a footpath into the car park.

'We're all targets,' Mallory said, half-turning his head. 'Westerners. The BIAP road is the most dangerous in the world. Averages a couple of kills a day . . . They know when the flights come in from Amman, the bad guys, and it doesn't take much savvy to figure out that half an hour to an hour later the passengers will be coming out. They'll be looking for a target.'

It got darker and cooler as they entered the vast concrete car park. Stanza followed Mallory between dozens of civilian cars, many with armed thugs hanging around them.

Stanza's laptop slipped off his shoulder and he shuffled on, trying to ignore the added discomfort and wondering why his security guard had not offered to help with his bags. But the BIAP road was a more important subject at that moment as he thought about the dangers they were to face almost immediately after landing. 'Isn't there another road out of here?' he asked.

'Yep,' Mallory replied. 'It's quieter but if you do get hit you're more isolated. At least on the BIAP road there's a chance that a US convoy might come by if you've had a contact. Then it's down to luck if they get involved. They don't always bother when it's a fight involving civilians.'

Stanza wondered if the man was being serious or just trying to get the new journalist in town all wound up. He decided not to ask any more questions for the time being – he'd try to assess things for himself as they developed. When Stanza had first heard that he was to have a personal security officer in Baghdad he'd been hostile to the idea – not that he'd had any choice in the matter. But that had been back in Wisconsin and despite his uncertainty about this Brit he was beginning to suspect that there might be some sense to it. Apparently the security adviser was just part of the life-insurance package anyway, which was expensive enough for a journalist in Iraq. A personal security guard significantly reduced the premium. Patterson would not have hired one for any other reason. Certainly not out of any altruistic concern for Stanza's well-being.

They carried on into a darker, dustier section of the robust concrete structure. The only light came in through narrow openings on either side, which left the centre area quite dark. Trash was everywhere and there were strong smells of sewage, rotting garbage and urine.

Stanza and Mallory walked past the seemingly endless rows of concrete pillars that supported the vast low ceiling. Most of the vehicles they passed were SUV types, four-wheel drive and solidly built. More armed men were positioned among them, looking like modern gladiators, all adorned with weaponry of various types. One group they passed was guarding four heavy trucks modified with what looked like steel plates that were all painted matt black. *Mad Max* came to Stanza's mind as he studied them. The last vehicle had a large board tied to its rear with the words 'GET BACK OR I'LL KILL YOU' written on it in large letters and an Arabic translation beneath.

Mallory led Stanza around the corner of a broad ramp that came down from the floor above. Ahead, Stanza saw two very ordinary-looking cars parked away from the others. Two smartly dressed Arab men in their thirties were leaning back against one of the cars, chatting and smoking. They stood up and put out their cigarettes as Mallory approached.

On seeing Stanza struggling with his bags, one of the Arabs hurried forward to help him. The other Arab took Stanza's laptop from him.

'Easy with my computer,' Stanza called out, his voice echoing in the concrete cavern as the men opened the boot of one of the cars and loaded the luggage inside.

'These two are Farris and Kareem,' Mallory said, introducing the Iraqis who paused to beam and nod hello. 'They're our drivers.'

'Hi,' Stanza said, forcing a smile.

The men went to hold out their hands, unsure if Stanza was the polite type or not. Iraqis were quite formal when it came to greetings. When meeting one of their own kind they usually broke into a pantomime of traditional gestures and phrases.

Stanza took their hands in turn and shook them somewhat limply in what he reckoned was an adequate effort to bond with the natives.

'D'you have body armour?' Mallory asked.

'No,' Stanza said, apparently unaware that he needed any.

From the back of his car Mallory dragged out a heavy flak jacket covered in a durable blue cotton material and with a stiff high collar. He held it out to Stanza. 'Try that,' he said.

'Do I put it on now?' Stanza asked, looking at it in Mallory's hands.

'I would advise it,' Mallory answered dryly.

Stanza took hold of it. As Mallory released it, it fell to the ground, its weight almost wrenching Stanza's arms from their sockets. He hadn't been prepared for that and after taking a firm grip on it he heaved it up and plonked it on the bonnet of the car.

Mallory opened one of the car's front doors, took off his short-sleeved shirt to reveal a thin nylon T-shirt covering a taut muscular torso and lifted a light pair of armoured plates off the passenger seat. They were connected by a series of Velcro straps and Mallory placed them over his head and fixed them tightly on his shoulders and around his back and chest.

Stanza removed his jacket and after a brief study of the flak jacket's configuration he put an arm through an opening and heaved it on as if it were a saddle.

'I thought these things were lighter nowadays,' Stanza said.

'They are but the *Herald* can't afford 'em,' Mallory replied as he put his shirt back on and buttoned it up. 'That one must be ten years old.'

Stanza zipped up the front of his armoured vest and, clearly unable to get his jacket back on over the top, stood and waited for Mallory's next command. It was all so very foreign to him. 'As long as it works,' he said, trying to sound relaxed.

He watched Mallory pull out of a bag a rifle that he guessed was a Kalashnikov, load a magazine, cock the gun loudly, apply the safety catch and put the weapon on the floor beside the front passenger seat. Beside it was a large pouch with several spare magazines protruding from it. The sound of two more weapons being cocked startled Stanza – the noise was accentuated in the cavernous place – and he looked around to see the drivers casually placing semi-automatic pistols into their hip holsters, which they then covered with their jackets.

Stanza's discomfort became more palpable.

'You set?' Mallory asked Stanza, a serious tone to his voice. 'A quick brief, then.'

The drivers came over to Mallory, the confidence of those familiar with their responsibilities evident in their relaxed yet alert body language. Stanza remembered his wallet in his jacket pocket and decided to put it in his trousers.

Mallory looked at him. 'This is mostly for you,' he said, sounding like a schoolteacher.

'Oh, right,' Stanza said.

'You'll travel in the back of my vehicle,' Mallory said to Stanza. 'I'll be in the front. Kareem will be in that car following behind. His job is to tail us at a distance without looking as if he's with us. If anything goes wrong, if we get hit and our car fails – flat tyre, whatever, anything that stops us – Kareem will pull in front of us and we'll debus into his car. If we run into a contact, a firefight or an IED – improvised explosive device – we'll try and push through if we can. You get your head down but be ready to act if I tell you. Just do whatever I say, OK? If we have to debus you stay close to me. D'you understand all that?'

Stanza nodded since it was all he could do. He didn't feel as if he had any time to think. He had questions but didn't want to appear nervous or overly concerned. He knew they were driving to the hotel but he was not prepared for these warlike precautions. He felt as if he was taking part in a military operation.

'What route do you want to take?' Mallory asked Farris.

Farris shrugged to indicate his indifference as he glanced at Kareem for his thoughts. 'Blue four, seven, then railway red two,' he said, more in the tone of a suggestion than a statement.

Kareem also shrugged. 'That's good,' he agreed. 'My brother he called, said IED one hour past at black nine flyover. There may be 'nother so we not go there.'

'Sounds good to me,' Mallory said. Then, to Stanza, 'You done a hostile environment course of any kind?'

'A what?' Stanza asked, looking confused.

'Your paper not send you on a course to prepare you for here?'

Stanza shook his head. He'd heard of courses for journalists that taught them about weapons effects, military and insurgent tactics and how to be a hostage but they were not cheap, whereas Patterson was.

'How about a medic course?' Mallory said.

'No. Nothing like that,' Stanza said, adding a feeling of inadequacy to his growing nervousness.

'The medic bag's on the back seat. If we have to get out under fire or for any reason, if you can remember, bring it with you. OK?'

Stanza nodded as he looked inside the back of the car at the black bag with a small red cross on it on the floor behind the driver's seat.

'I don't s'pose you know how to use a weapon, either?' Mallory asked.

Stanza shook his head and was about to say he didn't approve of them anyway, which he did not. But at that moment it felt like a pretty lame thing to say.

'I'm not saying you should carry one,' Mallory said.

'But if I was lying next to a gun and a crazed insurgent was coming at me to slit my throat I'd want to know how to use one. You have a financial value to some of them but not to everyone.'

Stanza began to imagine such a scenario but it was all too heavy for him to hold a train of thought. He was beginning to feel as if he had arrived on another planet.

'OK. Let's saddle up,' Mallory said as he unzipped a butt pouch hanging below his navel, took out a pistol and cocked it.

Stanza climbed into the back of the vehicle, an awkward manoeuvre thanks to his bulky vest – which had him wondering just how far he could run in the damned thing anyway. There was some comfort, however, in the knowledge that his torso was protected against bullets.

Mallory sat in front of Stanza, closed his door and tucked his pistol under his thigh for ease of access. Farris climbed in behind the wheel, started the engine and drove slowly out of the narrow parking bay between a pair of heavy pillars. He turned a tight corner towards the exit.

Kareem allowed them to get some distance ahead before driving out of his space and following some way behind.

'Kareem, this is Bernie, check,' Mallory said into his hand-held radio which he kept low on his lap so that no one outside could see it. There was no reply. 'Kareem. *Diswamy*?'

'I hear,' came Kareem's tinny voice.

'That's good to me too,' Mallory said before tucking the radio out of sight.

'Is this car armoured?' Stanza asked.

'Your door would weigh quarter of a ton if it was,' Mallory replied. 'And the glass would be more than an inch thick . . . The *Herald* can't afford armoureds,' he added.

Stanza should have known better than to ask. He looked around the vehicle, wondering what protection they *did* have. 'So there's nothing to protect us?' he asked, hoping Mallory had some good news.

'Just your flak jacket,' Mallory replied.

'And this can stop all weapons?' Stanza asked.

'No. Yours is level-three armour. The *Herald* won't buy level-four,' he added in a tone that emphasised his contempt for how cheap their employers were. 'It'll stop AK rounds maybe, and low-velocity stuff such as pistol ammo. But I wouldn't worry about it. A lot of the shooters out here use AP – armour-piercing. They'll go through the car and you and me like they would through butter. Anyway, IEDs are our biggest threat and one of those'll disintegrate this crate in a second if we're close enough. That, or turn it into a fireball. Your body armour's about all they'll find of you in the wreckage,' he added dryly.

Stanza wondered if this was another wind-up attempt, although it sounded all too realistic. Either way, he wished he hadn't bothered enquiring. 'Any good news?' he asked, forcing a smile, deciding to try and sound a little more cavalier about it all.

'I haven't finished with the bad news yet,' Mallory

142

said. 'Didn't think you'd want to hear it all in one go.' Then, deciding to be a little lighter-hearted, he went on: 'There's always a bit of good news. Chelsea beat Liverpool last night.'

Stanza didn't find that amusing and looked out of the window as they left the car park. They burst into the sunlight and rolled through a small checkpoint, Mallory waving at the Fijian guard without stopping, and picked up speed as they joined the broad three-lane airport perimeter road still within the heavily guarded confines of the airfield. Stanza suspected that Mallory's bad news, as he put it, was an example of sick Brit humour. He realised that his palms were sweating and he rubbed them on his trousers, tried to get comfortable in his armour and his seat and exhaled deeply in a futile effort to relax.

Mallory adjusted a second passenger rear-view mirror that he had stuck to the windshield for his own use and took a look at Stanza. He couldn't help thinking that he'd just got rid of one wanker, Stanza's prede-cessor, and suspected he now had another.

Mallory moved the mirror again, this time to look at the road behind. Apart from Kareem it was empty as they followed the tall perimeter wall that shielded any view of traffic from beyond the airport grounds.

Mallory thought about telling Stanza that he was not going to get a handover brief from the journalist he was relieving as he might be expecting. But he decided to leave it until they got to the hotel. Mallory reckoned Stanza would have enough on his mind, especially if he was a first-timer – which Mallory assumed he was. The previous journalist, a twit named Jed from California, was supposed to have waited at the hotel for Stanza to arrive so that he could give him a situation brief prior to leaving the following day. But the man had left a couple of days early after his nerves had finally snapped, coming up with some bullshit story about urgent family matters that he had to get home and attend to right away.

In his defence, it had to be said that Jed had fallen into the deep end from the get-go although that had been his own stupid fault. He'd never listened to anything that Mallory had said about security since he was one of those types who thought they knew it all. A week after Jed arrived in Baghdad, one bright sunny morning he decided to take a walk around the hotel complex to familiarise himself with the neighbourhood – something that Mallory had previously said was inadvisable. It was not a particularly dangerous neighbourhood but unfortunately Jed ran into a bunch of locals just returning from the funeral of a relative who had been shot by US troops. They decided to take it out on Jed by giving him a good kicking. If it hadn't been for a local shopkeeper and his sons who didn't agree that violence against a lone individual was the right way to express their objections Jed might have been seriously hurt, or worse.

He didn't step out of his room for a week after that and even a ride to the convention centre a mile away had him sweating. A few weeks later, when Mallory thought that Jed was at last settling in, the journalist took Mallory aside to tell him that he suspected the drivers were planning to set him up to be kidnapped. He asked Mallory to get rid of them. Mallory explained that they needed drivers who knew the city well and if they didn't use Farris or Kareem they would only have to employ two other Iraqis. Jed's response was to say that in that case they should leave their guns at home when they were working with him. Mallory tried to convince him that the drivers needed their guns for their own protection since they were risking their lives by associating with westerners. He added, probably unwisely, that the drivers wouldn't need guns if they wanted to do Jed harm anyway. They'd just drive him to a bunch of insurgents who would take care of him from there. This only served to increase Jed's paranoia. Mallory could only imagine what crap he was writing for his newspaper. Jed had been Mallory's first experience of a journalist and now this replacement wasn't looking too bright either.

'How long will it take us?' Stanza piped up.

'To get to the hotel?' Mallory asked.

'That's where we're going, right?'

'Depends on traffic, roadblocks, checkpoints. If there are no big delays then half an hour should see us home. Traffic's getting worse every day, it seems.'

Stanza nodded as he studied a group of US vehicles parked alongside the road on the other side of the meridian where a dozen soldiers were milling about as if one of the vehicles had a flat tyre. 'How's the hotel?' he asked.

'Delightful,' Mallory replied.

Stanza recognised the sarcastic tone.

Mallory wondered how much longer he would have to spend in this shit-hole of a country. He'd been in Baghdad for two months now and it didn't look as if he was any closer to getting to Fallujah than he'd been on the day he'd arrived. The clock was ticking and the pressure to get on with his plan was increasing. The London-based company he worked for was already asking him to provide them with his return date so that they could organise the rotation of his replacement security adviser.

Mallory's initial plans to catch a flight into Baghdad or drive over the border had been stymied by heavily enforced coalition regulations that refused foreigners entry into the country unless they were employed by a licensed Iraq-reconstruction contractor. There *were* ways to get across the border but the risks were great and the chances of Mallory surviving on his own inside Iraq were slim. The conflict was getting more violent by the week and movement within the country for a single westerner was highly dangerous and tantamount to suicide. The obvious change he had to make to his plan was to examine ways of gaining legal access, which basically meant getting a job. There were, however, obvious advantages to that, especially if he could get employment in Fallujah.

Having decided that a bona fide job was the way ahead, Mallory spent the final weeks before his departure from the Marines compiling a list of security companies that operated in Iraq. Considering his background and his limited experience in other 'reconstruction'-related skills, he reckoned that employment as a security adviser was the best way to proceed. He needed a job in which he would have some freedom to move around on his own. But all the companies he found either provided security for large convoys that ferried clients or equipment between locations across the country, or supplied static guards at installations or compounds. The convoys were usually manned by trigger-happy teams of security personnel who hardly got out of their vehicles between their home base and the delivery point. That was not going to work for Mallory and he widened the scope of his search. Using contacts he'd acquired through former Marines already working in Iraq he eventually found a small 'boutique' company in London that provided security advisers to businesses and media organisations operating in hostile environments. At the time it seemed like a perfect solution, especially if he could work the media angle: he knew that reporters sometimes travelled all over the country.

As soon as Mallory left 42 Commando's barracks for the last time he mailed a slightly exaggerated CV to the London-based security company, along with a letter in which he said how well he knew Iraq, specifically Fallujah and the dreaded Sunni triangle, since he'd served there during the war.

A few days later he received an invitation from the company to travel to London for an interview. In his account of his military experience Mallory had included a stint with 42 Recce Troop, omitting to reveal how little time he'd actually spent with the more elite group. But the detail proved to be helpful to his cause when the company's operations officer came to assess his ability to work independently. To Mallory's surprise he was offered a job on the spot as a security consultant to a media organisation and was asked when he could leave for Iraq. He replied that he could go at any time, with a few days' notice – something else that the operations officer wanted to hear.

Mallory later found out that one of the reasons he had been offered a position so quickly was that the company had a shortage of personnel – quality security companies were having problems finding adequately qualified people despite the number of applications pouring in. People with no military experience whatsoever – or those with only short stints in the Territorial Army, for instance – were applying for work, lured by the relatively high pay and pretending to have the know-how required.

Mallory was contacted a few days later and received his instructions and flight details the following week. Unfortunately for him that was the week when violence in Iraq increased significantly and Baghdad became a much more difficult place in which to operate, especially for the media. The insurgents had embarked on an enthusiastic campaign to kidnap any westerner they could get their hands on, either to cut off their heads or ransom them for financial gain. It was not immediately clear to Mallory how this was going to affect his plans to get to Fallujah but he found out within a few days of arriving in Baghdad. He was basically locked down and unable to move except to safe meetings within the Green Zone, the ministries and one or two other secure locations. But, worse than that, there was big trouble brewing in Fallujah, which had become a fortress town for Sunni rebels led by the new leader of the Iraqi resistance, Abu Musab al-Zarqawi. Several PSD teams had been shot up and blown to pieces while driving through the town, their charred and dismembered bodies hung from lamp-posts and bridges as a warning to all westerners. To make the prospects for Mallory's little scheme even worse, it also looked as if the Americans were soon to mount a serious full-scale military operation against Fallujah to flatten the place.

Mallory had successfully convinced his company in London that since it was his first visit for them three months would be a good spell for him to get his teeth into the job. But that deadline was now only three weeks away.

Mallory considered the option of going home soon and having a go at reaching Fallujah on his next trip. Things might even have calmed down a little by then. But in Iraq it was impossible to predict even the next day's events, never mind months into the future. There was a saying in the country that if you thought you were having a bad day, just wait until tomorrow.

But one positive communication that arrived via the office e-mail system that morning was a letter to all media representatives from a military media-liaison officer attached to the US Marine Corps unit based in Fallujah. The threatened assault on the town was no secret and the Marines were taking applications from reporters who wanted to join the news pool for the campaign if and when it kicked off. There were, of course, pros and cons with that option. A news pool meant a mixed bag of media personnel all being carted around within the security structure of a military unit – which meant no freedom to go where they wanted. The military were strict about that rule, describing it as a safety feature although most journalists saw it as a way of restricting what they witnessed. Another problem for Mallory was that he might not be able to go along anyway since he was technically not a media person. But there were ways around that, such as pretending to be a cameraman or producer. That would depend on how well he got on with this Stanza guy. The man might turn out to be another chicken-shit operator like Jed and refuse to go to Fallujah anyway. For Mallory's retrieval scheme to work he would have to be with the unit that actually passed through the area of the graveyard and then have the time and privacy to carry out the excavation. Frustration was building in Mallory as the situation looked like becoming impossibly complicated. Fallujah was little more than half an hour's drive up the motorway but it might as well have been on another world.

The two cars passed through the last airport checkpoint and out onto the wide three lane BIAP highway heading east towards the centre of the city. The checkpoint also signified the last point of refuge en route before reaching the hotel. There were no other cars on their side of the carriageway that was separated from the westbound route by a stretch of rugged open ground a hundred metres wide.

Mallory began to experience that familiar feeling of loneliness on this particular stretch of road as they gathered speed. Farris changed lanes to avoid a large scoop in the tarmac, an old blast hole from a vehicle bomb. On either side of the eastbound and westbound routes were even wider stretches of wasteland, with dilapidated houses in the distance. The ground was dotted with tree stumps, the foliage having been removed by the US military to reduce ambush cover for the enemy as well as to allow military convoys a clearer field of fire. At intervals there were the shattered skeletons of vehicles destroyed by fire or explosions, victims of the post-war rebellion.

'We call this the lonely mile,' Mallory said.

Stanza looked out of one side of the car, then the other. There was no sign of life in either of the stretches of waste ground but beyond them he could see vehicles cruising the roads in front of the houses. 'Is this where most of the hits take place?' he asked.

'A lot of 'em,' Mallory said. 'Any vehicle on this stretch between the airport checkpoint and the next on ramp is either coming from or going to the airport. That tells anyone targeting this stretch that any vehicle on it probably has something to do with the military or the reconstruction – which isn't true, of course, but the insurgents don't mind getting it wrong. They usually do. They kill more innocent Iraqis than anyone else.'

Heavy traffic appeared up ahead with a stream of vehicles joining the motorway from the first on ramp. Farris slowed the car as they closed on it and moved to the inside lane where the traffic was a little faster.

'PSD coming up,' Kareem's voice suddenly rasped over the radio.

Stanza felt the tension move a notch higher as Farris immediately looked into his rear-view mirror and Mallory turned in his seat to get a better look.

'Shit,' Mallory muttered as he looked to either side of their car, hemmed in by the building traffic. 'We need to get over to the right.'

'Can't' Farris said, his gaze flicking between his mirror and the road ahead.

Stanza looked in all directions, unable to see what they were concerned about. 'What is it?' he asked.

'PSD,' Mallory said.

Stanza knew what it meant but not why it was such a worry.

'Four,' Kareem's voice came over the radio. 'Fast your side.'

'I have eyes-on,' Mallory said into his radio as he saw the four matt-black-painted *Mad Max*-type vehicles that he had seen inside the airport car park. 'I was hoping to be clear by the time those bastards left,' Mallory said, more to himself than to Stanza.

PSDs were civilians but when they drove around in SUVs and in a convoy formation they acted as if they had the right to do whatever they wanted, as if they were genuine military. Since they were mercenaries they were, in fact, often more unruly than regular forces were. Iraq was practically lawless, its police largely ineffectual, and under the rule of the occupying forces there was nothing that anyone could do to stop them. The military did not want to get involved because the

PSDs were effectively aiding in the reconstruction by protecting contractors who were travelling to and from locations such as the airport. Indeed, the military often even hired PSDs to carry out protection duties for US government interests due to the shortage of official military personnel who were trained in such techniques. The PSDs tended to be more aggressive than military convoys in their response to attack by insurgents because they were more vulnerable, lacking the heavier firepower that a military unit might possess. They were also high-profile, drove at breakneck speed, and could not call in fire support such as helicopters or other ground patrols if they were hit. Because of their hair-trigger belligerence the Iraqi public hated them and loved to see them killed.

Dozens of PSD convoys had been hit, especially along the BIAP road. It was a long bottleneck and an ideal location for insurgents to ambush such targets. The local terrorists were pretty adept at mobilising quickly from the nearby housing areas along the BIAP road and could hit the convoys with an array of weaponry that included RPG rockets and armour-piercing machine-gun fire. Another reason why the PSDs didn't like hanging around in traffic and why they drove so aggressively and at such speed was the threat of vehicle-borne suicide bombers. The only tactic the convoys had developed against this form of attack was to bully their way through traffic to the point of physically bashing other cars out of their way. Many of the PSD vehicles had rear gunners whose job it was to ensure that no civilian vehicle tried to follow them or get too close. Most locals had a story of their own or of someone they knew about being run off the road, having their car damaged or being shot at by a western PSD team. Dozens of Iraqis had been killed and hundreds seriously wounded in these acts of violence.

But not all PSD teams behaved like this. Many chose to move around using clandestine or low-profile methods such as driving ordinary-looking vehicles that blended in with local traffic. Some did so out of choice, others because they could not afford to finance the larger convoys. The success of the covert method depended on the skill of those involved at staying unnoticed. Tinted windows, for instance, were an unwise choice because the bad guys often used them to disguise themselves when approaching targets. Not the type of person you'd want to be mistaken for. The biggest problem with the clandestine method was how it left its practitioners vulnerable if they did find themselves in a dangerous situation.

'They're coming up on our side,' Mallory said to Farris.

'I see them,' Farris replied anxiously, his stare flicking from his rear-view mirror to the traffic ahead as they merged with it at speed.

The car was hemmed in on three sides by others, with the waste ground of the wide meridian on their left.

'You have to get over,' Mallory said. PSD convoys favoured the left-hand fast lane.

'Trying,' Farris said, attempting to force the car to

his right into the car beyond by threatening to hit it. But the driver was stubborn and refused to budge, honking his horn at Farris.

'Bastards are coming right at us!' Mallory said in a raised voice. 'Over! Pull over!'

Farris's nerves began to show as his efforts to get out of the fast lane stayed unsuccessful. In a panic move he decided to pull over to the far left, his two left wheels leaving the tarmac and running onto the bumpy waste ground.

'No!' Mallory shouted. 'The other way!'

But as Farris moved back onto the road the lead PSD truck, which was now practically touching their rear bumper, swerved to take them on the inside. Farris quickly adjusted again to let him through, but the PSD vehicle turned with him, unable to guess Farris's intentions: the driver seemed to have the impression that Farris was trying to block him. The PSD driver lost what little patience he had and accelerated into the back of the car. Stanza grabbed the back of Mallory's seat as he realised that things were not exactly under control.

'Let him pass!' Mallory shouted.

'I'm trying!' Farris replied, taking his foot off the gas to make the car slow down.

'No, don't slow down!' Mallory shouted. 'Move right, move right!'

The PSD truck accelerated again, this time swerving to the outside of Mallory's car, its far-side wheels leaving the road surface and kicking up dirt from the meridian. As the truck came alongside, the aggressive driver slammed into the flank of Mallory's vehicle and the barrels of two assault rifles poked out of the rear window.

Mallory showed them his empty hands as he looked up at the white faces snarling at him, hoping they would see that he was a westerner. The truck accelerated hard and pushed past Mallory's car as the next in line followed closely, hardly a gap between them. Again, all the guns inside were poking out at Mallory's car as it passed. The third vehicle sped by, inches behind the other, and then the fourth and final matt-black truck covered in welded steel sheeting thundered past, throwing up clouds of dust. As it moved ahead of Mallory's car the rear gunner, crouching behind a belt-fed M60 that was fixed to a post bolted to the floor of the vehicle, gestured to Mallory to move away.

'Move over,' Mallory said loudly to Farris.

'I try,' Farris said, panic in his voice.

Mallory showed his empty hands again but the gunner continued to wave him over, this time more vigorously.

'What does he want?' Farris asked. 'I can't move over.'

'Slow down,' Mallory said, keeping his hands up. As Farris complied, the car behind hooted in protest.

Farris reacted by moving back towards the verge and behind the tail PSD vehicle.

'No!' Mallory shouted, but it was too late.

The PSD gunner either got nervous or was itching for an excuse to use his weapon. He fired a short burst at the car.

The first round went into the grille, the second smashed into the bonnet and two more punched through the windscreen between Mallory and Farris.

Stanza let out a piercing scream. Mallory spun to see the man clutching the side of his thigh, blood oozing between his fingers.

Farris slammed on the brakes as he swerved the car onto the meridian, his eyes wide in horror.

Stanza moaned loudly as he leaned over onto his side, his face contorted in agony. The engine began to judder and make a rattling sound.

Mallory's brain was flooded by a deluge of alarming thoughts, the worst of which were that Stanza was possibly mortally wounded and that they would break down on the BIAP road that was patrolled by bad guys. The prospects were not good.

Mallory scrambled over the seat and heaved Stanza onto his back as Farris tried to manoeuvre the car back onto the road. It was slowing by the second.

Stanza groaned loudly as Mallory pulled his shaking, bloody hands away from the wound to take a look at it. Blood was seeping steadily through a gash in his trousers but it did not appear to be spurting. Mallory vigorously ripped open the cloth to expose the wound. Blood was oozing from a hole in the flesh: Mallory's concern was that the bullet had gone through the leg into the pelvis or had severed an artery. If the pelvis had been shattered any interior bleeding could be fatal if it wasn't taken care of quickly. Mallory took a few seconds to check and see if Stanza had been hit anywhere else but there were no obvious signs. He knew that he should pull away the rest of Stanza's clothing to check more thoroughly but the hole in the thigh was, as far as he could tell, the only serious wound that the journalist had sustained.

The car came to an abrupt stop and Farris clambered out, leaving his door open.

Mallory ripped open the medic bag, found a trauma dressing, tore open the packet, unravelled the bandage to open up the large square pad and pressed it hard against the wound. Stanza cried out, his head banging against the door as he jerked in agony.

'It looks OK,' Mallory said, trying to reassure Stanza. One of the rear doors opened and Mallory looked up to see that it was Kareem.

'Your car all right?' Mallory asked.

'Yes.' Kareem nodded quickly.

Farris leaned in through the driver's door, out of breath and clearly frightened. 'The car no good,' he announced, scanning the traffic behind him.

The build-up of cars was heavy, with all three lanes filled. Mallory's group was attracting close attention.

Mallory had to act quickly. 'Kareem, we're taking your car,' he said as he bound Stanza's wound tightly. 'Get everything out of this one and into yours. Hurry!' Mallory shouted as he pressed down on Stanza's wound again, making him cry out once more.

Mallory clambered out of the car and hurried around to the other side. As he opened the door Stanza almost fell out. Mallory grabbed him. 'We're changing cars,' he said. 'You have to help me.'

But Stanza appeared to be lost in a world of pain

and confusion and did not respond. Mallory didn't wait on ceremony: he grabbed Stanza under the armpits and hauled him out of the car. When Stanza's feet hit the road he let out another yell and started to struggle with Mallory. Farris hurried across to help, grabbing Stanza's legs none too gently, and together they lifted him off the ground, an action accompanied by more howling. They half-carried, half-dragged the journalist to the other car where Kareem was waiting by the open rear door, practically threw Stanza onto the back seat and shut the door.

'Inside,' Mallory shouted as he hurried around to the other rear door. Kareem was already climbing in behind the wheel and as Farris jumped into the front passenger seat Mallory slammed his door. Kareem let out the clutch and the car screeched away.

Farris looked back at his car. It slumped at an angle on the scruffy verge, steam issuing from its radiator grille. Farris said something to Kareem who shrugged as he gave what appeared to be a philosophical reply. But Kareem had other things on his mind. The team was not yet out of danger. Kareem was a naturally aggressive driver and Mallory had been nagging him from day one not to draw attention to the car by driving recklessly. Kareem's excuse was that that was the way everyone in Iraq drove, which was not far off the mark. Still, Mallory had kept him on a tight rein. On this occasion Kareem was in his element and with a combination of skill and attack he worked his way down the side of the line of traffic, passing cars by a hair's breadth. There was a chance that someone had seen them and telephoned their descriptions ahead. Since there was only one direction they could go, an ambush could be waiting for them at the next overpass – a favourite tactic of the local insurgents.

Kareem, Farris and Mallory stared up at the overpass as they approached. Traffic was moving across it: a vehicle could stop at any time and let the enemy debus into firing positions. As it turned out, they passed safely beneath it and Mallory looked back through the rear window as they sped away.

'Where to?' Kareem asked as he emerged from a cluster of cars to find the road clear ahead.

'Gate twelve,' Mallory said.

Kareem responded by swerving hard over to the outside lane and clocked over a hundred mph as he drove towards a broad Y-junction, taking the left fork up a ramp that led away from the motorway. There were hardly any vehicles on this stretch of road because it led directly to the Green Zone and a major checkpoint, with only one other turn-off – into a residential area – beforehand.

'Slow down,' Mallory warned as they sped along the broad empty road. 'Let's not scare anyone else into shooting at us.'

The checkpoint appeared up ahead and Kareem reduced speed swiftly so as not to unnerve the soldiers manning it.

Stanza was no longer moaning and yelling but his expression remained a picture of agony.

'Stanza?' Mallory said.

Stanza did not react. Mallory wondered if the man

had lost consciousness and took hold of his ear lobe and pinched it hard. 'Stanza?' he repeated.

Stanza winced and opened his eyes, blinking hard as he tried to focus on Mallory.

'Stay with us,' Mallory urged. 'Don't go to sleep. We're almost at a hospital.'

Some kind of response that Mallory read as positive flickered in Stanza's eyes. He thought about giving the man some painkillers but decided against it. There were other priorities at that moment. Mallory was confident that Stanza was going to be OK. The bleeding appeared to have stopped and the journalist would have been in a lot more obvious pain if his pelvis had been shattered. Mallory gripped Stanza's thumb and pressed the nail before releasing it.

It remained white for a second before returning to a normal pink colour as the blood flowed back – a good sign that Stanza's blood pressure was in fair shape.

Mallory turned his attention to the next obstacle, the Green Zone checkpoint, and pulled his DoD identification pass from his pocket. It was an illegal ID since he was not working for an Iraq reconstruction contractor. But there was a healthy black market operating among those western security companies who were permitted to issue the highly prized certificates without which no civilian could enter the Green Zone. Mallory had paid seven hundred and fifty dollars for his but it had been worth it. The Green Zone was the only place he could shop in an American PX store or take a break from the bad hotel food and have a burger or pizza, all in relative safety and sometimes in the company of colleagues, former bootnecks who were also working as security advisers.

Kareem slowed the car to a crawl as they approached the first set of low concrete blast walls arranged in a tight chicane. He halted in front of a ramp where a stop sign in English and Arabic ordered all vehicles to obey or be fired upon. Half a dozen American troops beyond the next concrete chicane eyed the car with caution. It wouldn't be the first time a suicide bomber driving a car filled with explosives had tried to see how far he could get before detonating his load. An Abrams tank was parked behind the soldiers, its barrel pointed directly at the car. A high-explosive artillery shell would be in the breech: one word from the checkpoint commander and the tank gunner would – literally – blow away Mallory and the others.

Mallory held his DoD pass out of the car window while a soldier inspected it from a distance, using a pair of binoculars. The other soldiers relaxed a little as he told them that the card was in the hands of a white man: so far there had been no white suicide bombers. One of the soldiers waved Mallory forward, stepping closer to a blast wall and gripping his assault rifle while concentrating on the car and its occupants.

Kareem halted the car alongside the soldier who leaned down far enough to study the occupants, scrutinising the two Iraqis in front before looking in the back at Mallory and at Stanza who was lying awkwardly in the corner.

'We had a contact on Route Irish,' Mallory said, using the military designation for the BIAP road.

The soldier, a fresh-faced lad who seemed little more than twenty years old, was unfazed by the bloody trauma dressing and Stanza's wound. He took a closer look at Mallory's badge, comparing the picture to the man holding it. 'These guys with you?' he asked in a Southern drawl, indicating the two Iraqis.

'They're my drivers,' Mallory said. 'We left a car back on the BIAP. I'd like to get this guy to the CASH if I can.' He pointed to Stanza. Mallory was overly polite and respectful, in his experience the best way to communicate with soldiers. The youngster would let them through if and when he wanted to, no matter what condition Stanza was in, and being rude or trying to apply any kind of pressure was usually counter-productive.

'He got any ID?' the soldier asked, referring to Stanza.

'He just arrived in country,' Mallory replied. 'He's a US citizen. He has a passport somewhere. You want me to dig it out?'

Stanza managed a timely moan as the soldier took another look at him and his bloody thigh. 'Welcome to Baghdad,' the soldier said, a thin smile on his lips. 'You can go ahead,' he said before stepping back and waving to his commander who was standing between them and the tank.

'Thanks,' Mallory said as he tapped Kareem on the shoulder. 'Go,' he told him and Kareem pulled slowly away.

They drove through the last chicane, over a speed

ramp and passed the massive sand-coloured tank, speeding up as they drove onto a wide empty road.

The Green Zone was an area that had been traditionally blocked off to locals even during Saddam's time. It was several miles square and contained palaces and important government buildings, including Saddam's equivalent of the Pentagon with an elaborate bunker system. The Zone was traversed by broad roads that had been designed with military parades in mind and had more than its fair share of ornate arches, sculptures and heroic statues. Much of it was still intact although its former splendour was scarred by thousands of towering interconnecting concrete blast walls lining roads, fronting buildings and forming protective entrances to numerous checkpoints.

Ten minutes after entering the Zone Kareem steered the car in through the emergency entrance of the large US military hospital and stopped outside the main building. Mallory jumped out and had a quick word with a guard who called for an orderly. A few minutes later a couple of relaxed, experienced medical staff were easing Stanza onto a gurney and wheeling him into the hospital.

Mallory watched Stanza until he disappeared inside. With some relief he turned to face Kareem who was standing by the car. Farris was still in the front passenger seat.

'Farris needs to get back to his car, right?' Mallory asked.

'Farris would like this,' Kareem agreed.

'Stanza's baggage is in the back,' Mallory reminded him.

'*Inshalla.*' Kareem shrugged.

God willing indeed, Mallory mused. The luggage would still be there only if the car had not yet been ransacked.

'I'm gonna hang around here. Go sort the car out before the army blow it up as an IED,' he added, if they hadn't done so already. Farris would be compensated by the newspaper if his car had been trashed. He would even make money on the deal, something that he and Kareem would discuss on the way back to it, no doubt.

'How you get back hotel?' Kareem asked.

Mallory took a moment to think about the logistics of that minor problem. The hotel wasn't far away but it was in the Red Zone, a designation for anywhere in the country that was not inside a coalition-protected compound. 'You won't be able to get back into the Green Zone without a pass,' Mallory said, thinking out loud. 'I'll figure something out,' he said finally. 'Go get Farris's car.'

Kareem nodded and was about to walk away when Mallory stopped him and jutted his chin towards Farris. 'How is he?' he asked, his voice low so as not to be overheard.

Kareem glanced at his colleague and gave a shrug. 'He was frighten. Me too,' he said, a grin forming on his face.

'You weren't the only ones,' Mallory said. 'You did well today. It was good to have you there.'

Kareem nodded, trying to disguise his glee at having his bravery recognised.

'I'll catch you later,' Mallory said.

Kareem climbed into the car, started it up and drove away.

Mallory faced the hospital entrance, pausing to consider Kareem's question about how he was going to get back to the hotel. There were a number of people he could ask for a ride home. But that would have to wait until he was finished at the hospital and there was no telling how long that would take. His job was to look after Stanza. The first call he would have to make would be to the *Herald* in Milwaukee to let them know what had happened. He would put all the blame on the PSD convoy although in truth the contact could have been avoided if Farris had pushed his way to the inside lane when Mallory had told him to. The good news was that they were all alive. Mallory's next call would be to his boss in London: he'd give him the same story.

He sighed as he dug his phone out of a pocket, hit the memory key, scrolled to the *Herald*'s Milwaukee number and pushed the 'send' button. Seconds later the recorded voice of a young Iraqi girl declared first in Arabic and then in English that the number he was dialling was incorrect. Mallory cancelled the call, frowning. The girl's voice was the most hated in Iraq. The Iraqna mobile system was useless, to put it mildly, the service often shutting down for days at a time. At its best, calls were sometimes unavailable for hours and one of the system's most irritating features was the girl's voice informing the caller that the number they were dialling was wrong when it was clearly correct.

Mallory put the phone back in his pocket, mounted the steps and entered the hospital. He'd survived another day in Iraq.

5

Tasneen's Dreams

After a brief discussion with the hospital receptionist who was too disorganised to be much use to him, Mallory was sent to another desk where a clerk told him to wait in the lobby until someone came to see him. Twenty minutes later a man who might have been an orderly or even a doctor – he didn't introduce himself – informed Mallory that Stanza was not in any serious danger. The journalist was being X-rayed at that moment and would head into surgery at the first opportunity. The man could not say how long it would be before an operating theatre became available and since Stanza did not have a priority wound he was low on a list that could fill up at any time without notice. Mallory understood and was directed to a waiting area where someone would eventually tell him when Stanza was ready to leave.

Mallory found the waiting room but only after exploring two long corridors that met at an L-shaped junction. Countless doorways led off to a variety of rooms and offices and eventually he ended up not far from his starting point. The waiting room was small, narrow, empty, uninviting and it was easy to see why he had overlooked it in the first place. There were two rows of uncomfortable wooden chairs facing each other, a dozen in all, and only when Mallory sat down did he notice a small television bolted to the wall high up in a corner above the entrance. Its volume was muted.

He sat on a chair near the door and looked up at the screen that was displaying a US Army-sponsored broadcast of a sports update. Mallory looked around for the remote but if it was in the room its whereabouts were not obvious. Uninterested in getting up to search for it he rested the back of his head against the wall and stretched his feet out under the chair opposite. As he watched the muted screen where the picture had changed to a jolly army chaplain playing a harpsichord he considered getting up and fiddling with the controls on the front of the set to find another channel. But that would have required him to stand on a chair, an action that struck him as not worth the effort.

Mallory pulled his phone out of his pocket to try the newspaper's foreign desk again and pushed the redial button. After a long silence he concentrated on trying to make out what a faint voice that sounded as if it was at the other end of a tunnel was saying.

'Excuse me,' a girl's voice said.

Mallory looked up, unaware that someone had entered the room. He instantly pulled back his legs and sat upright to let an extremely pretty girl pass by. 'Sorry,' Mallory said as he watched her.

Tasneen smiled politely as she sat down on the furthest seat on the row opposite to Mallory.

Mallory stared at her, unable to avert his eyes. She glanced at him, smiled embarrassedly and looked away.

Mallory looked back down at his phone, conscious of his rudeness, but he had been unable to control his reaction to her. She was the most beautiful girl he had ever seen – or, at least, that was what it felt like – and he could not resist taking another glance at her. When he looked back at the screen of his phone he saw that he had accidentally dialled a wrong number. He cancelled it, found the *Herald*'s number again and hit 'send', stealing just one more sideways glance at the girl as he waited for the call to go through.

It was not so much how pretty she was as that a girl so beautiful could be alone with him in a room in Iraq. It was simply the complete unpredictability of it. Her lustrous black hair had a slight curl to it as it fell over her shoulders, her face was an utter pleasure to gaze upon and her large dark eyes were captivating. She was petite, wore tight trousers that accentuated her shapely bottom and legs and, although the colourful blouse she wore beneath a tailored jacket was modest, it did not completely hide the fullness of her breasts. The only women that Mallory had seen up close in Iraq so far had been the hotel chambermaids but they were all middle-aged and wore frumpy clothing. This girl was in a completely different league of attractiveness and poise.

She looked Arab but if Mallory had been told she was Italian or Brazilian he could have believed it. But despite appearing more liberated in her style of dress than most girls he had seen in Baghdad she still possessed that certain timidity or measured aloofness characteristic of well-brought-up Arab girls. Wherever she came from – and Mallory had not ruled out heaven itself at that point – just being in the small room with her was a complete treat as far as he was concerned.

He realised that a girl's voice was jabbering away in his ear and he fought to shift his concentration to the phone as the recorded Arabic response changed to English to inform him that he had dialled the number incorrectly. He ended the call, put the phone in his lap and stared at it as he contemplated what other ways he could contact the newspaper in Milwaukee. But the angel a few feet from him was spoiling his concentration.

Mallory was not what anyone who knew him would describe as a lady's man. He was by no means a complete failure in that department but chatting up girls had never been easy for him. He'd been a late starter in the pursuit of the fairer sex and by his mid-twenties he had decided that his chat was so bad that he had more chance of success by shutting up and hoping that a girl he fancied would talk to *him*. When he reflected on the girls he had successfully dated they had all been either friends of friends or he had met them in situations where they had grown to know each other over a period of time.

Mallory had never considered a relationship with an Arab girl before and certainly not while he'd been in Iraq. But finding himself close to such a beauty, the fact that when all was said and done he was a man and she was a woman could not be overlooked. As there was a distinct possibility that they might share the room for some time, Mallory didn't think that it had to be in silence. With no realistic ambitions beyond a conversation he shouldn't have felt intimidated. But as he drummed up the courage to say something he experienced a familiar apprehension.

He stared at his phone, wondering if he should just scrub round the whole idea, when, as if another part of him had suddenly taken charge of his personality, he announced emphatically, 'The voice.'

Tasneen glanced at him with a blank expression on her face before looking back down at her hands.

Mallory felt awkward at the outburst but decided to continue now that he had started. 'The voice on the phone,' he said, holding it up. 'The girl. It's a great voice but it's gotta be the most irritating one I've ever heard.'

Her only response was a brief, polite smile.

'I'm talking about the girl on the mobile phone,' Mallory persisted. 'The one who tells you that you can't get through because you've dialled the wrong number when you know you haven't.'

'Yes,' Tasneen said politely.

Mallory put the phone back in his pocket as the bullying presence in his head that had propelled him this far urged him to keep going. 'Would you like me to put the television volume on?' he asked, indicating the TV high in the corner.

Tasneen glanced up at the screen.

'I'm sorry,' Mallory said. 'There I go, assuming you can speak English.' He felt silly and decided to shut up.

'You can turn it up if you want,' she said, her accent as sweet and soft as her voice.

Mallory looked at her, pleased that she had responded and even more pleased she could speak English – although the impression remained that she did not particularly want to. 'I just wondered if *you* did,' he said. 'Sorry. I didn't mean to disturb you.'

The girl's gaze dropped to his hands and he followed her stare to the several large bloodstains on his trousers and the similar blotches on his hands and the sleeves of his shirt. He'd forgotten all about cleaning up and suddenly felt like a scruffy clod.

'Excuse me,' Mallory said as he got to his feet and walked out of the room.

Tasneen was glad that he had left. Normally she wouldn't have minded a conversation, especially with a westerner: they could sometimes be interesting, depending on what they did and where they were from. But on this occasion she was distracted by so many things, all of them to do with her brother and none of them remotely comforting.

Abdul was out of any danger from the wound itself. There had been an infection but the antibiotics had taken care of it. He had been lucky, or at least that was the view she was taking. After several days of silence Abdul had eventually told Tasneen how the squad had argued over some money that they had found and that one of them had gone insane and hacked off his hand with a single blow from a machete, something that the man had apparently not meant to do. She suspected there was far more to it than that but was thankful that the blow had not been to Abdul's head. She could not understand why they had threatened to kill Abdul if he told the chief but it was conceivable they were afraid of losing their jobs at a time when work was hard to come by. But with all the time she'd had to reflect on the event, hours spent in the same waiting room while Abdul lay in his hospital bed, she was certain that she had seen something behind his eyes that had warned her he had not been truthful and that the danger was far from over.

Abdul had given the police chief a completely different story, telling him that he had been jumped by masked men on his way home and had had his hand cut off as punishment for being a police officer. But the chief wasn't buying that story either and was pressuring Abdul for the truth.

Tasneen's concern was that if Hassan and his men knew about the police chief's interest, and they probably did, they might think that Abdul would eventually change his mind and report them. She had never met Hassan but after all the stories Abdul had told her about him in the past she believed he was capable of anything. It was a fear that had caused her many sleepless nights and the stress was beginning to wear her down.

The obvious solution was to leave their home but where they could go was the question for which she had no answer. Iraq wasn't like other countries where a person could leave their home and just move elsewhere. Apart from a cousin in Fallujah, Tasneen and Abdul had no close enough relations outside Baghdad to make a safe move and the problems posed by religious and tribal differences were, as far as she could see, insurmountable. Lack of money was a major difficulty as well. Then there was Abdul himself and all his personal issues and since they were together his problems were hers too. He was an invalid now, a young man with only one hand, and the psychological strains of that alone were only just sinking in — for both of them. When the time came for him to step back into normal life among his friends it would only get worse.

Abdul was already showing signs of becoming a recluse, spending most of his time shut up in his room. Even when he was in Tasneen's company he hardly talked, staring into space as if he was in a dream state. She hoped that would change in time. But there was something else about Abdul that worried her. It was as if he had suffered more than the loss of his arm. She wasn't sure, it was just a feeling, but it was as if he had been wounded far more deeply that night in a place that was not as visible. Tasneen's suspicions that he was psychologically disturbed beyond what she would have expected were aroused not just by his brooding silence but by several odd things that he had said. They were mostly in the form of incomplete sentences and references that did not quite fit his story, phrases such as 'It was my fault' and 'I should have done something.' But when she asked him to clarify these comments he would shut down. Whatever was going on inside his head it was obviously deeply painful to him and therefore distressing to her.

Mallory stepped back into the room. Tasneen raised

her head and slipped out of her bleak thoughts as he took his seat again. A quick glance revealed that his trousers and shirtsleeves were wet and that he had made some effort to clean himself. It was obvious that he was at the hospital because someone he knew had been injured but she had no interest in knowing about it. Two weeks had passed since the morning when she'd brought her brother in with the help of the Americans for whom she worked in the Green Zone. She had spent practically every hour of that first couple of days in the hospital, a place filled with bad news and horror stories. Every day she had seen mutilated bodies wheeled in or evidence of the presence of such: bloody trails up the front steps and in through the main doors. And from the waiting room she had heard the screams of victims and their relatives and the shouts of medical staff reacting to the arrival of the latest casualties of the terrorist campaign that was being waged in her country.

In a strange way, before her brother's accident, Tasneen had felt separated from it all, as if she was not really involved and it was happening to everyone else but her. That was until the morning she opened the door to find Abdul lying on the floor and clasping his bloody stump against himself. She would never forget that sight for as long as she lived. In one awful, bloody second she became as much a part of this gross conflict as everyone else and from that moment all thoughts of escaping it had disappeared from her mind. Her little brother needed her and she could not desert him even if someone handed her an air ticket, money and a passport with visas for anywhere in the world.

If Tasneen was to be brutally honest with herself, that loss of the hope of eventual freedom was the true root of her depression. A deeper analysis of her feelings would have revealed a certain resentment towards Abdul, as if he was to blame for holding her back. It was not a new feeling. She had hoped that by this stage in Abdul's life he would have found a wife. That would have released her from her self-imposed obligation towards him, one she had adopted even before their parents had died. But the dream that he would one day become self-sufficient and allow her to finally stretch her wings and fly away had withered in the past couple of weeks. It was as if she too had become an invalid, her wings clipped before they had even been used.

Mallory exhaled deeply as he stretched out his legs and rested his head back against the wall. He tried not to look at Tasneen, having decided to leave her alone, and glanced up at the TV that was now showing a large black US Army sergeant making clay pottery. He wondered if the programmers actually believed that legions of US soldiers were crowded around TV sets all over Iraq, watching this act of creativity in stunned silence. The desire to feast his eyes on the girl once more was too great and he turned his head slightly to have another look.

She was staring at the wall, looking lost and unhappy. Sitting in this room in a building filled with foreigners inside an American fortress town called the Green

Zone she was a foreigner in her own country. Mallory wondered why she was in the hospital or who she was waiting for. As a US military establishment it was not usually available to locals. Technically, it wasn't even available to Stanza and was only intended for coalition military personnel and civilians involved in the reconstruction programme. Perhaps the girl was married to an American or maybe she was American herself – although that would have surprised him if it turned out to be so. Her clothes were western but something about her told him she was Iraqi.

Mallory felt sadness oozing from her and had a sudden urge to help. He chose to make one last attempt to communicate with her. As he studied her, trying to decide how he was going to start the conversation, he was struck once again by her beauty. 'You're . . . ' he began, just about to tell her how pretty she was before crushing that rebel voice inside his head. She looked at him, her expression blank. 'You have someone in the hospital?' he asked.

She looked back down at her hands. 'Yes,' she said, her voice a little croaky. 'Yes,' she repeated after clearing her throat.

Mallory nodded. 'Family?' he ventured.

Tasneen was about to tell him that she did not want to talk, even at the risk of offending him, but there was something about him that made her change her mind. He did not look pushy or insincere – quite the opposite, in fact. He had a calm about him, as if he didn't have a care in the world, which was obviously a façade – or a mistaken perception on her part – since it was impossible to be in Iraq and remain worry-free. His manner did not offend her and his eyes did not display the lasciviousness so common in the looks she usually got from western men. She had never approved of the way Arab men kept their women down but had nonetheless taken the general respect they expressed in their routine etiquette for granted – until westerners came in significant numbers to Iraq. Working among them – mostly Americans – had been a stark lesson in the cultural differences between Iraq and the West. She had quickly learned not to trust their motives and she found their forwardness offensive. It was difficult to know for sure but most of them seemed to be generally insincere and duplicitous.

It was strange how in some ways westerners had more respect for women than Arab men did but in other ways were worse. Tasneen's boss was a nice man whose desk was covered in family photographs and gifts from his children but many of the other men in the office were vulgar and she did not feel comfortable in their presence. She had never been abused in any way nor had anyone been directly rude to her or even propositioned her. But the open eyeing up and down of her body without even an attempt to hide the lust behind the looks often angered her. Then she rationalised that the kind of men who joined the military or came to work in war zones were not typical of all westerners, certainly not of the characters who most attracted her in western books and on television.

This man seemed different, though. He looked about

her age, maybe a few years older, appealing because of his apologetic demeanour – and his looks were not unattractive. He appeared to be making an effort to be respectful and unobtrusive, which she appreciated. She decided that feeling down was no excuse for being rude.

'My brother,' Tasneen said.

Mallory looked up at her in surprise. She had replied when he had given up the hope that she would. 'Nothing serious, I hope.'

'He has lost his hand,' she said.

'I'm sorry,' Mallory replied. 'Was it an accident?' he asked.

Tasneen did not want to discuss the incident itself but she did not feel uncomfortable talking about her brother. 'He's a policeman,' she said. Or he was, she almost added.

'It happened while he was working?' Mallory asked.

'Yes.' Tasneen nodded.

'Today?'

'No . . . a couple of weeks ago. But he has to keep coming back for surgery.'

Mallory nodded, looking down at his own hands and thinking how horrible it would be to lose one of them. 'A bomb, was it?'

She looked away. 'A horrible thing to happen,' she said, avoiding the question. 'Especially to a young man.'

'How old is he?'

'Not very old . . . He's my younger brother.'

That's even worse, Mallory thought, being so young. She looked about twenty-five, though it was hard to tell. Her face was youthful but at the same time she had a mature air about her. 'How long will he be in here?' he asked.

'I don't know. No one ever seems to know anything, or they don't want to tell me. I don't know which.'

'There's nothing unusual about that,' Mallory said, thinking how nice she seemed and wondering what her own story was. 'I would bet it's because they don't know. Then, out of the blue, someone will make a decision.'

Tasneen nodded. 'Why are you here?' she asked.

Mallory was surprised that she had actually asked him a question. 'We were attacked on Route Irish, the road to the airport.'

'I know Route Irish,' she said. 'Nothing very bad, I hope?' she said looking genuinely concerned.

'No. One of my people got a bad graze, or at least I hope that's all he got . . . You work here, in the Green Zone?' he asked.

'Yes. The Adnan Palace,' Tasneen said.

Mallory had suspected that she worked for the Americans, which would explain why her brother was here – that, and him being a policeman. Her English was also very good and she was at ease talking to foreigners. The Adnan Palace was where much of the American and Iraqi bureaucracy was based.

'What kind of treatment is he getting?' he asked.

'What?' she responded.

The way she looked at him, her face so open and beautiful, Mallory wanted to reach out and touch it as one would a piece of fine art. But he looked away

181

in case she could see his feelings in his eyes. 'Your brother. How are they treating his wound?'

'They're doing the skin – er . . . ' Tasneen paused to find the word.

'Skin graft,' Mallory offered.

'That's right,' she said. 'Sorry. My English is not very good.'

'You're joking,' he said, grinning. 'It's better than how a lot of English people I know speak.'

Tasneen grinned back at him.

They sat in silence for a moment but Mallory was determined to keep the conversation going. 'Is he staying in the hospital long?' he asked.

'I hope not,' she said. 'They don't like keeping people in if they can help it.'

'Have *you* been waiting long?' he asked. 'I mean, did you arrive just now, when you came in here?'

'No. I got here early this morning. I had to go back to the office for a bit.'

Mallory nodded, suddenly thought of something and checked his watch. It was gone four p.m. 'Have you eaten since you got here?' he asked.

'No, but I'm not hungry,' Tasneen said.

'What about a drink?'

'I'm OK.'

'Have you had a drink of anything since you got here?'

'I'm fine,' she insisted.

'You don't have to be so polite.'

'I'm not being polite.'

'Let me get you something,' Mallory urged, getting to his feet.

'I'm OK,' she said again.

'I'm getting something for myself anyway. I don't even know you but I feel it is my duty to at least make sure you have a drink.'

Tasneen was about to refuse once again but Mallory held up his hand like a policeman stopping traffic. 'Please. What can I get you? Water? A Coke? Coffee? What would you like?'

She relented, sitting back in her chair. 'OK,' she said, giving in. 'I'll have a Coke. I don't think they know how to make coffee here.'

'Being American they don't know how to make a cup of tea either, which was why I didn't ask.'

'I thought you were English,' Tasneen said, giving a cheery smile that she forced off her face almost as soon as it had appeared. By now she felt very relaxed with this man.

'You don't have a problem with that, do you?' he asked, immediately wondering why he'd asked such a boneheaded question.

'Of course not.'

She said it with complete sincerity. 'One Coke coming up,' Mallory said as he walked out the door.

As soon as he was gone Tasneen felt guilty about her brief flight of frivolity at a time when she should have been dour and miserable. But it was exactly the kind of distraction she would have advised a friend to seek in a similar situation. Nevertheless, the guilt remained.

She stood up, walked out of the room and headed along the corridor in the opposite direction to that taken by Mallory.

Tasneen arrived in the reception area and stood in the centre of the hall, looking around for anyone who looked as if they might be able to tell her about Abdul. The receptionist was behind her desk as always but Tasneen knew by now that the woman was hopeless and always offered the same suggestion: to stay in the waiting room until someone came to see her. All Tasneen wanted to know was if her brother was to be kept in for the night. If so she would see him after his operation, then go home and return the following morning.

A man who looked as if he was employed by the hospital walked hurriedly out of a door but before Tasneen could intercept him he disappeared through another. Tasneen's frustration was rising despite her experience of endless waiting in the hospital but she brought it under control and decided to stay in the reception hall until someone in authority appeared.

Mallory arrived, saw her standing with her back to him and was about to walk up to her when he stopped. It was suddenly obvious to him that she wanted to be alone, otherwise she would not have left the waiting room. As he stepped back to walk away she turned and saw him. He made a pathetic effort to wave, self-conscious that she had seen him.

'Hello,' Tasneen said, suddenly flushed with embarrassment. She wished that she had continued on out of the building, avoiding him altogether. Now that he had seen her she felt foolish. 'I came to see if anyone knew anything about my brother,' she said as she approached him.

'Would you like me to have a go?' Mallory asked, holding the door open, wanting to be of help though still feeling he was a pain to her. 'I might have more luck than you . . . I mean, I can probably shout louder than you can.'

'It's not their fault,' Tasneen said. 'They're busy. But I'm just worried — it's an old habit of mine, worrying about him. I should just go back to that room and wait.'

Mallory shrugged. 'OK . . . well. Er — I didn't have much luck with the drink. They have a canteen but you can't take drinks out . . . I came to let you know in case you wanted to have something to eat . . . I don't suppose you'd like to do that — go to the canteen?'

She hesitated and he took it as confirmation that she wanted to be alone. 'That's OK,' he said. 'I'll see if I can sneak you something out.'

Mallory started to head off as a voice in Tasneen's head urged her to go with him. At least it would kill some time and he was not exactly a horrible person. 'Where is it?' she asked.

'Around the corner and halfway along the corridor on the right,' he said, looking back at her but hardly stopping. He walked on without a glance back, hoping his message was clear that he was giving her space to do what she wanted.

She set off at his pace, several yards behind.

Mallory could hear footsteps behind him on the tiled floor but resisted the urge to look back. He passed the waiting room and turned the corner into the longer, busier corridor where hospital staff seemed to be constantly walking out of one door and in through another. He continued a little further before turning right under an arch into a narrower passageway. He could no longer hear Tasneen's footsteps and wondered if she'd taken the opportunity to slip away. As he reached a junction he felt certain he was alone and looked back as he took a right turn. He was surprised to see her entering the short passage. He paused and stepped aside to let her pass. She stopped alongside him, wondering which way to go.

'That way,' he said, pointing along the passage.

She went ahead, leaving a gentle waft of perfume in the air for him to walk through. The entrance to the canteen was around the next corner and at the end of a short corridor lined with glass-fronted refrigerators packed with every kind of drink.

A narrow doorway opened into a large room and Mallory followed her inside. There were half a dozen tables and about the same number of people spread among them. Close by was a worktop jammed with plastic trays, plates, cutlery, napkins and assorted condiments in small sachets. Beyond that was a serving counter with a dozen different food items spread out on it in silver serving trays. A young Iraqi man wearing an apron and a white paper hat and armed with several serving implements stood behind it.

The food looked bleached and overcooked but Tasneen suddenly felt hungry as she realised it had been many hours since her light breakfast. She looked around at Mallory standing behind her. 'Shall I . . . er?'

'Take a tray and a plate,' Mallory said, seeing her

discomfort but also noticing the way she had looked at the food. 'It's OK. They don't expect you to starve to death while you're waiting.'

She picked up a tray, separated one of the plastic plates from the pile with a manicured fingernail, moved to the food counter and indicated some meat and vegetables to the server who promptly piled a generous mound onto her plate. She looked up at Mallory, surprised at the amount of food. He shrugged. It was enough to satisfy a rugby forward. Mallory gave Tasneen a set of plastic cutlery and collected some food for himself while she hung about looking lost. Then he led the way to an empty table in a corner.

'What would you like to drink?' Mallory asked as she sat down.

'Oh . . . hmmm . . . That's what I came in for,' she said with an embarrassed grin as she looked at the mountain of food in front of her. 'Coke, please,' she said.

Mallory went to one of the large fridges and returned with a couple of chilled Cokes. He sat opposite Tasneen and unwrapped his cutlery. She followed his lead, then waited for him to start eating before dipping a fork into her vegetables and tasting a piece of carrot.

'Edible?' Mallory asked.

'It tastes as good as it looks,' she said, grinning. He smiled back.

He stuck his plastic fork into a large slab of meat and began to saw at it with the knife. Before he was halfway through, the fork snapped. A piece of it went flying into the air and Tasneen broke into a giggle.

'Excuse me,' Mallory said, deadpan as he got to his feet. He went over to the stack of plastic cutlery, collected several packets and sat back down, placing them beside his plate. 'I think I'm going to need spares,' he said as he undid one of the packets. 'Maybe I should double up,' he added, opening another, placing two forks together and poking them into the meat. The experiment was a success and after sawing off a piece he put it in his mouth and pantomimed chewing it with difficulty, all much to Tasneen's amusement. She placed her hand over her mouth to hide her broad grin.

'You know,' Mallory said, pausing to make an exaggerated effort to swallow, 'they deliberately make the food bad in hospitals to take your mind off why you're here.'

'It works,' she said. Her smile faded as she remembered why she was in fact there.

'Life has to go on, though, doesn't it?' he said, trying to make light of the philosophy.

'You're right,' she said as she tried a potato chip. 'I don't know your name.'

'Sorry. Bernie,' he said, wiping his hand on a napkin and holding it out to her.

She put her knife down, looked around at the others to see if they were looking, and shook hands. 'Tasneen,' she said.

Mallory shook her hand lightly, enjoying the contact. 'That's a lovely name. I've never heard it before.'

She smiled a thank-you and went back to her meal. 'It was my mother's name, and her mother's too.'

'I take it you're Iraqi?' he asked.

'Yes . . . I'm from Baghdad.'

'Where did you learn English?'

'At school. My father spoke it very well. He used to go to England when he was a young man.'

'You speak it too well to have just spoken it in school.'

'My father wanted us to learn English. My brother and I . . . the three of us, we would have conversations only in English sometimes. We watch a lot of English-language programmes and films on TV.'

'What does your father do?'

Tasneen's expression warned him of the bad news coming. 'Both my parents died during the war.'

'This last one?'

'Yes.'

'I'm sorry,' Mallory said, putting his cutlery down, feeling it was impolite to eat at that moment.

'What do *you* do?' Tasneen asked lightly as she picked at her food, not wanting to talk about herself any more.

Mallory's instinct was to be cautious about his identity and personal details but then he reminded himself that she would not have been given a job at the Palace without being heavily vetted. 'I'm a security adviser to media,' he said, revealing more than he would to most but still remaining sufficiently vague.

'Television?'

'An American newspaper,' he said, picking up his cutlery again and resuming his meal.

189

'Is it one of your friends who has been injured?'

'A journalist. I only just picked him up at the airport this afternoon.'

'No, seriously?' Tasneen asked, looking shocked.

Mallory studied her, curious about something. 'I wasn't sure at first but now I think your English sounds American at times.'

'Well . . . I work with a lot of Americans. I'm a bit of a sponge for accents. By the time you and I finish speaking I'll probably be talking with an English accent . . . So where do you stay? Here in the Green Zone?'

'The Sheraton,' he answered.

'Isn't it dangerous there?'

'Where is it safe?'

'I suppose you're right,' she mused. 'But that place is a big target, isn't it?'

'There's a lot of media and westerners there, plus a US Army detachment. I suppose it gets more than its fair share of attention . . . rockets and mortars.' He shrugged. 'We've been hit four times in the last couple of months.'

'You've been in Iraq two months?'

'Something like that.'

'When are you going home?'

'I don't know. I'll be here a while yet, I should think.'

'Then you'll go home?' she asked.

It had always been a foregone conclusion with Mallory that as soon as he got his hands on the money he would be out of Iraq, never to return. But a primal force had suddenly come into play, one of the most basic known to man, over which he had little control. 'It's good to take a break, let someone else have a job. Then I'll come back, no doubt. The work's interesting,' he said. It wasn't a lie, at least. If he didn't get the money this trip he would certainly be back.

They spoke for over an hour at the table, mostly about trivial things, hardly ever referring to the conflict. Tasneen was very interested in where Mallory lived in England and what everyday life was like for him, comparing it where she could with life in Iraq before the war. They were eventually interrupted by the server telling them that the canteen was closing and, realising they were the only customers left, they headed back to the waiting room where they continued their conversation.

This time, Mallory sat opposite Tasneen, their knees almost touching, both of them sitting forward more often than back. Mallory talked about his childhood and school and the events that had led to his decision to join the military while Tasneen described her childhood and life in Baghdad under Saddam. Mallory was charmed by how positive she was about everything, how she emphasised the good times while glossing over the threat under which she and her family had lived constantly. Both of them managed to avoid politics for the most part, mainly because neither had any great interest in the subject but also because it was too depressing a topic and would spoil the mood they both wanted to be in.

Mallory was fascinated with Tasneen's knowledge of

the culture and history of the West. He was amused by how that knowledge bore all the marks of having been derived from television and magazines, lacking the detail one might get from a first-hand visit. But it sparked an interest in him as he listened to her describe the topics with such enthusiasm. She knew more about historical and modern London than he did, for instance, specifically the sights and tourist traps. He was embarrassed by his own lack of knowledge about things that were available to him without hardly an effort. She was not interested in nightclubs, a sentiment he shared, and even though she did not drink she expressed a desire to have her first glass of wine in Athens, the cradle of European civilisation. So many things she talked about left Mallory wishing that he had studied history as well as geography and he made a promise to himself to do something about that at the first opportunity.

Neither of them had noticed the time fly by until a doctor appeared in the doorway, looking for Mallory.

'You here with Jake Stanza?' the doctor asked tiredly, looking as if he'd had a long day.

'Yes,' Mallory said, getting to his feet.

'We're gonna leave him where he is for the night,'

'He OK?' Mallory asked, suddenly realising that he had forgotten all about his client during the past couple of hours.

'He's fine,' the doctor said. 'He had a mild reaction to the anaesthetic so we're gonna leave him on the monitor for the time being. You can come pick him up in the morning . . . You're Miss Rahman, right?' he said, turning his attention to Tasneen.

'Yes,' she said, standing and looking a little pensive.

The doctor's experienced eye recognised her concern. He smiled gently to help put her at ease. 'Abdul's fine. It was a pretty long procedure for the both of us but it went well. He's bushed so we'll let him rest here for the night.'

'Can I see him?' she asked.

'Yeah, we can arrange a five-minute visit, I guess. Why don't you come with me now?' he said, stepping back out into the hallway. 'I'll show you where he is and then I'm gonna get outta here myself.'

Tasneen followed the doctor into the corridor.

Mallory watched her as she headed out of the room, frustrated at the abruptness of her departure. But Tasneen stopped to look back at him in the doorway. Their sudden parting was curiously unpleasant for her too and she stared into the eyes of the man whose polite and interesting company had taken some of the edge off her problems for the past few hours.

She moved towards him, holding out her hand. 'It was very nice to meet you,' she said.

'You too,' Mallory said, taking her hand, enjoying the touch even more than before.

She broke the contact as she turned away and hurried to catch up with the doctor.

As Mallory watched Tasneen head towards the reception hall she turned quickly to look back at him, smiled, waved and continued on her way.

Mallory swallowed his disappointment and walked down to the corner and into the longer corridor that was practically empty now. He continued to a set of glass-panelled doors at the far end.

As he approached the exit he could see that it was dark outside, something he should have considered. He stepped out into the slightly chilly air, through the US Army pedestrian checkpoint manned by a male and female soldier who were dressed in full combat gear and onto the main road.

A couple of Hummvees cruised by with their headlights on, a soldier standing in each roof embrasure behind a belt-fed .50-calibre machine gun. Mallory looked up and down the road that was empty of other vehicles and pedestrians and as the patrol drove out of sight everything fell silent. It was not a good idea to hang around and, sighing philosophically, he closed the door on the romantic episode, turned his back on the hospital and walked on up the street.

Mallory took his mobile phone from his pocket and considered who he could call to ask for a ride back to the Sheraton. The hotel was only on the other side of the river, no more than a ten-minute drive using the nearest bridge, but the problem was the time of day. The dark hours brought out the criminal and insurgent population of the city in even greater numbers. But they were not the only dangers. The curfew was only an hour away, and the military and police patrols, though fewer at night, were more trigger-happy. Some PSD teams ventured out at night but the wiser ones did so only if it could not be avoided. Mallory himself had been out on several occasions after curfew, mostly to the convention centre on work-related trips, but these excursions had been undertaken only with great reluctance. The US military hierarchy was in the habit of holding press conferences in the evenings, the convention centre being situated inside the Green Zone, and they obviously had scant regard for the dangers faced by media crews who lived outside the zone.

Mallory scrolled through the phone numbers of a couple of PSD friends living in the Green Zone but after selecting one was reluctant to make the call. The odds were small that anyone was going out but that was not the only reason for his reluctance. The PSD guys would ask him how he'd ended up getting stuck in the Green Zone without a ride and frankly he would look like an amateur no matter what explanation he gave short of a pack of lies. He could ask to sleep over until morning but that would still leave his competency suspect. Reputation was everything in the security-adviser world and – something he had not overlooked – if he failed in his mission to retrieve the money from Fallujah he might find himself stuck in this business. The last option was to call one of his Iraqi fixers and ask them to meet him at the Assassins' Gate less than a mile's walk from the hospital. But Mallory would be asking him to take the risk of driving from his home to the hotel and back home again.

There was only one choice left short of walking back to the Sheraton, which would be a stupid and unprofessional risk, and that was to find somewhere in the Green Zone to lie down and wait the night out. But although the worst of Iraq's winter months had passed the nights could still get bitterly cold. Neither was the Zone as secure as people assumed, despite the heavy military presence. Iraqis occupied several large residential areas within the Zone and there had been reports of lone westerners being attacked. Only recently Mallory had read an intelligence report of an American contractor assaulted by three Iraqis while out jogging in broad daylight. They had tried to get him into the boot of a car in an attempt to kidnap him but he had managed to fight them off and make a run for it. Every western company compound in the Zone was heavily guarded – and for good reason.

Mallory paused in the street with his hands on his hips and broke into a grin as he shook his head. 'What a wanker,' he said out loud. One cute babe and all his soldiering skills flew out the window.

A car's headlights blinked on in the distance as it pulled away from the sidewalk and as it approached the other side of the road it began to slow. Mallory could not see the driver and his hand went to his butt pouch where his pistol was. The car was a small white Japanese job and as it came to a stop the driver's window wound down. It was Tasneen. Mallory beamed as he crossed towards her.

'Hi,' she said as he rested his hands on the roof of the car and leaned down.

'Hi,' he echoed, unable to conceal his pleasure.

'I'm glad I saw you,' she said. 'I felt bad about not being able to say goodbye.'

'Yeah . . . I . . . I really enjoyed talking with you.'

She smiled broadly but at the same time felt embarrassed by her forwardness.

A vehicle appeared, heading towards them. It was another Hummvee and Mallory hugged the side of the car as it passed closely by, the driver no doubt making the point that Mallory was standing in a stupid position on the road.

'How was your brother?' Mallory asked, resuming his stance.

'I didn't get to speak to him. He was asleep. But he looked fine. Peaceful. That's the only time he does, when he's asleep. The rest of the time he's either grumpy or in a trance.'

'Can't be easy, losing a hand.'

Another Hummvee approached and Mallory hugged the car again to let it pass.

He leaned back down and looked at Tasneen, unsure how to say what he wanted to. 'I feel like I could talk to you all night . . . I mean . . . you know . . . '

Her embarrassment increased.

'Which way are you going?' Mallory asked.

'I live outside the Green Zone.'

'Yes, you said. Which gate do you leave through?'

'The convention centre.'

'Oh,' Mallory said, looking disappointed and releasing the car. 'OK.'

'Where do you need to get to?'

'I'm heading for the Assassins' Gate,' he said.

'That's not a problem. I can drop you.'

'You sure?'

'Of course. It's not a big detour.'

Mallory hurried around to the passenger side, opened the door and climbed in. 'You're very kind,' he said as he closed the door.

Tasneen set off and they drove in silence, both feeling awkward travelling together, something neither of them had expected to be doing.

'It's cold,' Mallory said, in the absence of anything more interesting to say.

'Yes. But not as cold right now as where you come from.'

'That's the truth. Still, the desert can be so hot in the day and so cold at night. I couldn't believe it when I first got here. I didn't think of bringing a pully. Then I was stuck outside one evening and I was so cold that I was shivering.'

'You should go up north,' she said. 'We get snow in the mountains this time of year.'

'You ever been skiing?' Mallory asked.

'I would *love* to go skiing,' Tasneen replied with childish enthusiasm. 'I love to watch it on TV. Not racing but just skiing for fun.'

'Well, your luck's in. I happen to be an ace skiing instructor.'

'Ace?'

'The best. OK, perhaps not the best, but I'm good. Well, I can handle a novice like you, at any rate. I'll teach you for free, how's that?'

Tasneen slowed at a junction, made a right turn, and accelerated on. Mallory felt an idiot, making such a pointless offer, and her silence was proof of it.

'You would probably be shocked if I called you one

day and asked for my lesson,' Tasneen said. She wasn't sure why she had opted to continue the fantasy but sharing it with another person was excitingly different.

Mallory glanced at her, pleased that she had carried on the game. 'Shocked? I'd be stunned.'

'Why?' she asked.

'Because I haven't even given you my phone number.'

Tasneen broke into a delightful laugh.

'Where's your car?' she asked as she slowed. The Assassins' Gate checkpoint was still some distance away but the first set of barriers was already visible in the beams of her headlights and it was dangerous to stop a car close to them, even more so at night.

'Drop me here. I can walk,' said Mallory.

Tasneen could not see any vehicles on the approach road to the checkpoint. 'Where's your car?' she asked.

'At the Sheraton.'

'The Sheraton Hotel?'

'That's where I live.'

'Yes, but you can't walk there from here.'

'I'm not going to. I'm going to jog,' Mallory said. It wasn't so bad. The foot of the bridge was practically outside the Assassins' Gate. It was a long bridge, exposed, but once on the other side he could drop down onto the tree-covered embankment.

'Run?' Tasneen said, her voice a tone higher. 'But what if someone tries to attack you? You are a westerner. You look like one, even in the dark.'

'I'll jump into the river,' he said. It was meant to sound flippant even though it wasn't.

She carried on driving. 'You are mad,' she said as she closed on the first unmanned concrete-barrier chicane.

'You'd better stop,' he said.

'Not now. They might shoot at us.'

'Then drop me on the street.'

They carried on, obeying a sign that demanded they reduce speed to five mph.

'You're crazy,' Tasneen said, turning off her headlights as they approached some soldiers behind a low blast wall.

She was right, of course. Mallory had put himself in an awkward situation and none of his solutions were particularly smart. What a man will do to spend even a few minutes with a beautiful woman . . .

They passed through the Assassins' Gate, an ornate affair but smaller than Marble Arch. It was damaged in places where a shell had struck it during the war: tiles had buckled or fallen away to expose the wire framework beneath.

They cruised between several high blast walls and over a line of road claws towards several more soldiers standing beside a bunker. Tasneen was waved through and the car left the safety of the Zone.

'Anywhere here will do,' Mallory said.

But Tasneen did not slow down. Instead, she speeded up the gentle incline that was the start of the broad four-lane bridge.

'What are you doing?' he asked, realising her intentions.

'You're *not* walking at this time of night,' she said in the domineering tone she used with her brother.

200

'But now it's dangerous for *you*.'

'No more dangerous than when I go home every night.'

'But you don't go this way.'

'I think I know Baghdad better than you.'

'I'm not sure that I agree with you.'

'You know it from your work point of view. I know it as an Iraqi who lives here. It's different for me.'

'But I'm a westerner in your car,' Mallory said as they reached the crest of the bridge, the buildings on the other side now looming large. The tallest of them was abandoned and in darkness, shell holes that had been punched into it during the war visible even at night. An American soldier had told Mallory that it had been a YMCA and had not been an intended target. But during the battle for the city Iraqi snipers had made use of it to cover the bridge and so American tanks had come forward and taken care of them.

Tasneen reached behind her seat, pulled out a head-scarf and dropped it onto his lap. 'Put that on,' she ordered.

Mallory inspected the purple and yellow scarf, put it over his head and, making light of it, wrapped it around his face in a gesture of feminine flair.

Tasneen was unable to hide her grin.

'This is still unnecessarily dangerous for you,' he said.

'It's done now. You'll be home in a few minutes.'

They headed down the other side of the bridge towards a large roundabout.

'Don't take Sadoon Street,' Mallory said. 'Continue around the roundabout and go under the bridge.'

'Why? Sadoon Street goes straight to your hotel.'

'Don't argue,' he said, firmly but gently. 'I know this area better than you.' The roundabout was a block away from a street known for its criminals, particularly drug dealers. Car-jacking was common in the city and the roundabout had a reputation as a stake-out point for such activity.

Tasneen passed the Sadoon Street exit and continued around the circle. A couple of cars were on the round-about and Mallory scrutinised them.

Tasneen decided that Mallory could be quite domineering – but then, he was being protective at that moment. Pressure revealed a person's true self and in these new circumstances he remained as polite and calm as he had been in the hospital.

But Tasneen would be the first to admit that she had little experience of men, having really only known two in her life – her father and her brother. Her father had liked to appear tough but beneath the stern looks and the occasional raised voice he had not been. Abdul was a pussy cat whose temper flared at times, although now she would have to say she no longer knew him. Mallory did not appear to be like either of them. She had conversed more with him in a single period than with any other man in her life, including her brother and father. That was very odd, made even more bizarre because he was a foreigner and she had only just met him. In her culture, if a man from outside her family spent that amount of time with her it would be practically a marriage proposal, one reason why Tasneen had avoided such situations all her adult life. Mallory was safe from that standpoint. But if that was why she had begun talking with him it did not explain why she had stopped her car when she'd seen him in the street. Tasneen now had to question how well she knew herself.

'Go straight,' Mallory said as he twisted in his seat to see the other cars continue around without following Tasneen's vehicle.

Tasneen followed his instructions and turned along a quiet shadowy street, the buildings on both sides seemingly abandoned.

'Left,' Mallory said as they reached a T-junction.

A sign in English on one of the dilapidated buildings declared it to be the headquarters of the Iraqi Communist party. The windows and main entrance were draped in barbed wire with wind-blown trash stuck to its barbs. They passed beneath the bridge they had just crossed through a dank and rubbish-strewn cavern, and when they emerged on the other side the river glistened on their right. Battered three-storey buildings were packed tightly together on the left. The road was separated from the river by a parched green area dotted with trees, the remnants of a public park.

Mallory kept watch to their rear until he was satisfied that they had not been followed. Then he switched his attention to the poorly lit empty road ahead. When they had gone half a mile from the bridge he told Tasneen to pull over.

'The hotel is still a long way,' she said. She did not slow down.

'Pull over, please,' Mallory said insistently. Tasneen was evidently on the stubborn side, he decided, even if her obstinacy was well intentioned. 'The Baghdad Hotel is coming up and they're a little trigger-happy around the checkpoint,' he explained. The Baghdad Hotel was rumoured to be the operational HQ of the CIA outside the Green Zone and if it wasn't it certainly housed a lot of heavily armed Americans with local guards supplemented by PSDs running the checkpoint.

Tasneen obeyed and brought the car to a stop against the kerb. A floodlight came on a few hundred yards ahead, illuminating a barrier surrounded by blast walls. A figure stepped onto the street and into the light to make himself visible.

'Turn your headlights off,' Mallory said.

Tasneen turned them off but left the engine running.

'I'll get out here,' he said as he removed the scarf from around his head and turned to look at her. 'Thanks.'

'Not a problem,' she replied, taking the scarf from his hand.

'Which way will you go home?' he asked.

'Back the way we came. You know where the zoo is?'

'Yes.'

'I live near there.'

Mallory could picture the route to the park were the zoo was. It wasn't very far and didn't pass through any bad areas but he wished he didn't have to let her drive home alone. There was nothing he could do about it and he sighed as he opened the door. 'I need to know that you get home safely,' he said firmly. 'Can I have your mobile phone number?'

Tasneen considered the request for a moment, then reached behind the seat for her handbag.

'I have a notebook and pen,' he said, reaching into his breast pocket.

She gave up trying to lift her large handbag around the seat and held out her hand. He placed the pen and notebook on her palm and she turned on the interior light, scribbled down the number and handed the notebook back to him.

'Would you rather call me?' Mallory asked, wondering if he had been too forward.

'You can call. It's OK.'

Tasneen's eyes were illuminated by the dim bulb in the ceiling and her beauty struck him again. He wanted to kiss her soft lips but he knew that if he tried she would take off like a startled dove. He turned off the light, plunging them into darkness.

'Drive safely,' he said.

'Yes, daddy,' she replied.

'I really appreciate the lift. And . . . can I say, this has been my most enjoyable day in Iraq. In fact, the nicest day I can remember in a long time.'

Tasneen looked away but she nodded. 'I enjoyed myself, too.'

'Do a U-turn and head back the way you came to the roundabout.'

'I know how to get home,' she said. 'But thank you for your concern.'

Mallory wanted some kind of physical contact with her before she left and he offered her his hand. She took it and he held onto her fingers for longer than was polite. But she did not pull her hand away.

Mallory released her, climbed out of the car, closed the door and stepped away as the car moved off. It pulled a tight turn in the road, its headlights came on and Tasneen waved as she sped off up the road.

Mallory watched the car until its red tail lights had dipped under the bridge and the vehicle had turned the corner beyond and was out of sight. He glanced around the dark rubbish-strewn lifeless street as the wind picked up for a few seconds to blow an empty plastic bag and a sheet of newspaper into the air. He walked towards the floodlit checkpoint.

Mallory kept to the centre of the road to remain visible to the guards, took out his identification pouch and hung it around his neck.

As he approached the first of the chicane barriers a couple of young Iraqi guards in scruffy civilian clothes and armed with AK47s stepped into the light to watch him. He showed them his empty hands as he closed in and put on a warm smile as he entered the lit area.

'*Salom alycom,*' he called out.

'*Alycom salom,*' one of the men replied dryly.

Mallory raised his badge. The man inspected it briefly before offering him entry.

'*Shukran,*' Mallory said in thanks and headed past half a dozen more guards who were smoking and talking around a glowing brazier.

Mallory nodded, some responded, and he walked

on down the road, lined by towering blast walls, that ran past the back of the Baghdad Hotel. He reached the end of the block, passed through another barrier and walked towards the first checkpoint, manned by Iraqis, for the Palestine and Sheraton Hotel complex.

He repeated the safety procedures, was ushered through and headed for the main checkpoint to the complex manned by US soldiers. 'How's it going, guys?' he said, recognising one of the Americans.

'How you doin'?' the soldier replied. 'You havin' fun tonight?'

'Yeah. Checking out the local nightclubs,' Mallory quipped.

'Guess you can afford it,' the soldier smirked.

Mallory maintained an ongoing banter with a couple of the soldiers about relative wages: western private-security guards could earn ten times as much as a soldier. Another source of envy was the freedom that PSDs seemed to enjoy moving around as civilians. Mallory had been approached by several soldiers asking how to get a job as a PSD if they left the army but Mallory couldn't in all conscience recommend most of the tasks the PSDs were employed to perform. Much of what they had to do was running convoys through bandit country where many had met their end, caught up in explosive ambushes and fierce gun battles. The media heard about few of these incidents – the US Army didn't publicise their discoveries when they came across the remnants of western PSD convoys that had been wiped out and the companies that hired the men didn't advertise their losses because it was bad for business. Many of these companies were in any case not of a high standard: they sent their teams out in lightly armed soft-skin vehicles without sound intelligence or back-up into places where coalition soldiers would not even venture without heavy air support.

'You take it easy, guys,' Mallory said as he headed towards his hotel. 'I've gotta go call my stockbroker, make some investments.'

'Yeah, you do that, pal,' one of the soldiers called. 'You probably earned my day's wages the time it takes you to walk to your room!' another shouted. The comment was followed by some laughter.

Mallory waved without looking back as he followed a line of ten-foot-high blast walls that shielded the road from the river. He passed a large statue of a couple of Arab youths on a flying carpet. An Abrams tank was parked beside it under a canopy, a soldier standing in the turret. Its gun barrel pointed back towards the checkpoint in case a suicide bomber tried to ram his way through. Mallory headed down a broad avenue towards the entrance of the Sheraton and a minute later was stepping into the cavernous lobby and past a central waterfall towards glass elevators from which guests could look onto the lobby as they ascended. As usual, only one of the four lifts was operating at that time: one of them had been permanently disabled after its cables had been severed by a rocket strike earlier in the year. The lobby was five floors high and then the elevators passed through a transparent roof and continued up the outside of the building for another fifteen floors.

Mallory's lift stopped on the fifth floor and he

stepped out onto a landing that ran around the inside of the building. He walked to his room on the east side of the square, unlocked his door and closed it behind him. He took his notebook from his pocket, found Tasneen's number and keyed it into his phone.

Mallory went to the balcony window and pulled the sliding glass door aside to improve the signal reception. He looked down onto the large blue dome of the Firdous Mosque or Mosque of Paradise on the other side of Firdous Square. An explosion went off in the distance somewhere, followed by the rattle of heavy machine-gun fire, normal sounds for Baghdad by day and by night. As Mallory held the phone to his ear, expecting to hear the irritating recording of the girl telling him that he had dialled the number incorrectly, it actually rang.

'Hello,' said the unusually clear sweet voice.

'It's me, Bernie,' Mallory said.

'I'm just closing the door to my car and walking to my apartment.'

'That's all I wanted to hear.'

'And you got home OK too?' she asked.

'I'm in my room.'

'Good. Then we're both nice and safe.'

Mallory wondered if Tasneen was being facetious.

'Thank you,' she added then, sounding sincere. 'It's nice of you to care.'

There was a pause as both of them seemed to wonder what to say next.

'Would I be out of line if I called you again?' Mallory asked.

There was another pause. 'That would be nice,' Tasneen said finally as she reached her front door and put the key into the lock.

'What time will you be at the hospital tomorrow?' he asked, remembering that he still had to collect Stanza and that her brother was there too.

'I'll get there early,' she said. 'I have to work tomorrow.'

'Maybe I'll see you.'

'That would be nice.'

'OK . . . well, good night, then,' he said.

'Good night.'

Mallory ended the call and remained on the balcony, looking out over the city as he contemplated forming a relationship with a local girl. It was without a doubt pointless. But desire knew no boundaries and he would pursue her until either the obstacles became insurmountable or she refused his advances. There was, of course, his own mission in Iraq to worry about, too – it appeared to have slipped his mind for the moment. He yearned for Tasneen's company, though, and would meet her at the hospital even if it was only for a minute. Life in Iraq had to be taken one day at a time.

Mallory suddenly realised that he had not yet called the newspaper or the boss of his company. He scrolled through his phone numbers and then paused as he thought of two greater priorities at that moment. He needed to call Farris to determine the state of the car that they'd left on the BIAP and he had to organise a ride to the hospital in the morning. When that was sorted Mallory would devote the rest of the evening to reporting the incident to Milwaukee and London: both calls would take time – there would be a lot of explaining to do. Then he would organise himself some supper.

Tasneen closed the front door behind her, throwing across the new deadbolt she'd had installed, as well as the others, and double-checking that they were firmly in place. She walked through the living room, dropped her handbag on the couch and went into the kitchen. She filled a glass with water and took a sip. Mallory was a nice man but it would be impossible to see him again. If she ever managed to get out of Iraq it would be good to have someone she knew in the West but Mallory would probably not be right for what she had in mind. He would want to provide more than just help. It was pointless even to fantasise about it. A relationship with any man at that moment would be impossible and to have a friendship with a foreigner would be ludicrous. Mallory surely knew that for himself and if he didn't then she would have to doubt his common sense. But when she had told him that she would see him in the morning she had to admit that it hadn't been just to get him off the phone. She had enjoyed his company, more than she should have. It had been nice but this was the wrong time and very much the wrong place.

Tasneen looked at the fridge, wondering what to have for supper. But the thought of preparing anything now faded away. The sadness that had engulfed her like a fog for the past few weeks was back. For a little while Mallory had made her feel like a normal girl. More normal than she had ever felt before, probably. It had been a taste of forbidden fruit. But that was what she had devoted a life of daydreaming to. She'd had a glimpse of the real thing and ultimately it had frightened her. What she could not decide was whether she had the courage to either explore her dreams or abandon them.

6

Mismatched Pairs

Mallory stood in the hotel car park, checking his watch as Kareem's car emerged from the outer checkpoint in the distance and headed for the US-manned barrier. He walked through a gap in the blast wall, nodded at the American soldiers there and made his way up the road to meet Kareem.

On seeing his boss, Kareem made a three-point turn. As he completed it Mallory opened the car door and climbed in beside him.

'Hospital?' Kareem asked.

'Yep,' Mallory replied. 'You're half an hour late.'

Kareem shrugged in classic Arab fashion, opening his hands to the sky. 'IED in Karada,' he said matter-of-factly.

Mallory never knew when to believe his Iraqi drivers. They were basically good guys but their philosophy seemed to be that if the truth was not of great importance then there was no need to be scrupulous about it. There may well have been an IED in Karada but Mallory doubted that was why Kareem was late. He had caught both him and Farris lying in the past, always about something too trivial to challenge for fear of denting their delicate pride. Arabs tended to rate themselves highly in all manner of things. Both drivers were former Iraqi military and regarded themselves as experts with small arms but in reality their technique was abysmal. Their drills were dangerous and their accuracy terrible. But to tell them as much would have offended them and could have affected their relationship with Mallory. In Arab culture a man who does not share the high opinion one has of oneself is not a friend, and someone who is not a friend is a potential enemy. It was important to maintain mutual respect because Kareem and Farris were not simply employees. Mallory put his life in their hands every day and so let them get away with the small things and dealt with the more serious matters with great diplomacy. They were well paid, their families would be looked after if something happened to them and their laziness and incompetence were often overlooked. Trustworthy staff were hard to find and, as locals went, Kareem and Farris were OK.

Mallory's anxiety today was entirely about Tasneen, anyway. He had woken up that morning thinking of the girl and after some brutal self-examination and self-directed accusations of mere lustfulness nothing had changed. He could not get her out of his mind and the urge to see her had to be satisfied.

'How's Farris?' Mallory asked.

Kareem exhaled dramatically, a familiar sign usually telegraphing a problem. 'No happy,' Kareem said. 'He very upset.'

'How upset?'

'I no know,' Kareem said, using facial expressions and hand gestures to punctuate his comments. 'Maybe he want time to off.'

That was only to be expected and was not a bad idea. The team was going nowhere for a while in any case. 'You too?'

Kareem shrugged, playing his hand. 'If you like. I no care.'

They drove over the Jumhuriyah, the bridge that Mallory had crossed with Tasneen the night before, and pulled over to join a line of vehicles waiting to enter the Assassins' Gate checkpoint. Passing through any of the Green Zone checkpoints was an exercise in tension because of the number of times that they had been bombed. Police vehicles usually hung around the busy junction but their presence only added to its attractiveness as a target. It took ten minutes for Mallory and Kareem to get through into the relatively safe Green Zone and to the hospital. Mallory jumped out on the main street outside the hospital, leaving Kareem to park the car, and hurried to the entrance where he was searched before entering the building.

Mallory turned the corner at the end of the long corridor and paused to look in the waiting room. It was empty and he carried on to reception where, after the usual pointless discussion, he was directed back to the waiting room. After fifteen minutes the wait became intolerable and he began to wonder if Tasneen had already been and gone.

He looked out the door along the corridor that had become busy and saw Stanza standing in the reception hall with a member of the hospital staff. As Mallory reached the reception doors he could see Stanza supporting himself with a pair of alloy crutches and holding what looked like a paper bag of medication. This was apparently the subject of his conversation with the orderly or doctor who left Stanza as Mallory pushed in through the doors.

'Hi,' Mallory said.

Stanza turned to face him, a move that evidently caused him some pain. 'Hi,' he said.

'So you survived, then,' Mallory said.

'I guess so,' Stanza said, markedly less cocky than he'd been the day before.

'How is it?' Mallory asked, looking at Stanza's heavily bandaged thigh.

'Not too bad at all. They dug a bullet out of the muscle but there was no major damage done. Hurts like a son of a bitch, though. Gonna be living off painkillers the next week or so. But the good news is that I should be running around in a couple of weeks.'

'Have you decided if you're staying or heading home? I talked with your foreign editor in Milwaukee. Patterson.'

'Let me guess. He hooted with laughter.'

'He sounded concerned.'

'I'll bet.'

'He wants you to call him soon as you can.'

'I plan to stick around,' Stanza said. 'Hopefully I've had all my action for this trip.'

'Well . . . Car's outside,' Mallory said, pointing along

the corridor. Stanza took a step and froze as his face tightened against a bolt of pain.

'Want me to get you a wheelchair?' Mallory asked, displaying a motherly attitude he had developed only since working with civilians.

Stanza fought the pain until it eased, his face relaxing as he breathed deeply in and out while blinking away the wetness in his eyes. 'I'll be fine,' he said. 'Perhaps another painkiller . . . I just need to get the hang of these crutches. They're my first.'

'Let me carry your bag.'

'They gave me a bunch of dressings and stuff. I said you could handle that for me.'

'We'll change your dressing every morning. Not a problem.'

Mallory took the paper bag as Stanza concentrated on keeping the injured leg rigid while he leaned forward, put his weight on the crutches and took a step with his good leg.

Mallory took a single step to stay alongside him and, as he pondered the time it was going to take to reach the main street entrance, he saw Tasneen step out of a ward, a young man beside her whose heavily bandaged right arm was shorter than his left. They headed across the reception hall to the exit doors, Tasneen too concerned with her brother to notice anyone else.

Mallory felt a spasm of excitement at the sight of her. 'I need to see someone,' he said to Stanza.

'Huh?' Stanza grunted without looking up, concentrating on his next step.

217

'Just head down to the end, then go right. I'll catch you up,' Mallory said as he hurried away.

Stanza turned to look for Mallory but a painful twinge forced him back. He sighed, took a breath and concentrated on making his way along the corridor.

'Hi,' Mallory called out to Tasneen as she held the door open for her brother.

'Hi,' she replied, startled and looking immediately uncomfortable.

Mallory followed her outside where Abdul had stopped to look at the stranger.

'Is this your brother?' Mallory asked. The young man looked ill and exhausted.

'Yes,' Tasneen said, her uneasiness clear to Mallory. 'This is Abdul.'

'Hi,' Mallory said. '*Salam alycom.*' Mallory suspected that Tasneen had not said anything to her brother about the time at the hospital that she'd spent with an Englishman. 'I'm sorry to bother you,' he went on. 'Your sister was unfortunate enough to get stuck with me yesterday while she was waiting for you.'

Tasneen held her breath for fear that Mallory would mention the drive. She could not look at him.

'Anyway,' Mallory continued, 'I'm sorry to have stopped you but I just wanted to say that if your brother is looking for some light work when he's feeling better we could do with a translator.'

People were moving in and out of the emergency entrance. Mallory was suddenly aware of someone standing behind him and looked over his shoulder to see Kareem.

Mallory ignored him and faced Tasneen who was looking less panic-stricken than she'd been a few seconds before.

'Let me give you my number,' Mallory said, pulling out his notebook and scribbling on a page. 'You don't even have to let me know if you're not interested. It just struck me that your being a former police officer could be useful to us.' Mallory ripped out the page and offered it to Abdul who looked confused.

Tasneen took the paper. 'Thank you,' she said, looking away.

'Goodbye, then,' Mallory said. 'Nice to meet you, Abdul, and I hope you feel better soon.' Mallory felt that he was acting too cheerful but he was stuck in character.

'Goodbye,' Tasneen said, giving him a quick look. 'And thank you.'

'Hope to hear from you,' he said, praying that she understood the personal element in the request.

Tasneen took hold of Abdul's left hand and led him away.

Mallory's gaze lingered on her until he turned to face Kareem who was staring at him in his usual blank manner. 'I park there,' Kareem said, jutting his chin towards the hospital car park.

'I need you out front,' Mallory said.

'Is busy so I come here.'

Mallory thought about explaining why Kareem was not permitted to bring his car into the hospital car park without permission and also reminding him to listen to the instruction that Mallory had given him to wait out at the front of the building. But he chose to ignore the impulse. It was sometimes easier just to move on. 'OK,' Mallory said, trying to sound patient. 'Drive your car back out to the front of the hospital and I'll meet you there. Yes?'

'No problem,' Kareem said. But he stayed where he was.

'Off you go, then,' Mallory said, adopting the paternal tone he used with his locals.

Kareem finally moved away and Mallory took one last look at Tasneen. He smiled inwardly at having achieved his aim of talking to her. Now all he could hope for was that she would call him. The job offer that he'd made to Abdul had been a stroke of brilliance, an idea that had come from nowhere and was clearly a gift from the gods.

He went back inside, through the reception hall and into the corridor. Stanza was not in sight, which meant that he had either made it to the corner at the end or had collapsed and been taken away. The last look Tasneen had given Mallory was replaying itself in an endless wonderful loop and even the thought of being Stanza's nurse for the next week or so was nowhere near enough to put him in a bad mood.

Tasneen guided Abdul towards the car, resisting the urge to look back. It was not that her feelings for Mallory had blossomed in any way. But she was grateful for the offer as well as for the way he had revealed their relationship to her brother. Just the possibility of a job for Abdul was a monumental boost.

'You OK?' Tasneen asked, wondering if her brother had read anything into the chance meeting with the Englishman.

'My head feels like it is full of weeds,' he said.

'It's the medication. The doctor said you would feel better later in the day.'

'Who was that man?' Abdul asked.

There came the question but Tasneen did not think she could read anything untoward in it. 'I was stuck with him in the waiting room yesterday. He was waiting for his friend . . . He was very kind to offer you a job, don't you think?'

Despite feeling mentally sluggish, Abdul's interest had perked up at the mention of employment. Of the many things that had occupied his thoughts during the past few weeks the need to find a job had become the most important. He had many problems to deal with, real and psychological, but Tasneen had been right when she'd said that a job was the most important rehabilitation phase he had to aim for. He had not reacted positively when she'd first made the comment because he'd thought that she was just saying it for the sake of his morale. It had been hard enough getting a job when he'd had both hands.

'He did say translator, didn't he?' Abdul asked.

'Yes.'

That was certainly a job he could do with one hand. 'What does he do?'

'I didn't take a great interest, I'm afraid. I do remember him saying something about a newspaper. Yes, that was it. He works for an American newspaper.'

'I don't speak English as well as you,' Abdul said, looking for the negative aspects of Mallory's offer.

'You speak it well enough,' she said. 'And you can work on it while you're getting better. It will give you something to aim for.'

Tasneen was right, as usual. Abdul was already feeling better.

They arrived at her car and she unlocked the passenger door for him. He eased himself into the seat while she closed the door, walked around to the other side and climbed in beside him.

'Why don't we speak nothing but English for the next few days?' she suggested. 'Like we sometimes used to with Father. Remember? It won't take you long to get good at it again. Father said your accent was always better than mine. I don't know why we didn't think of a job like that for you before. There are so many jobs here for Iraqis who can speak English.'

Abdul leaned his head back and stared at the ceiling, wondering if he should get his hopes up.

Tasneen placed the key in the ignition and started the engine. 'He seemed like a very good person,' she said. 'That's the impression I got. What do you think? He was polite and well mannered. Not offensive as some of them can be. I feel he was sincere. Why else would he walk up to us like that? And he mentioned you being a former policeman. I told him, of course. He seemed very interested in that.'

Abdul looked over at her and Tasneen wondered if she could detect suspicion in his eyes. She was talking too much, especially about Mallory, selling him too hard. But Abdul smiled in a way that she had not seen in a long time. 'OK, my big sister,' he said with an affection she had not heard in his voice since before the war. 'We'll see what happens.'

'That's all we can do,' she said.

'Take me home,' he said tiredly, closing his eyes.

'Only if you say it in English.'

He opened his eyes and stared ahead in thought. 'Home, Jeeves,' he said.

Tasneen grinned. 'Yes, sir,' she said in an exaggerated American accent as she pulled out of the parking spot.

Kareem watched Tasneen and her brother drive away as he climbed in behind the wheel of his car. He was not sure if he should be disturbed or not by the little he had overheard or understood of Mallory's conversation with the couple. Kareem had told Mallory more than once that if ever another job opened up with the newspaper he could provide a good and trustworthy man. He started the engine and drove out of the parking lot. Kareem liked Mallory – a bit. As much as an Arab could like a white man who was his boss in his own country and who probably earned ten times as much money. All westerners were in Iraq to get what they could, to make as much money as possible and ultimately they did not give a damn about the Iraqi people. Kareem knew, or was very sure, that Mallory often held things back from him too, never revealing to him or Farris anything about the day's agenda until just before they were about to leave the hotel. That was because

Mallory didn't trust them. It was not difficult to work that out. Mallory suspected that Kareem or Farris would set him up or something. It never failed to amaze Kareem how stupid the Englishman was. If Kareem wanted to do him harm it would not be difficult. But like all Iraqis who hated the westerners in his country he needed them – for the moment, anyway – to put food on the table to feed his wife and four children. These were bad times but at least he had a job, and a well-paid one at that. What made it so much more difficult was that although he wished the westerners would go he feared for his family's future if they did. These were certainly troubled times.

Mallory opened the door of Stanza's hotel room, two doors away from his own. He stood back to let the man inside. Stanza struggled through the door into a short narrow corridor and examined the place that would be his home for the next two months. The first impression was of somewhere dark, musky and dreary. Immediately by the front door was a small bathroom, a toilet and bidet cubicle next to it. The soiled carpeted corridor led to a poky bedroom, its walls covered in tired grubby wallpaper with seams that either failed to meet or overlapped. It was sparsely furnished with a low double bed, a desk, a chair, and a long dresser with an old television set on it that had a wire coat-hanger for an antenna.

Stanza's bags were on the floor by a glass balcony door that was partly concealed by a drape whose quality matched that of the wallpaper.

Stanza hobbled on his crutches past the bed and pushed the drape aside to look through the balcony door at a view dominated by the Palestine Hotel across the road. Sadoon Street was to the right of it, the Tigris river to the left, the Green Zone beyond the river's far bank and the Jumhuriyah bridge in the distance.

'Tell me this is one of the best rooms in the house,' Stanza said.

'They're all pretty much the same,' Mallory said, shrugging. 'The hotel doesn't have a problem with you doing it up if you want.'

'I'll bet,' Stanza mumbled.

'Room service is limited. The food can sometimes be OK but we have a good supply of Ciproxin, Flagyl and Maxolon in case you get a bug. Chances are you'll need one of 'em before the month is out.'

Stanza looked at Mallory to see if he was serious but as usual there was nothing in his manner to suggest that he was not.

'I'll leave you to it, then,' Mallory said, stepping back to the door. 'I'll pop by later in the day and give you your contact numbers, emergency procedures, intel brief . . . stuff like that.'

'I'll probably be on my bed for the rest of the day after I've cleaned up,' Stanza said.

'That's a good idea. If you need me I'm on the end of my phone. If I'm not in my room I won't be far. Maybe down the gym later this evening . . . Don't forget to phone your editor,' Mallory added, pausing in the doorway to see Stanza staring at his bed. He

225

wondered what the man was thinking. Mallory headed out of the room and was about to close the door when Stanza called after him.

'Bernie?'

Mallory held the door open and looked back in.

'Thanks. For yesterday. I appreciate what you did.'

Mallory shrugged. 'Just doing my job,' he said.

'Yeah, I know,' Stanza said. 'Thanks, anyway.'

Mallory left the room.

Stanza stared back down at the bed, wondering how best to get from the standing position to lying on it in the least painful way. The journey from the hospital bed to the hotel room had been excruciating – at times he'd thought he was going to pass out.

Stanza let the crutches fall onto the bed and leaned forward slowly. The stretching movement caused a bolt of white fire to shoot up his leg and he dropped onto the mattress like a sack of potatoes and remained in the same position until the pain became bearable. Then he rolled carefully on his back, an inch at a time, and eased himself towards the pillow until his ankles reached the edge of the mattress. He suddenly felt utterly drained, raised a hand to look at his watch and, after a quick calculation, decided it would be another four hours before Patterson arrived at the Milwaukee office. He wondered about the conversation he would have with his foreign editor. If Stanza wanted to stay in Iraq, which he had decided he did, he would have to play down the injury. He should have asked Mallory exactly what he'd told the office – but then, it didn't really matter. It was up to Stanza how he felt and what shape he was in. He would describe the incident as more of a shock than anything else and say that the wound was not as serious as they'd first thought, which was all true. He would emphasise that it would not affect his work and he'd claim that he'd be running around in a week as well as any other journalist in the country.

Stanza's mission in coming to Iraq, to claw back something of his career, remained unchanged and a mere bullet was not going to deter him. Looking at it from another perspective, his hell-raising introduction to Baghdad would make a powerful introduction to his first report. It could not have been better, really. As for the content of the rest of the article, that was going to be the hard part. Every journalist in the country was looking for that insightful piece that would get them talked about. The stories were out there. With all that was going on in this crazy place there *had* to be great stories. But they had to be found and he was going to need some luck. The shooting on the BIAP road had been luck of a kind and he didn't mean just because he'd survived it. He had been shot while in the noble pursuit of his duty to inform the ignorant and he would push on regardless, handicapped by pain, in pursuit of the truth.

He sighed. If only he believed that garbage he would be a better journalist. But Stanza's salvation lay not in trying to gain back the ground he had lost but in forgetting the past and forging himself a new reputation. He needed a rebirth. His past had not been forgotten by his bosses because he had not replaced it with anything better. He decided that he didn't need anything more for his first article. His arrival and the shooting on the BIAP road was it. 'I arrived.' A bit Dickens, perhaps, but that was the point entirely.

Stanza closed his eyes and tried to forget the rest of the world for the moment. He needed to heal and sleep was the key. But try as he might he could not break away from his pain or his problems and so he just lay there until exhaustion finally led him into unconsciousness.

Mallory left his room, walked along the landing and before reaching the lifts pushed through a heavy wooden door bearing an illustration of a stick man running from a flame down a flight of stairs. He continued along a short corridor to another door that led into a dank, poorly lit concrete stairwell that stretched out of sight above and below. The air was warm and smelled of cigarette smoke and urine. He jogged down the steps to the floor below and in through an open door. A short corridor led to another door which he pushed through and emerged onto a carpeted, palatial landing identical to the one above. He carried on past the lifts and towards the open door of a suite that had been converted into an office. As Mallory entered what had originally been the suite's bedroom a burst of cheering and clapping went up from the three white men already there, one seated behind a desk, the other two in comfortable low armchairs opposite.

''Ere 'e is!' declared Des, the sinewy large-eyed man

behind the desk who was wearing a broad grin. 'It's Bernie the bolt. Sit yersel' down, cherub. We 'ear yer dented yer new client five minutes after pickin' 'im op at the airport.'

Mallory sat down tiredly in the remaining empty seat and forced a smile while preparing himself to absorb the well-rehearsed abuse that he knew was about to come his way.

'Give 'im a chance, lads. Let's 'ear your version, Bernie,' Des said.

'Nothing much more than that, really,' Mallory sighed. 'Got whacked by PSDs on the BIAP.'

'Bad, is 'e?' asked Dunce, an ape of an ex-paratrooper from Cardiff who sat nearest the balcony window that was slightly open so he could blow cigarette smoke outside.

'He'll live,' Mallory said.

'What 'appened, then, laddy?' Des asked with his habitual interrogative expression, his unusual eyes slightly out of sync with each other. He was a salt-of-the-earth Northerner, mid-forties, very experienced on the private security circuit and former Royal Artillery, which was why he talked loudly all the time. 'Com' on, out wi' it. We 'eard that soon as the shootin' started you dragged the poor booger in front a' ye to save yersel'. That right?'

Every comment from Des was accompanied by grins and chuckles from the other two.

'PSD. Is that right?' Dunce asked.

'Yep,' Mallory said. 'Usual nonsense. Only this time they aimed inside the cab.'

'Foockers, ain't they?' Des said. 'Shoot back, did yer?' he asked, knowing it would have been suicide but he liked to wind anybody up in any way possible. 'Tell me yer put som rounds inter 'em . . . Ey, wait a minute. Yer grenade. You 'ad it out, didn't ye? Tell me yer did, lad, and all's forgiven.' It was one of those conversations that Mallory knew was pointless to take seriously in any way. Des had got the others in their usual giggly mood and was determined to have a laugh at Mallory's expense. Mallory had pretty much expected it on walking into the room but the truth was that he didn't mind it at all. In fact, there was something therapeutic about the way Brits gave each other stick, especially about their misfortunes. It appeared heartless to some, especially to foreigners, but not to Brits, especially those who had served in the military. It was character-testing – and a bloody good laff, of course.

''Ey. Harpic 'ere were shot at yesterday 'n all,' Des shouted. 'Client shat 'isself, din't 'e, Harpic?'

'Fuckin' right,' Harpic croaked in his Luton accent. Harpic was nicknamed after the well-known toilet-bowl-cleaning product because it claimed to 'clean round the bend' – which was how Harpic was often described.

'O' course,' Des went on, 'stupid bastard were drivin' down wrong foockin' lane towards a Yanky checkpoint int' t' GZ. Weren't yer, Harpic, yer daft bastard?'

'Fuckin' soljer waved me in 'at way, din' 'e?' Harpic said defensively, giving a sniff at the end of the sentence. 'Client shat 'imself, all right. 'E 'ad to wipe 'is arse with a trauma dressin' while I went 'n 'ad a go at the wankers who shot at us.'

'I'd advise yer boss to keep a trauma dressin' strapped to 'is arse all the time, the way you drive rount Baghdad, yer mad bastard,' Des said. A hooting laugh came from Dunce.

There was a knock on the door and a rotund Iraqi stepped in, looking most apologetic for intruding on the group.

'Jamel, me ol' codger,' Des boomed. 'What yer want, lad? We're in top-level meetin' 'ere.'

'Hello, hello, hello,' Jamel said, a forced grin on his face. He was a stoutly built Iraqi who looked as if he had not missed many meals in his life. 'Sorry, Des,' he then said sombrely, the smile fading as he bowed his head, his right hand spread over his heart in a sign of deference. 'Please, I want pill,' he said.

'Pill? What's that, the morning-after pill?' Des said, then burst out laughing. 'You been fuckin' aroun' wi' Akmed again?'

Dunce was drawing on his cigarette and snorted so abruptly that mucus shot from his nose. He did his best to catch it as it ran down his chin.

Jamel forced a smile though he didn't have a clue what Des was talking about. 'I need pill, Des.' Jamel held his stomach with both hands while putting on a pained expression.

'For your fat?' Des asked. 'You know why yer fat, don't yer, Jamel? Yer mouth is bigger 'n yer arse' ole, that's why yer fat.'

Dunce snorted once again but this time held his nose.

Jamel grinned, again not knowing what Des was talking about. 'I'm going to toilet too much, Des. Give me pill, please.'

'Oh. Diarrhoea? Yer know why yer've got diarrhoea, don't yer? Same reason. Yer mouth is bigger 'n yer arse' ole. 'Ow long yer been shittin', then? 'Ow long on toilet?' Des said, pausing between each word.

'All today,' Jamel said.

'Well, if yer still shittin' by tonight, come see me and we'll stick a cork op yer arse, OK?'

Jamel maintained his smile, oblivious to Des's meaning, and nodded. 'Thank you, Des,' he said. 'Thank you.'

'Are all the cars filled op wi' benzine?' Des asked.

'Yes, Des. Yes,' Jamel insisted.

'I'm gonna check, you know I will,' Des said with a sudden serious look as if talking to a child. It was impossible to imagine Des with a natural expression.

'All cars full,' Jamel insisted.

'Spare tyres pomped up? You remember what happened on the way back from Basra last month and we 'ad a flat, don't yer? Put the spare on and it were flat too. Eh? Eh?'

'Very sorry, Des,' Jamel said, bowing slightly several times. 'Not happen again.'

'OK. There's a good lad. Shoot off now, then, and don't eat anythin' and we'll see yer later, all right?'

Jamel remained grinning at them, unsure what Des had said. Understanding Des was a common problem among the Iraqi staff, even those who could speak good English. In fact, they did not believe he was English at all and called him The Scottish.

'Jamel,' Des said with emphasis and Jamel gave him his fullest attention. 'Foock off and com back later, me ol' flower, OK?'

Jamel suddenly realised that the meeting was over and that he wasn't going to get his pill. 'Oh. Hello, hello,' he said as he took a step back towards the door. When Des nodded at him to indicate that he was going in the right direction, Jamel put his hand across his heart again and smiled and nodded, saying 'Hello, hello' to everyone as he backed out of the room.

Mallory had not been in Iraq very long before he'd noticed a flagrant misuse of the word 'hello' by most if not all the locals, especially those who could speak hardly any English at all. It was used in its correct form as a greeting but the same person might also use it as a reply to a query about their health and well-being and, most notably, it was often used in place of 'goodbye'. To the uninitiated it could prove highly confusing and irritatingly extend what would normally be a brief encounter.

'Good lad, is our Jamel,' Des said after the Iraqi had gone. 'Now, Bernie, me lad. You all right, are yer? Cuppa tea?'

'I thought you'd never ask,' Mallory said.

'Harpic. Get the lad a cuppa. 'E's 'ad 'ard day.'

'I'm off,' Dunce said, getting to his feet and moving his large frame between the desk and the chairs as he wiped his hands on his backside and followed Harpic. 'See you lads later,' he said as he left the room.

'See you at scoff,' Des yelled after him. Then he leaned back in his chair, grinning one of his classic

233

grins, his eyes like golf balls and looking at Mallory. 'So. 'Ad a bit of a rough day, 'ave yer?' he asked.

'Not really,' Mallory said stretching out his own feet.

'Ow's the client? Aw right, is 'e?'

'He's fine. Took a round in the thigh. The event itself has probably left a deeper scar.'

'I'll bet,' Des said. 'Can't take gettin' shot, these boogers, eh? Make such a song and dance about it.'

Harpic walked in with four mugs of tea on a tray and put them on the desk. 'Where's Dunce?' he asked.

'Hidin' in t' top drawer of desk but 'e don't want to be disturbed,' Des said. 'E followed yer out, yer blind bastard . . . Now,' Des continued, suddenly serious and looking directly into Mallory's eyes. 'What's your plan for Fallujah?'

For a split second Mallory thought that Des meant Mallory's private plans until simple reason reminded him it was not possible for Des to know anything about them.

'Your man's not gonna be fit to get op there, is 'e?' Des said. ''Ave yer got any slots for the embed?'

'Everything's a bit up in the air at the moment,' Mallory said. 'Have you heard anything that might give a clue as to when the Yanks are going in?'

'Bush called me this mornin' but 'e tol' me not to tell anyone. O' course I don't foockin' know when they're goin' in, yer twat, but it's got to be sometime in the next few weeks. They 'aven't put ten thousand men and a couple 'undred tanks around the bloody town to keep wind out.'

Mallory took a sip of his tea while his mind buzzed

about Fallujah. He needed more information. He had decided that embedding with the troops was not the best option for him simply because he would not have the freedom to go anywhere alone. But then, his other choices were probably worse. If Stanza was fit enough in time to go Mallory would be stuck with him as well as with the US Marines.

'I'll be honest, Des, I don't know what we'll do. It depends on how my new guy's health stands at the time.'

'Yeah, I s'pose you're right. Bit soon, really, seein' as he was only shot yesterday.'

'What about yourself?' Mallory asked.

'What, Fallujah? One producer wants to go but 'er correspondent's crappin' 'isself at the thought. 'Ope they both don't want to go or I'll get mesel' in a tangle.'

Des was working as a consultant to a handful of small media outfits who had arrived in Iraq looking for inexpensive security coverage. That meant no full-time security but Des was available as a consultant and also as a body if needed – at extra cost. It was workable most of the time since all the low-rent set-ups usually wanted was advice on how to operate, occasional threat updates and a hand to hold if every-thing went wrong, such as the threatened civil war that had been rumoured for months. But if more than one media company wanted Des to take them out somewhere at the same time he had to do some juggling.

'Let me run somethin' by you,' Des said. 'If your

guy ain't able to make it, would you take one o' mine if needed?'

'How am I gonna do that? If my guy doesn't go I still have to be here for him.'

'I thought you were goin' 'ome soon,' Des said.

'Perhaps.'

'Why don't you let your relief com on in? But instead o' you goin' 'ome, you stay 'ere and 'elp me out. Same money you're gettin' now.'

Mallory was immediately attracted by the idea, its advantages being the let-up in pressure from the London office and an increase in his freedom of movement. Mallory could take Des's client to Fallujah, escort him to the embed rendezvous and then slip away. The client would be with half a dozen other media types as well as the Marines to look after him. It was a very possible plan.

'You know, Des, you might have something there,' Mallory said.

Des grinned.

'Why don't you keep me in the picture, let me know how things are developing and we'll see what we can do. But I like it,' Mallory said.

'I'll let you know soon as I do, me old chum,' Des said.

Mallory's phone rang in his pocket and he pulled it out to check the small screen. When he saw the name he sprang to life, put his mug down as he got to his feet and headed for the door. 'Got to grab this. See you later,' he said as he went out of the door and pressed the 'receive' button.

'Hello?' he said as he walked along the landing to put some distance between himself and the office. The line was bad, the signal jumping from weak to strong and back again. Mallory cursed the Iraqi phone network and called 'Hello' into the phone several times in case he could be heard even though he couldn't hear much himself. Then, as if his prayers had been answered, the line suddenly became clear and he heard the sweet voice that was music to his ears.

'Tasneen. How are you?' he asked.

'I'm fine,' she answered. Her voice sounded like a song of springtime.

'What's going on? To what do I owe the pleasure?' he asked.

'I wanted to tell you how sorry I was for not talking to you very much this morning,' she said.

'You don't need to. I understood perfectly. I'm not a complete idiot, you know.'

Tasneen laughed. 'I know that. You're not an idiot at all. But thank you for making how we met seem so normal to my brother. I know it *was* normal, but you know what I mean. You put it very nicely.'

Mallory was beaming because she sounded so friendly. 'Well . . . I'm sorry too that we didn't have time to talk. I didn't think I was going to see you again . . . You at work right now?'

'Yes. I got in a little while ago . . . I also want to thank you for something else.'

'This is my lucky day. What else did I do that I was not aware of?'

'Well . . . you made Abdul feel so much better. The

237

offer of a job. I don't know if you meant it or not but just by suggesting it you made him feel, well, useful, I suppose. Ever since you spoke with him he has been in the best mood I have seen him in since his injury. You can imagine that my brother does not feel on top of the world right now. He feels hopeless about his future. You made him feel better, that's all.'

Mallory's job idea had been a top-of-the-head ploy but as a means to see her again it was working like a charm. 'I wasn't joking,' Mallory said. He was the team's security adviser but he did have some influence with the general running of the bureau. The problem was, as always, a question of money but he was confident that he could figure something out.

'Then you were serious?' Tasneen asked, her voice hopeful. In fact, there was such a tone of excitement in her words that Mallory was suddenly struck by a pang of guilt at the possibility that he might not be able to deliver.

'His English is really quite good,' she went on. 'And it will be even better . . . When were you thinking of hiring him?'

Mallory struggled with his conscience. 'Why don't you give me a few days to work it out?' he said. 'I assumed he would need to fully recover first, anyway. Can Abdul read and write English as well as speak it?' Mallory asked.

'Not very well,' Tasneen said regretfully. 'Is that important?'

It would improve his chances, Mallory thought to

himself. And it was a way out if all went pear-shaped. 'I shouldn't think so.'

The line went suddenly bad and Mallory could not hear her. 'Say again,' he said loudly. 'You were cut off.'

'We should get together and talk about it,' she shouted. 'These phones are terrible.'

'How would we do that?' he asked.

'Don't you have a restaurant at the hotel?'

'Yes.'

'I'll come over for lunch.'

'Sounds perfect,' Mallory said. 'When?'

'I'll call you,' Tasneen said, her voice breaking up.

'OK,' Mallory said. But then the line went completely dead, a repetitive beep indicating that the signal had been lost.

Mallory thought about calling her back but decided against it and leaned on the landing rail to contemplate the brief conversation. It appeared that he was developing a social life of sorts, and all because Stanza had been shot. Fate was a strange beast, to be sure. Mallory was confident he could wangle a job for Abdul. The need for an interpreter was obvious since Kareem was not working out as originally hoped. It was the *Herald* being cheap again, trying to double up on jobs. From a security point of view it wasn't smart – but then, when did the media ever put security as a priority? After the event, was Mallory's immediate and damning answer to his own question. It could become problematic if the newspaper wanted to get rid of one of the drivers to make room for Abdul on the payroll, especially when Mallory explained that the young man

239

only had one hand. It looked like it was going to depend on how easily Mallory could manipulate Stanza.

'There 'e goes,' Des said, leaning on the rail a few metres away and looking down into the lobby. 'See that guy there?' he said, pointing at the reception desk. 'The short-arse in t' black suit.'

Mallory made out a short, well-groomed man in a black suit talking with one of the hotel managers.

''Is name's Feisal,' Des said. 'Ali Feisal something or other. One o' the puppet deputies at the Ministry of Interior. You know what 'e does? Takes suitcases o' dollars out of Iraq and deposits 'em in banks in Dubai.'

Mallory took another look at the small man. 'How do you know that?'

'Mate o' mine works at Palace in the GZ, the one at US embassy. They 'ave a big room in t' basement filled wi' US dollars. Guarded by US soldiers. Loads o' money, so they say. Billions is what I've 'eard. The ministries get an allowance or summat like that. The Yanks keepin' 'em 'appy, I s'pose. Money belonged to Saddam anyway, so they say, or it's part o' the Yankee 'andout. Once a month 'e comes in to embassy wi' 'is suitcase which they fill op and 'e takes to airport . . . Good job if you can get it,' Des said.

Mallory watched the little man moving around energetically, pressing the flesh with several suited individuals as if he was of some importance.

'We never did it for money, did we?' Des said.

Mallory glanced at Des, wondering what he meant.

Des was a funny chap, unserious most of the time but prone to the occasional bout of philosophy.

'In the mob, I'm talkin' about. When we first joined op. We did it for love of it, di'n' we? An' it were great, wa'nt it? I remember me first wage. Fifty quid the army gave me for ma first two weeks. I di'n't think yer got paid till yer'd finished trainin'. Fifty quid. We were rich then, 'cause we weren't there fer the money . . . Different now, eh? That's all we're 'ere for, i'n't it? Money. We're all 'ere for that. We're no different than 'im.'

Mallory had to agree with Des, the part about his early days in the forces. He'd never thought about the money, not for a second.

'Good news, was it?' Des asked. 'The phone call. Yer looked 'appy.'

'Oh . . . Nah. Just work.'

Des nodded. 'I'll let you know about the Fallujah job, OK?'

'Roger that,' Mallory said as Des walked away and he headed along the corridor towards the emergency stairs. He would go to his room and watch a bit of TV, catch some news if it was worth watching, take some lunch, read a bit of a book and then visit the gym before dinner. He had some interesting prospects to think about: a meeting with the delightful Tasneen and possibly a move to Fallujah in the next week or so. There was some prepping to be done, mental as well as kit-wise. He needed to be able to move decisively and at short notice. All in all things seemed to be on the up and up.

7

A Life Reborn

Abdul popped a couple of painkillers and washed them down with a glass of water. He remained motionless at the sink for a moment until the worst of the throbbing went away.

He stared at his bandaged stump, as he often did, still unable to believe this horrible thing had happened to him. For days following the amputation he had been consumed not only by his own loss but by the horror of the other events of that night. The image of the woman being shot through the eye inches from him, followed by the brutal slaying of the old couple. The mental picture of the westerner being handed over to the insurgents, his pathetic, shivering obedience as he trotted off with them like a dog to the slaughter. Then there was the guilt for the part he himself had played in the kidnapping, intermingled with bouts of self-pity. Abdul would sometimes burst into tears, often without warning. It was worse still when it happened in front of Tasneen – such an unmanly thing to do.

Night-time brought a fresh intensity to the memories of the atrocities and Abdul slept little more than an hour before being awoken, usually by the voice of the woman declaring her love for the American just before the gun went off.

It was at the lowest point of one of those days that Abdul took hold of himself and reasoned that he could either be a victim of the memories or fight to escape the mental prison they threatened to keep him in.

Unsurprisingly, Allah became a great help and Abdul found comfort in the Koran, reading it for hours at a time, especially after being woken in the night by horrible dreams. When he got to the end of the book he started at the beginning again, always, to his joy, discovering something new or a subtly different inter- pretation in the wise pages. He began to feel his soul reaching out to Allah more and more and believed it would be only a matter of time before he, Abdul, made true spiritual contact with Him.

Abdul began to see Allah's influence in everything around him and decided that the job offer from the Englishman was a hand reaching down to guide him. There were things he needed to set right over the coming weeks and the word that cried out above all others was 'change'. He was going to have to become a different person than he had been so far in his life. The pathetic way he had acted since the amputation sickened him and the need to stand on his own two feet and let go of Tasneen's apron strings became para- mount. The only way to achieve that was to leave her. It would be the most positive single event in his quest for development. She had always urged him to think for himself and forge his own way in life but then her very next action would be to treat him like a helpless little boy. And despite resenting her for it he had been content to allow it to continue. With Allah's help he was going to break free of these chains and the curse of the amputation and become the man he should be.

Abdul went into the living room, sat on the couch, reached for the remote control and turned on the television. The day's plan was to watch English-language programmes until Tasneen came home and then he would tell her he was ready to start work for the newspaper as soon as possible. As he flicked through the channels he paused at an Arabic news broadcast, the image on the screen suddenly turning him cold. It was poor-quality video footage of the man's face that he saw every night in his dreams, the face of the American he had helped kidnap. The man was sitting on a floor, wearing a one-piece orange overall, his hands tied in front of him while several hooded men holding guns stood behind and on either side of him. The commentator was explaining how the tape had recently been released on the Internet by a group calling itself the Holy Jihad Brigade and that they were demanding all American troops should withdraw from Fallujah within a week or the hostage would be executed.

Abdul was stunned to his very core. Having decided to look to the future by cleansing himself of the past he found that it was thrown right back in his face. And then, just as immediately, something became very clear to him. This was not a coincidence. He had been meant to see the footage. He did not know precisely what it meant but one thing he strongly suspected was that it was not over between him and the American.

Stanza swam easily to the shallow end of the Sheraton's outdoor swimming pool and took hold of the side, his breathing laboured. This was his fourth consecutive day of self-supervised physiotherapy and he was doing it days earlier than the doctor had recommended. But Stanza was anxious to get his leg back to a semblance of working order as soon as he could. His earlier belief that he could get almost as much work done in his room, relying on the Internet and talking to other people in the hotel, had turned out to be unrealistic. Patterson had shown a surprising degree of patience with the lack of substance in Stanza's reports so far but he would not put up with it for much longer. There was little chance of finding any story of substance while Stanza was immobilised in the hotel. His leg was still painful but not all of the time and was nowhere near as bad as it had been only a few days before.

He brought his legs beneath him into the standing position and gradually lowered himself, bending his legs at the knees. The dull throbbing around the wound was immediate but bearable until a sudden increase in pain forced him to straighten back up. Undeterred, he repeated the exercise several times and was pleased to note that the aching reduced slightly and he could bend a little lower each time. Worried that he might open the wound again if he overdid it Stanza called it a day, pushed himself out of the water and twisted his body so that he ended up seated on the edge of the pool. He winced as a sharp pain stabbed through him and he waited for it to ease, checking the wound that was still ugly and swollen with tiny scabs of blood around the stitches where they entered the skin. There was going to be a nasty scar but at least he had a good war story to go with it. There were not too many 'war correspondents' around who had a bullet wound.

Stanza eased himself onto his back, closed his eyes, gently extended his legs until they were flat on the hot concrete surface and let the sun, which felt immediately strong on his face, bake him dry. He felt tired and could have drifted off to sleep but forced himself to concentrate on a plan of action for the next few days. He was confident of soon being fit enough to make a trip to the convention centre in the Green Zone.

But there were some administrative and logistical problems that had to be taken care of, the first of which was his security adviser. When Stanza had told Mallory that he planned to go to the convention centre within a day or two the man had appeared unenthusiastic. Stanza had argued that all he had to do was walk a few metres from the drop-off point to the first checkpoint inside the Zone where he would be safe but Mallory had explained how he doubted Stanza's ability to move quickly enough in the event of a 'situation' developing on the way to or from the centre. Mallory's point was that if Stanza needed help getting away he would be putting the rest of the team in jeopardy.

Stanza still felt he had a valid case, though, and rested it on the argument that he had come to Iraq to do a job that he could not do from his hotel room and that Mallory was employed to find solutions, not create obstacles. To drive his point home he suggested that if it was Mallory's job to keep Stanza completely safe he should have kept him at the airport on his arrival and held him there for a couple of months. Mallory had no answer to this facetious reasoning and agreed wearily to take Stanza to the convention centre, a decision that heartened the journalist. He had wondered about Mallory's flexibility. Stanza had heard other journalists complain about their security advisers and how they could be complete pains in the backside. Stanza's philosophy was that he was in the risk business and therefore so too were his staff. It appeared that Mallory now understood that.

Another problem – and this was according to Mallory – was the team itself. It was going through something of a shake-up, with Farris the driver having lost his nerve somewhat: under pressure from his family, he was planning to relocate to Jordan. Rumours of civil war were rife and even Mallory, it seemed to Stanza, was not immune to them.

Mallory had come to Stanza's room on the journalist's first morning in the hotel and had presented him with a list of 'operational procedures', as he called them. They were in a typical military format, covering things that Stanza should and should not do, such as never leaving the hotel without informing Mallory and never making an appointment in the city without getting every possible contact detail and location to enable Mallory to conduct a security-risk assessment. There was also a detailed equipment list of things that Stanza should carry with him at all times. This included his passport and sufficient money, a torch or flashlight with spare batteries, a phone with a list of emergency contact numbers and a map that Mallory provided that showed friendly and not so friendly locations, hospitals and notable bad areas. Mallory also provided an emergency evacuation plan several pages long, containing information on escape routes to Jordan, Turkey and Kuwait that Stanza had promised he would read but hadn't. There were also comprehensive health and hygiene tips. Mallory's 'briefing' had gone on for almost an hour, by which time Stanza felt as though he was on some kind of clandestine mission. He did ask, somewhat impudently, at the end of the briefing if Mallory was going to provide him with a Rolex that was really a tracking device. Mallory replied soberly that there were tracking devices on the market if Stanza really wanted one.

It wasn't as though Stanza thought that Mallory's concerns were pointless. On the contrary. But Stanza's view was that Mallory had his job to do, an important part of which was to make Stanza's life easier. Mallory's responsibilities included the general running of the bureau staff, ensuring they were trained in their respective tasks and that they maintained security standards at all times. But, according to Mallory, the team was apparently not as solid as it should have been. If Farris did quit, and that appeared to be his intention, they would need to hire another driver. When Stanza suggested that Mallory should ask Farris to make up his mind Mallory was against it, arguing that they needed to show the men some loyalty. These were trying times for Iraqis and Farris was under enough pressure from his family without any westerners adding to it. Stanza agreed to let Mallory handle it. Another question that Mallory had raised was the need for a translator. He explained that he had been told on arrival the *Herald*'s budget had originally made allowance for the post.

Stanza was interested. Anyone who could help him was welcome. As for the budget, it wasn't Stanza's money and he reckoned that if the allowance was there they should use it.

Stanza was struck by how keen Mallory was: he already had someone in mind for the job. However, Stanza did question Mallory's judgement when the recruit was described as a twenty-five-year-old Sunni with limited experience of working with the media, who could not read or write English well despite being able to speak it adequately and, most bizarrely, had only one hand. Mallory defended each criticism as if prepared for it. The man was indeed young but he was a former police officer and therefore had a useful knowledge of the streets and would also be helpful if the police ever stopped them. It would also help if they were in pursuit of a story that required some assistance from that department. As for being a Sunni, the advantages were obvious when a story involved that particular religious persuasion. And as far as his disability was concerned the man was being hired as a translator and in Mallory's opinion one hand less would not affect this function.

Mallory's presentation of his discovery's case was so thorough that Stanza had little choice but to give the man a try. Still, after his security man's sincere thanks he got the distinct impression that he had done Mallory some sort of favour.

Stanza's mobile phone chirped beside him. He picked it up and hit the 'receive' button. 'Jake Stanza.'

'Jake? It's Henry.'

Stanza was instantly fully alert and would have sat bolt upright had it not been for the pain. 'Hi . . . ' Stanza stammered. Patterson had not introduced himself to Stanza as Henry since before the infamous incident. After that dreadful day Patterson had been unrelentingly rude to him, a constant reminder of his terminal dislike for the journalist who had almost ruined his precious paper's reputation.

'What are you doing?' Patterson asked without a hint of a barb in his tone.

Stanza struggled to gather his thoughts. This was his first conversation with Patterson since his injury, all previous communications having been with Patterson's assistant and mostly by e-mail.

'You there?' Patterson asked with a hint of irritation, sounding a bit more like his old self.

'Yes, sorry, I was just . . . '

'You been watching the news?' Patterson interrupted. 'I know you haven't been writing much of it – anything worth reading, that is.'

Stanza rolled his eyes. Whatever the reason for Patterson's initial civility, it had obviously passed. 'I . . . '

'Listen. What do you know about Jeffrey Lamont?'

Stanza felt that he knew the name from somewhere and as his silence became unbearable even to him it flashed into his head. 'Kidnapped a month or so ago. Worked for—'

'Shut up and get off this damned phone. The walls have ears over there. You at your computer?'

'No. I'm . . . '

'Get to your computer. I'll Skype.'

'I'm down in the lobby.'

'Then get your ass back to your room. Three minutes,' Patterson said. The phone went dead.

Stanza lowered the phone, wondering what on earth the man was so fired up about. He wanted to talk through Skype because it had high encryption, making it more secure than other communication systems.

Stanza moved as quickly as he could, gritting his teeth against the pain as he pushed himself to his feet. He pulled on his T-shirt and flip-flops, gathered up his things and shuffled into the hotel.

The pool entrance was on the mezzanine floor but for some reason known only to the hotel management the lifts did not stop there: it was a choice between walking up to the first floor or down to the lobby in order to call one. Stanza chose to employ gravity and, supporting himself heavily on the banister rail, hopped down the broad curving marble stairs to the ground floor as quickly as he could. He hobbled over to the elevator bank and joined a short podgy man who was pushing the call button repeatedly as if his action might speed up the machinery.

'Goddamned elevators,' the man mumbled as he adjusted a thick pair of glasses on his nose to squint up at the floor indicators that sometimes told the truth about the lift's whereabouts.

Stanza checked the indicator on the elevator on the other side of the lobby to see that it was on the top floor, which was not unusual. KBR, a major general contractor, rented the top section of the hotel and it was their habit to jam one of the lifts on their floor so that they did not have to wait for one. It was a constant irritation to the rest of the guests but KBR was the nine-hundred-pound gorilla.

The man kept his finger on the button as he looked over his shoulder. 'Hey, Jack Stanza, right?'

Stanza looked down at the short man whom he did not recognise. 'Jake,' Stanza corrected him.

'Jake, right,' the man said, holding out his other hand. 'Aaron Blant, *Washington Post*.'

Stanza shook the hand, wondering if he had met the man before. There were several papers staying at the Sheraton and the *Post* was below on the fourth floor. 'Have we met?'

'No. I heard about you. The guy who got shot on his first day, right? How's the leg?' Blant asked, leaning around Stanza to take a look at it. 'Ouch,' he said as he saw the ugly scar.

'It's not so bad,' Stanza said.

'Looks pretty painful to me.'

'It's OK now.'

'You were pretty lucky,' Blant said. Something about his tone was beginning to annoy Stanza. 'Couple more inches towards the middle and you wouldn't have been laughing,' he said, grinning. Blant seemed to trivialise the incident in a way that made Stanza feel more like a loser than a hero.

'That's right,' Stanza said, looking up at the floor indicator that was on the move at last.

The lift arrived and Stanza imagined his computer ringing away while Patterson cursed his name. Blant stepped into the elevator and made a meal out of holding the doors open for Stanza as if he was a cripple.

'Which floor?'

'Fifth,' Stanza said, attempting to collect his thoughts, wishing he had some kind of bone to throw to his foreign editor. He'd been working on a couple of pieces, one about the closing of several local schools because of terrorist threats against the teachers and children and another about a suicide bomber whose device failed to detonate and who was now in jail. But frankly they were both crap and frustration welled up in him as he stared at the shattered plastic ceiling in search of divine help.

'Still painful, huh?' Blant said, watching him.

'What?' Stanza asked, wondering why the little jerk was still talking to him.

'You look like you're still in a lotta pain.'

Stanza sighed inwardly and chose to ignore him, hoping that his silence would be hint enough to make the guy shut up.

'What are you still doing in Baghdad?' Blant persisted, oblivious to Stanza's lack of interest. 'I'd have been on the first flight outta here as soon as I left the goddamned hospital.'

'Yeah. Maybe you're right,' Stanza said, wondering about Patterson's interest in Lamont and his need to go to a secure communication link. Stanza had read a couple of lines on the wires about the guy but there were so many kidnapped victims in captivity, a couple dozen of them American, and there was nothing about Lamont's story that made it more significant than the others.

Stanza looked down at Blant, who was wearing a shirt and tie under a sleeveless argyle pullover. 'Know anything about this Lamont guy who was kidnapped?' Stanza asked, suspecting that if there was anything unusual this little swot would probably be aware of it.

'Nothing new as far as I know. Kidnapped from the Karada district three or four weeks ago. You see him on TV? The vid's out already.'

Stanza was more out of touch than he thought. He should've known there was a terrorist video out on Lamont even if he had no interest in the man. It was his damned job to.

'Only a matter of time before he buys it,' Blant went on. 'You're with the *Herald*?'

'Uh huh.'

'I'd have thought you woulda been all over that story.'

'Why's that?' Stanza asked, suddenly afraid that he had missed more than just the video.

'Rumour has it he's a Wisconsin boy. Any truth to that?'

The lift came to an abrupt stop but Stanza might well have jolted with equal force if he'd been standing on firm ground. 'I . . . I don't know if that's true yet.'

'Well, you take it easy,' Blant said as the doors opened and he started to head out.

'You know anything else about him?' Stanza asked, hoping that he didn't appear as desperate as he sounded to himself.

Blant appeared to suspect something but then shrugged. 'Ain't much of a story,' he said. 'Rumour is he was seeing a local chick. She got blown away, maybe because she was a hooker.'

'I . . . I'd heard something about that,' Stanza said, grabbing the doors to keep them open.

'Maybe it was the girl's brother. You know how uptight these people get about one of their own screwing a westerner.' Blant smirked. 'Catch you later,' he said as he walked away.

Stanza let the doors close and the lift continued up to the next floor. He squeezed through the doors before they opened fully and hobbled, wincing, along the corridor towards his door.

As he entered his room he could hear the simulated standard phone tone coming from his computer speakers. He tossed his things onto the bed, sat at his desk and fumbled to pick up his headphones as a window on his computer monitor screen alerted him to the call from the *Herald*'s foreign desk.

He placed the headset over his ears and fumbled with the jack as he spun the mouse pointer around the screen in an effort to click the 'answer' button.

'Hello,' he said, adjusting the microphone in front of his mouth. 'Hello, hello,' he repeated, unable to hear anything.

'Where the hell have you been?' Patterson grumbled, his voice stretching like a rubber band as the Internet fought to convert the signal.

'Sorry, I—'

'I take it you're alone?'

'Yes.'

'OK. Jeffrey Lamont . . . '

'Yeah,' Stanza interrupted in an effort to show that he was up to date. 'Kidnapped in Karada. A Wisconsin boy. Was sleeping with—'

'So what did you do when you heard he was a local boy?' Patterson asked accusingly.

'I . . . I figured since he was sleeping with an Iraqi girl, she was killed because of that relationship and—'

'And you didn't try and find out what he was doing there, check out his *family*?' Patterson emphasised the last word.

Stanza suspected that Patterson would have made a perfect Gestapo officer. 'If Lamont was sleeping with an Iraqi girl in her house he was, well, frankly stupid. I didn't see any attractive angle in portraying a local guy who was so dumb . . . '

'Where are your goddamned instincts, Stanza?'

Stanza rubbed his forehead in frustration, wondering if Patterson hated just him or everyone.

'I was gonna give this story to one of our people here,' Patterson growled. 'But it's gotta come from Baghdad. And since none of my chicken-shit writers wanna go there it looks like it's gonna have to be you. I'll e-mail you what we have so far but I'll read you the meat of it. This is uncut from research. Jeffrey Lamont is a Milwaukee boy born and bred, but his name wasn't always Lamont. He went to St John's North-Western Military Academy in Delafield, Wisconsin, an all-boys boarding school and considered one of the best in the region: at St John's North-Western, young men learn that with discipline comes character. He ran away from the place twice, was caught and re-enrolled. From there he went to Harvard where he majored in film theory, experimented with psychedelic mushrooms, dropped out to piss off his folks and spent a couple of years burning through his trust fund on a beach in Indonesia. Between Harvard and Indonesia he had a row with his father who wanted him to join the family business. Jeffrey wanted nothing to do with it. Sounds like he finally grew up after Indonesia because he started his own communications business. But things didn't go well and he ended up working for an outfit based in San Francisco called Detron Communications. Six months ago, on his father's birthday, eight years after walking out on the family, he made contact with the old man again and it looked like they were going to patch things up . . . His real name is Stanmore . . . Jeffrey Stanmore.'

As Patterson said the name it dropped inside Stanza's head with a crash. 'Stanmore beer,' he said. It was one of the largest breweries in Milwaukee and was still owned and run by the old man – who was also an influential player on the state political scene.

'The man's a genius,' Patterson said sarcastically, referring to Stanza. 'Now. Why do we have this story before anyone else?'

Stanza could have come up with some theories but Patterson was clearly in a pugnacious mood.

'The *Herald*'s owner is a long-time friend of old man Stanmore,' Patterson went on immediately. 'But that's not why Stanmore called us in on this. You're probably already writing this – least, I *hope* you are – but this is no ordinary kidnapping story. We're talking about a son of Milwaukee, an estranged son, alienated from one of the most powerful figures in the state. We're talking about a father who wants his son back and is prepared to pay a lot of money for him. But it's also the mighty versus the merciless. Democracy versus Islam. When this story breaks we're gonna lead it for two reasons. One, because we're the *Herald* and we'd *better* damn well break it first with the advantage we have. And second, when other media get a hold of it there could be some muck-throwing: young Stanmore sleeping with an Iraqi girl, the enemy, a hooker, gone native, living in the danger zone, et cetera, et cetera. But by then we will have already put the story into perspective, something old man Stanmore is very keen on – and is willing to pay for. It's not just a story about the son, it's about the father too. A dynasty is gonna be exposed. The *Herald* is gonna tell the true story, Jake. It's a story about a young man lost in search of a dream of proving his worth to his father, putting his life on the line in a vile and ugly war in search of love, perhaps, love lost. That's what it is, Jake. It's a story about love and sacrifice . . . Do you hear what I'm saying?'

Stanza knew the smell of bullshit well enough. He was beginning to wonder if Patterson hated him not because of the quote he'd stolen but simply because he had been caught. He decided to play his boss a little, give him some more rope. It was a dangerous move, perhaps, but Stanza had home-field advantage. 'To be honest, I'm not sure if I do, exactly.'

But Patterson was nobody's fool and could read the likes of Stanza from a mile away. 'You know why I'm giving you this story, Jake?' Patterson asked rhetorically. 'You know why I don't hire a freelancer or order one of our people to get on a plane right now and fly into Baghdad to take over from you? It's partly because you are a good journalist, Jake. Good enough to get this job done. It's also because you need this if you still want a future in the news business . . . Jeffrey Stanmore was a passionate boy. I believe he loved that Iraqi girl and he was willing to put his life on the line for her . . . Jeffrey was a hero, a son of America . . . And that's only the first part of this story. This story is also going to propel you into the spotlight. It will end up a story as much about you as about Stanmore, and when I say you I mean the *Herald* . . . Jake, you're going to negotiate his release. The *Herald* is going to get young Stanmore back to his father. Jake Stanza, of the *Herald*, is going to reunite father and son. Do you hear me? You do this job right, Jake, and I'll hand your career back to you on a golden platter. Do you hear what I'm saying, Jake?'

Stanza could hear only too well.

'Jake?'

'Yeah,' he said.

'Am I right? Are you the man for this job?'

For one second Stanza had thought he'd had hold of the rod. But he was always the fish on the end of Patterson's line. Still, Patterson had something. He was right. This could be a big story. Huge, if played well, and Patterson and the *Herald* were behind it one hundred per cent. There wasn't a journalist alive who would pass this one up. It was showtime. 'I can do this,' Stanza said, his voice low and thoughtful.

'Does that pass for enthusiasm where you come from?'

'I couldn't be more enthusiastic. I'm already writing.'

'Good . . . We'll talk later, after you've read the file and thought about it.' The phone gave a click and the window on the monitor indicated that the caller had disconnected.

Stanza pushed himself to his feet, too quickly at first – stiffness was followed by a bolt of pain. He manoeuvred himself to his bed, lowered himself onto it, put his head on the pillow and shuffled his legs until he was in a straight line. Then he exhaled deeply.

Without having to think too hard Stanza could see the warning signs for the minefield ahead. Patterson – or, more to the point, Stanmore – knew what he wanted. The big question was how much the facts would support the current storyboard. Overall, the story was going to have to be a combination of perspective, timing and faith, with parallel strands of past and future narrative. The past was old man Stanmore and the Iraqi girl and would be defined by the struggle between love and worth. The future was the hostage negotiation and its final outcome, defined by a contest of life versus death.

Stanza was going to need help, that much was obvious. Mallory came to mind and Stanza wondered how much he should confide in his security adviser. To write this story Stanza was going to have to stretch beyond the boundaries he had expected to in Iraq and Mallory and his obsession with security would be more of a hindrance than a help.

But if Stanza got it right the rewards were beyond anything he could reasonably have hoped for. A smile formed on his lips, the first in a long time, as he closed his eyes and saw the hero's homecoming welcome that he would receive at the office.

8

Forbidden Fruit

Mallory stood at the last checkpoint before the hotel complex, looking with anticipation from his watch to the street beyond the barrier. Tasneen had sounded so happy to meet him for lunch that it had sparked in his imagination all kinds of daydreams about them together. He had even dared to speculate how he could get her out of Iraq and back to England. All this was absurd on many levels, he knew, especially considering how little he really knew her. On top of it all it was highly possible that he was misreading the signs – and the same could be said for her. Ostensibly, the reason for the forthcoming meeting was to discuss the employment of Tasneen's brother but Mallory's motives had little to do with the young man's qualifications for the job.

Abdul's suitability as a translator was worrying Mallory. Farris and Kareem were going to be annoyed, without doubt. They both had family members looking for employment and would see it as a personal insult that they had not been consulted. Then there was the whole Sunni–Shi'a thing, as well as Abdul's youth and his disability. Mallory wondered what the two drivers would think if they knew it was all because he wanted to get closer to Abdul's sister. That would probably freak them out. On the other hand, Mallory wondered why he cared at all since he was effectively quitting his job as soon as he left for Fallujah.

As Mallory looked again, hoping to see Tasneen's car appear, he saw her walking along the river road towards him. He had specifically told her to drive into the hotel complex, which was why he was waiting at the checkpoint, but the mere sight of her obliterated any criticisms. Her suit accentuated her slim, curvaceous body, while her lustrous dark hair bounced on her shoulders with each step and her face was even more beautiful than he remembered.

He ducked under the barrier and strode past the soldiers towards her. She beamed on seeing him. 'Where's your car?' he called out.

'I left it in the street,' Tasneen replied as she stopped in front of him. 'The Iraqi guards would not let me drive it in because I have no pass for this place. I showed them my Green Zone pass but they said this was not the Green Zone.'

Mallory looked in the direction of the outer barrier, considering whether or not to get her car for her.

'It will be all right,' she assured him, reading his thoughts.

Mallory's concerns were, as usual, alien to her. She would have found it bizarre if he'd told her he was worried someone might put a bomb under her vehicle. Security was all about mitigating risk. He decided to walk out with her after lunch and inspect the car before she drove it away. 'It's good to see you,' he said. 'Do you mind if I tell you that you're the most beautiful girl I have ever seen?' It was forward but he didn't care at that moment.

Tasneen looked away, clearly embarrassed, and then to Mallory's surprise she quickly recovered to look back at him and hold his gaze.

'Thanks for coming,' he said.

'Thanks for inviting me.'

They moved off side by side.

'Did you have any trouble getting off work?' he asked.

'They're used to me taking time off for my brother these days. That's what I told them – but in any case I was not lying, was I?'

Mallory guided her to the women's pedestrian entrance where a girl was waiting inside a small cubicle to search her. One of the soldiers gave a low whistle of approval, intended for Mallory to hear, as Tasneen exited the cubicle, closing her handbag. Mallory ignored him.

'It's so different now,' Tasneen said as they passed the Abrams tank under its awning beside the flying-carpet sculpture. 'I haven't been here since I attended a wedding a couple of years ago. You could drive all the way along the river between the bridges at that time.'

'Was it a nice city?'

'It used to be, yes. But I don't know anything else to compare it to. Maybe you would not have liked it.'

Mallory was not sure how to respond. 'You don't

wear a headscarf,' he commented, something he had wanted to ask her about when they'd first met.

'Iraqi Sunni women are generally less conservative than Shi'a women. Although these days most women in Iraq wear headscarves, since the war at least. I work in the Green Zone so I don't get much trouble from Iraqi men. I wear one when I go to the market.'

'Why since the war? I'd have thought you would have felt more liberated – if you'll excuse the word-play.'

Tasneen smiled, but with a polite expression of understanding. 'When there is no law and order the more extreme people have a louder voice,' she said. 'A woman must be more careful not to bring attention to herself.'

They walked up the steps to the Sheraton's entrance past a pair of smartly dressed security personnel who cheerfully bid him welcome. Tasneen avoided their stares as Mallory opened the glass doors and followed her into the foyer.

The restaurant was on the far side of the cavernous lobby beyond the elevators. A waiter greeted them and led them into the dining room. It was a large well-appointed room that gave the illusion of a level of service and cuisine that the current management could not actually provide. Only a handful of the dozen or so tables were occupied, despite the hotel being almost full. Most of the guests, nearly all westerners, opted for some degree of self-catering even if that meant nothing more than sending their staff out to collect food from local restaurants. The hotel food was expensive and monotonous, room service was abysmal and few guests had the time or inclination to eat in the dimly lit formality of the restaurant. But the hotel was still an acceptable place for Tasneen to dine in public with Mallory. Besides, there was nowhere else in the city that was considered safe for a westerner to openly enjoy a meal. The Green Zone was an option – one of the fast-food stalls outside the PX, maybe – but there was a good chance of meeting people either Tasneen or Mallory knew and Mallory wanted to keep their relationship, such as it was, a private affair.

They chose a table in a corner and the waiter left a couple of menus with them before attending to a group of Arab businessmen across the room.

An awkward atmosphere descended on the pair as they sat opposite one another.

'Would you choose for me?' Mallory asked. 'I've eaten here a couple of times but I've not been very adventurous . . . don't know the dishes.'

Tasneen flicked through the menu, studying the offerings. 'How about some lamb?' she asked.

'Sounds great,' he said. Ever since arriving in Iraq he'd eaten lamb kebabs until they were coming out of his ears and he feared the lack of choice was not limited to the hotel. He had not discovered much variety in Iraqi cuisine but he didn't know if that was because there really wasn't any or whether current poor supplies limited the choices.

Tasneen looked for the waiter but he appeared to

have left the room. 'Well,' she said, sighing. 'It's nice to be here. Thank you for inviting me.'

'I'm glad you could come . . . So. Abdul. How is he?'

'He's fine.'

'Good.'

'You still have a job for him?'

'Of course.'

She smiled. 'What is it you want him to do, exactly? He can do anything you need, I'm sure – except drive, of course. Although, knowing him, he will be driving before long.'

'We don't need a driver. We *do* need a translator and someone who knows the city.'

'That's perfect,' Tasneem said. 'He speaks English better today than he did last week and he knows the city very well.'

'Tell me something. It might be a small point – I don't know, and I'm sorry if it's the wrong thing to ask but – you'll forgive an ignorant foreigner, but – well, just to clarify. Abdul being Sunni: how would he feel about working with Shi'a? My two drivers are Shi'a, you see.'

'That's not a problem for Abdul. Westerners make a big thing out of the differences between Sunni and Shi'a. They mostly get along just fine. Like everything, it's the work of a handful of fools that makes life impossible for the rest.'

'I thought as much . . . just wanted to hear your view.'

'There's every religion in Baghdad, you know, even

some Jews, though not many of them now, I suppose. Christians live alongside Muslims where I live . . . Have you asked your drivers how they feel?'

'Not yet. I will. I doubt they'll have a problem.' And if they do, Mallory thought, he'd find a way of dealing with it. 'OK. That's the interview over with,' he said, sitting back with a grin.

'That's it?'

'He has the job if he wants it.'

'You didn't mention the pay.'

'Ah. Money. Yes. Would six hundred dollars a month be OK – to start with?'

'Six hundred,' she repeated, holding on to her surprise. 'I think he'd be happy with that.'

'He would be on probation at first. We have to consider the team.'

'Of course. You will be pleased with him, I'm very sure of that.'

The waiter arrived and asked Mallory in Arabic for their order. Mallory referred him to Tasneen who rattled off a reply and the waiter left them.

'I'm very happy, Bernie.' She was beaming. 'When do you want him to start?' This was something to which Mallory had not given much thought, indicating how little he had considered Abdul in this whole affair. 'When will he be fit for work?'

'He would like to start right away. He's well enough.'

Mallory nodded, his expression blank, and Tasneen suspected he was unconvinced. 'The pain has practically gone from his hand. He hardly ever takes a painkiller now. He needs to get out and do something. This job will be perfect for him and he will work very hard to please you. It will help heal his mind as well as his body.'

'OK. I'm sold,' Mallory said. 'Why don't you send him over tomorrow morning and we'll have a talk. He can meet the others and we'll take it from there.'

'That sounds perfect.' She leaned forward, despite no one else being close enough to hear. For one moment Mallory thought she wanted to kiss him and leaned forward himself. 'You are very kind, Bernie.'

'You make it easy for me,' he said, after she stopped what might as well have been a million miles short of kissing him. She did, however, hold his gaze for a few seconds and Mallory began to believe that Tasneen actually reciprocated the feelings he had for her. He had a sudden urge to say something to that effect but stopped himself, worried that it might ruin the moment. But even if he had shouted undying love for her at the top of his voice she would not have heard a word of it. Not at that moment . . .

A massive explosion blew in all the floor-to-ceiling plate-glass windows that made up two sides of the restaurant and the vast hotel building rocked to its very foundations. Walls and ceilings cracked, lights and cornices fell as the stark sounds of crashing and smashing took over from the initial thunderous boom. Mallory was blown off his seat and as he lay on the marble floor his brain fought to grasp what had happened. It felt as if he had been struck by a wall, dust filling his eyes and nostrils as he struggled to get his mind to refocus.

The thought of Tasneen came into Mallory's head like a detonation and he scrambled to his knees. She was not in her chair and he ducked beneath the table to see her pushing herself up onto her hands and knees. He got to his feet, hurried around the table, grabbed her up and pulled her over to one of several robust pillars supporting the ceiling. His first fear was of structural collapse but as the seconds passed and the building stayed up his next concern was another blast. The hotel had been attacked by rockets or mortars three times since his arrival although none of the previous assaults had been as bad as this.

Tasneen was slightly concussed and did not resist Mallory's protective grasp, although even had she wanted to she would have been unable since he was holding her so tightly to him. The waiter was standing in the centre of the room as if catatonic, his face bloody, his mouth agape as he looked up at the ceiling. Mallory followed his gaze to see the elaborate central chandelier swaying dangerously. A couple who had been at a table by the windows were on the floor, both of them covered in blood and glass. Mallory thought the explosion was down to a car bomb in the street or a mortar, or a walking suicide bomber just outside the restaurant. There had been rumours for weeks now that a member of staff had smuggled explosives into the hotel, a small amount at a time. But in a city that experienced dozens of explosions a day and where rumours of all kinds abounded the general feeling that one could get caught out anywhere at any time tended to offset such threats. It was all up to God and westerners used the word 'inshalla' as much as did the Arabs.

There was a sudden loud whooshing sound as if an aircraft had flown past outside and Mallory held Tasneen even tighter against the pillar. A second later there was a loud boom that sounded close but not close enough to do the hotel any more damage. Mallory decided that it had been a rocket since mortars tended to drop silently or with a whistling sound and, just as he said this loud enough for Tasneen to hear, yet another rocket slammed into the hotel with a force equal to that of the first. A shock wave followed, blasting in through the gap where the window had been and spending its great force against the opposite wall in the restaurant. A wooden dresser was tossed aside, its china contents shattering. Tables blew over and something struck Mallory's back but without harming him. He pulled Tasneen's head against his chest and she held on to him tightly as something heavy struck the floor close by. As the shock wave dissipated the sound of automatic gunfire could be heard over the noise of breaking glass and falling debris.

Mallory's eyes widened as he looked up, his ears straining to gather vital information. Another long burst followed by an answering volley of single shots, indicating that a firefight was taking place. When it came to explosions the best thing to do was get to cover and wait it out. But flying bullets required a different reaction. Another circulating rumour concerned the threat of an assault from the Mardi Army, a Shi'a militia occupying Sada City barely a mile west of the hotel complex. It was generally considered suicide to attempt, bearing in mind the amount of western firepower in and around the hotel but on reflection a suicide attack could not be overlooked. There were thirty or forty US troops stationed in the Sheraton and Palestine hotels plus a hundred or so western PSDs. If the Mardi Army attacked with all its estimated eight-hundred-strong force it would find it costly to take even a section of the grounds and would then find it impossible to hold on to for long. But the rebels were not to be under-estimated: they had attacked hotels and coalition camps in the past, beginning the assaults with various explo-sive devices such as mortars before pressing the attack with infantry. They had failed to penetrate even the perimeters in every case but that had not appeared to deter them.

Mallory pulled his pistol from his pouch as the rattle of gunfire intensified as more weapons joined the fray. He ignored the moaning injured around him and held Tasneen at his side as he headed towards the restau-rant entrance. They passed through the small opening into the lobby where gunfire echoed inside the cavernous hall and, their feet crunching on broken glass, kept close to the walls, avoiding the central area that was exposed to debris falling from the domed ceiling. A couple of hotel staff ran across the lobby shouting something and several US soldiers clutching M4 rifles hurried down the curving stairs from the mezzanine above towards the entrance while pulling on their flak jackets and helmets. One of them tripped and sprawled across the marble floor but a colleague quickly dragged him to his feet and they sprinted on outside together. Broken glass was everywhere, lying on the white marble floor like crystals. A fine dust filled the air along with flakes of black and grey ash from a fire somewhere. Most of the massive sheets of plate glass forming the exterior walls of the lobby had shattered. Mallory was heading for an emergency exit that led to the basement, which he had decided was their best choice. Had he been alone he would have looked for a way to join the fight but Tasneen was his greatest concern now.

The main source of the gunfire seemed to be near the Firdous Mosque on the other side of the round-about below his room. A loud burst from a heavy machine gun came from a floor above and Mallory suspected that it was return fire from the US troops who had a firing position on the sixth floor.

Mallory suddenly wondered if the basement was such a good choice after all. If an assault managed to penetrate the lobby he could get cornered down there. On the other hand, if he went above ground level it could prove disastrous if there was a fire. But he was going to have to make a choice.

Des ran in through the main entrance, holding an AK47 and wearing his chest harness of multiple pouches containing spare magazines and a couple of grenades. Only a trusted few knew about the grenades as they were shunned by the US military.

'Des!' Mallory called out.

Des glanced in Mallory's direction and changed course towards him. 'Ee, this is fun, ain't it, lad?' He skidded to

273

a halt beside them. 'You all right, flower?' His eyes were moving faster and bulging even more than usual.

'Any idea what's going on?'

'It's a battle, me lad,' Des said, grinning with his usual flippancy.

'I gathered that. Is it an assault on the hotel?'

Nah. Doubt it. They're not that stupid. Doing a bit of rescuing, are we?' Des eyed Tasneen with a grin. 'Any left?'

A loud burst of gunfire from above startled all of them.

'Des. What's going on?' Mallory asked trying to be patient.

'Rockets, me old sausage. Little bastards drove a truck alongside t' mosque and fired a bonch o' the boogers. One 'it the first floor, the other somewhere near it. Another went into the park just over the blast walls. A palm tree caught fire out front but there might be another burner on t' first floor.'

'So who's firing at who?'

'Don't know. Could be comin' from the block o' flats opposite. US lads on t' sixth-floor roof opened op on the launch platform and it sounds like some was returned. I wouldn't go out there, though. Yanks are shooting at anything that moves. I'm gonna go check on my clients, make sure none 'ave wet 'emsels. See you later. Nice to meet yer,' Des called out to Tasneen, grinning widely, before he hurried away.

Mallory checked Tasneen who was still frightened but was staying in control of her emotions. 'You OK?' he asked, making sure.

She nodded. 'I'm OK. What are we doing?'

Good question, Mallory felt like saying. 'We can't hang about here or go outside. Only one place, really. Come on,' he said, taking her by the hand.

He led her past the lifts, up the broad stairs to the mezzanine and into the emergency stairwell. The main lights had failed but the emergency lighting was just about adequate, although not on every floor. The gunfire outside sounded amplified in the bare, concrete, windowless stairwell as they trotted up. By the time they reached the fifth floor both of them were breathing heavily. Tasneen paused to catch her breath while Mallory went through the first fire door and along the corridor to the next that led onto the landing. The smoke was immediately thicker and he went to the rail to look down into the lobby. Hotel staff members were hurriedly attempting to organise a fire hose, although Mallory could not see where the fire was.

'Come on,' Mallory called. Tasneen responded and they moved off along the landing. He paused outside his room to dig the key out of his pocket and check below once again. The fire team had managed to divide into two groups, one at either end of the hose as they dragged it across the lobby. But on reaching the fountain the groups moved either side of it and an argument began over which one should take the lead. Mallory shook his head as he found the key and opened his door.

Tasneen followed him inside. He closed the door and went directly to the balcony windows, pausing before opening them. 'Stay back,' he warned.

Tasneen stayed in the narrow hallway. 'Should you go out there?' she asked as Mallory slid open the glass door.

'I'll only be a second.' He inched carefully through the gap, keeping low. The firing had stopped and there was shouting from the street below. He leaned forward until the mosque came into view. Men were running, a pick-up truck parked at an awkward angle across the road was on fire, its doors open, and beyond it were two cars that had been hastily abandoned. A body lay on the road between them. American soldiers came into view, moving stealthily across the roundabout towards the mosque. Others were inspecting more bodies further up the street. Smoke was drifting directly across the front of Mallory's balcony and he looked over the rail to see the top of one of the hotel's palm trees on fire and more smoke coming from inside the hotel directly behind it. Mallory assumed it was the impact point of one of the rockets.

He stepped back into the room. 'It's OK. I think it's over.'

Tasneen did not appear relieved by the news.

'I need to check on my people,' Mallory said, heading for the door. 'Stay until I get back and then we'll get you out of here, OK?'

She nodded.

'You sure you're all right?' he asked.

'I will be,' she said, forcing a smile with difficulty.

'There's a fire downstairs. I think it's only a small one. If it gets any worse I'll be straight back.'

Tasneen nodded again.

'See you in a bit, then,' Mallory said as he opened the door.

'Oh, Bernie,' she whispered. 'My handbag.'

'I'll find it,' he said before closing the door behind him.

A few metres along the landing he knocked on a door. 'Stanza?' he called out. 'Stanza!'

A moment later the door was hurriedly unlocked and opened. Stanza stood in the doorway, looking visibly worried.

'You OK?'

'Yes. What's happened? Are we being attacked? Is there a fire?' Stanza didn't wait for a reply and limped back to his open balcony. 'There's a lot of activity outside.'

'I'd be careful about showing yourself. There'll be some itchy trigger fingers out there.'

Stanza ducked back and then decided to vacate the balcony entirely and close the door.

'As far as I can tell it's all over,' Mallory said. 'There might be a fire risk. I'd have your things packed and ready to go, just in case.'

'Right,' Stanza said as he hobbled to his wardrobe and pulled out his holdall.

Mallory decided the man would move quickly enough if necessary and went back to the door. 'Stay here until I get back. You've got food and water for the night?'

'Yes,' Stanza said without looking up at him as he emptied the contents of one shelf into the bag and went to another. 'Let me know as soon as you hear anything.'

'You'll be the first to know.' Mallory closed the door behind him and a quick check over the rails revealed the abandoned fire hose around the base of the fountain. The smoke was still thick and began to irritate the back of Mallory's throat. He decided to see if Des had found out anything more about the attack. It might also be prudent to head over to the Palestine Hotel and book a couple of rooms in case they had to vacate the Sheraton.

An hour later Mallory was back on the fifth floor outside his room with his key in one hand and Tasneen's handbag in the other. He was concerned about a bit of information he had received and how Tasneen might react to it. He had spent fifteen minutes with a US Army captain who had given him the low-down on what had happened and the plans for the hotel's immediate future. It turned out that six or seven insurgents had been involved in the rocket attack. Four of them had been killed as they'd tried to drive away while the rest had escaped on foot through a block of flats on the other side of Sadoon Street. The fires had been put out and although there had been several injuries only one of them had been serious and no one from the hotel complex had died. Des had placed a sign on his office door that read '4–0' with a footnote reminding everyone not to be complacent since we had enjoyed home-field advantage.

Mallory informed Stanza that all was well, after which the man immediately focused on his work – which seemed odd after his previous two weeks of complete inactivity. The journalist launched into a not entirely coherent listing of requirements that he claimed needed taking care of right away. It included the hiring of a fixer or a city guide. Mallory was anxious to get back to Tasneen and agreed with everything Stanza said. He finally extricated himself with a lie that the army was waiting to see him on a security issue. Stanza let him go but not without getting an assurance that they could hit the road first thing the next day.

Mallory put his key in the lock and tapped the door lightly as he pushed it open. Tasneen was looking out at the city through the closed balcony windows and faced Mallory as he came into the room.

'Is everything OK?' she asked.

'Kind of,' he said, holding up her handbag for her to see. 'At least the fire's out . . . There's just one small problem: the Americans have put the hotel complex on full lockdown.'

A look of horror spread across her face. Tasneen knew from working in the Green Zone what full lockdown meant. 'Full?' she asked, hoping he had exaggerated that part of it.

'Nothing in or out of the complex until further notice. They've done it before and, trust me, they mean it.'

'How long for?'

'I'm going to call them every hour but – well, they said at least until dawn.' Mallory screwed his face up a little as he said the last word, aware of the implications, or at least the more obvious ones.

Tasneen sat down heavily on the edge of the bed,

an expression of utter disbelief on her face. 'I can't stay here until night-time, even.' She looked up at him, hope in her eyes.

'I don't know what to say . . . I tried to get you a room but there aren't any.'

She began shaking her head even before he had finished. 'It doesn't make any difference. I can't stay here, Bernie. Not even in the hotel. You don't understand.'

'I do,' he said coming closer and sitting on the bed.

'No, you don't. This is Iraq. I am a Muslim girl.'

'I know, I know, but there isn't anything we can do. If we went down to the checkpoint to try and force them to let you out it would only draw more attention to you when they refuse – which I know they will. Right now no one knows you're in here. If you walk outside you won't be able to come back in because you'll be seen. You can't stay in the lobby. It's a mess and they've already begun clearing it up. It's open air down there and the furniture is all stacked up.'

The gravity of the implications of all this was almost too much for Tasneen to bear.

'Listen to my plan,' Mallory urged. 'As I said, no one knows you're in here. No one. You stay until you can go, in a few hours or even at dawn. You can sneak along the corridor to the emergency stairs and by the time you appear in the lobby no one'll know where you stayed. That's not so bad, is it? Huh?'

Tasneen pondered it all until she came to accept that there were no alternatives. Mallory's plan had made her feel a little better, at least the part about no one knowing where she was. But there was one glaring problem with it.

'Why don't I leave you alone?' Mallory said, getting to his feet. 'I'll come back when it's OK for you to leave.'

'Where are you going?'

'I might be able to use a friend's room.'

'And what will you say if he asks why you can't use your own room?'

'I'll think of something.'

'What if someone comes looking for you?'

'No one's going to come into the room,' Mallory assured her.

'But the hotel staff have the key. They might come in.'

Mallory suddenly wanted to take her in his arms, hold her close and assure her that everything would be all right. 'What is it you are specifically worried about? I understand the reputation thing and all that, especially with a westerner.'

'It's my brother. He will be worried and he'll want to know where I am.'

'You can't tell him?' Mallory said, making it sound like a question although he meant it as a statement.

'Of course not.'

'Then tell him you're staying with a girlfriend.'

Tasneen shook her head. 'He will want to know who and why and . . . Abdul can be very protective.'

'There's a saying that if you want to hide the truth stay as close to it as possible.'

She did not understand.

'Tell him the truth so far, that you were at the hotel seeing the *Herald* about his job. Then the hotel got hit and you had to stay – but in your own room, of course. That would be the only lie.'

'But what if he comes to find me?'

'He can't get in,' Mallory reminded her.

'He can be very persistent.'

'Not as obstinate as the Yanks. Trust me on this. He's not getting through those checkpoints. A lockdown is a lockdown with these guys and there are no exceptions. Plus he's an Iraqi. I'm sorry but you know what I mean. If he tried too hard the Americans would arrest him.'

Tasneen knew he was right.

Mallory could see her relax slightly, although her expression remained pensive.

She pulled her phone from a pocket, selected a number, pressed the call button and pushed it under her hair to her ear.

'Go to the window,' Mallory said quietly. 'Better reception.'

She got off the bed and went to the window. 'Abdul,' she began and then after he answered rattled off in Arabic. The conversation went back and forth for a while before it ended abruptly. Tasneen looked up at Mallory and then smiled slightly. 'I think he's happy with the story. I emphasised the job. I told him he could start tomorrow. Is that OK?'

'I think that's what we agreed just before the restaurant blew up. Which reminds me. You must be starved.'

'I'm not really—' Tasneen began.

'I've been through this with you before. The last time you said you weren't hungry you embarrassed me by getting the server to pile so much food onto your plate that I had to do the same.'

She grinned and her face lit up.

'I know somewhere I can scrounge a meal,' Mallory said, going to the door. 'I'll check on a few things, see if the checkpoint is going to remain closed. Be back in a while.'

When Mallory left the room Tasneen lowered her head as her thoughts remained on her predicament. She did not regret coming to see Mallory, although she could have done without this situation. If it all turned out OK then securing the job for Abdul would have been worth it.

She felt that her feelings of attraction towards Mallory had increased. He had acted well during the bombing and had protected her. He was so easy to be with and he amused her. But there was something else which she was not sure ought to continue. She had taken to daydreaming again, fantasising about being in different places in the world, but now she was not always alone. Bernie was often there and what surprised her was her willingness to become involved with him, something she had never contemplated with anyone else.

The dangers were obvious but at the same time she felt safe with Bernie. He would not pressure her. It could remain just a fantasy. He had implied that he'd be in Iraq for a while, although she understood that he would have to go home occasionally. But Abdul could never know there was anything between them, even though it was only a game. In the Islamic faith only the man could marry outside his religion – a family's religion was dictated by the male, not the female.

Life was a never-ending series of complications. Tasneen sighed and went back to the window to look out over the city. It was a long time since she'd had such a view of Baghdad. Her heart began to ache for its people and she wondered when they would ever see peace again.

Mallory was back within an hour, carrying a trayful of several plates covered in foil. He'd appropriated the food from Des who, it had to be said, was a generous man. Unsurprisingly, Des had a contact in KBR's kitchen upstairs. As Mallory was leaving the office Des had made a joke about wanting to see the video. Mallory ignored it but was concerned that Des even suspected that Tasneen was with him. It might be worth having a word with him just in case he added it to his repertoire.

They began the meal in silence but after Tasneen asked Mallory what countries he had been to they embarked on a lengthy discussion that included politics, food, fashion and music as well as geography. Before long they had forgotten the brutal conflict outside the room except when a distant explosion or rattle of gunfire interrupted them. But they were determined to keep their thoughts elsewhere.

It was the looming prospect of bedtime that eventually stilled the conversation. Mallory took the initiative by tossing a pillow on the floor, lying down on the carpet and announcing that the spot would suit him perfectly. Tasneen removed her shoes and stretched out on top of the bed. They were out of sight of each other but continued talking until Tasneen quite matter-of-factly said that he could join her if he wanted to. He insisted he was fine. When she said he could stay on the floor if he wanted but said again that she did not mind him being on the bed he changed his mind lest the invitation should not be repeated. He placed his pillow on the bed and lay beside her but left a respectable gap between them.

Mallory had no illusions that the invitation was anything more than a friendly gesture but her close proximity set his imagination going and he fought to control it. They talked for a while longer and then Tasneen rolled onto her side. Mallory glanced over to see that she was facing him. He decided to remain on his back. This was not the time or the place to become intimate with her. Taking advantage of her predicament in such a way would be wholly unscrupulous. If she became frightened she would be trapped and Mallory could not bear the thought of her being in the room with him and not wanting to be. This was far more than he had expected and it was satisfying enough. They eventually drifted off to sleep, although he remained aware of her presence throughout the night. At one point she turned over and brought her knees up to her chest and Mallory looked at her, feasting his gaze on the heart-like shape of her bottom and wondering what it would be like to caress it with his hands and, better still, feel it pressed tightly against him. He eventually rolled away to ease the feelings of desire and it was not long before dawn reached for the balcony windows and Mallory sat up and went to look at the city. It was Baghdad's most beautiful time of day. The minaret of the Firdous Mosque came to life, its speakers crackling before a voice called for morning prayers. Mallory dialled a number on his cellphone. When the call was answered Mallory asked about the state of the lockdown, closed the phone and went back to the bed to look at Tasneen. She did not stir but as he moved a strand of hair from her face she rolled onto her back with a sigh and opened her eyes. She sat up, startled as she focused on the unfamiliar surroundings but relaxed on seeing Mallory, remembering where she was.

'Good morning,' he said. 'Sleep well?'

'Thank you,' she said as she slid off the bed and stood up.

Mallory watched her find her shoes and pull them on.

'They just opened the checkpoint . . . I shouldn't come down with you,' he said as she pulled on her jacket.

'I can find my way out.'

'Take the fire escape down to the mezzanine floor. It's written on the door in the stairwell.'

'I'll find it,' Tasneen said as she picked up her handbag and checked that she had everything.

Mallory followed her to the door, unlocked it and paused before opening it. 'Maybe one day we can look back and be amused by all this . . . I enjoyed you being here.'

When she looked up at him he could not read her expression. 'I think I will say that I enjoyed it too,' she said. He felt relieved and was suddenly bursting to hold her and kiss her lips. If there had been an invitation in her eyes he would have. He wanted to ask when he might see her again but it seemed pointless. He would let fate play the next hand. 'Wait,' he said as he moved around her to open the door enough to look out onto the landing. 'Mind how you go. Drive carefully,' he said.

Tasneen moved past him in the confined space, her breasts touching his chest, her smell filling his head. Seconds later she was gone and only then did Mallory remember that he'd intended to check her car for bombs. He doubted whether anyone would target her but, as he always told himself, that was not the point. He would have to let it slide this time, though.

Mallory took a look in all directions for prying eyes before closing the door. But he was too far from the edge of the landing to see down onto the third-floor walkway where an Iraqi security guard was leaning on the rails, smoking a cigarette. The man could see the top of Mallory's door from his position and since its opening and closing was the only movement at that early hour it caught his attention. Then he saw the moving head of a woman who was walking along the landing and a moment later she passed through the lobby and out of the hotel.

9

The Team Deploys

Mallory climbed out of the shower and towelled himself dry as he went through the list of things he had to do that day. First he had to contact the office in London and tell them to give his relief the go-ahead to move to Baghdad. Next he needed to inform Des that he would be available to accompany his client to Fallujah — although Mallory was still unsure if that was the best way to proceed. But he had extracted all the pleasure he could from daydreaming about Tasneen and the million dollars and it was time to turn some at least of the fantasy into reality.

There was a knock on the door and he checked his watch. It was ten past seven. Too early for the drivers. The knock came again.

'Who is it?' he called out, standing to one side of the door out of habit. No one to his knowledge had been shot through a door but it was the sort of thing that went through his mind on such occasions.

'It's Stanza.'

'One second.' Mallory went back into his room and pulled on a pair of trousers and a T-shirt, wondering if something was up. Stanza had never called on him this early before. When he opened the door Stanza was standing there, dressed as if ready to go out.

'What time are the men coming in?' Stanza asked.

'I told them to be in at nine.'

'Nine,' Stanza repeated, making a calculation.

'I still don't know about Farris.'

'When will you know?'

'If he turns up then I'll know.'

'This is not gonna work out like this, is it?' Stanza said testily.

Mallory sighed inwardly, wondering when Stanza was going to get the message regarding local staff.

'We need to get together to discuss a plan of operation,' Stanza said. 'We have things to do, places to go, people to see and I need reliable drivers and a guide. I'm sorry, Mallory, but that's your job and it's not going very well.'

Mallory decided that Stanza had a flea up his backside about something. Having started the day in such a good mood he would not allow the little knob to wind him up. 'Give it until nine. By then we'll know about the drivers and we should also have a fixer.'

'A fixer? Who?'

'I told you.'

'Oh. The one-armed guy.' Stanza had left a message about finding a fixer with Blant from the *Post* but he had not received a reply yet. His confidence in Mallory's guy had eroded from the moment he'd agreed to meet him. 'I have some feelers out for a fixer myself. I'll also look for a driver. We'll talk at nine, then,' Stanza said, turning on his heel.

Mallory closed his door and took a moment to calm the anger that was threatening to ruin his morning. The twat had managed to wind him up with his final comment about looking for a driver and fixer himself. Stanza was beginning to show his true colours: he was either a real bastard or he was trying to bully Mallory in particular. If Stanza kept on like this Mallory would simply tell him to shove his job. But that would mean letting Tasneen's brother down, which would not help his cause with her.

He took out his mobile phone and scrolled through the numbers. Stanza was right to a certain extent, though. The team had slipped a notch and that was Mallory's responsibility. In truth it wasn't of huge importance to him but he had standards to maintain.

'Kareem. It's Mallory. Are you coming in this morning at nine? Nine o'clock . . . Good. What about Farris? OK. See you here at nine. Be a little earlier if you can. Bye.'

Farris was apparently on his way in but seeing was believing. Mallory's next call was to Tasneen who was very cheery when she answered the phone. She asked him to hold on while she moved to somewhere more private in her apartment. She had made it home without a hitch to find Abdul asleep on the couch and when he woke up he'd been relieved to see her. He had been visibly excited about starting work that morning and she intended to drop him off at the hotel on her way to work. When Mallory asked if she planned to drop him off and pick him up on a regular basis she said no but since this was his first day she would make an exception. In future Abdul would use the taxi service which was reliable enough. Mallory made a mental note to instruct Kareem to drive Abdul into work and back home when practical. Mallory eventually said goodbye to Tasneen after they agreed to discuss Abdul's first day at the end of it.

At a quarter to nine Mallory stepped out of his room and looked down into the lobby. The wind blew unchecked through the hotel but apart from the missing windows everything looked in place. If there was one thing the Iraqis could do efficiently it was clean up immediately after a bomb.

Kareem and Farris stepped out of the emergency stairwell – the lifts were still out of order – and walked towards him, both lighting up cigarettes even though they were out of breath. It was at times like this that the KBR staff suffered through living at the top of the building, particularly their grossly overweight members – of whom there were many. But because of their selfish antics with the lifts no one had any sympathy for them. Des, of course, had been quick to react by posting a sign in the emergency stairwell on his floor that was aimed at KBR staff. It announced: 'Only 16 more floors to go, you fat bastards.'

Farris looked sheepish as he greeted Mallory but said nothing about his future intentions. Mallory chose not to ask. If Farris wanted to leave the country it would be a problem for Mallory's relief. Some media organisations were easier-going and local staff could organise stand-ins to take their place but Mallory did not allow that. Mallory had trained his drivers in security-driving techniques that included actions to take in the event of various different situations, from a traffic accident or flat tyre to an actual enemy contact. He did not want to endanger the client or the team by having a stranger take over, someone who did not know the drills and procedures.

Mallory looked back down into the lobby and saw a young man who resembled Tasneen's brother standing near the fountain, one of his arms wrapped in a colourful cloth. 'We have a new guy starting today,' Mallory said to the drivers. They looked at each other quizzically. The suspicions that Kareem had confided to Farris on the subject had obviously been correct. 'If you need someone I can find you good man,' Kareem said.

Mallory knew that was coming. It irritated him how these people never seemed to grasp the boundaries of their rank, often making suggestions concerning matters beyond their authority. 'He will be a translator and fixer and will be working directly with Stanza . . . He's a Sunni,' Mallory added, caring less if that last bit of information annoyed them further.

Farris and Kareem glanced at each other again to ensure that they were in agreement. 'No problem,' Kareem said, shrugging, a sentiment clearly opposite to what he truly felt.

'Be back in a minute,' Mallory said, leaving them.

Abdul recognised Mallory as soon as he saw him step onto the lobby floor and put on a smile for him. Mallory reached out with his left hand, Abdul took it and they shook. The vividly coloured silk scarf that wrapped the bandaged stump was no doubt a touch from Tasneen.

'How are you?' Mallory asked.

'I am fine – thank you for asking,' Abdul said, each word carefully enunciated.

'Your sister drop you off?'

'Yes.'

'Have you had breakfast?'

'I had breakfast with home – *at* home, thank you.' Abdul smiled apologetically at the mistake.

'How is the wound? Still painful?'

'Very little now. I do not need the pills any more.'

'That's good.' Mallory was pleased with his first impression of the young man who was polite, dignified and unobtrusive, qualities that Mallory hoped would sustain. 'We live on the fifth floor. Come and meet the rest of the team.'

'Of course,' Abdul said, extending his left hand in a courteous gesture to indicate that Mallory should lead on.

Mallory headed for the stairs. 'The lifts aren't working at the moment but you need to know the emergency stairs anyway.'

Kareem and Farris were leaning on the rail, smoking cigarettes and chatting, as Mallory and Abdul exited the emergency stairwell. Mallory made the introductions and the men exchanged greetings in Arabic. Kareem and Farris glanced at Abdul's stump several times without mentioning it. The meeting between them seemed cordial enough and, not wanting to waste any more time, Mallory knocked on Stanza's door.

When it opened Stanza looked out, saw his assembled team and stepped back to let them in.

'This is Abdul,' Mallory said as the young man passed the journalist. Stanza forced a smile, extended his right hand and before he realised his mistake Abdul took hold of the journalist's offered fingers with his left hand and shook them.

Mallory closed the door after Kareem and Farris and followed them into the room.

'Find a seat,' Stanza said. The drivers sat on the edge of the bed, leaving the two chairs for Mallory and Stanza. Abdul stood politely to one side until Stanza insisted that he should take a chair.

Stanza sat on the edge of his desk. 'I guess we should first of all welcome – Abdul, is it?'

Abdul nodded. 'Abdul, yes,' he said.

'I take it you guys all know each other?' Stanza asked, looking between the drivers.

'They just met,' Mallory said.

'OK. Welcome to the team . . . um . . . let's see how we all get on and . . . well, let's get straight to it . . . We have a story the paper wants to pursue. But before I get into it I need to stress one important thing, which is that everything about this story has to be kept between ourselves. No other media group out there –' he pointed to his door '– has the knowledge we have about the story and they must not find out. In fact, no one outside of this room must know. Understood? Friends, family, whoever. It has to stay with us only. Is that clear?' He acted like a headmaster, looking hard at each individual until he nodded.

Stanza looked at Mallory last. Mallory was miffed at being relegated to the level of the others and decided that he'd been right in his earlier impression of the journalist: Stanza was a twat.

Appearing satisfied, Stanza adjusted his position before delivering the next part of his brief. 'The story,' he announced, 'is Jeffrey Lamont, the American who was kidnapped from a house in Karada last month. A lady and two other people were murdered at the same time.'

Abdul stiffened, then checked to see if any of the others were looking at him. Suddenly he wondered if this was some kind of bizarre set-up. But all eyes were on Stanza who was looking down at the floor while composing his next sentence.

Kareem and Farris did not know who Stanza was referring to but, typically, nodded as if they did.

Mallory didn't know who Stanza was talking about either. There were dozens of kidnap victims. The mention of the murdered girl rang a bell but triggered nothing specific in his memory.

'I'm not gonna say too much right now,' Stanza went on, 'other than that we're a Wisconsin newspaper and Lamont is a Wisconsin boy.'

That was obviously the appeal of the story but Mallory could not see the reason for secrecy. Stanza was clearly taking this too seriously. From Mallory's experience, Kareem and Farris would have understood about five per cent of what Stanza had said: they made little effort to concentrate, even though they nodded constantly. Abdul, on the other hand, appeared locked onto Stanza's every word.

'I'm gonna need your help on a few things,' Stanza went on, addressing the nodding drivers, clearly unaware of their level of competence. 'Research. First thing. The woman Lamont was seeing, the one who was murdered. Very important. I want to know who she was. Where are her family, parents, whatever? We need to talk to someone who knew her. Next. The house where the kidnapping took place. Where is it? This is where you guys earn your dollars. Any ideas how to find answers to these questions?'

Kareem and Farris were looking at each other as if they had been asked to find the Holy Grail.

'Mallory,' Stanza said.

Mallory looked at him. 'Sorry. What?'

'Any ideas?'

Mallory shrugged. Story research was not his part of the ship. 'Finding the house?' he said, blowing through pursed lips. 'Was the address on the wires?' he pondered, throwing out the first thought that came into his head.

'Research back at the office has come up blank. Someone in this town has to know. What about the police?'

Mallory looked at Abdul who was wearing a bemused expression. 'Abdul?'

Abdul snapped out of his trance and looked at him enquiringly.

'Any ideas?' Mallory asked. 'You're an ex cop . . . Do you know anyone who could tell us where the house is?'

Abdul stared at Mallory for an uncomfortably long

time but his eyes were out of focus again and were seeing something else. He was back in the house in its dark, quiet street, seeing again the tattered entrance, the creaking stairs, the room at the top, the people inside and then hearing a gunshot that made him blink.

Mallory wondered if there was something wrong with the man. Tasneen had mentioned something about psychological stress but she'd never said how bad. 'You OK, Abdul?'

Abdul refocused and saw everyone looking at him. 'I know where it is,' he said matter-of-factly.

'The house where Lamont was kidnapped from?' Mallory asked, unsure if Abdul was on the same page as the rest of them.

'Yes,' Abdul said. His mental reaction to thoughts of the house had varied since that night but his present feelings tended towards morbid curiosity. He had passed by the end of the street a couple of times since that night and had strained to see the building in the few seconds it had been in view. There had to be an explanation of why he was going to offer to take these people to visit it. The thought had come from outside his soul and therefore was not his. Perhaps it came from Allah, he mused.

'The house where Jeffrey Lamont the American was kidnapped?' Stanza repeated.

'Yes,' Abdul said. 'Where Lamont was kidnapped.'

'And where the woman was murdered?' Stanza added, still not entirely convinced that the young man knew what he was talking about. It all seemed too easy, too convenient.

'And another man and woman,' Abdul added.

'Were you on duty the night it happened . . . a police officer?' Mallory asked.

'Yes,' Abdul said.

'Were you involved in the case?' Stanza asked anxiously.

'I was out that night and I know where it is.'

'And you can take us there?' Stanza asked, tense.

'Yes,' Abdul said, calming down as the questions kept coming.

'This is fantastic,' Stanza said, standing up and flexing his leg, which had stiffened a little. 'What about the woman?' Stanza asked.

Abdul considered the question. 'I don't know,' he finally said.

'I'll settle for the house for now,' Stanza said. 'I want to go there. Right away.'

Abdul shrugged. 'OK.'

'So let's go.' Stanza made a move towards the door.

'One second,' Mallory said.

Everyone paused.

'Let's remember where we all are, shall we? Kidnappings, bombings, shootings take place outside the hotel, any time, anywhere. So can we all put our security heads back on? I need to give Abdul a security brief: how we do things, go through a few of the drills, OK?'

Stanza sighed heavily. 'Do we have to do that now?' he asked.

'What if something happens on the way?' Mallory argued. 'He needs to know – for his safety as well as ours – how we operate and what to do in an emergency. You can't take short cuts in this place.'

'OK, OK,' Stanza said, holding up his hands. 'Enough with the lecture. I'll see you guys in the car park.'

'Quarter to ten at the cars,' Mallory said. Kareem and Farris acknowledged and followed Stanza out of the room.

Mallory looked at Abdul, curious about his mental balance though not unduly alarmed by any of the signs of distraction that he'd displayed. Abdul looked far too pathetic to be threatening. 'Let's take a slow walk to the car park. I'll tell you what we do in emergency situations – bombs, shootings, flat tyres, accident, car crash, if we're being followed, et cetera. I would normally take a whole day going over these things. Anything you don't understand, ask me. OK?'

Abdul nodded.

'I don't mind repeating myself a hundred times but you have to know what I'm saying. Don't say you understand something if you don't because I will ask you questions and if you can't answer them correctly I'll be angry. Do we understand each other?'

'Yes,' Abdul said, wondering if the Englishman liked him or not. Abdul was instinctively suspicious of this invader. All foreigners were in Iraq to make money out of Iraqis. Abdul did not feel hate for them, nor malice, but he did not like them either. His attraction to western trappings was not as strong as it had once been. The West and democracy were threats to Islam and they had to go, it was as simple as that. But, simple as the solution was, its achievement would not be easy, he knew that much. He believed in patience but above all else he trusted in Allah. Abdul's faith was founded on the teaching that every single object and action was part of a great and universal design that would eventually prove Islam to be the true guiding light of mankind. It was the only religion that secured man's salvation against himself. Allah oversaw every strata of life and was even watching the faithful at this moment, listening to their plans and ambitions and guiding them where necessary.

The pair left the building and as Mallory talked Abdul listened carefully. He did not want to give Mallory any reason to criticise him and he asked several questions, some of which he already knew the answers to. But he wanted to prove that he was being attentive. All the while, however, in the back of his mind was the forthcoming visit to the house of the murders. It was a living nightmare that he had to confront at some time. There was also the threat from Hassan to consider. As long as Abdul did not implicate the other members of his squad in any way there should be no problem. But that was assuming Hassan was a reasonable man, which he was not. Abdul was aware of another change in himself. He was no longer as afraid as he used to be. He still feared the unknown, though: the house, his future. His recent maturity was Allah's doing, he knew that much. He also had a strange feeling that the journey he needed to take had begun.

Half an hour later the Milwaukee *Herald*'s two cars were passing through the hotel's last security checkpoint. Farris's car still had bullet holes in the windshield and bonnet: Mallory had asked him repeatedly to have them repaired because they drew attention. It was this type of insubordination that took Mallory to the brink of losing his temper and in this case threatening to replace Farris's car and therefore the driver if it was not taken care of. He decided that if the vehicle was not repaired by the end of the week he would deliver just such an ultimatum. Farris and Kareem were slacking and needed a kick up their backsides.

The team drove down a narrow pothole-scarred residential backstreet that connected to Sadoon Street. Des had nicknamed it 'Fingers-in-your-ears Street' because of the number of explosive devices that had been planted in it during the past year – it was the only route out of the hotel complex most of the time and was therefore an attractive ambush site.

Abdul was in the lead vehicle with Farris while Mallory and Stanza followed in Kareem's car. At his feet Mallory kept a holdall containing a short-barrelled AK47 with an extra-long forty-round magazine attached, a chest harness holding six AK47 magazines, a smoke grenade and a shrapnel grenade that he had appropriated from a US soldier.

The general M.O. while driving in the city was for both vehicles to act as if one had nothing to do with the other. Mallory had given Abdul as much of a security brief as he could in half an hour and was relying on Farris to guide him if they ran into a problem.

Stanza wiped his brow and adjusted his body armour. 'This jacket is damned hot,' he complained.

'Wait until the summer,' Mallory said dryly.

'How come the drivers don't wear any?' Stanza asked. Kareem glanced at the journalist in the rear-view mirror and gave a smirk.

'Same reason they don't wear seat belts,' Mallory said. 'Allah will decide when it's time for them to die and no safety equipment will help when that moment arrives. That right, Kareem?'

'*Al hamdillilah*,' Kareem nodded.

Abdul had given Farris and Kareem a rough idea of where the house was and on reaching the Ali Baba roundabout they took the first exit into a popular shopping district. The street was lined on both sides with vendors of every description, most of them util-ising the wide pavement to display their wares that included newly made furniture, washing machines still in their boxes and stacked several high, satellite dishes, refrigerators and clothing.

'What's this street?' Stanza asked.

'Tariq Al Karada,' Kareem replied.

'Are we actually in Karada?' Stanza asked.

'We not far from the house – if Abdul is telling truth,' Kareem said.

'Do you think he's making it up?' Stanza asked, curious why Kareem should say such a thing.

Kareem shrugged his shoulders and stuck out his bottom lip. 'We shall see,' he said.

The traffic was heavy and Kareem did not allow more than a couple of cars to get between him and Farris. After crossing a major junction they turned along a quiet residential street. A few blocks further on Farris slowed as he approached the entrance to another.

The area was middle-class by Baghdad standards, or appeared to be. The trick was to imagine it without the trash and rubble that was everywhere other than in the truly affluent sections. Farris's car pulled over to the kerb and Kareem came to a stop close behind it. Mallory was first out, looking up and down the street for anything suspicious. A few months back a westerner could have gone shopping in this part of town and could even have grabbed a bite in a restaurant but now even just passing through had its dangers.

'Let's keep it to fifteen minutes,' Mallory said to Stanza. Abdul was staring up at the first-floor window of a house directly in front of them.

'This it?' Stanza asked.

'Yes,' the young Arab said.

'Who do we see about taking a look inside?' Stanza asked.

Abdul walked to the front door and pushed it open.

Mallory made a mental note of Abdul's direct-approach style. 'Kareem, Farris, you stay here. Come up and get me if anyone looks like they're taking an interest, OK?' he said.

The two men nodded.

Abdul led the way into the hall, followed by Mallory and Stanza, and stopped at the foot of the staircase. Mallory looked along the dilapidated hallway where there were two doors, both closed.

'You sure this is the place?' Mallory asked.

'Yes,' Abdul said, staring up the narrow staircase.

Mallory followed his gaze to the darkness at the top of the stairs and when he looked back the young Arab appeared to be in a quandary of some sort.

'Abdul?' Mallory asked quietly. Abdul's response was to raise a foot and place it on the first step. It creaked loudly. He continued up and the next step squeaked too. Mallory and Stanza followed him to the top where they all stopped outside a closed door.

'You've been here before?' Mallory asked.

'Yes.'

'Does anyone still live here?' Stanza asked.

'I don't know,' Abdul said.

Mallory wasn't comfortable with this half-cocked way of operating but Stanza clearly didn't care.

Abdul reached for the doorknob and paused as he touched it.

'Open it, for Christ's sake,' Stanza said impatiently.

Abdul turned the knob and pushed open the door. They looked inside, Stanza craning his neck to see past Mallory's shoulder.

The room was a shambles, as if it had been ransacked, and smelled of rotting trash. A broad shaft of daylight came in through a broken window that was partly covered by a tattered curtain. Clothes and bedding were strewn around the floor and draped over toppled furniture. Everything was covered in a thick layer of fine sand that had blown in through the window.

The floorboards creaked lightly as Mallory eased past Abdul. Stanza followed.

'Doesn't look as if anyone lives here at the moment,' Mallory offered.

Stanza moved carefully around as if he was afraid of leaving a footprint. He crouched to take a look at a bundled-up sheet that was heavily stained. 'This look like blood to you?' he asked.

Mallory moved the sheet away with his foot to reveal the floorboards beneath. They were covered in a dark crusty substance. 'Yeah. Loads of it,' he said, following a trail to an even larger pool of dried blood.

Stanza wiped his hands on his thighs as he got to his feet, even though he had not actually touched anything. 'Something about murder scenes,' he said. 'They've all got the same spooky feel, as if the ghosts of the dead were standing next to you and watching.'

Mallory pushed open the bedroom door to reveal a window covered by a gaily coloured curtain, a bed with its sheets on the floor and a bedside table on its side with a broken lamp beside it.

'This tells a sad story,' Mallory mused. 'I heard somewhere that she was a hooker.'

'No,' Stanza said, perhaps too firmly.

'Would spice up the read,' Mallory joked, unaware that it irritated Stanza.

'You don't think Lamont could have found love in Baghdad?' Stanza asked, only remotely interested in Mallory's plebeian view.

Mallory was at the window, standing on tiptoe and trying to look down into the street when Tasneen's image filled his mind's eye. 'Why not? You can find love anywhere, I suppose.'

'My point is, could it happen between an American man and a Muslim woman here and now, I mean?'

Mallory turned his gaze to the greying sky, wondering if there was a sandstorm brewing. Then he realised what story angle Stanza was hoping for. 'You mean, is love stronger than religion? Before I came here I would have said yes. But . . . well, they're a fanatical lot generally, more than I used to think . . . People back in the West might buy it, though . . . How can you find out?'

'Find someone who was close to her,' Stanza said, glancing at Abdul in the hope of some kind of lead. But the young Arab seemed to be back in a daydream.

'Lamont's not dead yet, is he?' Mallory asked.

'Not as far as we know,' Stanza replied.

'Better get the story right, then. He might turn up one day.'

That didn't matter to Stanza. Writing a story correction only provided more bites of the cherry.

'Would Lamont have been the romantic-hero type or a total ass, d'you reckon?' Mallory said.

'I take it that *you* think an American screwing a Muslim chick in a house like this would be a total ass.'

'These days? For sure,' Mallory quipped.

Abdul was reliving the horror of that night once again but the memory was already becoming blurred. The physical pain of his terrible wound had also lessened but the shame of his part in the atrocity had not. If anything, it had become clearer to him. However he looked at it he couldn't escape the feeling that he could have done something. He'd had a gun but he had been a coward. It was as simple as that. 'She was wrong to give herself to the American,' he said.

307

Stanza and Mallory looked at him.

'But she wasn't a whore,' Abdul added.

'How do you know that?' Stanza asked.

Abdul moved his gaze from the floor where the woman had fallen and stared sullenly at the two foreigners, confidence returning to his expression. He had been growing steadily irritated with their banter, particularly their comments about love between members of different faiths. The woman had been wrong to give herself to the American but Abdul had felt sympathy for her. She was a lost soul, a sinner, but nevertheless brave, more so than he. She must have sensed that Hassan might kill her for sleeping with the American and yet instead of begging for forgiveness she had declared her love for him. Abdul could not allow these people to cheapen her.

'She loved him,' Abdul said.

Stanza believed Abdul and not just because he wanted to.

'There were rumours of a western man seeing an Iraqi woman,' Abdul went on. 'He came here often.' Abdul could only surmise that but something like it had to be the case since Hassan had been confident that he'd find the American in the house. And then there was the woman's declared love for Lamont – that could not have happened in an instant. 'There are not many hookers in Baghdad. We . . . the police know those who are and she was not known. It is a great risk for an Iraqi woman to have a relationship with a westerner and only one force could have kept them together.' Abdul, satisfied with his deduction, turned around and walked down the stairs.

Stanza glanced around the room, half-hoping that a clue would present itself to him. Abdul's analysis had made sense.

Mallory went to the door to look down the stairs. 'We've been here too long,' he said.

He headed down the stairs while Stanza went to the doorway before pausing to look back into the room. The ghosts seemed to touch him this time and he shivered. Then he followed Mallory.

Mallory stepped out of the house and saw Abdul climbing into Farris's car. Stanza walked out behind him and closed the door. 'I want to drive back with Abdul,' Stanza said.

Being detached from his client wasn't the way Mallory liked to operate but he let it go. He could feel Stanza was close to clashing with him on the security-versus-work issue. 'If you have a problem you must get into this car as soon as you can.'

'Sure,' Stanza said as he opened the rear door of Farris's car and climbed in.

'Sure,' Mallory echoed. He got into Kareem's car.

As Farris pulled into the street and accelerated away Stanza stared at the back of Abdul's head, wondering how best to tackle him. Stanza had been impressed with Abdul's assessment of Lamont's relationship with the murdered woman but at the same time he felt it was too insightful. Stanza leaned forward in his seat. 'Abdul?'

Abdul half-looked around.

'That was interesting, what you said. Can you add to it? Or perhaps you know someone who can.'

'I was speaking as a policeman.'

In Stanza's experience there were several reasons why a person would not elaborate on something that they knew to be important. Fear, whether of retribution or of being implicated. Protecting someone. Holding out for personal gain. And then there was the bullshitter. Stanza had dealt with all of them but he could not say which applied to Abdul – probably not the last one. 'Something I said upset you back there . . . Abdul?'

Abdul made a point of looking at Farris. 'Can we talk later?'

Stanza read the glance and sat back. 'Sure.'

Abdul did not trust the drivers because he did not know them. But most of all he welcomed the break from further questioning. As for the house, he was glad he had visited it. But as he contemplated the possible divine purpose behind it a sudden throbbing in his wound took over everything else on his mind. He closed his eyes in an effort to control the pain.

Traffic was heavy and forty minutes later they rolled into the hotel complex. Mallory climbed out with his heavy holdall and watched Stanza and Abdul walk away from Farris's car to have a private conversation.

'I'll give you a call if I need you again today,' Mallory said to Kareem.

'What about . . .' Kareem said, finishing the sentence with a jut of his chin towards Abdul.

'Not today,' Mallory said, wondering if he would

have a moment with Tasneen when she came by to get her brother.

Kareem said something to Farris who gave Mallory a wave. Both men climbed back into their cars and drove out of the car park.

Mallory thought about waiting for Stanza, decided against it and headed for the hotel. Their conversation had nothing to do with him, anyway. It was hot and he fancied a cold shower and a cup of tea.

Stanza was standing close to Abdul and talking in a quiet yet determined manner. 'If we're going to be a team we have to help each other. If there is something about this story that is a problem for you let's talk about it. One of my most important responsibilities is to protect my sources and certainly members of my team. I wouldn't do anything to put anyone in jeopardy. Do you trust me as far as that goes? We plan to stay here for a long time . . . Abdul?'

'I understand,' Abdul said. 'It's just that . . . lives are under threat, in danger. Not just me. I'm afraid, not for me but for others.'

'I understand that,' Stanza said, looking around to ensure they were still alone, pausing as he spotted a couple of Iraqi guards some distance away, standing around smoking and chatting. 'Walk with me,' he said and they followed the towering blast wall towards the other end of the car park that was deserted. As they left the shade of the eucalyptus trees the sun touched them and the temperature increased notably.

'What I'm about to tell you I've told no one,' Stanza said, pulling the top of his shirt open to let some air in. 'I'm telling you because I believe I can trust you. The other reason I'm telling you is that I want *you* to trust *me* . . . We're not just doing a story on Lamont,' Stanza went on, deciding to keep the American's real name to himself for the moment. 'We're going to negotiate his release, or at least try to.' Stanza had deliberated for some time before deciding to confide this much in Abdul. He needed help from a local and his instincts told him that Abdul was the man. Even if Abdul was connected to the insurgents in some way, that was precisely who Stanza was trying to get in touch with. 'Does that shock you?' Stanza asked.

Abdul's mind was beginning to spin at the consequences of such an undertaking. 'It . . . it is a shock, as you say. But also dangerous.'

It was indeed, and stimulating too, Stanza suddenly thought. 'What do you think about finding the people who kidnapped Lamont and asking for a meeting to discuss a ransom?'

The image of Hassan and the others appeared. But it was not Hassan to whom Abdul would need to talk. He would know the identities of those who'd ordered – and paid for – the American's kidnapping.

'How would we go about that?' Stanza asked. 'In theory, at least. Is it possible?'

'I don't know.'

'We couldn't involve anyone else. No one official.' The US government's policy of non-negotiation with hostage-takers, hijackers and the like was well documented. But it was not against the law for a private individual to do it. 'If we could at least try and make a start. I don't expect it to be easy but . . . What do you think?'

Abdul was thinking about Hassan. The idea of approaching his erstwhile boss filled him with dread. It seemed that he had not become fearless after all. Abdul might now be enjoying the comfort of Allah but Hassan was still a tool of the devil. Hassan could contact those who had bought Lamont, it was his business to. But why would he want to? 'It would be very dangerous,' Abdul repeated, more to himself than to Stanza.

'But would it be possible? Can't we take it in small steps? A feasibility study? What would your first step be?' Stanza was pushing the matter because he was not meeting the resistance he had expected. Whether Abdul could manage such a thing was something to worry about later.

Abdul took hold of his stump that had started to throb again. Stanza was right. Abdul could take a small step. Test the ground. Money was the key to Hassan, though. 'Would you pay for the information?'

'Pay? Pay who?' Stanza was unprepared for talk of money.

'Palms will need to be oiled. You are asking people to put themselves at risk. People who owe you nothing.'

Stanza understood. But journalists like him rarely paid for information. In any case, his budget was small and he only had enough dollars to pay the local staff's wages, plus the hotel bills and expenses. 'How much?' he asked.

'Not for me,' Abdul said. 'But if I found a person

313

with information he will want money. How much I do not know. I am not experienced in these matters.'

Neither was Stanza but the point was he didn't have any money anyway. He could rustle up a few thousand dollars, more if he withheld the wages until he got a resupply from the *Herald*. He would have to get permission from Patterson, of course, who would in turn have to get it from old man Stanmore. They had not even discussed the size of the ransom yet. The paper wasn't ready. Stanza would be moving ahead unsupported. An immediate conversation with Patterson was required. 'Can you find out how much we might be talking about? For information and such?'

'Maybe.'

'OK. We'll take it a step at a time. See what we need to do to make contact with the kidnappers. Let's not put ourselves at risk. Call me the minute you have anything,' Stanza said before walking away.

If one's fate was always in Allah's hands, then Abdul could not imagine what was in store for him further along the path. But, thinking positively, it would be wonderful if he could achieve something with this Lamont business. Here was a chance to redeem himself, partly at least. Perhaps the idea was not as wild as it first appeared. Meeting Hassan – the only way into the maze that he could think of – was a terrible prospect, of course. But if there was money involved that would interest Hassan more than anything.

This was the most ambitious undertaking of Abdul's

life. But, most important, it was very much an adult mission.

As Abdul stepped off towards the checkpoint he straightened his back and pushed out his chin. This was indeed the start of a remarkable journey.

10

The Lion's Den

Tasneen stepped into her apartment, closed the door behind her and bolted it. As she pulled off her jacket a sound came from the kitchen. 'Is that you, Abdul?' she called out, her breath catching as she became suddenly nervous.

Abdul popped his head around the kitchen doorway. 'Hi,' he said. His smile was unusually broad.

Tasneen's unease was immediately replaced by a different concern. He was supposed to have called her when he was ready to be picked up. She put down her jacket, dropped her keys into her handbag and placed it on the small table by the door. 'How was it?'

When Abdul did not answer she walked to the kitchen doorway. He was cutting a sandwich, using his handless forearm to keep it in place while he sliced through the bread with his good hand. Her instant reaction was to take over but as she reached out he shifted his body to block her and continued sawing. 'I can do it,' he said, a hint of annoyance in his tone.

Tasneen folded her arms and leaned against the door frame, glad to see him showing some independence. 'Well? Are you going to answer me?'

He cut through the sandwich and brushed the crumbs from his stump. 'I was concentrating on not cutting any more of my arm off.'

She grinned. 'You had a good day, then.'

'I have never had a day quite like it,' Abdul said, taking a large bite out of the sandwich as he offered her the other half.

Tasneen shook her head. 'Sounds exciting . . . What did you do?'

He walked past her into the living room while trying to keep the pieces of lamb and tomato from falling out from between the slices of bread. 'We did journalist things,' he said as he sat on the couch, his mouth full of food.

'Tell me. I want to know.'

Abdul swallowed the mouthful before he had chewed it completely. 'We investigated a story.'

'So . . . what's your job?'

'I don't think I have a title. I do things the white guys can't do. I talk to Iraqis, find locations, stuff like that.'

'Sounds like fun,' she said.

'Not exactly how I would describe it.'

'You said you hadn't had a day like it.'

'It was different.'

'So tell me what you *didn't* like about it, then.'

He sighed. 'OK, OK . . . You and your cross-reference analysing . . . It's just, well, not what I expected.'

She studied him patiently. His moods were so difficult to understand these days. It was as if she didn't really know him at all any more.

He appeared about to reveal something deep, then winked at her.

Tasneen gave up, rolling her eyes. 'If you don't want to tell me, fine. You like the job, kind of. At least you don't hate it. And since it was the first day it could get better, or worse . . . What about the others? The Iraqis? Can you tell me how they were?'

'They don't like me. They're suspicious. They're not very bright, either . . . The journalist is strange. I have mixed feelings about him.'

'In what way?'

Abdul shrugged. 'I don't think I trust him. He's hard to understand. I don't think he is very experienced. He knows nothing about Arabs, that's for sure.'

'What about Bernie?'

'He doesn't like me or trust me.'

'I don't believe that,' she said.

'He's hard to read, too. He seems impatient, as if he has other things more important to do. That – or he has no interest in being here.'

'He wouldn't have hired you if he did not like you.'

'It doesn't matter what he thinks, anyway. Stanza is the boss and Mallory will be gone soon.'

Tasneen did not allow her expression to change. 'Oh? When?'

'I don't know. I heard the drivers talking. He's been here longer than he should have, apparently.'

Mallory had told her that he would have to leave but also that he would be back. 'Are you going to stay working with them?' she asked as she picked up her jacket and handbag and carried them into her bedroom.

'Sure . . . Why not?' Abdul said as he sank into the couch, finished off his sandwich, wiped his hand on his lap and looked at his stump. The first thing he did every morning when he woke up was to check his hand to see if it had all been a dream. It was why every day began at a low point for him.

Abdul lowered his arm as he pondered his next step, dark images returning to his thoughts. Since leaving the hotel he had considered the best way to approach Hassan. The telephone was pointless since details could not be discussed over it and Hassan would not meet him unless he was told the purpose of the rendezvous. There was only one solution, not a particularly attractive one. But then, no part of the undertaking was particularly appealing.

'Tasneen?' he called out.

'Yes?' she answered from inside her room.

'Can I use your car for a couple of hours?'

She appeared in her doorway. 'My car? Why?'

'Mine has a problem. I think it's the fuel pump.'

'I meant, why do you want a car?'

'It's not so difficult to drive with one hand. I used to do it all the time when I was using my phone.'

'Where are you going?' Tasneen asked, trying to sound matter-of-fact. But she was concerned for several reasons.

'I have to work.'

'Work?'

'That's why I was home early. My day is not yet over.'

'What work?' she asked, growing suspicious.

319

'It's confidential.'

'Is that right?'

Abdul sighed. 'I work for a newspaper. The stories are often confidential. Scoops.' He could see the doubt in his sister's eyes. 'If you don't want me to work for them then why did you get me the job?'

'Don't twist this around, Abdul. Why can't I drive you to wherever it is you want to go?'

'Because then you'd know what the job was.'

'What about your drivers?'

'The boss doesn't want them to know, either. He hasn't even told Mallory.'

Tasneen wondered if that was true.

'Why do they all call him Mallory but you call him Bernie?'

Tasneen decided there was something dark about Abdul today. 'How long will you be? Are you allowed to reveal that much?'

'Why? Are you going out somewhere?' he asked cheekily.

'You don't have the keys to the car yet,' she parried.

Abdul conceded the point. 'A couple of hours. No more . . . All I'm doing is going to see someone who might have some information for the journalist about a story he wants to do . . . Look, I'll tell you a little but if you tell anyone else I could get fired . . . The news story is about an American hostage. He comes from the same town as the newspaper and so the journalist is very interested in him. OK? Now you have it.'

Tasneen didn't know what to make of it. It sounded

odd to her. But if her brother was lying he had suddenly become very good at it.

'The problem is that I don't know what time this person will get home so I will have to wait for him.'

'So you could be late.'

'I'm not a child!' Abdul snapped, startling her. Immediately he regretted losing his temper, although he was not sorry for the sentiment behind the outburst.

Tasneen walked back into her room and a moment later emerged from it and tossed the car keys at him.

Abdul sighed again as he leaned back and looked up at the ceiling in silent prayer.

He got to his feet, went into his bedroom, opened up his wardrobe, reached in, took out a shoebox and put it on the bed. As an afterthought he pushed the door until it was almost shut, sat on the bed beside the box and opened it to reveal his pistol and spare magazine. Tasneen had found it on the floor of his car days after the incident. It still belonged to the police and Abdul was supposed to bring it in with him when he went to collect his final pay cheque. He pondered the wisdom of taking it with him. It had no part in his plan but it might be useful if things went wrong. He dithered over the pros and cons before finally allowing his male vanity to decide for him. He shoved the loaded magazine into the weapon, placed the gun in his jacket pocket, closed the box and put it back in the wardrobe. He checked his watch and then the window. It would be dark soon but it was still too early to go. However, the thought of hanging around the apartment with Tasneen made him uncomfortable so he pulled on his jacket and opened the door. 'I'll see you in a while,' he called out as he walked to the front door. 'I'll call you if I'm going to be late.'

He closed the door behind him and a moment later was walking out of the apartment block to Tasneen's car.

Abdul took his time getting the feel of the vehicle and practising his one-handed technique before starting the engine and slowly manoeuvring the car out of the parking space and around the block. The most difficult operation was turning the wheel quickly enough to steer around the tighter corners without crossing to the other side of the road. Once on the wider main streets his confidence increased and he joined the busy late-afternoon traffic.

He took his time, ignoring the usual fierce competition for gaps and lanes, allowing anyone who wanted to push in front of him, and headed due south towards Dora once he arrived at the roundabout beside the Baghdad radio tower. The control building at its base had been destroyed by a guided missile during the war. He crossed the BIAP highway near the great mosque and headed for the towering smokestacks on the edge of the infamous neighbourhood.

Abdul had been to Hassan's house a couple of times although he'd never been inside it. The street was easy to find because of a prominent blue ceramic-tiled mosque at one end and a small produce shop almost directly across the road from the house itself.

The first phase of Abdul's simple plan was to see if Hassan's car was outside his house. It wouldn't necessarily mean that Hassan was home if it was but he would knock on the door anyway. If the car was not there Abdul would wait. But that was the potentially tiresome part. When Hassan wasn't working as a cop he was conducting his nefarious business dealings around the city and he could be out at all hours.

It was dark by the time Abdul arrived in Hassan's neighbourhood. The area looked as bad as its reputation. Several streets around Abdul's neighbourhood had a street light or two that worked most nights but Dora was in darkness except for the glow of benzene lamps from some of the houses.

The mosque loomed ahead, its colourful dome illuminated by a couple of light bulbs powered by a small generator. A cruise along Hassan's street revealed only a couple of vehicles, neither of them his. Abdul carried on to the end of the street, circled around the block, pulled to a stop beside the kerb, from where he could see the house and turned off the car's engine and headlights. He sat in the dark silence for a moment. He felt uncomfortable and, in case he was being watched from one of the unlit houses, he climbed out and walked down the street to the small store across from Hassan's house.

The shop was a hovel of dust-covered tins, sweets and cigarettes. Abdul bought a packet of Marlboro Lights and headed back the way he had come. He considered walking past the car and continuing around the block but decided against it in case he was challenged. He climbed back in behind the wheel. If anyone came up and asked him what he was doing

323

he would tell them the truth. Hassan was well known and respected – or feared – in the neighbourhood and Abdul might attract a measure of the same esteem if it was understood that he was an associate.

Abdul placed the packet of cigarettes on the dashboard, eased down into the seat and rested his head in a position that allowed him to watch the street.

He checked his watch, deciding to give Hassan until nine o'clock. But then, if the man did not arrive by then Abdul would have to come back another night if he was to pursue his plan. He would give the man until ten, or perhaps later. It didn't really matter if he gave him until midnight. His final decision was to leave it to fate, to Allah. If it was His will that Abdul should make this connection then it would take place. But that was the big problem with fate, Abdul decided. In this case, for instance, it was up to him to choose the time until which he would wait. If Hassan arrived in that time it would be Allah's will. But if Abdul decided to then extend the time limit was that then also extending it beyond the divine will? Everything was of course Allah's will, but the outcome might be different if Abdul kept changing his mind.

Abdul decided that the best way had to be to stick to his guns. If he declared to fate well in advance that he was leaving at nine o'clock then that would be the time he should leave.

At a quarter to nine a car drove into the far end of the street and Abdul watched its headlights move slowly towards him. Before reaching the small shop the headlights pulled into the kerb, came to a stop and went out.

Abdul leaned forward in his seat, unable to make out if the car had stopped in front of Hassan's house. Its interior light flickered on as a door opened and a figure climbed out. Abdul suddenly wondered what to do if there were other thugs – such as his dreaded team mates – with Hassan but as he peered into the darkness it did appear that the figure was alone. It disappeared into a house.

Abdul's heart rate had increased, his nerves were tingling and a ripple of fear passed through him as he contemplated the next phase of his plan. A voice inside his head was suddenly arguing that the whole thing was pointless.

But he knew it was the voice of fear and not of reason that was nagging at him. He took several deep breaths, crushed the internal debate and went through a mental rehearsal of what he was going to say to Hassan. Abdul remembered the gun in his pocket. He thought about leaving it in the car in case Hassan decided to search him. The weapon would only make the man suspicious and perhaps even alarmed. But if Hassan did lose control Abdul would be defenceless. He took the pistol out of his pocket, cocked it as quietly as he could by gripping the top-slide between his knees and put it back.

He climbed out of the car and closed the door, making hardly a sound. He crossed the street towards Hassan's house, his nerves tightening even more as he took several deep breaths in an effort to calm himself.

As Abdul arrived outside Hassan's house he looked in every direction, at the same time straining to listen. A light was burning inside on the ground floor. The car that had pulled up was Hassan's red Opal. Abdul stepped into the shadows of the doorway and faced the shabby door that had not been painted in years. His feeling of apprehension grew even stronger and he prayed it would not get any worse – Hassan would sense it and feed off it. He breathed deeply several more times, reached his hand out and struck the door with his knuckles. The knock was pathetic and he cursed himself for his feebleness as he repeated it with more vigour.

An orange glow appeared through several cracks in the door and a noise came from inside the house. Abdul's heart beat faster at the sound of the key turning in the lock. The door opened.

Hassan was holding a pistol. The pale orange light filled the end of the hallway behind him. He stared at Abdul with an ominous expression on his face. Hassan's shirt was unbuttoned to reveal a stained T-shirt beneath and the top of his trousers had been unfastened to ease the strain on his fat stomach. He looked as oily and sleazy as ever.

Hassan's stare shifted to Abdul's stump and his podgy unshaven face broke into a smirk. 'What do *you* want?' he asked, losing the smile and spitting out something.

Abdul swallowed, opened his mouth but was unable to speak. It felt as if he had suddenly been choked by a tightening pressure around his chest.

'Say something or get lost,' Hassan growled.

'I . . . I have to talk to you,' Abdul finally managed to stutter.

'About what?'

Abdul glanced behind him nervously. He cleared his throat but found that he had become tongue-tied with tension again.

'Are you going to say something or are you going to just piss your pants?' Hassan asked.

'I have . . . I have business to discuss with you,' Abdul stammered at last.

'Business?' Hassan said with contempt. 'What kind of business would *you* have with me?'

'I need information.'

Hassan suddenly grew suspicious and looked past Abdul.

'I'm . . . ' Abdul began. But he found himself struggling to remember the verbal strategy that he had rehearsed.

Hassan raised his pistol and levelled it at Abdul's forehead. 'You've got five seconds. If you don't tell me what you are doing here by then I'll shoot you where you stand.'

'The man w-we kidnapped. I have people who want to know where he is.'

'I'll leave your body in the street right here,' Hassan growled. 'No one will care around these parts. I could butcher you with a cleaver into a dozen pieces and no one would bother me . . . Who wants this information?'

'An American. Civilian, not military,' Abdul quickly added.

'I think I *will* shoot you,' Hassan said, turning the weapon to check the safety catch was off before pointing the muzzle back at Abdul's head.

'Please. They will pay for the information,' Abdul pleaded. 'I'm frightened. That's why I can't speak. Give me one minute. Please, Hassan.'

Hassan studied the younger man as if he was a piece of dirt. 'You said the one word that could save your life, you little shit. Pay.' Hassan lowered his gun. 'In,' he said, stepping aside.

Abdul stepped into the house's narrow hallway, past Hassan who smelled of sweat and alcohol, and waited as the man checked outside before closing the door.

Hassan brushed past him, walked to a room partway down the hallway and stopped in the doorway. 'Here,' he grunted.

Abdul shuffled past him and into a squalid room. The only furnishings were a tattered couch, several worn and grubby rugs overlapping each other to cover the floor and a side table.

Hassan went to the side table that was covered in dust-covered junk as well as several bottles of Scotch, one of them half-empty and with its cap off. He put the gun down, picked up a filthy glass containing a fair measure of the amber liquid and took a large swig. He winced as the liquid passed down his throat and then he glared sullenly at Abdul. 'You want a drink?'

Abdul shook his head. 'No.'

Hassan dropped his gaze to Abdul's stump. 'How's the hand?'

'What hand?'

Hassan broke into a guttural laugh. '"What hand?" That's good. I never knew you had a sense of humour.'

Abdul had intended it simply as a stoic statement.

'I hope what you want is not some kind of joke, though,' Hassan said, ominously serious once again.

'I am here to do business.'

'About the American *we* kidnapped,' Hassan said, chortling. '"We." I like that. I hope you don't expect to get paid now that it's *we*.' He took another swig from the glass. 'Who are these Americans?'

'A newspaper.' Abdul felt less tense now that he had engaged Hassan in conversation. 'They want to do a story.'

'What's the deal?'

'They want to know where the man is.'

Hassan drained the glass and refilled it from the bottle. 'Where he is? That's another joke, of course.'

'They want to make contact with the people who have him,' Abdul corrected.

'And how much will they pay for this information?'

'I don't know.'

Hassan looked at him suspiciously.

'This is why I am here, Hassan. You know that I don't know much about these matters.'

'Who are they?'

'I'm not supposed to say.'

'I asked who they are?' Hassan said darkly.

'I . . . I cannot say,' Abdul said, sensing danger but pushing his luck.

Hassan took another swig, put the glass down and picked up the pistol. 'I could fire bullets into you all night and no one would come to investigate. You come into my house and dictate to me! "I cannot say".' He mimicked the words with a fair approximation of Abdul's pathetic tone. He looked at Abdul coldly. 'Who are they?'

'A newspaper . . . called the *Herald*,' Abdul blurted.

'Why do they want to speak to the kidnappers?' asked Hassan.

Abdul was about to reply but Hassan interrupted.

'They want either to interview them, interview him, or they want to pay a ransom. Right?'

'You are right.'

Hassan nodded. 'The ransom will be in the millions.'

'I don't know anything about the money. Not right now,' Abdul said.

'They sent you out looking for the American without money? You are either crazy or stupid . . . I hope you don't think I am either.'

'They also do not know the cost of doing this kind of business. That's why I am here.'

Hassan studied Abdul, weighing him up. 'I'm supposed to give you a price for my information and then you tell those you work for, and then they give me the money – is that how this is supposed to work?'

'Does that not suit you, Hassan? If not, please guide us.'

'Tell me something, you little shit. How did you get into this line of business? I cut your hand off and

330

now you're working in a business that deals in millions. It was good fortune for you. I should take a piece of your money.'

'Can you at least tell me if you can get in touch with the men who have the American?' Abdul asked, desperate to get Hassan on track.

'I think you are trying to make a fool of me, little man.' Hassan swayed a little as the drink soaked into his brain.

Abdul warned himself to be more careful. He had never seen Hassan drunk before but suspected that it made the man even more dangerous. 'Please, Hassan. I am only the messenger. They would not trust me with more than I have discussed with you.'

'I believe that,' Hassan slurred, putting down his pistol and lurching around as he took another swig of Scotch. 'It's a dangerous errand they've sent you on.'

'Perhaps I should come back another time.'

'Is that what you would ask the lion as you stood in his cave?'

Abdul's concern went up a notch as he gauged the distance to the front door, wondering if he could make it outside at the run before Hassan picked up his gun and shot him. Abdul reckoned he might reach the door but he feared it would be as far as he got before Hassan's bullets cut him down. 'Then how must this work, Hassan? Please tell me.'

'You want information and I want money for it,' Hassan said, draining the glass again. 'It is a marriage of the two,' he continued, reaching for a packet of cigarettes. 'You have asked for the information but you do not have money. So how can it now proceed? This is the question.'

Abdul watched Hassan as he laboriously set about lighting a cigarette. 'Why don't you give me a price for your information? Then I will tell those I work for.'

'Idiot,' Hassan scoffed as he picked up the gun and somehow managed to hold on to it while he poured yet another drink.

Abdul felt his own pistol inside his jacket pocket. His advantage lay in Hassan's drunkenness but he would be foolish to underestimate the man's experience with violence of all kinds. Hassan was unpredictable even when he was sober. He could lose his temper at any second and put a bullet into Abdul just because he was there.

Hassan looked over the rim of the glass, fixing Abdul with his heavy-lidded stare. 'One hundred thousand dollars,' he declared.

The price was unimportant now. Abdul had not imagined Hassan being this difficult to deal with and his every thought was focused on getting out of the house. 'I'll tell them,' Abdul said as he took a step towards the door.

'Where are you going?' Hassan said as he put down the glass and swung his gun towards Abdul, holding it level for a moment before lowering it as if it had suddenly become too heavy.

'To tell my people your demands.'

'You think I'm so stupid? Eh? You don't think I know you want revenge for your arm . . . You leave and then the next people through my door are American soldiers who will torture me for the information.'

Abdul was not prepared for such a response. 'If that was true I would not have needed to come here,' he said, thinking swiftly. 'The American government does not negotiate. That is why they do not know. The newspaper is dealing with this. They would not tell the military.'

It took a while but Hassan began to see the sense in Abdul's reasoning. 'I have an idea,' he said. 'I will have my own hostage to make sure that you don't cross me.'

Abdul had no idea what the man meant. He watched as Hassan tucked the pistol into his belt and reached for his jacket. 'I don't understand,' Abdul said.

Hassan burped loudly as he looked at Abdul, a knowing smirk forming on his face. 'I need a hostage to ensure I get my money . . . We'll go to your apartment and I'll stay with your sweet little sister until your newspaper comes up with the money.'

Abdul was horrified. 'You cannot do that,' he gasped, unable to hide the alarm in his voice.

'I do what I want. And if you don't come back with the money . . . well, then you have a problem. And don't be long. I don't know how long I can spend in a room with your pretty little sister without showing her some affection,' Hassan said, a grin forming on his sweaty face.

The blood pounded through Abdul's veins and throbbed in his temples at the thought of Hassan even entering his apartment. The image of the man grabbing Tasneen grew frighteningly clear. There was no way he'd let the pig leave this house with that objective in mind. Abdul took the gun from his pocket and pointed it at Hassan.

Hassan's brain was addled with alcohol and he'd already taken a step towards Abdul before the sight of the pistol stopped him. He swayed as he looked into Abdul's eyes. 'So I was right. This is what you came to do. Murder me.'

'No,' Abdul said. 'But now it seems like a good idea.'

'You don't have the guts.'

'Maybe I didn't before the night you cut off my hand.' Abdul's voice quivered slightly. 'It doesn't take courage to murder a man like this. Look at you. You're not brave. It only takes great cruelty or hate and I have plenty enough of one of those.'

'So. The boy thinks he is a man now. Perhaps you are ready to join us at last.'

'Go to hell,' Abdul said, the pistol shaking slightly in his hand as he tightened his jaw. The boom as the gun fired was the loudest sound Abdul had ever heard, or so it seemed in the small dingy airless room where even the clatter of a cockroach's legs as it scurried up the cracked walls was amplified.

Hassan shrieked, grabbed his thigh and dropped heavily to the floor, falling onto his backside. There was no blood: the round had punctured the skin neatly and the meaty flesh closed around the entry hole. The intense pain that Hassan was feeling came from the red-hot bullet lodging inside the thick muscle and the shattered femur as his weight collapsed the limb that could no longer support him.

Abdul kept the gun aimed at Hassan. The man had not made another sound after his initial scream but his face was screwed tightly against the pain.

Hassan opened his tear-filled eyes and blinked furiously in an effort to focus on Abdul. 'You shot me!'

Abdul was surprised by how easy it had been to fire a bullet into a man – or into this particular man, at any rate. There was something else about the experience that he had not expected. It had felt very good indeed. This chunk of metal in his hand was more than just a tool that fired a projectile. Weapons like it had made kings and brought down nations and now it had in a second reversed his vile relationship of servitude and torment with Hassan to turn Abdul into the undisputed master. But if it was to stay that way Abdul would have to finish the job. So he fired again.

This time Abdul was prepared for the explosion and he watched something red fly off Hassan's shoulder as the bullet struck it. Hassan screamed as he brought a hand up to clutch at the new wound that, unlike the first, immediately bled heavily. The masterful feeling only increased as Abdul took a step forward, adjusting his aim to point the muzzle at Hassan's head. Abdul was about to pull the trigger a third time when he suddenly remembered why he was there in the first place. 'Where is he?' Abdul asked, his voice now cold and decisive.

Hassan looked at him through drooping eyelids, his mouth open while his head and torso moved with every heavy gasp. 'The . . . Islamic . . . secret . . . army have him,' he said, the effort obviously causing him more pain. 'Black Banners.'

'I know that. They were on the television. I want to know who I can contact.'

'And . . . and then . . . you will . . . kill me.'

'You are not in a position to barter.'

'My money. You will . . . keep it for yourself . . . I have taught you well.'

'There is no money, Hassan. Your life is at an end. You are bartering for nothing. Tell me and I will send you on your way. If you do not, then I will leave you here for the rats to finish off. Think about it.'

Hassan understood and quickly came to terms with his drastically shortened future. Death did not horrify him, not as much as it would have appalled a person who had something however small to live for. Hassan had been an unhappy boy who had grown into an unhappy man. To him, no human life had any value beyond what it would fetch in ransom money, not even his own. He had never feared dying and this stoicism had nothing to do with religion. He did not really care what Abdul did to him. Perhaps the alcohol that he'd drunk made this acceptance easier but Hassan would not admit that. He knew this moment was his last and he grinned at the irony. 'My . . . my father told me . . . my . . . my weakness would one day kill me.'

Abdul was not interested but allowed the man to ramble on in the hope that he would eventually tell him what he wanted.

'The others . . . they wanted . . . to kill you . . . I said no. That was . . . my weakness. The old fool . . . he was right after all.'

Abdul realised that Hassan had accepted his fate: it was time to go. Despite his earlier threat to leave the man alive for the rats to gnaw he could not risk abandoning him like this in case he stayed conscious long enough for his brother Ali or the others to find him.

Abdul was about to deliver the *coup de grâce* when Hassan struggled to say more. 'Fallujah,' he said. 'I'll see you in hell.' Hassan looked for his gun beside him, reached for it and wrapped his bloody fingers around the grip.

Abdul squeezed the trigger. The gun jumped in his hand, the noise making him flinch even though he had braced himself against it. Hassan's head jerked back as blood gushed from his eye socket, his mouth gaping open. He moved no more.

Abdul walked out of the room and down the hall, opened the door without any difficulty, stepped outside and headed for his car. He tossed his pistol onto the passenger seat, dug the car key from his pocket, started the engine and accelerated down the road, tyres screeching. He passed Hassan's house, turned the corner at the end of the road too wide, almost hitting a parked car on the other side, switched on his headlights and sped away up the road.

Twenty minutes later he came to a stop outside his apartment block, turned off the lights and engine and sat in silence while he absorbed the implications of the evening's activities. He had achieved much more than he had ever hoped for or would have believed possible. There was no doubt that he had broken down many barriers since losing his hand but Abdul was shocked at the type and speed of the progress he had made. Then it dawned on him how he could have discovered these qualities in himself long ago had he put his mind to it. All those years of weakness could have been avoided. This night had proven how lethally competent he was when left to his own devices.

Abdul took a deep breath, pocketed his gun and made ready to head upstairs, no doubt to an interrogation by Tasneen. He would not tell her anything, of course. She would never be able to imagine how her little brother had killed a man that night.

Abdul climbed out of the car and took a moment to consider his likely fate from now on. The suspicion that he was on a great journey was even stronger now and that he was developing the skills to complete it. Fate had removed one of his hands but he was now more powerful than when he'd had them both.

Abdul looked to the sky as if he was staring into the face of Allah. '*Allah akbar*,' he said softly. Then he walked to the entrance of his apartment.

11

Plans Within Plans

Stanza removed his headset, got up from in front of the computer, poured himself a cup of coffee and looked through the closed balcony windows over the city. He took a sip of the hot black liquid, enjoying just about the only reminder of home in this God-awful place while pondering the hour-long conversation he'd just had with Patterson. It was early in the morning in Milwaukee and the foreign editor had not appreciated being woken up by his bedside phone to hear Stanza on the other end of the line telling him to get to his computer for an important conversation.

When Patterson came online, though, he was in a better mood and immediately pressured Stanza for the story so far. When Stanza began by describing the immediate problems that faced them it was as if Patterson had not heard him. The man launched into a plethora of thematic suggestions of his own, based on the premise of a young heir to a fortune who fled a stifling future in the family business in search of love and adventure. Stanza asked if old man Stanmore would appreciate the monstrous-father inference but Patterson brushed the question aside. He said that every good plot and subplot had a protagonist and antagonist and that this piece was not simply news. It was an epic.

Patterson went on to impress upon Stanza the need to be prepared for several possible scenarios, at which Stanza rolled his eyes. The first and most ideal was young Stanmore's imminent release into Stanza's hands after the payment of a ransom. This would read like a hero's triumphant return to his family after escaping death at the hands of vile Islamic insurgents. The *Herald* would, of course, enjoy the acclaim for their pivotal role in securing the young man's release. Then there was the tragic scenario: young Stanmore getting his head cut off. *That* would read like a eulogy for a young life prematurely extinguished while in pursuit of love and adventure. Patterson suggested it should be written in the first person: 'I did this' and 'I did that', 'I went here to speak to these people', 'I was approached', 'I investigated further.' Stanza had no objections to this idea. Neither did he think Patterson had gone too far when he expressed a belief that the piece would have the potential for a Pulitzer Prize nomination.

Stanza eventually steered the conversation back to his main concerns: the need to find the people who were holding young Stanmore and open up a line of communication with them. To Stanza's utter amazement Patterson said that he thought Stanza was already involved in that stage. Stanza's frustration grew with every revelation of Patterson's ignorance of the realities of Iraq. Finally, unable to contain himself, he burst out exclaiming that it was not a case of simply picking

340

up the phone, calling directory enquiries and asking for insurgency headquarters and the offices of the Black Banner Brigade. Patterson did not appreciate the sarcasm.

When Stanza introduced the subject of money Patterson was not so responsive and simply made excuses about why there was no progress to report in that area. Stanza's mood turned ice-cold at this point and he warned Patterson in no uncertain terms that the success of the story depended on hard cash. Stanza did not allow Patterson to interrupt and went into detail based on Abdul's suggestions. The summing-up was simple: no money, no story. It was the first time that he had experienced Patterson unable to deliver a tirade in defence of an indefensible position. When Patterson finally asked how much money he needed Stanza held on to the first figure that came into his head, doubled it and then doubled it again. 'One hundred thousand,' he said.

Patterson went quiet for several seconds but then calmly said he would get as much of it as he could to Baghdad as soon as he found a quick way of doing it.

'And the ransom amount?' Stanza asked.

'It's being discussed.'

'I need a ballpark figure at least.'

'We don't have one yet.'

Stanza felt it was safe to assume that no one at head office had been willing to start such a discussion. 'Fine,' Stanza said. 'My advice is to be prepared to part with five to ten million.'

Patterson was stunned.

'Those are the figures the French and Italians are rumoured to have paid,' Stanza said. 'I'm afraid they've set a tough precedent for high-profile kidnapping payments.'

Patterson had little more to say after that and assured Stanza that he would get back to him as soon as he had talked with the publisher and old man Stanmore.

Stanza was satisfied by the way the conversation had gone and felt that his stock with the *Herald*'s management had greatly improved. It was now up to him to produce the goods. The only scenario Stanza wanted to see unfold was one where he made contact with the kidnappers and eventually negotiated young Stanmore's release. But for the moment the chances of that appeared to be hanging on the abilities of one young disabled fixer and somewhere between the previous afternoon and that morning Stanza had for some reason lost confidence in Abdul. He began to doubt that he would ever hear from the man again: he'd sent him on an errand that was clearly out of his league. The question was who he could contact next. Mallory was his only source at present but having come up with that one-handed Arab youngster in the first place it reflected badly on him.

A knock on the door snapped him out of his thoughts. He put down his coffee and went to answer it. 'Who's there?'

'Abdul.'

Stanza was surprised. Suddenly he hoped he was wrong about the young Arab. He would learn soon enough, he reckoned, and opened the door to see Abdul standing back politely. 'Come in,' Stanza said.

Abdul entered, closing the door behind him.

'Want a coffee?'

'No, thank you.' It was less than twenty-four hours since his introduction to the team when he'd been so nervous but his self-confidence had soared since the previous night's experience.

'What have you got for me, then?' Stanza asked.

'I managed to track down someone involved with the kidnapping.'

'You did?' Stanza asked, his amazement followed immediately by suspicion. 'How did you manage that, if you don't mind me asking?'

'I was in the police, remember.'

'And you tracked down the insurgents who kidnapped Lamont?'

'No,' Abdul said, shaking his head and wondering if Stanza was being facetious or just plain stupid. 'Most kidnappings are not carried out by insurgents. They are done by criminals who then sell those they've kidnapped to insurgents. Many of these criminals are known to the police.'

Stanza nodded. That made sense. He wanted to ask why the police had not done anything if they knew who the kidnappers were but he chose not to go there, for the moment at least. 'And this person can help us?'

'No . . . But he pointed to where we can look.' Abdul paused to align his thoughts. 'If you want to make contact with those who now have Lamont we will have to go to Fallujah.'

343

'Why?' Stanza asked. 'I take it you have a reason to believe that Lamont's there.'

Abdul had thought about it long and hard and it was an obvious choice in the end. It had been obvious to Hassan and had been the man's last thought before he died. Fallujah had become a popular location with kidnap gangs over the past year. The bodies of several beheaded western kidnap victims had been dumped outside the town. The place was also the headquarters for the Sunni rebellion. Many of the rebels were also criminals and, being a Sunni himself, Hassan would know them or at least know how to make contact. Abdul had no doubt that Lamont was there. 'It is the Black Banner Brigade that has Lamont,' Abdul said. 'And they are based in Fallujah.'

'But we only need to make contact with those who have him. Surely they have a representative in Baghdad?'

'I agree. But I don't know who to ask.'

'This man you met. He actually told you that Lamont was in Fallujah?'

'He made that suggestion.'

'Did you ask him if he knew a Brigade contact in Baghdad?'

'No.'

'Then go back to him and ask.'

'That is not possible. He has gone and will never return.'

Stanza wished he had been at the meeting and had taken control of it. 'What about others? This guy didn't kidnap Lamont alone.'

Abdul shook his head. 'It is very dangerous, even

with money . . . Fallujah is the best chance you have. The Brigade controls Fallujah. The military and the police will not be able to find Lamont easily. The Brigade will do business. They paid money to get Lamont and they will sell him for a good profit. They are businessmen.'

Stanza sipped his coffee as he contemplated the prospect of going into the infamous town. 'How would we get hold of someone from the Brigade if we went there?'

'I have a cousin who lives in Fallujah. He would find someone who knows. That will not be a big problem . . . You are offering money, yes?'

Stanza nodded. 'How much would we need?'

'My cousin will want some. Not much. A thousand or two. But the insurgents? I don't know. A lot. This will be discussed at the first meeting.'

'And what about our safety – or should I say mine. I'm the wrong colour, not to mention the wrong nationality.'

'My skin or my religion will not save me from them either. We will have the rights of negotiators. This is something they will respect as businessmen,' Abdul said, reflecting on Hassan's comments on the business sense of the insurgents. 'Before you are introduced, I or my cousin would get assurance that they will accept you as a negotiator.'

Stanza could see a distinct change in the young man since the day before. He was far more relaxed and self-assured. 'So you would go to Fallujah and prepare the ground for me to go there at a later date?'

'That is possible.' Abdul contemplated the idea. 'But if I set up a meeting for you soon after getting there I would have to come back for you. Perhaps they will have questions I cannot answer. They might not trust me or believe me. They will believe you because you are a white man. And moving in and out of Fallujah is not easy right now. I think it is best that we go there, do our first piece of business and leave.'

Stanza could see the argument but that didn't make it any easier to accept. Stanza might be white enough to initiate negotiations but at some stage the deal's bona fides would have to be confirmed even further. Verification would be required that the transaction was ultimately being conducted by Stanmore's family. Stanza would like to see some evidence of that for himself.

He decided to play along for the moment, as if he were planning on going to Fallujah with Abdul, and in the meantime see how it panned out. 'How would we get into Fallujah? The Americans have the town surrounded.'

'I will call my cousin. He will know how to get past the Americans.'

'That doesn't sound reassuring. I mean, I'm sure your cousin is a capable guy but there's an entire army out there.'

'It is impossible to cover every inch of ground, even for the Americans. There will be ways in.'

'You're sure about that?' Stanza could not control the constant doubts he had about Abdul.

'You have read of many insurgents from all over,

called by their masters to move into Fallujah for the great battle against the Americans. They arrive every day and bring many weapons with them and the Americans cannot stop them. I have also heard that many of the car bombs that are used in Baghdad still come from Fallujah.'

Stanza had read stories about that on the wires too. He had also heard it from official American military sources. The insurgents' defences were being strengthened and weapons were arriving from Iran and Syria almost daily. 'OK . . . So we find a way in. Then what?'

'Then we will find the Black Banner Brigade and begin negotiations.' Abdul shrugged as if nothing could be simpler.

Stanza felt that he was in danger of becoming infected with Abdul's optimism and had to bring himself down to earth for a reality check. Nothing went that easily, especially in Iraq. 'We would drive, I guess?'

'Yes. But you cannot use your existing drivers. They are Shi'a.'

Stanza suspected that Kareem and Farris would refuse to go anyway. But as far as he was concerned the fewer people the better – which raised the question of Mallory. Judging by the way the guy treated a simple drive to the Green Zone convention centre a jaunt to Fallujah would be way out of the question. But that would mean going without him. Still, a single security guard wouldn't be much help against an army of insurgents anyway and another white man could only increase the danger. Mallory probably wouldn't go anyway. The best thing was simply not to tell him. 'You've not discussed any of this with anyone else? The drivers? Mallory?'

'Of course not. You said I was not to.' Abdul hoped that Mallory would not be brought into it anyway. 'What would you like?'

'What do you mean?'

'What would you like me to do now?' Abdul watched Stanza, gauging him. The man looked doubtful about the operation and Abdul suddenly felt that he would choose not to go. The thought disappointed him and for the first time he found himself anxious for Stanza to act bravely. Abdul wanted very much to reverse the fortunes of Lamont but he had not realised until that moment that his heart was so very much in it.

Stanza went to the window in the hope of inspiration but all he could see was danger. 'I'll think about it. See what else you can find out about the route into the town, checkpoints, that sort of thing.' Stanza needed more time to decide. His journalist side was shouting at him to get on with it. But it was the self-preserving side of Stanza that was holding everything up. He was now fully confident that Abdul would arrange things if he was given the go-ahead but the thought of climbing into a car and driving to Fallujah filled Stanza with dread. His hand reached for his gunshot wound that had begun to itch.

'I will call my cousin. Perhaps he can make contact with someone in the Brigade today.'

Abdul's words only increased Stanza's anxiety. 'That would be great.'

'I'll call you later,' Abdul said as he went to the door. Stanza continued staring out of the window without acknowledging Abdul's parting words.

Abdul left the room, headed for the lifts and pushed the call button. He had not been entirely straight with Stanza and wondered if the journalist had suspected his minor manipulations. It might well have been possible to find someone who knew how to make contact with a member of the Black Banner Brigade in Baghdad but Abdul had no desire to try. Neither was he sure of Stanza's safety. Arabs did indeed respect the inviolability of a negotiations parley. But Abdul could not be certain whether that applied to the fanatical Takfiri who were the backbone of the Fallujah insurgency. Takfiri were the most dangerous individuals on the planet. Zarqawi and Bin Laden were Takfiri, an extreme faction of the Wahabi who were themselves extremists and, like the Taliban, believed that Muslims should live by the strictest rules of Islam. Abdul could only pray that those who were holding Lamont were more fiscally liberated. His focus now was truly on Fallujah. He believed the town was part of the path he had to take and that Allah was his guide. It was not difficult to understand why. Lamont was his salvation and everything that had happened since that night pushed him closer to it. His sister meeting Mallory at the hospital, Stanza, the destruction of Hassan were all signs. Stanza was the perfect means to establish Abdul's contact with the Brigade and he suddenly had no doubt that the journalist would decide to make the journey.

The sound of a door shutting caused Abdul to look up and he saw Mallory heading from his room along the corridor. Abdul stepped out of view and when Mallory did not arrive at the lift he assumed that the man had taken the emergency stairs. Something about Mallory bothered Abdul but he could not put his finger on it. Perhaps it was nothing more than the mistrust Abdul believed they had for each other. The lift arrived, a porter walked out pushing a baggage trolley, and Abdul stepped inside and touched the ground-floor button. A moment later he stepped out into the lobby and marched briskly across it to the main entrance. If Mallory should call after him he would act as if he could not hear him.

Abdul walked out of the hotel entrance onto the road and maintained a brisk pace to the US check-point as he ran through his plans. His first task was to get hold of Muhammad, his cousin, if the man was still in Fallujah, which he prayed he was, and get him to remain there. Muhammad was a greedy man and would do anything for money. All Abdul would have to do would be to hint at the possible financial rewards of helping to release an American hostage and Muhammad would cheerfully take his chances with any American assault on his town. Abdul was sure of that.

Mallory walked out of the fourth-floor emergency stairwell door onto the landing and headed for Des's office. He'd had a restless night thinking about his plans for Fallujah and had got out of bed at one point to pore over a map of the town and make notes. At dawn he telephoned his boss in London and arranged for his relief to come out to Baghdad as soon as possible. His boss called back shortly after to let him know that a guy called Johnson would be arriving in Amman in two days and would get into Baghdad the following afternoon to take over from Mallory. Mallory was committed one way or the other – Fallujah or home.

Mallory glanced over the rail and paused as he saw Abdul leaving the hotel. He wondered why Abdul had not contacted him and looked up at Stanza's door. Then again, Abdul was Stanza's fixer and it was really nothing to do with Mallory unless they wanted to go somewhere.

Mallory walked on, knocked on Des's door and on hearing a muffled 'Come in' pushed it open.

Des was at his desk concentrating on his computer monitor and looked up for a second as Mallory entered the room. ''Ello, me ol' cock, 'ow are yer?'

'Not so bad,' Mallory said, falling tiredly into the armchair.

Des concentrated on hitting a couple of keys and when he was satisfied they'd had the desired effect he pulled off his glasses to rub his eyes. 'Cuppa?'

'I'm fine, thanks. How's everything?' Mallory asked, getting on with the formalities.

'Can't complain.' Des sat back in his chair and exhaled heavily. 'We ain't lost anyone this week so it's nay s' bad.'

'Anything more on Fallujah?'

'What, about the Yanks goin' in?'

'Anything, really. Your man still embedding, is he?'

'Not sure now.' Then Des lowered his voice like a real gossip. 'I think 'e's 'ad a touch of the old cold feet about it. 'E's from a small radio network in Oklahoma and I think he's only finally got around to asking 'imself why 'e's riskin' 'is arse to send news over there when 'e can sit back 'ere in t' 'otel and pull it off wires.'

That was not what Mallory wanted to hear. His plan had been designed around the embed.

'Can't blame 'im, really,' Des went on. 'So many bloody rumours goin' around about what the Yanks are plannin' on doin' to the town and when they're goin' in and the resistance an' all. Yer don't know what to believe.'

'Have you still secured his embed?'

'Aye. 'E's still got a spot if 'e wants it. But I'm pretty certain 'e ain't goin'.'

'When is it for?'

'We're on standby. Some journalists 'ave already gone in, some of the big networks, a couple from each. If there's too many o' the boogers runnin' aroun' they'll be gettin' in the way of the Marines. Sounds a bit of a gang-fock media circus but there yer go. Are yer all right?' Des asked, his classic bulging-eyed grin appearing as if by a switch. 'Look a bit tired, lad. Not sleeping well?'

'I'm fine.'

'Tell me,' Des said, leaning forward, his voice lowering once again in a conspiratorial manner. 'Who were that lovely little thing you 'ad 'ere t' other day? Eh?'

'When was that?' Mallory asked, feigning ignorance.

'When was that, 'e says,' Des echoed with a chuckle. 'During rocket attack. In lobby. Little beauty, she were.'

'Oh,' Mallory said. 'She's the sister of one of our locals. She'd popped in to see him and I just happened to be on my way out when the boom-boom hit.'

'Know her well, do yer?'

'Nah. Just enough to say hello.'

'Just enough to say hello? You don't say too much when she stays over, then. I like that. All action.'

'What do you mean?' Mallory asked, looking Des in the eye.

Des winked at him. 'Can't get one past Des, me ol' cock. Jedel, our night watchman, saw 'er leave your room in the wee hours. 'Ay. Me 'at's off to yer. If yer can gerrit, go for it. Just watch yersel', though, laddy. They'll slit yer throat aroun' 'ere if yer dip yer wick in the wrong crease. Know what I mean?'

'Don't read too much into it, Des, me old cock. There was a lockdown, remember. She had to stay somewhere.'

'Well, just watch yersel', that's all, like I said. If Jedel knows then every bastard does.'

It was a concern to Mallory but he had other problems at that moment. 'Des . . . Let me ask you something. Getting back to the embed. If your man doesn't take that spot would you mind if I did?'

'Lookin' for a slot for your bloke then, are yer?'

'It's for me,' Mallory said.

Des raised his eyebrows. '*You?* As in yersel'?'

'Yes.'

353

''Ave I missed summat?'

'My relief arrives in a couple days and . . . well . . .
I'd like to see the fight.'

'You want to go to Fallujah on yer time off?' Des
asked with continuing incredulity.

'If you don't fill the slot.'

'You've been 'ere too long, me old cock. You need
to get 'ome, 'ave a few ales and a bit o' tatty. When
yer've got the taste back then call me and tell me yer'd
rather be in that shit-'ole op road.'

Mallory stared at him blankly in reply.

'You serious?' Des asked.

'Yep.'

'Why, fer God's sake?'

'Like I said. I'd like to see the fight.'

Des shrugged and shook his head. 'OK. If yer that
focken' mad I'll put yer name down and I'll give yer
a shout when the call comes in. You got a press pass?
They won't let you on chopper unless yer press.'

'I've got a pass.'

'OK. It's a thirty-minute standby.'

'I'm ready to go,' Mallory said. 'Oh. One other
thing. You got a spare room? I hand mine over to my
relief when he gets in.'

'Anything else I can do fer yer?' Des said sarcastically.

'Just in case I'm still on standby.'

Des sighed. 'Dougal is heading up to Arbil tomorrow
for a couple of weeks. You can use 'is room.'

'Thanks, Des. Much appreciate it,' Mallory said,
getting to his feet. 'I'll catch you later, then.'

'Yer not trying to be a reporter, are yer?' Des asked.

Mallory wondered if that might not be such a bad cover story. Des would tell just about everyone and it was better than being thought of as simply a mad bastard. 'Well, truth is I'm going to take a camera. Might be able to sell some pics.'

'Mad sod,' Des said as he put his glasses back on. 'Don't become one of that lot. You know what they say about media, don't yer? Responsible for 'alf the world's problems and all of its ignorance.'

'Photos tell the truth,' Mallory said, defending his cover although he would agree with Des at any other time.

'Do they fock,' Des said. 'It's not what the media tell or show anyway, it's what they don't tell and show that's the problem.'

'Well, it's more for the crack than anything else,' Mallory said, heading for the door. 'Catch you later.'

Des watched Mallory until he was out of sight before focusing on his computer monitor. 'Mad bastard,' he said, his mouth twisting in concentration as he stabbed at one of the keys, none too confident of its effect.

Mallory leaned on the rail and looked down into the lobby as he gathered his thoughts. All he could do now was wait and hope that the embed happened. It would see him to the outskirts of Fallujah in a US helicopter and then with the usual chaos of battle he would slip away from the media gang and head for the cemetery. It had been a long time getting to this stage and, as expected, a tingling of apprehension had arrived with it.

Tasneen entered his thoughts, followed by Des's comments about her being in his room. He would rather no one knew but it was not a major drama. Their conversation the evening before had set him thinking of her until he'd fallen asleep. It had begun with Abdul, of course, but once Mallory had reported how well her brother had done on his first day they had moved on to other matters. They'd ended up not only talking about cycling holidays but practically agreeing to plan a tour of France together one day. It had been bizarre in many ways and Mallory wondered if they were truly hitting it off or just living some kind of fantasy. He had an urge to call her but decided to put it off for the moment. His retrieval mission was, with luck, about to begin and his concerns for its success as well as for his own survival were gnawing at him.

The plan's biggest flaw was that it depended heavily on factors over which he had no control. There were essentially three main phases to his mission: the move to Fallujah; the move to the cache; the extraction back to Baghdad. The embed with the US Marines would cover phase one but the problem there was where precisely that would put him on the map. The Marines had many options for taking the town and Mallory needed to be in the right place on the outskirts before his move in. The Marines might decide to form up on one side of the town and push through on a broad front, herding the enemy back into ambush positions. Or they might drive a wedge through the centre of the town and then continue to subdivide it into pockets to prevent the enemy from regrouping and coordinating their defences. Another option would be to press in from all sides, bulldozing the enemy into a central point while artillery and air power concentrated fire into an ever-shrinking area. Then again, they might just bomb the town flat for several days before walking in to see what was left. Whatever the method, Mallory needed to be in a position to get to the cemetery as soon as it was overrun.

Mallory headed back to his room to pack. Des could call him to move at any time and he needed to be able to just snatch up his gear and go. It was entirely possible that within a few days he could be heading back to the UK with a bag full of cash. It was a nice thought and one that Mallory tried to keep in the forefront of his mind. But it kept on getting overtaken by a feeling that something was going to go terribly wrong.

12

The Betrayal

Abdul cleared the last hotel checkpoint and headed towards Sadoon Street where he hoped to find a taxi. A horn beeped and he looked across the road to see Kareem's car pull over and stop. The window opened and Kareem leaned out. 'Abdul! Come here!' he shouted.

Abdul would have liked to avoid the man but he was too close to walk away and ignore him for no reason.

'Are you going home?' Kareem asked as Abdul approached.

'Yes, but I can get a taxi.'

'Get in. I will take you.'

'No, truly. That's OK,' Abdul said.

'Please. It is my job and I insist.'

'You are very kind but I can get a taxi.'

'Please, it is no problem for me. I would rather drive you than have you wait for a taxi.'

Abdul was sincere and was not indulging in the Arab propensity for extreme politeness. But Kareem clearly took his resistance as simply good manners and, determined to give Abdul a ride, was not backing down.

'Are you sure?' Abdul finally asked, giving up after deciding there was no harm in it. He wanted to be alone but would have to wait until Kareem dropped him off.

'I insist. It would be my pleasure,' Kareem said, smiling thinly.

Abdul walked around to the passenger side and climbed in. 'You are very kind,' he said.

Kareem carried out a multi-point turn in traffic to head back the way he had come. 'Al Mansour?' he asked.

'Thank you.' Abdul nodded.

They drove in silence until they reached the Jumhuriyah bridge, Kareem glancing at Abdul every now and then as if trying to think of something to say. 'How are you enjoying the job?' he finally asked.

'It seems very nice.'

'You have been very useful. Finding the house. Jake was very pleased.'

'Yes. That was lucky.'

'You knew Mallory from before, of course?' Kareem glanced at Abdul for a reaction.

'No.'

'Oh?' Kareem sounded surprised. 'But I thought he hired you because you were friends.'

'I did not know him before I arrived.'

'You mean before the hospital.'

Abdul did not understand. 'Hospital?'

'I first saw you at the hospital talking to Mallory.'

Abdul did not remember seeing Kareem that day. 'That was the first time I met him.'

'Ah . . . Then the woman you were with . . . she knew Mallory.'

'She is my sister.'

'Then that explains it.'

Abdul wondered what it explained but not enough to ask.

'You live with your sister?'

'That's right,' Abdul said, becoming irritated with the cross-examination.

'So she has known Mallory for a long time, then,' Kareem persisted.

Abdul glanced at him, wondering what was up with the man. 'No,' he said.

Kareem looked surprised. 'Are you sure?'

'Why are you asking me? I know my own sister.'

Kareem sighed as if something was weighing heavily on his mind. 'I am confused, then. That is all. So you were at the Sheraton when she was with Mallory?'

'What are you talking about?'

'The day of the rocket attack. Your sister was at the hotel.'

'I know. She was with a friend. A girlfriend,' Abdul said, annoyed with this fat Shi'a sticking his nose into his affairs.

'I am sorry, but the woman I saw you with at the hospital was at the hotel with Mallory and not another girl.'

Abdul stared at Kareem, his eyes narrowing.

'I saw her go into the restaurant with Mallory,' Kareem went on. 'Then the rockets hit. I would have asked you how she was after the attack, but later I heard she was fine.' Kareem glanced at Abdul long enough to see the other man's stare burning into him.

'What are you trying to say?' Abdul asked coldly.

'This is very difficult, you understand,' Kareem said.

'Tell me.'

Kareem was having doubts about taking the subject any further. His purpose for revealing what he knew was straightforwardly malicious. He enjoyed gossip and even though the implications of his information were dire only now did he appreciate the full gravity of it. 'I am only saying this because I am more your brother than I am Mallory's. You are Sunni but you are also Muslim and Arab. That is important to me.'

'I asked you what you are trying to say,' Abdul said softly but firmly.

The horn of the car behind honked and Kareem moved over to let the driver pass. 'A woman left Mallory's apartment early the next morning, after the rocket attack. She was seen by Jedel, a security guard at the hotel.'

'My sister?' Abdul asked.

Kareem shrugged nervously.

'And how can you be certain it was her? Did you see her?'

'No. The description was the same, though.' Kareem suddenly feared he had underestimated the other man who had more of an aura of power about him than he had first suspected. 'You are right. People should not jump to conclusions. This is a serious accusation . . . You would have known if your sister had not come home that night, of course,' Kareem said, glancing at Abdul who was looking ahead. 'I am sorry. Forget all that I have said.'

They did not speak for the rest of the journey and when Kareem stopped the car outside Abdul's apartment block the one-handed young man climbed out and walked away without saying another word.

Abdul walked up the stairs, opened his front door, stepped inside, closed the door behind him and remained rooted to the spot, horrified. The news had rocked him. It was possible the hotel security guard had lied or Kareem had made it up but Abdul knew in his heart that it was true. His sister had lied to him. Tasneen had spent the night with Mallory, a white man, an infidel.

Abdul sat on the couch as his stump began to throb slightly. But this was too serious an issue for him to be distracted even by this reminder of his mutilation. His sister, the most important person in his life, had betrayed him, the family, their name, their heritage, and Allah. She had defiled herself. Not only had she been with a man out of wedlock but it had been Mallory, a man he did not trust. Abdul realised that what he sensed about Mallory's attitude to him, what he took for suspicion, was something far worse. Mallory had been laughing at him.

Abdul rested his head on his hand and closed his eyes tightly as the torment swirled like a storm around him. He had thought that he knew Tasneen better than anyone but now it seemed he did not know her at all. She was everything to him: she was perfection. Now he could barely comprehend how in one short space of time she had destroyed their entire past together. She had lied from the beginning about Mallory and therefore every second, from the moment of their meeting on, had been a lie. Voices in his head began to chant, a single cry at first. Then others joined in, voices of his family but not just those of his father and mother. It was a collective cry from generations of his line. He was head of the family: his was the last remaining name on earth to represent them and they were calling to him from a thousand graves and over a thousand years, gathered in chorus, baying for justice, punishment. Tasneen must pay, they cried. She must pay. They both must pay!

Abdul got to his feet, went into the bathroom, turned on the tap and vigorously splashed his face with cold water. But the voices did not relent. Retribution, they clamoured. Revenge was the cry, and then he heard faint music, an Arabic song that he recognised. It was his cellular phone ringing in his pocket.

He pulled it out and looked at the display. Stanza. Abdul did not want to talk to anyone at that moment and he let it ring on. When it went quiet he walked back into the living room and considered what to do. The phone came to life once again and he checked the screen. It was Stanza again. Abdul knew the man well enough already to know he would call until Abdul answered. He pushed the receive button and put the phone to his ear. 'Yes?'

'Abdul?'

'Yes.'

'I've decided to go – to Fallujah.'

Abdul should have told him that he could not discuss it at the moment but the draw of the town suddenly grew in his mind to equal the overriding obsession of his sibling problem.

'Did you hear me, Abdul?'

'Yes.'

'I've just heard from a reliable source that the Americans may be attacking in under a week. I want to be out of Fallujah before the offensive begins.'

'I have not yet talked with my cousin,' Abdul said.

'Well, do it now, and let me know.'

'OK . . . I will.'

'Is everything all right?' Stanza asked, sensing an oddness about Abdul.

'All is fine.'

'I'll wait for your call, then,' Stanza said and ended the conversation.

Abdul lowered the phone and stared at the flower-pattern carpet as if in a trance. Going out of town would give him time to think, which he needed to do. Grave decisions had to be made. It would be best if he was not in the apartment when Tasneen returned. Masking his feelings would be difficult if he had to face her so soon.

Abdul scrolled through the numbers on his phone and hit the call button. A moment later it picked up. 'Muhammad. It's Abdul, your cousin. Tasneen's brother,' he added.

Muhammad was besotted with Tasneen which was another reason he would be eager to help. He sounded

364

pleased to hear from Abdul and after the initial pleas-
antries asked about his sister. Tasneen detested the man
but Abdul lied that she had asked after Muhammad's
health and sent her regards. Muhammad expressed his
strong feelings for her, as usual, and at the first opportunity Abdul declared he was coming to visit. The
announcement, as expected, gave Muhammad pause
and Abdul went on to explain how he needed his
cousin's help – and that it involved money. Muhammad
was now all ears. Abdul explained about the American
hostage and the newspaper journalist, emphasising the
funds available to pay those who assisted in the
endeavour. As Abdul had expected, Muhammad was
entirely at his service.

The first thing Abdul asked for was an accurate and
reliable route into Fallujah. Muhammad offered several.
Abdul chose the one closest to the route he knew –
he'd been to Fallujah only once since the war. The
town was forty minutes west of Baghdad by motorway
in normal traffic and the back roads would more than
double the time, depending on any obstacles encountered. Muhammad warned of an American checkpoint
on the motorway that could be avoided by heading
north a mile before it at Abu Ghraib. The route would
then take them along country lanes and eventually
lead into the town from the north. The Americans had
Fallujah pretty much surrounded but there were gaps
in the encirclement with which Muhammad was
familiar. Muhammad warned Abdul, however, that their
problem was not so much the Americans as the insurgents and sympathetic villagers who had set up their

own checkpoints inside and outside the American cordon. These checkpoints were not coordinated – they were run by local thugs monitoring their own patches. Most of the hard-line insurgents were in the town itself, preparing defences for the battle. Abdul should be prepared to bribe his way through these checkpoints but Muhammad was uncertain about the wisdom of attempting the journey with a white man. Still, a western reporter might be allowed in. Some insurgents would want the battle to be recorded from a point of view other than the American military's but others might kidnap the journalist simply because he was a westerner. Abdul told his cousin that he would call if he needed more advice and after Muhammad wished him luck he disconnected the call.

Abdul hit a couple more buttons on his phone and a few seconds later Stanza picked up. 'We go tonight,' Abdul said.

'Tonight!' Stanza echoed, surprised by Abdul's speed.

'Going at night will be best.'

Stanza pulled himself together and silently reassured himself that he could cancel at any moment. 'OK. How will we get there?'

'My car.'

'You want me to drive?' Stanza asked, his voice rising.

'I can drive. Or you can if you prefer.'

There was another long pause before Stanza spoke. 'What time were you thinking of leaving?'

'We should leave soon after dark.'

'OK. Come to my room. I don't want to be hanging

around outside.' A beep indicated that Stanza had cut the call and Abdul checked the phone to make sure.

Abdul took a moment to think what he might need to take with him and pared it down to just a pistol and money. He needed to get fuel for the car – he could quickly get the small mechanical problem it had fixed – but other than that his cousin would take care of all their needs in Fallujah. The rest was up to Abdul and his wits. It was Allah's mission but He used mortal tools to achieve His aims and if they were not up to it then He would allow them to fall.

Abdul went into his room, opened his wardrobe and removed the box that contained his pistol. He pocketed the gun and went back into the living room where he opened a drawer in the side of the coffee table and took out a notepad and pen. He needed to let Tasneen know that he would not be home for several days, otherwise she would be worried and look for him. He would also have to tell her he was going out of the city or she would wonder why he could not come home.

He considered telephoning her and then dismissed the idea in favour of the note. If he spoke to her he would have to deal with a myriad of questions but worse than that his anger might reveal itself and Abdul did not want to deal with the problem of her relationship with Mallory until his return. The ramifications of that issue crowded his mind and the pain of accepting that his relationship with his beloved sister was at an end was like a burning knife in his heart.

But Abdul warned himself not to linger on the past.

His religion, tradition and a thousand ghosts would not allow it: Tasneen and Abdul's lives were inconsequential when compared with the greater scheme of things. He could not begin to fathom why she had done such a thing – but then, there could never be an explanation that would satisfy him. There was no acceptable explanation why she had gone alone to a man's private room. Staying the night put it beyond all reason. Death was a more acceptable option than dishonouring herself and her family. She was a Muslim, an Arab, an Iraqi. What made it even more horrendous, if that was possible, was who she had done this foul deed with. Had he been an Arab and a Muslim Abdul would still have wanted revenge. But to defile herself with an infidel – with Mallory, an Englishman – was beyond comprehension.

Abdul suddenly felt painfully alone, more than ever before, beyond the loneliness that had engulfed him when his father had kicked him out of the house for deserting the army. And it was going to get much worse between him and Tasneen before he could put it in the past. He thought about seeking advice – from a mullah, perhaps. But that would mean airing his family's shame in public and he could not do that. It was bad enough that the likes of Kareem knew. And how many others by now? The shame of it all intensified at the thought of the gossip that was being spread around at that very moment. The stain on his line would be there for ever. It was more than an obligation to exact revenge. It was Abdul's duty.

Mallory should be the first to suffer because Tasneen

would have to know that he had been punished before her own sentence could be carried out. She would have to recognise the enormity of her sin and be aware that her partner in this crime had paid the ultimate price. Abdul would give her time to ask Allah for forgiveness before he sent her to Him.

The horror of what Abdul had to do was vivid in his mind but he believed in its necessity wholeheartedly. He had a great deal to do during these coming days. So much that it began to seem impossible to achieve. But it was not impossible. He had dealt with Hassan, a test of fire that he would have believed beyond him had he consciously made it his mission when he'd set out that night. He would find the American hostage, he would kill Mallory and then Tasneen: when it was over he would have truly reached manhood and would be free of the chains of his youth, his soul cleansed of sins, and free to pursue a purified life.

Abdul took a deep breath and scribbled a few lines on the page. He decided to reveal that he would be staying with Muhammad in Fallujah while he, Abdul, was with his reporter boss. Muhammad would use Abdul's visit as an excuse to call her anyway. It was of no consequence if she knew where he was. He no longer needed to deceive her about anything. Before her execution he would tell her the truth about his hand and inform her that he had killed Hassan in revenge. She would depart this world knowing she was leaving behind not a little brother but a man.

Abdul put the pen down, leaving the page on the

table, and got to his feet, feeling in his pockets for his car keys, gun and identification card. Satisfied that he had everything he needed he went to the front door. Then he paused to look up at the Koran on the shelf. He took it down, held it most reverently, closed his eyes while he asked Allah for the strength that he would need, kissed it and returned it to the shelf.

He closed the door behind him.

Stanza drew the cord tight on his backpack and wondered if there was anything else that he needed to take. He had his satellite and mobile phones, tape recorder, camera, plenty of pens and notebooks, his toothbrush and toothpaste, a flashlight and all of the bureau's money – six and a half thousand dollars – except for a thousand left behind as a reserve. He checked his watch and looked outside to see that the light was fading. The tingling fear had not left him since Abdul had called to say they were going into Fallujah that night. Sometimes it got so bad that he had to sit down and go through his mission to reassure himself. He knew it was madness, that he was taking a great personal risk. But then, great things were never achieved without those elements being present. He told himself he had to keep that in mind. It was the madness of his adventure that would later be interpreted as dedication to his work and set Stanza apart from all the others. He was going into the gorgon's lair for sure, but what he would retrieve would be the envy of everyone in his profession. There wouldn't be a journalist or media organisation in the entire world who would not know his name.

It was the moment of truth. Stanza could grab the chance for fame and glory or let it pass. Few people ever got such opportunities and if Stanza turned away from it his life would effectively be over. At the end of the day the choice was between possible death or certain oblivion for if he ignored this opportunity he would fall into the void. In the end, actual death was better than that.

A knock startled him into standing up. He walked to the door, opened it and Abdul marched straight in. Stanza's stare was fixed on the young Arab as he followed him into the room. 'Is everything OK?' he asked.

When Abdul looked at him his lips formed a thin, reassuring smile. 'Are you ready?'

'I am,' Stanza said, nodding slowly and deliberately.

Abdul could see that Stanza had wrestled with the decision and that his courage had emerged victorious. But he wondered how long it would last. 'Good.'

'How long do you think it will take? I know we can't know for sure – but an estimate?'

'I am hoping that one day will see our first contact made,' Abdul said. 'After that . . . it depends on the result of the meeting. If we are lucky we can return tomorrow.'

'Good.' Stanza nodded. It was precisely what he wanted to hear. 'You have a route?'

'Yes. We head up the motorway and before the main

checkpoint we turn off and head east, then north. I have directions.'

'Why do we need to avoid the American check-points?' Stanza asked. 'Surely they would be points of safety for us.'

'The answer is simple. They will not let us through. We do not live there so we cannot pass.'

'And the insurgents' checkpoints? How do we deal with them if we meet them?'

'But that's who we are looking for,' Abdul said. 'We have to meet them sometime and begin our negoti-ations.'

Stanza had come to the same conclusion but wanted to hear it from Abdul. His confidence in the young man had increased but the fear would not leave him.

'I am in as much danger as you,' Abdul said, reading Stanza's concerns.

Stanza looked at the young Arab. 'Why *are* you doing this?'

Abdul was not sure how to answer. He did not care to reveal his reasons to the American but he still felt an explanation was needed. 'Guilt,' Abdul said. 'Anger.'

'I don't understand.'

'I have no purpose. Up until now I have only been a victim.' Abdul felt his stump. 'I want to become involved . . . This is a beginning perhaps.'

Stanza was still not clear about Abdul's reasons but the young man appeared sincere enough.

'Are you ready?' Abdul asked.

'Let's do it,' Stanza said, removing his jacket from the back of the chair, pulling it on and picking up his backpack. As the two men stepped towards the door there was a distant boom, followed by a low rumble that gently rocked the balcony windows. Stanza paused for only a second before walking out of the room. He locked the door and followed Abdul along the landing.

Tasneen closed the apartment door and tiredly pulled off her jacket as she headed for the kitchen to make herself a much-needed cup of tea. She saw the sheet of notepaper on the coffee table and at first ignored it. But as she turned on the electric kettle she had second thoughts and went back into the living room. On reading the few lines she was instantly filled with dread. Fallujah had been on everyone's lips that day at the Palace: the general consensus among the Americans seemed to be that not only was the battle imminent but the town with its estimated thousand insurgents was going to be levelled.

Tasneen scrambled for her phone and dialled Abdul's number. It rang for a moment until the irritating female voice broke in to inform her that the phone she was trying to call was either switched off or out of the coverage area.

She paced the room, wringing her hands, and then scrolled through the phone list until she came to her code name for Mallory. She waited impatiently for it to ring.

'Mallory here,' he said almost immediately.

'Bernie. It's Tasneen.'

'Tasneen,' he said, delighted.

'Bernie, where's Abdul?'

'Abdul? I don't know.'

'What's he doing? I must talk to him.'

'I haven't spoken to him since yesterday.'

'You must know where he is?'

'What's wrong, Tasneen?'

'Don't you know he's in Fallujah? I just got home and found a note from him.'

'Fallujah?' Mallory said, obviously astonished. 'Why is he going there?'

'I have no idea. Are you sure?'

'I must find him. If he's not going with you, what is he doing?'

'Look. No one's going to Fallujah. Certainly not Abdul. Stanza's said nothing to me.' But as soon as the words left his lips Mallory knew he was wrong. Stanza had been acting weird all day. Then there'd been the sighting of Abdul that morning. Mallory had known that something was up but frankly hadn't cared enough to find out what.

'Abdul would not make it up, Bernie. Not something like this.'

'Can I get back to you?' Mallory said, heading for the door. 'I'll find out what's going on and call you back.'

'Please, Bernie,' Tasneen said pitifully.

'I will. Soon as I know. I'm going now. Bye.' Mallory ended the call as he walked out of his room towards Stanza's. Perhaps Stanza had sent Abdul to Fallujah for something. The man was stupid enough to do that.

He knocked on Stanza's door and when there was no immediate answer he knocked again more loudly. 'Stanza,' he called out. 'It's me. Mallory.'

Mallory dug out his phone, brought up Stanza's number and hit the send button. The line rang and then suddenly stopped as if the phone had been turned off. Mallory dialled Abdul's number and, according to the young lady's recorded voice, it was either switched off or beyond signal range.

Mallory's feelings of concern deepened. Something was going on that he was not privy to and he felt that he was being tugged in several different directions. On the one hand he shouldn't have cared because he had his own mission to complete. But on the other, Abdul's life could be at risk and Mallory had responsibilities on that score, his own as well as those he had to Tasneen. The other issue was of course Stanza's security but Mallory wasn't particularly bothered about that – beyond a niggling sense that it was one of his professional duties. The first thing to do was find out where the pair were. He scrolled to another number and called it.

'Kareem? It's Mallory. I'm looking for Abdul.'

Kareem explained how he had dropped him off at Abdul's apartment and when Mallory asked him if he knew anything about a trip to Fallujah Kareem said that he knew nothing. Kareem had not talked to Stanza all day but he did have one bit of bad news: Farris was leaving with his family for Jordan in the next couple of days. Mallory had no interest in Farris at that moment so he ended the conversation and went to the rail to look down into the lobby. Stanza's absence from his room was bothering him since there was nowhere to go in the hotel, unless the journalist had made some friends. Stanza didn't go to the gym and usually had one of the drivers bring him food from outside at around this time. Kareem hadn't heard from him and Farris was out of the loop now, it seemed. As for his work, Stanza was not booked on an embed – Mallory would have known about that – and he could not have taken an Arab with him anyway.

The little creep of a reporter was up to something but worse, he was avoiding Mallory and Mallory resented that hugely.

Mallory's phone chirped and he snatched it up to look at the screen before answering, expecting it to be Abdul or Stanza. In fact, it was Des. This was not a good time. He hit the receive button and put it to his ear. 'Mallory.'

'Where've you been?' Des asked. 'I've been calling you for ages.'

'You know how the phones are.'

'You still want the embed, yer need to get to helipad in twenty minutes. Go like mad 'n' you could make it.'

Mallory suddenly didn't know what to do. 'Have you seen my journalist?'

'What?'

'Stanza. The one who got shot.'

'No, mate. Do yer want this embed or what?'

Mallory squeezed his forehead with his fingers as he fought to make a decision. Then something else dawned on him. 'Shit, I don't have a driver.'

'Right. One o' mine is just leaving the hotel. I'll

give 'im a call and tell 'im to meet yer outside the far checkpoint. If yer run yer might make it.'

'OK . . . OK. Bye.' Mallory killed the call and stood tensely, trying to decide what to do. This was what he had been waiting months for. It might be his last chance. God only knew what would happen to Fallujah after the Americans went in. The cemetery could get blown to bits. The town could get shut down for months or even longer. He could search for Abdul and Stanza all night and not find them. Or if he did and they were doing nothing more than having dinner in the Palestine Mallory would be furious. And – worst-case scenario – if indeed they had gone to Fallujah, which Mallory still could not believe, it was out of his hands anyway.

'Bollocks,' he said as he hurried back into his room, snatched up his backpack, and broke into a run towards the emergency stairs.

Abdul's car was parked away from any others in the hotel-complex car park, beneath a couple of parched eucalyptus trees, and Stanza paused in front of it.

'You sure you're OK to drive?'

'It's an automatic,' Abdul said as he put the key in the door.

Stanza did not look any more convinced.

'If we get stopped I will have to do the talking,' Abdul said. 'I also know the way.'

Stanza's expression did not change – Abdul could easily mediate and navigate from the passenger seat.

'Then you drive,' Abdul said, shrugging with indifference.

'What the hell. Go ahead,' Stanza said as he moved to the passenger door. 'If I get crazy with your driving we can always stop and swap over.'

As both men opened their doors a dark muscular-looking Mercedes sedan cruised into the car park, the wheels that supported the four tons of armoured glass and bodywork crunching over the gravel. It stopped a short distance in front of Abdul's car, bathing the two men in its powerful headlights.

Abdul and Stanza squinted at the vehicle as the engine died, leaving the headlights burning. Both rear passenger doors opened and two men climbed out. One stayed beside his open door while the other walked to the front of the Mercedes. He gave a discreet hand signal and the headlights died.

'Jake,' the man said.

Stanza strained to see who it was but could only make out that the man was Caucasian and was wearing a tailored jacket with a crisp white open-neck shirt beneath. 'Who am I talking to, please?' he asked, somewhat pathetically. The man standing by the open rear door moved away from the car a little and Stanza saw some kind of rifle in his hands.

'Name's Bill Asterman,' the man at the front of the Mercedes said in a distinctly Midwestern American accent. 'I'm from the embassy.'

'The American embassy?' Stanza asked.

'That would be correct,' Asterman said dryly.

Stanza looked around, wondering if other embassy guys were standing in the darkness. It was very sinister. 'What . . . what can I do for you guys?' The man's features became a little more visible. He looked middle-aged with that polished clean-cut bearing one associated with Secret Service types.

'Where are you headed, Jake?' Asterman asked.

'How do you know me? My name?'

'Jake Stanza of the Milwaukee *Herald* . . . That's not a secret, is it, Jake?'

'Well. That . . . that's me.'

'I asked where you were headed?'

'Headed?' Stanza repeated, sounding pathetic even to himself, unable to be more assertive.

'Yeah. As in where are you going?'

'I'm . . . I'm er, heading out, with my translator.'

'Yes. But where is "out"? Where are you going?' Asterman's voice was a patient monotone.

'Do you mind if I ask who wants to know?' Stanza ventured bravely.

'I'm an official of the US government. *Your* government . . . We have responsibilities to you, Jake. But you also have responsibilities to us . . . So why don't you just tell me where you're headed?'

Stanza wasn't sure of his ground. He'd never come across government types like this before. 'The convention centre . . . We're heading over there for a meeting.'

Asterman took a packet of cigarettes from his pocket, toyed with it for a moment then brought both hands up to his face. A second later a flame appeared illuminating his cropped blond hair and when his hands went back down he had a cigarette in his mouth. One of his hands went back into his pocket while the other returned to his mouth to remove the cigarette and allow a long stream of smoke to escape. 'The convention centre? There are no pressers today. Who you meeting?'

The man had all the airs and attitudes of an interrogator and Stanza had the sudden feeling that this stranger actually already knew a whole lot about what Stanza was really doing. 'Why are you so interested?' The journalist tried to lighten his tone by forcing a smile but he could not sustain it.

'That's my job, Jake . . . So, if you don't mind, I'll ask you again. Where are you going?'

'I told you,' Stanza said, clearing his throat nervously.

Asterman took a slow draw on his cigarette and blew the smoke out towards Stanza through pursed lips. 'I'll tell you something, Jake. In my job I rarely ask questions I don't know the answer to.'

Stanza told himself to get a grip: he was perfectly within his rights to go wherever he wanted in Iraq. He was the press, after all. 'OK,' he said, putting a little starch into his backbone. 'You wanna know where I'm going, then you say you know where I'm going. Fine. I don't know why it's any of your business but I'm going to Fallujah.'

'Why are you going to Fallujah?' Asterman asked in the same monotone. It was beginning to irritate Stanza.

'I'm a journalist. Dozens of journalists are going to Fallujah. There's a damned battle about to take place there,' Stanza said. The growing irritation in his voice was a substitute for genuine confidence.

'But are you going to Fallujah just as a journalist?' Asterman asked.

'Why else would I be going there?'

'What's the story, Jake?'

'What the hell is this all about? Huh? I don't have to tell you anything.'

'And you know why that is, Jake?'

Stanza gritted his teeth. 'Because you know everything? You tapping my phones and my e-mails? Is that it?'

'You're aware of our policy about negotiating with kidnappers,' Asterman said.

'I'm aware of your policy. But that's *all* it is: a policy, not a law.'

'Where did you get the idea that you could do whatever you wanted in this country?' Asterman asked.

'So what are you trying to tell me? That I have no right to try and free an American from captivity? You think that's gonna fly? Tell me some more. I'd love to write that story.'

The man took a final draw from his cigarette and tossed the glowing butt to the ground. 'I have a responsibility for your safety, Jake. It's not true that I can't stop you. But I respect your freedom. I'd just like *you* to respect *our* efforts to maintain national security.'

'You've got to be kidding me. How the fuck does this affect national security?'

There was an uneasy silence for a moment until Asterman eventually spoke. 'What if I told you I could block the ransom money?'

'I'd say you were full of shit. If they cut his head off that would put the knife in your hands.'

There was another long silence.

'You gonna stop me or not?' Stanza asked.

'Like I said, Jake. I respect your freedom . . . Gonna be a tough drive, though.' Asterman looked over at Abdul, his gaze falling on the young man's stump. 'Off the record, Jake. One American to another. That's a mean road you're gonna have to take. A lotta tougher folk than you have tried it and failed.'

The sound of footsteps crunching the gravel caused the spooks to turn instantly. The one by the open door raised his M4 assault rifle as another climbed out of the front passenger side, a pistol in his hand.

Mallory walked past the Mercedes, his small back-pack over his shoulder. 'Evening,' he said to Asterman as he carried on across to Abdul. 'Keys,' he said, holding out his hand.

Abdul had remained perfectly still throughout the exchange, unable to understand the game being played and concerned that the American official was going to stop them going to Fallujah. Mallory's arrival caused Abdul's heart to race and he lowered his head, unable to look the man in the eyes for fear that his own stare might reveal his hatred. He dropped the car keys into Mallory's outstretched hand.

Asterman looked from Mallory back to Stanza and sighed deeply. 'You know what happened to Pierre Dusard, John Santez, Mike Kominsky, Paul Jerome, Natasha Kemp, all media freelancers who went into Fallujah a week ago?'

Stanza stared coldly back at Asterman, suspecting that he could guess the answer.

'Neither do we. And we know more than most.' Asterman walked back to his open door and climbed in. His men did the same. The Mercedes's engine and headlights came to life again and after the heavy doors had closed it reversed a short distance, pulled a slow, tight turn and cruised out of the car park.

When Stanza looked over at Mallory his security adviser was staring back at him coldly. 'Are you gonna tell me I can't go too?' Stanza asked. 'Because if you do I'll tell you the same thing I told him.'

Mallory had been jogging past the end of the car park heading towards the checkpoint, when he'd seen Stanza in the headlights of the Mercedes some distance away, just before they went out. He'd heard most of the conversation, unable to tear himself away, and when he realised Stanza was going to stick with his plan to go to Fallujah it seemed that the only thing he could do was join the journalist and Abdul. Travelling with them legitimised his trip to Fallujah – he was responsible for their security, after all. It was still crazy but now that it was probably too late to catch his embed he was left with the same choice as before but with a different way of achieving it. He chose to go for it.

'Get in the car,' Mallory said to them both.

Abdul climbed in the back as Mallory sat behind the wheel. Stanza remained standing outside. 'Are you getting in or not?' Mallory called out, starting the engine.

Stanza leaned down to look at Mallory. Several

things were playing on the reporter's mind, but eventually he climbed in and closed the door. Mallory put the car in drive and they headed out through the checkpoints.

After the last chicane the car turned along the potholed road that led to Sadoon Street and they crawled along, steering left and right to avoid the worst of the hazards. Before they reached the main road where traffic was passing in both directions Stanza held up his hand. 'Stop the car,' he said.

Mallory glanced at him. 'What, here?'

'I said stop the car.'

'This is not a good place—'

'STOP THE GODDAMNED CAR!' Stanza shouted at the top of his voice.

Mallory was angered by the sheer petulance of the command but the man was clearly upset about something. He brought the car to a halt.

Stanza clenched his jaw. 'What the fuck is GOING ON?' he shouted before turning in his seat to look at Abdul. 'You ever see that guy before?'

Abdul shook his head. 'No.'

'Tell me something. What the fuck are you doing here? Huh? Why are you here?'

'You asked me that already,' Abdul said.

'A sense of fucking purpose? Bullshit! A chicken-shit kid like you wants to go with me to the most dangerous goddamned town in the goddamned world because you're feeling left out of things?'

Mallory stared ahead, knowing that his turn was surely coming.

Abdul remained calm. 'I will not die for you if that's what you think. I believe in what we are doing.'

Stanza stared at the young man for a few seconds, unable to decide if his reply was in any way convincing. Then he turned to Mallory. 'And what the hell is your excuse? Huh? You have more chance of getting whacked than I do. At least I have some value as a journalist if we get caught. They'll label you CIA and slice your goddamned head off in a heartbeat . . . Well?'

'You'll think my reason is stupid.'

'No kidding. Why should you be the only person in this car with an intelligent reason for going to that shit-hole? . . . No, please tell me. I'd like to hear anyway.'

'Well. The truth is . . . I'd like to see the fighting. I missed most of the war and to be honest this might be my last chance to see a full-on battle.'

'You want to go and watch the battle?! Christ, now I really am worried . . . Do you know why I'm going?'

'Lamont . . . I heard most of the conversation between you and the spook and I can figure out the rest.'

'What were you doing in the car park?' Stanza asked, suddenly wondering.

'I saw you both leaving the hotel and I was curious.'

'And you just happened to have your backpack with you.'

'If you were going out I was going too. You two've been sneaking around devising some kind of conspiracy,' Mallory said, starting to raise his voice. 'I'm the one who should be pissed off here. I'm in charge of security and you two planned a trip to Fallujah without even consulting me.'

'And you can't figure out why?'

'Damn right! I would've said no.'

'Then what the hell are we doing now?'

Mallory exhaled as he lost the edge of his feigned anger. 'I decided that what you were doing was . . . well, a pretty good thing. Maybe you should do it or at least try. And I couldn't just sit back in the hotel room and let you go alone.'

Stanza looked ahead quizzically, then glanced between Mallory and Abdul again before facing the front. 'I don't know what to think any more. But something stinks about this whole thing. You. Him.'

Mallory decided to shut up and let Stanza work his way through it. The man was indecisive but now it looked as if the decision to go was all down to him. Mallory could only wonder how he'd got into this position.

Abdul remained quietly in the darkness of the back of the car, unsure of what to make of the pair of them.

Mallory studied the darker shadows around them. The lone car with its engine running and lights on would eventually attract attention, not only from bad guys but from any army or police who happened to be in the area.

'I'm not sure if I have the strength to say that we should go any more,' Stanza finally said. 'If you leave it up to me I think I'll say go back to the hotel.'

Mallory shifted in his seat, wondering how he could manipulate Stanza's uncertainty. 'Why don't we just head out of Baghdad, assessing the situation as we go? We don't need to take stupid risks if we play it right. If it starts to look dodgy we abort and come home.'

Stanza looked at Mallory. 'You want to go that bad?'

'Stanza,' Mallory began, sounding tired of him. 'I don't care if you want to go back to the hotel. It's fine with me. But I bought into your mission to try and save Lamont. I think it's a noble idea and I have not been on a noble mission for quite some time now. So why don't you just run through all the reasons you wanted to go to Fallujah in the first place – quietly in your head, if you don't mind – and if they no longer work for you then let's turn around. But do me a favour. Make your decision fast because I don't want to sit in this street like a fucking target for a moment longer. And if it's a yes, I don't want to hear you whingeing to go home half a mile up the road. I run the road trip until we start the negotiations and then it's all yours.'

They sat in silence for a moment. Stanza shifted uncomfortably. 'I'm sorry. You're right . . . Asterman spooked me,' he said.

'That's what he was trying to do,' Mallory said.

'I'll leave it up to you. You're the security expert. If you think we should go then we'll go.'

'Oh, for fuck's sake,' Mallory said as he put the car in gear. The bat was back in his hands and he had already decided what he would do with it despite the constant doubts. The car crawled out of a water-filled pothole and bumped its way to the end of the road. Mallory paused at the junction for a gap in the traffic and quickly cut across the oncoming lane to join the handful of cars heading north.

13

Into the Breach

Mallory adjusted the rear-view mirror: he watched it as much as he looked ahead – his normal technique whenever he pulled away in a vehicle. This time his concern was more acute than ever. His usual plan in the event that they picked up a tail was to head for the nearest US checkpoint. But on this night they were heading out of Baghdad, away from nearby safe locations, and picking up a couple of bandits would create problems. It was impossible to detect a follower quickly if the driver behind had any level of skill. The trick was to find a distinguishing feature of any suspect vehicle that would be easily recognisable further into the journey.

Stanza picked up on Mallory's vigilance. 'You think he might follow us?'

'Who?'

'That jerk Asterman.'

'I can't think why.'

'Because we might lead him to Stanmore.'

'Who?'

Stanza sighed. 'Lamont's real name . . . It doesn't matter right now.'

Mallory nodded. The details held little more than a mild interest to him. 'Asterman won't follow. If he gets too far from the safety of the Green Zone he'll attract more attention in that armoured Merc than we will in this piece of shit . . . No offence meant, Abdul.'

Abdul ignored the comment and Mallory glanced at him in the mirror as he steered around the Jumhuriyah roundabout and onto the bridge.

'Abdul knows a route into Fallujah,' Stanza offered.

'Abdul?' Mallory said, looking for a response to Stanza's comment.

'You are heading for the ten motorway?' Abdul asked.

'Yes.'

'Take the ten and I will tell you where to turn off.'

Mallory checked the lights in the rear-view mirror again to see that the configuration had changed. He memorised the new image and settled down as they left the bridge and turned right at the Assassins' Gate towards Haifa Street.

'Don't take Haifa,' Abdul said calmly.

'I wasn't going to,' Mallory said. Haifa Street was probably the most dangerous stretch of residential road in Baghdad after the BIAP. US convoys could expect some sort of attack every time they went down it. Mallory took the next turn left at the Al Mansour Hotel, cut across town towards the disused Baghdad Airfield that was now a US military camp and headed east on the main surface streets to the entrance of the ten motorway. Traffic was light and after they mounted the access ramp a glance in the rear-view mirror revealed that they were alone.

The black surface of the motorway stretched ahead of them with only a sprinkling of tiny red and white lights along it. Ten minutes later they passed a sign for Abu Ghraib and Abdul sat forward in his seat as if suddenly taking an interest in the journey. 'That's the prison,' he said and they all looked to the right at the long, brightly lit and ominous wall topped with razor wire and sentry towers. The car passed through an underpass and Mallory noted they were now the only vehicle on the road in either direction.

'Mobile phones don't work beyond here,' Abdul said, referring to the poor signal reception. 'The first American checkpoint is about a mile further on. We must turn off soon.'

'What do we turn off onto?' Mallory asked. 'A road, track, what?'

'A track through a gap in the barriers,' Abdul said, peering into the distance in an effort to find it. 'There!' he suddenly called out, pointing to the near side.

Mallory slammed on the brakes and the car's tyres screeched loudly. Before it came to a stop Mallory slammed it into reverse and the occupants jerked forwards as the vehicle accelerated backwards, snaking from side to side as Mallory avoided the crash barriers. They passed the gap, Mallory applied the brakes – with less of a screech this time – threw the lever into drive, which caused a crunching sound, and the car shunted forward. He turned off the road and down a steep bumpy embankment after which the ground levelled out again. The headlights exposed deep tyre tracks in the sand and Mallory followed them into the blackness.

'How far along this track?' Mallory asked, deciding to get all the information he could from Abdul ahead of time to avoid any more emergency stops.

'You will come to a road soon. We go left.'

The sandy track was awkward to drive along at any great speed with several soft patches that threatened to suck them to a standstill if Mallory got too slow. He maintained the vehicle's momentum to push them through and after half a mile they mounted a solid bank and bounced over an edge onto a narrow tarmac road. Mallory braked hard as he turned the wheel in an effort to keep all four tyres on the road. He had only partial success. But the verge was firm and eventually he managed to steer back onto the tarmac and accelerate away.

'What's next?' Mallory asked, peering ahead along a straight dark road that the headlights failed to illuminate adequately. Open countryside was on either side of them, with clumps of bushes and trees lining the road.

'Stay on this road for a few miles,' Abdul said.

'And then what?' Mallory persisted.

'We pass through some villages and then we come to a river, which we will follow.'

'What about the US military?' Stanza asked.

'What about them?' Abdul asked.

'For Christ's sake. Where are they?' Stanza asked excitedly.

Mallory glanced at the journalist, wondering exactly how strung out he was.

'I do not know where the Americans are,' Abdul said. 'They could be anywhere . . . They are not your only problem, though.'

'Don't you just love the way he says "your problem" and not "ours"?' Stanza mumbled.

Several squat angular shapes appeared up ahead and a moment later a dull orange glow became evident inside some of them. It was a small mud-brick hamlet of dilapidated dwellings, several with benzene lamps but with no other sign of life other than a corral of aimless-looking cows and goats. The car's headlights swept across the animals as it passed through the village.

Mallory was maintaining a pace that would only just allow him time to react safely if something appeared in the headlights. He took a moment to run through in his mind the technicalities of a handbrake turn. He'd done one only once before – for a laugh when he'd been a young Marine out with some of the lads.

A T-junction appeared eventually and Abdul instructed Mallory to take the left turn. The other minor roads they had been on since leaving the motorway had been quite straight but this one snaked tightly. Mallory soon realised they were following the line of a small river mostly hidden behind a lush bank of trees and bushes. They shadowed the waterway for several miles before eventually moving away from it and straightening up again. A fork in the road appeared and Mallory slowed, expecting Abdul to give him directions but none came. He turned to see Abdul looking ahead, a confused expression on his face.

'Well?' Mallory asked.

Abdul's expression did not change.

Stanza looked around at him. 'Which way?'

'We should come to a crossroads after the river,' Abdul said.

'Which way did your cousin say to go at the crossroads?' Mallory asked.

'Across.'

They stared at the junction for a moment.

'What came after the crossroads?' Mallory asked, breaking the silence.

'A fork.'

Mallory sighed in frustration. 'Which way at the fork?'

'Left,' Abdul said, suddenly irritated that Mallory assumed he had got the crossroads and the fork mixed up. 'My cousin told me a crossroads was first.'

Mallory made an executive decision and accelerated into the left-hand road. 'What came after the fork?'

'Another crossroads.'

They drove along the winding road into increasing darkness that the car's headlights struggled to penetrate. All eyes were glued to the beam as a faint glow on the horizon hinted at a town ahead.

Stanza clasped his clammy hands together, his breathing quicker than normal. Since leaving the city he'd more than once had the urge to slam the dashboard and demand that Mallory turn around and head back to the hotel. The fear of running smack-bang into death at any second grew with every bend in the road – he felt as if he was playing some insane game of Russian roulette. But he could not say what kept him from giving in to his fears. It was not embarrassment, nor the dim hope of getting the story of his life, nor the chance of saving Stanmore's life. What kept Stanza from cracking wide open was the connection he had made with his old self. It was not all that long ago that Stanza would look forward in an odd kind of way to dangers such as the race riots he had experienced. This mission to Fallujah was far more dangerous, of course, but the buzz was similar and he needed to find that part of himself again.

This was a new epoch in journalism, the age of the media warrior. More journalists were dying for the cause of getting a story than ever before and Stanza was a part of this brave new era. But simply holding on while the possibility of unknown horrors loomed closer was proving to be the most difficult thing he had ever done in his life.

Mallory realised he was gripping the steering wheel too tightly and forced himself to relax. His stress was intensifying with the feeling that he was possibly driving into hell on earth. He could imagine his reaction if someone had casually asked him in a pub back in Plymouth if he would risk his life for a million dollars. It would have been a resounding 'not likely'. Yet here he was. It was supposed to have been an exercise in planning and logistics but had grown slowly into an obsession. Pride was a killer of men, he remembered someone saying, a British affliction that the Royal Marines were so good at instilling into young men. Mallory was a finisher at heart, something he had learned about himself during commando training. But he also liked to think that he had *some* common sense, at least. This adventure was proving otherwise. Mallory didn't want to become a victim of his own pride, but it might already be too late.

The headlights suddenly illuminated several cans and large stones in a staggered line across the road and Mallory took his foot off the accelerator as his mind raced to decide if he should stop or keep going. As they moved closer a figure moved from the roadside bushes into the light of the beam, a young man in a scruffy *dishdash*, holding something long that was hidden in the folds of cloth at his side. Another man with a shabby *shamag* wrapped around his head and carrying a short pole stepped into view behind the first.

Everyone in the car tensed, Abdul gripping the back of Stanza's seat with his one hand.

Without any conscious thought Mallory hit the accelerator, pushing the pedal to the floor and willing the car to turn into a rocket. But time seemed to slow to a crawl and the car felt as if it had hardly speeded up at all. Two more men appeared from the other side of the road, stepping into the middle of it. The first man held up a hand, signalling the vehicle to stop, but Mallory bore down on him.

One of the front wheels struck an obstacle and the men made a concerted effort to dive out of the way.

But the corner of the car struck the first man's legs, the second faring only slightly better as one of the headlights shattered. The other pair scrambled in their sandals to take evasive action on the loose surface. Mallory swerved in an effort to avoid them but there was a quick succession of thumps and the remaining headlight exploded.

'Down!' Mallory shouted as he continued to swerve the car from left to right, expecting a volley of bullets to follow them. He could barely make out the road ahead by the dim glow from the sidelights and it seemed like an age before the sound of gunfire eventually started behind them. None of the bullets seemed to strike the car. Mallory hit the high verge on the edge of the road and kept going until they were out of direct line of sight. He pulled the car over in an effort to keep it in the centre of the road and they drove on, the weak sidelights struggling to illuminate the road more than a few metres ahead.

Mallory took his foot off the accelerator to slow the vehicle down. 'Everyone all right?' he called out, glancing at Stanza who had his hands pressed tightly against the sides of his head as if he did not want to hear. 'Stanza?'

Stanza flashed Mallory a startled look.

'You OK?'

Stanza nodded. 'We're not going to do that again, are we?' It was more of a request than a question.

'Abdul?' Mallory asked.

'I'm OK,' Abdul said quietly from a corner of the back seat.

'What now?' Stanza asked.

'What do you mean?'

'We can't continue!' Stanza said, an octave higher.

Mallory steered around a curve, his eyes searching ahead in the gloom and then slowed to a stop before turning off the engine and lights. He opened his door and climbed out.

Stanza suddenly felt vulnerable and climbed out on his side. Mallory was looking up the road in the direction they had come. 'What are we doing?' Stanza asked in a low voice. It had gone strangely silent after the ambush incident.

'I'm listening,' Mallory said.

'You think they might come after us?'

'No.'

'Do you think we hurt anyone?'

The back door opened with a creak and Abdul climbed out.

'Mallory?' Stanza was seeking an answer to his question.

'I think they'll think twice next time before they try to stop a speeding car with their bodies.'

Stanza was in no mood for any flippancy. 'What do we do now?' he insisted.

Mallory wished the man had a little more backbone. He'd given Stanza credit for beginning the journey but had suspected that he might crumble at some point. 'We go on . . . The problem's behind us.'

'What if we want to go back? What if we had to?'

'We can't. Not the way we've just come . . . I'd have thought that was obvious.'

'But if we did want to,' Stanza said. 'If we did, how could we?'

'Don't ask me. Ask Abdul.'

'I only know this route from here,' Abdul said.

Stanza looked up the road ahead, into the darkness, accepting that it was the only way to go but not liking it one little bit.

The sound of a very heavy engine starting up not far away got their attention and seconds later another grumbled to life with a throaty roar.

'Tanks,' Mallory said.

'They coming for us?' Stanza asked, alarm in his voice.

'Doubt it. Changing location, perhaps. They could be half a mile away. Difficult to tell at night.'

Mallory went to the front of the car and looked along the road into the darkness. 'We can't stay here and we can't go back,' he said.

'But what if we run into more of the last lot?' Stanza asked.

It was a good question that Mallory had no answer for.

'You should let me drive now,' Abdul said.

Both men looked at him.

'Get into the back, into the trunk. I will drive us through another checkpoint.'

Stanza's expression went from perplexity to astonishment. 'In the trunk?' he squawked.

Mallory's initial reaction was not far off Stanza's. But as he thought through their options, it seemed to him that, unsavoury as it was, Abdul's suggestion was probably the wiser course. The real question was whether or not Abdul could be trusted. There was something odd about the Arab that Mallory had not noticed before. He appeared more confident and self-assured but there was something else, something less definable, about him.

Stanza was looking at Mallory. 'You obviously don't think it's a bad idea,' he said accusingly.

'Maybe it isn't. Compared to our other choices.'

The rumbling engines grew louder and sounded as if they were heading towards the group.

'If the Americans catch us they'll probably hold us before sending us back,' Mallory said. 'Maybe for a day or so. Point is, this little adventure will then be over.'

That didn't sound like such a bad idea to Stanza.

'We can't be far from Fallujah,' Mallory said, looking at Abdul.

'A mile, maybe.'

The engines continued to draw closer and Mallory went to the trunk of the car and opened it. Inside was a box of what looked like spare parts, an empty fuel container and some rags. 'Now or never, Stanza . . . Make your mind up.'

Stanza could not get his feet to move. Why were there so many opportunities to quit? He groaned. It was like being compelled to jump off the roof of a skyscraper onto a blanket only to find oneself on another roof with yet another small blanket far below to jump onto. This time all he had to do was climb into an airless space and continue into hell blindfolded.

The distant engines sounded as if they were moving

behind them. Stanza looked at Abdul to assess him one more time, a man he hardly knew and in whose one hand he was expected to place his life. 'Ah, Jeezus,' he said as he gritted his teeth, walked to the trunk and placed a foot inside.

'Wait a minute,' Mallory said as he removed the fuel container and box and threw them into the bushes. 'In you get.'

Stanza obeyed.

Mallory joined him. When they were lying down Abdul took hold of the top of the lid and studied them for a moment. 'I'll do my best to get you there,' he said before slamming the trunk shut.

'I could have thought of more encouraging things to say under such circumstances,' Stanza said in a low voice, his lips close to the back of Mallory's head. The car lurched a little as Abdul climbed in.

He started the engine and was about to turn on the sidelights when he changed his mind. He put the gear change into drive and headed slowly down the road.

His eyes gradually grew more accustomed to the dark and he increased his speed.

Mallory and Stanza lay spooned together in the blackness, their hands braced against the sides of the trunk to keep from bashing into them. Mallory's concern inevitably increased now that he had relinquished all control to Abdul. He told himself he could trust the guy but that belief depended wholly on the fact that Abdul was Tasneen's brother. There was something oddly amusing about his predicament and had he been

401

with a fellow bootneck he might have joked about it. But Stanza was clearly not the person to share such bizarre humour with.

Abdul wound down his window, wondering if he would still be able to hear the tanks. He couldn't. The crossroads appeared and he passed straight over without slowing. As he reached the top of a gentle rise a yellowy glow lay spread out ahead of him. It was Fallujah – very close.

He turned on the sidelights to provide some illumination and the bushes and scruffy vegetation that had lined the road gave way to a broad expanse of open ground. Pinprick house lights appeared and Abdul remembered his cousin telling him to leave the road at that point and drive across the open hard-packed ground, heading directly for the town.

Shortly after leaving the road a long dark scar appeared ahead of him. Abdul realised it was the motorway that passed north of Fallujah and connected Baghdad with the Jordanian border. It was the same motorway that they had driven out of the city on and it was empty. His directions were to head right alongside an earthwork barrier in front of the motorway until he found a well-used gap through it. The gap in the silhouette was easy to spot, and Abdul drove through. When he reached the edge of the tarmac he stopped the car.

Muhammad had warned him that crossing the motorway at this point might be dangerous. The Marines were known to take pot-shots at vehicles avoiding their checkpoints and he would be in full view for several seconds.

Abdul took a moment to mention to Allah that he understood his life was in His hands and He was free to take it or otherwise. As soon as he had finished his short prayer he felt confident that Allah would not have brought him this far to die so uselessly. He pushed the accelerator pedal to the floor.

The engine roared as the wheels mounted the road, sped across the lanes, through the corresponding gap in the meridian and across to the other side. But as Abdul reached the edge he panicked as he realised that the motorway was far higher than the ground beyond and he was going too fast. The vehicle shot off the side and was practically airborne for a few seconds as the nose dropped to strike the dirt surface on the other side.

Mallory and Stanza were thrown against the roof of the trunk, against the petrol tank as the front wheels hit and when the rear wheels touched down they were hammered back against the floor.

The car immediately stalled and Abdul worked quickly to restart it, conscious that he was still in the open and a sitting duck. The engine came to life at the first try and, thanking Allah out loud, he accelerated ahead, the car fishtailing in the soft soil as he aimed for a gap between a row of squat buildings.

No sooner had Abdul rounded the corner of the end building when two youths, red *shamags* wrapped around their heads and faces, exposing only their eyes, one of them brandishing an AK47, stepped from the shadows and forced him to brake hard. They approached Abdul's side of the car, the boy with the gun holding it at the ready. He looked as though he meant business.

Abdul wound down his window. '*Salam alycom*,' he said to the boy with the assault rifle who had stopped a short distance from the car.

'Where are you going?' the boy asked.

'To visit my cousin, Muhammad Rahman,' Abdul said.

'Why are you here?'

'I have come to join the fight, of course,' Abdul said.

The boy remained suspicious and moved to look through the windows and inspect the back seat. Abdul noted his gaze wandering towards the trunk. 'Does your friend need a weapon?' Abdul asked.

The youngster's attention immediately went back to Abdul who was reaching into his pocket. He retrieved his pistol and held it out for the boy.

'What's in your other hand?' the boy asked suspiciously, bringing the end of the barrel up to meet Abdul.

Abdul held his stump out of the window. 'A gift from the Americans,' Abdul said. 'I have come to return it.'

The boy appeared to accept Abdul immediately and his stare fell back on the weapon.

'Take it,' Abdul said.

'What will you fight with?' the boy asked.

'My cousin has others.'

It was difficult to judge the boy's expression behind his *shamag* but Abdul thought it softened as he took

404

the weapon. His friend stepped forward, anxious to have it. The boy handed the pistol to his colleague who inspected it eagerly.

'Be careful. It is loaded. Kill as many as you can,' Abdul said as he started to pull away. 'Allah be with you,' he added.

The boy stepped forward as if to stop Abdul. But he changed his mind and let him go, joining his friend to look at the pistol.

Mallory and Stanza had frozen the moment they'd heard the voices. They waited tensely for the trunk to open, their faces red in the glow of the brake lights. Neither of them could scarcely breathe, fearing this was the moment of their discovery. When the car shunted forward and accelerated away they were both exhausted by the tension.

'Are we in the town, do you think?' Stanza asked.

Mallory shushed him. Their fates were in Abdul's hands and there was no point in discussing anything until they were out of the trunk.

Abdul drove slowly along a narrow residential street, trying to work out his location according to his cousin's instructions. Only after turning right at a major road did he recognise where he was. A group of men, some with rifles slung over their backs, were up ahead, working by the light from a benzene lamp. They appeared to be moving some heavy items from the back of a pick-up truck into a house and as Abdul passed he saw a stack of large artillery shells. One of the men looked around at him and Abdul immediately faced ahead, prepared to stop if the man so much as lifted a finger. The man went back to directing his workers and Abdul suddenly felt a heightened nervous respect for the spirit of the town. It was as if the very buildings were holding their breath in anticipation of a coming storm.

He turned a corner clumsily, having to use his knees to get the wheel around before his hand could assist. There was activity in this street too with more armed men stacking sandbags to make what looked like a firing position, a collection of RPG rockets and ammunition boxes inside it. It seemed that everywhere there were signs of the great defence that the insurgent leader Zarqawi had threatened.

Mallory and Stanza lay wide-eyed in their uncomfortable confinement, their faces dimly illuminated by the rear lights of the vehicle. Mallory strained to look through a small hole in the tail light but could make out very little other than that they were in a town. The car was moving more slowly than before, swerving from one side to the other as if negotiating obstacles in the road.

Stanza was practically numbed by the entire experience, unable to see anything, and had somehow placed himself in a Zen-like state in order to get through the journey. His eyes finally opened when the vehicle came to a stop and the engine and lights went off. The pair remained frozen once again, all their senses tuned to the goings-on outside their metal shell.

One of the doors opened and the weight shifted as if Abdul had climbed out. This was followed by the sound of footsteps, but they were moving away.

'He's not coming to let us out,' Stanza whispered anxiously. 'What shall we do?'

'We're doing it,' Mallory said, adding a 'Shh.'

Mallory thought he could hear voices, followed by what sounded like a wooden door closing. A moment later the vehicle sank slightly as someone climbed in, the door closed and the engine came to life. They shunted forward slowly, took an immediate turn followed by another and a few seconds later slowed and went over a bump before coming to a stop again. The engine died, the driver climbed out and this time the footsteps came around to the back of the car. There was some shuffling, followed by the sound of wood creaking and then what sounded like a pair of large doors banging together. A moment of silence followed. Then Mallory and Stanza flinched as the trunk lock clunked loudly and was opened.

The two men remained in their dark pit like a couple of helpless animals, blinking up at a naked light bulb dangling on a wire between Abdul and another Arab who were looking down on them.

'This is my cousin Muhammad,' Abdul said.

Muhammad, who was older than Abdul, much fatter and looked nothing like him grinned broadly as he offered a hand to Mallory. Mallory took hold, assuming it had been offered to help him out, but Muhammad shook Mallory's hand weakly and let go.

'*Salam alycom*,' Mallory said as he pushed himself up, grabbed the side of the trunk, and got out. He stretched to relieve the stiffness in his back.

'*Alycom al salam*,' Muhammad said, placing a hand on his chest as he bowed slightly. 'Welcome, welcome.'

Mallory forced a smile and nodded.

'Hello,' Muhammad said, grinning and bobbing his head in a servile manner. He extended an arm towards an open door. 'Hello,' he repeated, indicating they should go that way, using the word with more versatility than Mallory was used to.

As Stanza climbed out of the trunk Mallory took a look around the dingy room that was filled with junk of all descriptions, none of it valuable. Stanza brushed himself down and shook the cousin's offered hand. The man bid him hello and indicated the open door again. Muhammad shuffled towards the door and Abdul indicated that the others should follow.

Muhammad led them along a short corridor to a doorway with a curtain across it. The air here smelled like a strong mixture of mildew and kerosene fumes, an aroma explained by the contents of the room that Muhammad invited them into. He held back the curtain to reveal a dark interior more than amply furnished with cushions of every size and colour, though black and burgundy were the most prevalent. Rugs covered every inch of the floor and a good portion of the walls. The tobacco-stained ceiling was streaked with cracks. Everything was bathed in an orangey glow from a benzene lamp on a large circular copper-tray centrepiece that was suspended a few inches off the ground on a wooden frame. Muhammad was evidently proud of his living quarters and confidently invited his guests to choose a place to recline.

The sound of cutlery tinkling against glass came from behind another curtain suspended across a corner of the room. Mallory and Stanza lowered themselves onto a cushion each and stretched their feet towards the copper tray while Abdul and Muhammad, who were having what appeared to be an intense conversation, sat opposite. The curtain moved aside and a heavily veiled woman in an *abaya* stepped out of a tiny kitchenette, carrying a tray on which were four small glass cups that were half filled with sugar. A little teapot stood beside them. The woman's dark eyes were barely visible through the narrow slit of her headpiece and she avoided eye contact with everyone as she placed the tray on the table and filled the cups with a tan liquid. No sooner had she completed that task than she went behind her curtain and drew it back across.

Muhammad smiled broadly once again as he invited Mallory and Stanza to indulge in the tea. After the two westerners picked up their cups Abdul and Muhammad took up theirs, resuming their conversation. Mallory was certain that he heard the name Tasneen mentioned a couple of times whereupon Abdul glanced at him. The two men eventually faced the westerners.

'My cousin welcomes you to his house,' Abdul said.

Mallory and Stanza nodded politely.

Muhammad's smile disappeared while he sipped his tea and did not return when he replaced the half-empty cup back on the tray. He asked Abdul something and the reply was accompanied with a shrug. Then Abdul indicated Stanza with a jut of his chin whereupon Muhammad's gaze fell on the journalist. Muhammad said something while looking at Stanza and Abdul nodded.

'Muhammad asks if you have any money with you.'

'What does he want money for?' Mallory asked.

The men exchanged glances while Abdul relayed the response. The cousin appeared annoyed as he rambled on, using hand gestures to emphasise certain points. When he stopped he looked between Mallory and Stanza.

'My cousin asks . . . how can you negotiate without money?'

Stanza was the one who now looked irritated. 'We don't need money to begin negotiations. When we finally agree on a price the funds can be transferred.' Stanza looked at Muhammad in a wearily superior manner. 'Why is he asking me about money? Has he made any contact with the kidnappers?'

Abdul talked at some length with his cousin before facing Stanza, his fingers scratching an itch at the end of his stump. 'Muhammad has made contact with someone who can take us to a member of the Black Banner Brigade. He needs to find out which hostage you are interested in.'

'What do you mean, which hostage?'

'I did not tell Muhammad Lamont's name over the phone. But you have also called him by another name.'

'Stanmore, yes. But they will know him only as Lamont, unless Lamont has told them his real name . . . How many hostages do they have, anyway?'

Abdul said something to Muhammad who shrugged as he rattled off a list of nationalities that Mallory and Stanza did not understand for the most part. Abdul repeated them as best he could in English: 'British, French, Italian, German, Portuguese, Armenian, Turkish, Kenyan, Somalian, Nepalese, Chinese, Japanese, Americans and dozens of Iraqis.'

Muhammad said something as he picked up his tea.

'He . . .' Abdul began. Then he took a few seconds to rethink his words. 'He asks how much he is to get. He thinks it should be a percentage of the ransom.' Abdul looked down at his stump as if distancing himself from the question.

Stanza looked at Mallory, then back at Muhammad. 'Can you believe these fuckin' monkeys?' he said.

Abdul looked up at Stanza sharply.

'How can this guy ask for a percentage?' Stanza asked. 'Is he one of the kidnappers?'

'My cousin has nothing to do with kidnapping. But Muhammad believes that if he is to risk his life for the American he should get something for it.'

Muhammad said something which Abdul repeated. 'Are you getting paid for coming here?' he said.

Stanza sighed. 'I will pay him. But not a percentage.'

Abdul spoke to Muhammad who looked away as if he had been insulted.

Stanza threw up his hands. 'OK. What the hell. Sure, why not? Take a piece of the action. It's not my money and I'm sure Stanmore's old man would agree. What percentage does he want?'

Abdul asked his cousin who replied after a moment

of thought. 'He thinks ten per cent is fair,' Abdul said.

'*Ten?*' Stanza said, breaking into a laugh. 'These fuckin' people . . . OK. It's a deal. Who the fuck cares? Just do me a favour. Can we put his money to one side for now? Your cousin will get paid, I promise him that. Can we get this ball rolling now? I'm here to get Stanmore, not spend my time haggling with your cousin over his goddamned fee.'

Abdul said something to his cousin who thought about it for a moment before replying. When Abdul responded there was a hint of frustration in his voice. Muhammad eventually nodded in agreement and got to his feet, said 'Hello' to Mallory and Stanza and left the room by another door that appeared to lead to the front of the house.

Stanza and Mallory both looked at Abdul for an explanation.

'He has gone to contact those who have Lamont.'

'Just like that,' Stanza said. 'What they got, some kinda store down the road with a hostage section?'

Mallory dropped his head into his hands, suddenly feeling exhausted. The stress of the evening was catching up with him. He felt it was going to be a long night and he just wanted to lie back and sleep.

A distant explosion rocked the building enough to fill the air with dust from the many cracks in the walls and ceiling. Stanza looked at Mallory, then at Abdul, both of whom appeared to have ignored the blast. A shot was fired close by, then another in the distance, followed by more. Then silence.

Stanza ran a hand through his hair and massaged his neck. 'I'm bushed,' he said to no one in particular. Then he lay back, rested his head on a cushion, stretched out his legs and closed his eyes.

Mallory contemplated doing the same but then felt Abdul's stare on him. When he looked up the young Arab looked away. Again he sensed something odd about the man. He'd caught Abdul looking strangely at him a couple of times now and each time the Arab looked away as if he was hiding something.

Mallory slid down the cushion until his head was resting on it. He closed his eyes and decided to rely on his hearing for security for the moment. He reasoned that snatching a rest was only sensible as there was no way of knowing when their next opportunity might be. But as soon as he began to relax a distant voice warned him to be cautious, a voice clearly recognisable even though he had not heard it for many years. It was that of his first troop sergeant at 42 Commando, Muggers Mugrich – the unsmiling one, as he'd been known.

It was strange how that particular man's image had emerged from the lower reaches of Mallory's memory. He had not seen or thought about Muggers for years. Shortly after Mallory's arrival in the troop, his first draft since passing out of commando training, it had been tasked with taking part in one of the last tours of Northern Ireland, a pointless task to all concerned as the IRA had long since been defeated. Most of the deployment duties consisted of long walks across stretches of the border where little of any great significance had happened for an age. The last incident had been so far back, in fact, that the intelligence officer whose job it was to provide such historical background information during the operational briefing wasn't quite sure what it had been. The military wing of the IRA had seen the last of the wind removed from their sails when their essential funding and support from the USA was brought to an abrupt end after the 9/11 terrorist attack. What little was left of their struggle was diminished as much by the rising tide of Islamic terrorism as by their own internal corruption.

But Muggers treated the operation the same way he did every task, even the most boring exercises, and that was as if the screaming hordes might come over the top at any second. It was considered a certainty that if any member of the patrol fell asleep on sentry duty Muggers would catch them – and when he did, woe betide that individual. Harsh as his punishments often were he was a likeable character who offended few because he was always right and fair and, after more than twenty years in the mob, there wasn't much he didn't know about the business. Mallory had almost nodded off only once in his entire military career. Muggers caught the young Marine as his heavy eyelids were starting to close. 'Fight it, laddy,' Muggers said softly from behind him and Mallory's eyes snapped open. 'Think of something violent that makes you angry. Like someone attacking your mother, or your sister. It'll get your blood up and put a touch of adren- alin into your system and you won't sleep for a while.'

Mallory never forgot the advice and it had served

him well on many an occasion. But despite his memory of it he drifted away on the feelings of nostalgia it brought with it and while mentally reliving those good old days he forgot to think of something that made him angry. Mallory had no idea precisely how long he had been asleep. What woke him up was another soft voice coming to him as if from the end of a long tunnel.

'What?' Mallory said, his eyes opening abruptly to see the dull cracked ceiling with its flickering patterns created by the light of the benzene lamp.

'I asked if you had any family.'

Mallory fought to marshal his senses and remember where on earth he was. 'Family?' he said as he realised that he was in Fallujah and the voice was Stanza's.

'As in wife and kids,' Stanza said.

Mallory looked over at the man who was lying fully stretched out on the rug, staring up at the ceiling. 'No,' he said. Mallory looked around the room to discover that they were the only two in it. He got quickly to his feet.

'Not even a girlfriend?'

Mallory went to the curtain in the corner and pulled it aside to reveal that the tiny kitchen space was empty. He went to the door Muhammad had left by and opened it enough to look into a dark empty hallway with the front door at the end.

'If you're looking for Abdul he's gone,' Stanza said. 'His cousin came back for a couple of minutes. They had a brief talk, kinda secretive, and then they both left.'

Mallory lowered himself into the chair Abdul had been sitting in and felt the shape of his pistol inside his front pouch.

'*Do* you have a girlfriend, then?' Stanza asked.

Mallory wondered why Stanza was intent on pursuing such a trivial subject in the light of their situation. Then again, trivia was probably what they should be discussing at such a time. They had relinquished control of their lives and were at the mercy of so many different forces that it made a mockery of the central concept of Mallory's job, which was risk management. 'No,' Mallory said. An image of Tasneen's pretty face came into his mind's eye. At that moment his pursuit of her seemed as ridiculous an adventure as the one he was currently involved in.

'I suppose it's difficult in your job,' Stanza said.

'Is it any easier in yours?'

'I don't go away as much as I imagine you do.'

'You have a wife and kids?' Mallory wasn't particularly interested, but since they were on the subject he felt he might as well ask.

A smile twisted Stanza's face. 'No. Never been lucky in that department. Almost. Had a wife, that is, but never got far enough to contemplate kids. I don't think I'd make a good father.'

Mallory thought about asking why and then decided not to.

'I'm too selfish,' Stanza said anyway. 'That's also what went wrong with my relationships . . . all of 'em. Too tied up in my own world. The irony was I was never that interested in journalism. Not really. Not passionately like some. But I did want to succeed. So I kept on trying and didn't have time for anyone else . . . Is that a pointless life or what? Eh?' Stanza glanced over at Mallory to see if he had been listening.

Mallory had been only half-attentive – he'd drifted away to reflect on his own life. But he caught Stanza's question and look. 'My philosophy has always been never to regret anything,' Mallory mused. 'You take the right fork and even though it wasn't ideal you might not have survived the left . . . For what it's worth, that's my philosophy.'

'Yeah . . . Basic, but I guess it works,' Stanza said.

'Well, maybe if I reach your age I'll have managed to work out something a little deeper, but that's where I've got to so far.'

A sound came from the front hallway and Mallory got to his feet while Stanza sat up.

The door opened and Muhammad looked alarmed as he eyed the two men. He immediately stepped aside to make way for a fierce-looking Arab dressed in a dark, soiled *dishdash* with a well-worn leather jacket over the top. He was carrying an AK47 and his stare flicked to Mallory's hand as it moved to his pouch.

The man took a couple of steps into the room and looked around quickly. Stanza got to his feet as Abdul, looking as if he had seen a ghost, walked in behind the stranger. Behind him was another Arab who moved like a beast in search of raw meat. He was far more tense and murderous-looking than his colleague and his leathery face was covered with a wiry black beard. The hatred in his narrow dark eyes was unmistakable. He gripped a Russian PK belt-fed machine-gun rifle, heavier than his comrade's AK47, and looked as though he would like nothing better than to cut loose with it.

The first Arab, who was clearly the senior of the two, said something while keeping his gaze fixed on Mallory.

'He asks who is the one he should talk to about the hostage,' Abdul said.

Stanza forced a smile as he stepped forward to offer his hand. 'My name's Jake Stanza,' he said.

The Arab ignored the hand while he studied Stanza from head to foot. He said something else, his voice cold and assertive.

'He asks what you want,' Abdul said.

Stanza cleared his throat. 'I'd like to interview Jeffrey Lamont. Would that be possible?'

Abdul translated and the Arab replied. 'Is that all you want – to talk to him?'

'N-no . . . no,' Stanza stuttered in an effort to correct any misunderstanding. 'I have the authority to nego-tiate a payment for his release. A ransom.'

Abdul translated and the Arab scrutinised Stanza before replying.

'He will take five million US dollars,' Abdul said.

Stanza nodded. Sweet and to the point. But now that he was finally in the position he had been looking forward to he felt insecure and unsure how to conduct himself. 'Fine . . . Fine. That's a lot of money,' he said. The only concept of negotiating that Stanza had was, ironically, one of the basic Arab rules of bargaining: don't settle for the initial price.

The Arab's expression remained icy as he uttered a few words.

'What do you offer?' Abdul translated.

Stanza rubbed his brow nervously. 'I was thinking in the region of a couple of million. But . . . Well, I'll gladly put that to my people. I'm only the go-between,' he stammered, forcing a smile that quickly became a nervous grimace.

Abdul repeated Stanza's words and the Arab replied. 'He doesn't think you are in a position to negotiate, which is not a healthy position to be in.'

'B-but I am. I am.'

Mallory looked at Stanza, realising that his life was now in the hands of this twat. This was not a factor he had considered before and he decided that he wasn't about to let Stanza take him down with him. 'Ask him for proof that the hostage is still alive,' Mallory interjected.

The Arab looked at Mallory as Abdul interpreted the question.

'Would you like an ear or a finger?' Abdul translated the response.

'That's not proof of life,' Mallory said. 'Stanza – ask him something,' he ordered.

'Ask what?' Stanza was flustered. 'I don't understand.'

'A proof-of-life question.' The irritation in Mallory's voice was clear to all.

'Like what?'

'I don't know, for fuck's sake. The name of his pet fucking goldfish. Something that only his father would know.'

Stanza rubbed his forehead as he struggled to think. 'Ask him what his favourite beer is.'

'For God's sake,' Mallory said, looking up at the ceiling. 'We are fucking dead.'

'His father owns a brewery,' Stanza shouted.

'They could get that off the bloody Internet,' Mallory retorted. 'Something only his old man would know. His mother's pet name or maiden name. You've come here to negotiate for a man's life and you don't know the first bloody thing about it.'

'Shut up,' Stanza yelled as anger fused with his fear. 'I need to talk to him,' Stanza said to Abdul. 'I need to talk to Stanmore . . . Lamont. That's the proof I want that he's alive. Let me talk to him and then I'll get the money.' Stanza's desperation was clear – and distinctly unappealing.

Abdul relayed what Stanza had said. The first Arab replied and left the room before Abdul could translate. The murderous-looking Arab remained a moment longer to stare at the white men with his hollow black eyes, his hand tight around the stock of his machine-gun. A voice called from the hallway and he walked out of the room, leaving a miasma of tension and fear in his wake.

The four men stood in silence as Abdul closed the door.

'Was that a yes or a no?' Stanza asked.

'He said you are fools who have come here to die.'

'Great job, Stanza,' Mallory said.

'That's it?' Stanza asked Abdul. 'What about Stanmore? Do we get to see him? Does that guy want the money? I don't get it. How have we left things?'

Muhammad said something which led to a heated exchange between him and Abdul. Then they calmed down and seemed to agree on something. 'They will talk further with us,' Abdul said.

'What does that mean?' Stanza asked.

'That was the first negotiation,' Abdul said. 'We can talk more later.'

'How the hell do you know that?' Stanza asked, raising his voice. 'You said the man told us we were dead.'

'That is why I know,' Abdul said. 'You are *not* dead. That is his way of saying you can talk more later.'

'Jesus fuckin' Christ. *When* later?' Stanza asked.

'That I do not know,' Abdul said.

'We don't have time for this,' Stanza said.

'You are in a hurry but they are not,' Abdul pointed out. 'They are preparing for a battle.'

'All the more reason to get on with this,' Stanza said.

'I am only the translator,' Abdul reminded him, for the first time revealing some of his own anxiety. Abdul had been racked by fear since meeting the two Arab men, especially the murderous one. Muhammad had taken him to a house a few blocks away where a dozen or so fighters were digging a deep hole in the floor of the living room. Muhammad told Abdul there were many such excavations in the town but he did not know what they were for.

An hour had passed before the leader arrived and when Abdul saw the murderous one with him he was consumed with fear that the beast would recognise him. It was the demon in human form from the house in Dora where Hassan and the others had delivered Lamont the night they'd kidnapped him. Until that moment Abdul had forgotten the face that had peered in through the car window as they'd waited. When the beast looked at Abdul with those distinctive black eyes it was as if he was looking into his very soul and could see everything. Abdul could not hold his gaze and prayed that the man had forgotten him. The slightest suspicion would result in the immediate elimination of Abdul and his cousin. Infiltration and betrayal were the insurgents' greatest fear and they treated suspects with brutal finality. It seemed that every time Abdul glanced at the man he was looking back at him, the cold malevolent expression unvarying as if nothing existed behind those eyes but hate and a desire for violence.

Stanza exhaled loudly as he walked across the room. 'What now?' he asked, pausing to look at Abdul.

Abdul shrugged. 'We wait . . . They are busy preparing defences. Perhaps tomorrow Muhammad and I will go and see them again,' Abdul said, repeating his suggestion to his cousin who shrugged as a reply.

Stanza sighed as he came to terms with his predicament and slumped down onto a cushion.

Silence descended on the group for a while until it was broken by Muhammad. 'He asks if you want food,' Abdul said.

'Why not?' Stanza said, only half interested.

Abdul nodded to Muhammad who replied with a hand gesture.

'He needs money,' Abdul said.

Stanza reached into a pocket and took out a bundle of notes, a mixture of dollars and dinars. Muhammad took the offering, checked it, appeared satisfied and left the room.

Mallory took stock of their situation as he watched Stanza lower his head into his hands. He wondered if it wasn't time to get on with his own mission. But before he could take a single step towards the cemetery there were several obvious matters that needed to be checked out.

Mallory went to the doorway that led to the garage, decided it was the right time, pushed back the curtain and quietly slipped out of the room.

14

Rendezvous with Death

Mallory opened the door to the garage, shone his flashlight around, found the light switch and flicked it up and down a couple of times without luck. He sat on the edge of a table covered in junk, turned off his flashlight and used the darkness as an aid to concentration.

The first and most obvious problem involved in leaving the house would be having to trudge through a town bustling with insurgents who were preparing for a major assault by the US Marine Corps. Mallory's first option was to wait for the attack to begin and then stay under cover until it had rolled over and past him. That might involve surrendering to the Americans at some stage, which would with luck mean that he'd be told to stay put. But they might transfer him outside the town, which would not do at all. Another problem with waiting for the assault was that it might not happen for days yet or possibly weeks. Still, Mallory reckoned that he could let Stanza head back to the city with Abdul. He felt confident he could strike some kind of deal with Muhammad to lie low in his house, although he did not trust the man an inch. If he ever found out about the money Mallory might well have a problem.

His other option was to head for the cemetery as soon as possible. He could do it if he had a local guide, someone who could communicate with anyone they bumped into, a scout who could move ahead and clear the way for him. The only person available who could possibly do that was Abdul.

It made good sense. Abdul was in a weird mood, or so it seemed, but money was a great facilitator and Mallory had no doubt that ten or twenty thousand dollars would bring him alongside nicely.

The second option was the most attractive and Mallory got to his feet walked back down the corridor and into the living room.

Stanza was in the same position, still holding his head in his hands. Abdul was at the sink, staring into space while holding a glass of water to his lips. Mallory's appearance appeared to set Abdul in motion again and he emptied the water down his throat.

Mallory waited for Abdul to look at him again and beckoned him over. Abdul glanced at Stanza who remained staring at the floor. Mallory stepped back through the curtain and Abdul followed along the corridor to the garage.

When Abdul stepped into the garage Mallory closed the door behind him and shone the torch in his face. 'Do you mind talking in the dark – I want to save my batteries?'

'No,' Abdul replied, wondering what this was all about.

Mallory turned off the light and the room went completely dark. 'I need to ask you something – something private.'

Abdul remained silent.

'I have something very valuable hidden not far from here and I need your help to get it.'

Abdul found this most bizarre. He had been expecting something along the lines of questions regarding their mission in Fallujah but this was entirely unexpected. 'Valuable?' he asked, unsure if he'd understood the English correctly.

'Money,' Mallory said, getting to the point.

Abdul blinked in the darkness. 'I don't understand you.'

Mallory took a deep breath. He did indeed have a lot to explain. 'I have a box of money, US dollars, buried in a hole in the ground not far from here. I was here a year ago, during the war. I was a soldier and I found this box. I could not take it with me so I buried it and now I want to get it.'

This made immediate and perfect sense to Abdul. 'How much?' he asked.

'A lot.' Mallory wondered if he should reveal the amount, then quickly decided against it. 'I'll give you a portion of it,' he said. 'How about ten thousand dollars?'

Abdul's thoughts began to shoot in several directions at once and he decided that he needed time and space to sort them out. 'Where is this money?' he asked.

'In a cemetery.'

'Buried?'

'Yes.'

'How do you know it is still there?'

'I don't . . . There is only one way to find out.'

'Why have you asked me to help?'

'I need you to get me through the town. A guide. A simple job for a lot of money,' Mallory said, hoping that would be the case.

Abdul broke into a thin smile that Mallory could not see. Allah did indeed move in mysterious ways. Here was the answer to his prayers. And the cemetery was a delicious irony. He needed to know nothing else. 'When do you want to go?'

'Now.'

Abdul accepted the risks that could come with meeting insurgents but his confidence had improved since he'd been out in the town already. 'I will help you,' he said.

Mallory flicked on his flashlight and aimed it at Abdul for a second. 'We'll need a shovel.'

They followed the beam around the dilapidated room as it illuminated an assortment of junk. Abdul saw something, walked over to the pile and withdrew a spade from it. 'Will this do?'

'Perfect,' Mallory said, taking it from him. 'A bag would also be useful. A strong, fairly large one.'

Abdul wondered how much money there was.

Mallory moved the beam to another pile of odds and ends. Abdul picked up a filthy canvas bag, fine dust filling the air as he opened it up and tested the handles for strength.

'That'll do,' Mallory said.

As Abdul handed the bag to Mallory his gaze caught something in the brief torchlight.

Mallory went to the garage door to open it.

Abdul crouched to feel for the object.

'Let's go,' Mallory said.

'Coming,' Abdul said. 'Fixing my shoe.'

Mallory cracked open the door, checked that the narrow backstreet was empty and slipped outside.

Abdul found what he was looking for and picked it up. It was a cast-iron hammer with a nasty-looking spike on the reverse head. The shaft was bound in string for an improved grip. Abdul swung it down to assess its suitability. If brought down firmly enough a single blow using the spike would penetrate a skull with ease. He tucked it into his belt and headed for the door.

Abdul walked over to Mallory who was looking at an electronic device in his hand. 'What is that?' he asked.

'GPS,' Mallory said as he scrolled through a list of waypoints and stopped on the one marked RENDEZVOUS. He hit the accept button and a moment later an arrow appeared on the screen, along with several information windows. 'Seven hundred and fifty-seven metres as the crow flies . . . in that direction,' he said, pointing. Mallory looked at Abdul. 'Don't suppose you know a cemetery in that direction?'

'I don't know Fallujah that well.'

'Lead on, then. That way. You go forward, check if it's safe, then I'll join you. We'll keep doing that until we reach the cemetery. OK?'

Abdul nodded and headed off. Mallory put an arm through the carrying straps of the bag that had the shovel in it, pulled them over his shoulder and followed Abdul at a distance.

The sky had grown lighter, most of the cloud from earlier having cleared. The two men kept to the right side of the street where the shadows were thicker, hugging the building line as closely as possible. Abdul paused at the end of the first row of houses, all of which appeared to be empty, and Mallory stepped into a doorway out of sight.

Abdul remained still for a time, checking in all directions while Mallory kept him in view. Just as Mallory was beginning to wonder if Abdul had had second thoughts the Arab set off without looking back and turned right and out of sight. Mallory carried on to the corner, peered around it and saw Abdul walking away up the street. Mallory checked behind him, turned the corner and walked briskly along, maintaining his distance from Abdul. They were in another residential street packed with run-down homes.

A pair of headlights appeared up ahead. Abdul ducked out of sight and Mallory skipped over a low wall outside a front door and got down behind it.

The vehicle passed.

When Mallory got to his feet and looked over the wall Abdul was already out of his hiding place and looking back in Mallory's direction as if impatient to get going.

Mallory stepped onto the street as Abdul headed off to the end of the row of houses and stopped at the corner. Mallory checked his GPS and broke into a jog. By the time Abdul looked back Mallory was just behind him.

Ahead was a broad boulevard and the arrow on the GPS indicated they needed to cross it diagonally. The boulevard had three lanes either side of a meridian and several vehicles, their headlights on, were gathered some distance away outside a mosque.

'That way,' Mallory said, indicating across the boulevard and away from the cars.

'Should I run?' Abdul asked.

'Walk casually,' Mallory said. 'We'll go together, OK?'

Mallory walked out from the shadows onto the boulevard with Abdul by his side. They stepped off the pavement onto the road and headed towards the central meridian. As they reached it a shout came from behind them and the hairs stood up on the back of Mallory's neck. There was another yell, followed by a shot and both men broke into a sprint. A burst of automatic gunfire rang out. It seemed abnormally loud. Several bullets ricocheted off the road nearby as they leaped across the last section of road and onto the pavement. But they were still exposed and some distance from the nearest corner. More bullets, one of them a bright-orange tracer round, slammed into the wall beside them and as they reached the corner Mallory grabbed hold of Abdul and pulled him around it as a couple more slugs cut through the air, dangerously close. The two men did not stop and ran for all they were worth.

Mallory was ahead and, spotting an alleyway across

the street, changed direction towards it. 'This way!' he shouted.

Mallory came to a skidding halt inside the alleyway entrance and urged Abdul ahead. As they emerged from the other end into what looked like a square he nudged the young Arab more to the left.

As they reached the entrance to another street Mallory took hold of Abdul's jacket and steered him into a dark doorway.

They panted heavily and Mallory checked back the way they had come before reviewing his GPS display. 'We must be near the cemetery,' he gasped. 'It has to be behind those buildings. Come on.'

They headed up the street to a gap between the buildings on the other side of the road and a few metres further on stopped at a low wall. Beyond were the jagged silhouettes of tilted stones looking like rows of broken teeth, along with black flags on angled sticks. Mallory did not recognise the place but he remembered that he had approached it from a different direction the last time. He sensed Abdul close behind him and without further hesitation he unslung the bag, tucked it under his arm, hopped over the wall and moved in among the tombs at a slight crouch. He paused by a headstone a few metres in and cloaked the glow from the GPS while he checked the direction. After he moved off, a quick look behind him showed Abdul mimicking his caution.

Mallory slowed as the GPS indicated that the cache was only metres away. He searched around for anything that he might recognise. He was about to learn the answer to one of the greatest worries that had been on his mind since leaving England: had the stash been discovered or not? He held his breath in anticipation.

Mallory realised he was standing on the path that was lower than the surrounding ground level, the path in which he had dug the hole. Then his stare practically lasered into the exact spot where the box was buried. It was undisturbed and more natural-looking than when he had left it. That did not mean, though, that someone hadn't dug it up the day after he'd buried it and he double-checked the GPS, which confirmed their arrival at RENDEZVOUS. He turned it off, its job finally done, and pocketed it.

Mallory looked behind at Abdul who was crouching by a headstone. 'It's here,' he said as he removed the shovel from the bag and, without wasting a second more, rested its blade on the spot beneath which he believed the box lay.

Mallory placed his foot on the shoulder of the shovel and was about to push down on it when a familiar sound stopped him. He looked to the night sky as the thud of a helicopter's rotor blades beat the air somewhere above. With its navigation lights off the chopper was virtually invisible.

After a few seconds Mallory went back to his task, pushing the shovel into the ground that yielded easily.

Abdul stood on the grave directly behind Mallory, which made him a head taller, and watched as the Englishman got into a digging rhythm. He slipped his hand inside his jacket, felt for the hammer tucked into his belt, slid it out and held it against his side with his stump while he took a firm hold of the grip with his hand. It felt good, not too long or too heavy, and he rested it against his thigh, pressing it into his flesh to make sure that the spike was facing behind him. Mallory was moving in unpredictable patterns, making it risky to attempt a blow, and Abdul told himself to be patient. The ideal moment would present itself soon enough. The point of the weighty spike was sharp and one good whack would stun Mallory enough for Abdul to deliver another that would penetrate his skull, drive into the fleshy brain and kill him. Allah was such a thoughtful god. He had not only provided the perfect tool for the job, silent and final, but He had also arranged for Mallory to have his back to Abdul, distracted by his greed.

Mallory struck something metal with the spade and he dropped to his knees to feel around in the hole. A grin spread across his face as his fingers touched the box: at that moment he knew his money was there. No one would have reburied the box if they had emptied it. 'We've hit the mother-lode,' he said softly, turning his head to look up at Abdul.

Abdul moved the hammer out of sight behind his leg and smiled thinly at the man he was about to kill.

Mallory faced the hole again, pulled away several handfuls of earth from the side of the box and felt for the handle. He eventually dug it free, took a firm grip of it and put all his effort into pulling up the edge of the box. It resisted at first but a little more effort and the corner moved and then seemed to spring up. Mallory lifted the box onto its side, got to his feet, pulled it out of the hole completely and rested it on the path.

He stood upright and took a breather.

Abdul was about to raise the hammer when Mallory dropped to his knees again.

'Right. Let's see if the worms have left us anything,' he said as he unclipped the lid with some effort, gripped its edges and prised it open. He could not see inside the box well enough to confirm it was the money although it was obviously full. A layer of fine sand covered the paper and Mallory's smile returned as he pulled out a tight bundle of notes. He shook the remaining dust off, flicked through the bills and held them out to Abdul. 'There you go. Ten thousand US dollars.'

Mallory was not looking directly at Abdul who quickly tucked the hammer under his right arm and took Mallory's offering.

'And you can have another for your trouble later,' Mallory said as he dragged the bag alongside the box and began transferring the money into it.

Abdul stared again at the back of Mallory's head as he put his bundle of money into his pocket and gripped the hammer once again. The rest of Abdul's journey suddenly became clear to him and he knew what he had to do.

Abdul strengthened his grip on the haft and brought the hammer out in front of him. Mallory was busy transferring the bundles of banknotes, his head more or less in the same position, and Abdul stepped down onto the path behind him, adopted a wide-legged stance and raised the spike.

Mallory placed the last of the bundles in the bag, ran a hand around the inside of the box to be sure he'd emptied it and closed the bag. 'Can't believe I've actually got this far,' he said.

Abdul held the spike high and focused on the centre of Mallory's head.

'Wait,' Mallory said suddenly as his ears picked up a repetitive distant concussive sound that alarmed him although he could not immediately identify it.

Abdul froze before lowering his weapon, momentarily confused. He could hear nothing: aware that time was running out, he raised the spike again, grimacing with effort as he started to drive it down.

Mallory suddenly remembered what those distant thumps meant: he had heard similar sounds many times during the war. They were heavy cannon being fired from several miles away, one after the other. The shells would take only a few seconds to land.

As Abdul's hammer spike drove through the air towards Mallory's skull the first shell struck the cemetery, the powerful explosion producing a shock wave that lifted both men off their feet and tossed them aside like rag dolls. The ground rocked as a series of the shells struck in quick succession, half a second between each as they landed across the cemetery and through the houses opposite.

Mallory slammed against a headstone and was knocked close to unconsciousness. Abdul landed on a grave with a metal surround, smashing a collection of flowerpots within it. He tried to sit up as his brain fought to understand what was happening but he fell back as another blast shotgunned him with soil, pebbles and fragmented headstone rock. The barrage raged around them, the ground shaking as masses of earth were thrown into the air. The sound was deafening. Mallory came back to near-consciousness and rolled into a ball, his hands tight around his head as soil and debris rained down. A ton of headstone landed feet from him, then toppled over to hit the edge of a grave, thereby miraculously forming a shelter instead of flattening him. He remained unaware for the time being and stayed curled in a tight ball, jolting with each powerful boom and expecting the next to be the one that tore him to shreds. A nearby headstone exploded as a chunk of shrapnel slammed through it. The incoming shells sounded like screaming freight trains, only a thousand times louder, before they struck the ground. It was a symphony of doom: fiery, ear-splitting blasts, white-hot chunks of shrapnel that shrieked like banshees and shock waves powerful enough to rip stone walls apart.

Mallory was unable to move while death tore hungrily through the air, seeking victims inches above him. He could not think, only pray that it would end soon. There was a brief lull and he considered getting out of there, but just as he did the shells returned.

Mallory had no idea how long he lay in his cocoon of dirt and fear. It seemed like an age before the barrage gradually moved away and into the town. But he was alert enough to know that he too had to move – and soon. Artillery barrages were intended to clear a path for an assault that would follow close on its heels and out in the open was no place to be when tanks and infantry were bearing down on their targets.

Mallory raised his head, banged it on the massive headstone, brushed the dirt from his face and eyes and looked up at the grey slab. Had it landed a few feet to either side it would have flattened him. As he started to crawl out from under it he felt a sharp pain on the back of his head and touched it to find a wet spot that was obviously blood. He pressed it gently to feel if the bone was still intact, which it appeared to be, and went on to check the rest of his body. Satisfied that he had no broken bones or missing pieces he crawled out from under the slab and sat up. He saw the money bag a few metres away, covered in dirt. He got to his feet to look for Abdul and saw him lying on a grave several metres away. As he made his way to him across shattered tombs the young Arab began to stir.

'Abdul?' Mallory called out, hardly able to hear his own voice. His ears felt muffled as if they were filled with dirt. He took hold of Abdul's jacket and gave it a tug. 'Abdul?'

Abdul looked completely disorientated, mouth open, eyes blinking and darting in every direction.

'We have to get going.'

Abdul continued to blink rapidly in fear and confusion as he attempted to focus on Mallory.

'You OK?' Mallory asked.

Abdul looked around as if he was trying to decide where he was. He made an attempt to get up but his legs and arms began to shake and Mallory took his weight as he helped him. 'That's it. We have to get going.'

Abdul reached for a headstone to steady himself while Mallory held him under his arms. 'Stay there a moment,' Mallory said as he made his way back to the money bag, quickly checked it for damage, crouched to put the strap over his head and with a great effort got to his feet. The back of his head began to throb but he gritted his teeth, straightened up and stumbled back to Abdul.

The young Arab was still holding on to the head-stone and staring at the ground as if in a daze. Mallory took hold of his arm. 'Come on. We can't stay out in the open.'

Abdul did not appear to hear him but he responded when Mallory yanked him forward. They stumbled through the graveyard, Mallory scanning in all direc-tions to get his bearings. He decided that the motorway was on his left and north of the ceme-tery which would make an ideal kill-zone for anyone trying to break out of the town. Alternatively, it would be a good location from which to form up and mount an assault. The only thing to do was head into the town, find somewhere to hide and then surrender to the Americans as soon as it was safe to do so.

The rolling barrage was still heavy, heading towards the centre of the town. But just as Mallory thought they were at least safe from that, a series of powerful explosions behind them alarmed him and he feared it might be the start of a follow-up shelling. They had been lucky with the first barrage but might not survive another.

'Come on!' Mallory shouted as he picked up the pace and pulled Abdul along.

Abdul appeared to understand the need to hurry and increased his speed as they moved across the cratered ground. Mallory wondered if the young Arab was experiencing some kind of shell-shock and could only hope that he would keep moving.

Mallory managed to retrace their route despite much of the ground being churned up. He could make out the gap they had come through between the buildings and he steered Abdul towards it.

The thunder of exploding artillery shells intensified and every few seconds a jagged chunk of metal flew past them. The effort to make it to the narrow alleyway became desperate. They scrambled over a low wall, the money bag falling heavily off Mallory's shoulder as he pulled Abdul across. Abdul dropped to his knees as a shell landed inside the cemetery not far away and Mallory fell to the ground beside him.

'We have to keep going,' Mallory shouted as he got up and pulled Abdul to his feet. They broke into a run along the alley.

It felt as if they were surrounded by explosions. A section of a building up ahead gave way and crumbled into the alleyway but the men hurled themselves over the rubble. They were on a roller-coaster ride from hell and could be blown to bits, crushed or riddled by shrapnel at any second. But to stop seemed more dangerous than to keep moving.

As they ran out of the alley and across the open square an explosion ahead caused Mallory to hesitate and consider dropping down somewhere – anywhere – to wait out the assault. But a series of crunching booms behind changed his mind and they kept up the pace. As they turned a corner into a narrow street Mallory wondered if they shouldn't just keep going until they reached Muhammad's house. Stanza was probably hysterical by now. Mallory had considered leaving the journalist to his own devices, a decision that might have been easier to make had the man not been so pathetic. But Stanza was his responsibility, after all, and Mallory might as well wait out the assault with him as anywhere else – if they could make it back in one piece.

The explosions continued but for the most part appeared to be concentrated behind them. The barrage was as much a psychological weapon – a way of softening up the enemy – as it was a means of destroying defences and covering an assault. Mallory had not heard any small-arms fire and wondered if the Marines planned to bomb and shell the place for hours before sending in the first ground troops. Either way, Muhammad's house now seemed as good as any as a place of refuge.

Mallory and Abdul paused, exhausted, at the corner of the street that led onto the broad boulevard that now looked quite different from when they had crossed it earlier. Several fires were burning fiercely in front of the mosque where the vehicles had been gathered and judging by the twisted wreckage strewn around they had received a direct hit. Craters peppered the roadway and every telegraph and electricity pole appeared to have collapsed, their wires criss-crossing everywhere.

Several louder explosions behind them goaded them on. Mallory pulled Abdul onto the boulevard and they crossed over poles and ducked under wires towards the other side, which they could barely see. The air was filled with a dense acrid smoke that burned the back of Mallory's throat and he tried to cover his mouth as he ran. He lost his grip on Abdul as he tripped over something. When he looked back Abdul was close behind him, nearly blinded by ash, and Mallory took hold of him and led him along the side of the buildings until they reached a street which they hurried into.

The air quality improved dramatically but as they reached the next road junction gunfire erupted. It sounded like heavy machine guns, .50-cal or greater: either the defenders were shooting at anything in reaction to the shelling or the ground assault had begun.

Mallory and Abdul hurried along a street and turned a corner to see Muhammad's garage up ahead. The house across from it had received a direct hit and had collapsed, dragging a section of the next-door building down with it. A fire was burning inside. Mallory hurried to the garage door to discover that a chunk of it was missing. He dragged Abdul inside, leaned him against the vehicle, opened the trunk of the car, threw the bag in, slammed the trunk shut and carried on into the house.

He walked into the living room, expecting to see Stanza. But the place was in darkness, the benzene lamp extinguished and the only light coming from the open doorway – open because the door had been blown in – that led to the hallway. Mallory walked across the debris-covered cushions to look into the hallway only to discover that the front door had been blown off its hinges too and was lying on the floor, along with its frame. A figure ran past outside and Mallory stepped out of sight to consider what to do.

A groan came from somewhere near his feet and at the same time the living-room door moved. Mallory pulled the edge of the door up to find Stanza lying beneath. He quickly shoved it aside.

'Stanza? It's Mallory.' He removed pieces of wood and other debris from Stanza's face and torso. 'Can you hear me? Stanza?'

Stanza was breathing in short, sharp bursts. He opened his eyes, blinking rapidly.

'Easy,' Mallory said. 'You're fine but you need to lie still a moment.'

Mallory checked Stanza for signs of any broken bones or bleeding. 'Can you hear me, Stanza?'

Stanza's breathing slowed as Mallory came into focus. He tried to speak but no words came out and he broke into a coughing fit that forced him over onto his side. 'Mallory?' Stanza finally wheezed as he struggled to get his breath.

'You're OK.'

Stanza continued coughing but not as desperately. 'Where . . . where've you been?'

'Do you have any pain anywhere?' Mallory asked. 'Can you see me OK?'

Stanza nodded. 'I'm OK. I'm OK . . . What the hell happened?'

An explosion shook the house and dust seemed to leap from the walls to fill the room.

'The assault's begun,' Mallory said. 'Can you stand?'

The shelling continued in the distance and Stanza looked through the door at the fire across the street. 'Sweet Jesus. I thought the insurgents had attacked the house.' He made a move to get up and Mallory took most of his weight. Stanza wobbled on his feet while Mallory held him.

'We might need to get out of here,' Mallory said.

Stanza felt all over his head as if checking that everything was still in place Then he looked at Mallory's dust-covered face that had a dozen small, dried cuts all over it. 'What happened to you?'

'Same as you.'

Stanza looked around and let go of Mallory to stand on his own two feet. He looked up as a couple of nearby booms shook the ground. 'The assault.'

'We need to decide what to do.'

Stanza shuffled over to the sink, leaned heavily against it, took the remaining glass off the shelf and held it under the tap as he turned it on. A dribble of water came out before it stopped altogether. Another explosion rattled the building to produce more dust and Stanza looked around at Mallory with fear in his eyes. 'What shall we do?'

'I think all we can do is wait it out and surrender when the Marines arrive.'

'Can we survive until then – in here?'

'We won't live any longer out there.'

'Where's Abdul?'

Mallory suddenly realised that the young Arab had not followed him into the room. He went to the back door, moved down the short hallway and entered the garage. 'Abdul?' he called out. There was no sign of him. Mallory hurried to the back of the car and lifted up the trunk lid. The bag seemed to be as he'd left it and he opened it up to find the money untouched. He went to the garage door to look out through the hole. There was no sign of life. Then a nearby explosion splattered the house with shrapnel, forcing him back inside. He went to the car, lifted the bag out of the trunk and made his way back into the living room where Stanza was still standing by the sink.

Mallory put the bag down and went into the hallway to the front door.

He peered outside into the street that was a mess of debris; chunks of bricks and mortar, splintered wood, trailing wires and lots of smoke. A few feet in front of him lay a buckled lifeless body. The jacket looked familiar and Mallory edged out of the doorway to get a closer view of the face. It was disfigured, one of the eyes hanging from its socket and the lower jaw torn away, but he was just about recognisable. Mallory was certain it was Abdul's cousin.

Large pieces of ash floated by on the warm air like grubby snowflakes. The ground shook as a shell landed close by and showers of powdered masonry fell on Mallory. A man in a tattered *dishdash* who was carrying an assault rifle ran quickly down the street, past Mallory and out of sight.

Mallory decided that Abdul had legged it. The man was shell-shocked and couldn't be blamed. He'd taken a hammering at the cemetery and was lucky to be alive. They both were. Mallory could only wish him luck and hope that the Marines wouldn't shoot him before he had a chance to surrender. He thought of Tasneen and wondered what he would tell her. But then, he'd have to get back himself to do that and at present the prospects of that were in the balance.

Mallory went back into the living room to find that Stanza had not moved.

'This house'll collapse if this keeps up,' Stanza said.

'What do you want *me* to fucking well do?' Mallory shouted, the stress and Stanza's bleating finally getting the better of him. 'Why don't you just accept that if we get out of here in one piece we're going to be lucky, OK?'

Stanza blinked at him innocently as if he, Stanza, was being victimised. Another heavy boom shook the house and Stanza gripped the sink behind him as his stare darted to the ceiling where a crack had suddenly widened. 'Perhaps there's a basement,' he said.

'Why don't you go and look for one, then?' Mallory said, wondering if there was indeed a safe place to wait for the Americans to arrive. The garage, perhaps. Better still, inside the car. Short of a direct hit, being inside a metal box would be safer than being out in the open. A fire would, of course, be a problem if they got trapped. But then maybe they could drive out, at least. Mallory's mind was racing. He looked at Stanza who had not moved but was wearing a most odd expression, a combination of shock and fear. He realised that Stanza was looking behind him and he turned around to see the demonic insurgent they'd encountered earlier standing in the doorway. His *dishdash* was soiled, his machine-gun dusty in his grimy hands. A couple of bandoliers of linked ammunition spanned his chest and a short sword in a scabbard hung from a leather belt around his waist. Mallory took a step back as the Arab's crazed stare bored into him. Then the human devil moved out of the doorway and his leader walked in, dressed in a similar fashion as if ready for battle. A series of new explosions shook the building but no one reacted, not even Stanza.

The leader asked something in a calm, authoritative voice. Mallory did not understand a word and simply looked at him. The leader beckoned to someone behind him and Abdul walked into the room, looking calmer than the last time Mallory had seen him.

Abdul held Mallory's gaze with difficulty. His failure to kill him in the graveyard had left him confused. The Englishman had been saved from Abdul's blow by the very hand of Allah. It had all seemed so clear to him up until that point, what his purpose was and how he was to achieve it. He had seen himself as a tool of Allah but that clearly was not the case, not entirely at least. Somewhere along the road he had misread the signs.

But Abdul had come to his senses and seen the way to complete his mission. Mallory had indeed played a part in it but Abdul had not realised what that was until almost too late. Now he knew what he had to do. 'He asks where the money is,' he said.

Mallory's mouth started to drop open in utter disbelief. 'You little arsehole,' he muttered.

'It is payment for Lamont,' Abdul said, as if explaining to Mallory what the money had been intended for all along.

Explosions close by followed by a rattle of gunfire lit a fire under the proceedings and the leader raised his voice.

'He does not have time to waste,' Abdul said. 'Don't try his patience,' he added as a warning of his own.

Mallory exhaled in frustration. It was clearly not an issue for debate and he walked over to the bag, picked it up and dropped it on the floor in front of the leader. The leader nodded to his fighter who crouched to open and inspect the contents. He pulled out several bundles of money, did a quick count, looked up at his boss and nodded.

Abdul suddenly remembered the bundle Mallory had given him, took it out of his jacket pocket and held it towards the leader.

The fighter took it, shoved it in the bag and fastened it back up as the leader eyed Abdul.

Stanza looked from the bag of money to the others in blank confusion.

The leader barked a command and left the room.

'He wants you to follow,' Abdul said, stepping aside.

'Me?' Stanza asked. Everyone seemed to know what was going on except him.

'Both of you,' Abdul said.

'Where are we going?' Stanza asked.

An explosion rocked the building and the dark-eyed fighter shouted at them as he hoisted the bag of money onto his shoulder.

'Now,' Abdul insisted. 'He's taking you to see Lamont.'

Stanza opened his mouth to say something. But the fighter interrupted with an outburst that was clearly threatening and Stanza hurried out the door.

Mallory stared at Abdul, feeling a mixture of loss and humility. The money had driven his every move for almost a year, nearly cost him his life and was now gone. But he could not begin to chastise Abdul for what the man had done. Abdul could have run off with the money himself but instead had continued to risk his life to exchange it all for a complete stranger, and an American to boot. That was altruism above and beyond any level Mallory had contemplated. Tasneen had been right about her brother all along. She had said he was good and honourable and would not let him down. In a way, Mallory felt it was he who had let Abdul down.

Mallory walked out of the room and Abdul followed, the demonic fighter close behind.

Several more fighters were waiting in the hallway and in the doorways at either side of the house and they followed as the leader headed down the street. Devastation was everywhere: fires burning in roofless buildings, pieces of furniture and rubble strewn all over the road, the air thick with ash and smoke. Homes had collapsed, telegraph poles were snapped or bent, water was pouring from severed pipes, mangled human remains lay scattered around. Mallory covered his mouth to stop from choking on the smoke-filled air and as he followed a fighter directly in front of him he had to lengthen his stride to avoid stepping on a severed arm and then on a face that had been stripped from its skull.

An explosion sent a chunk of metal whistling overhead and the leader and those close to him ducked as it smashed into the building above. The staccato of heavy machine-gun fire joined the cacophony and was answered, or so it seemed, by a dozen less powerful weapons. A heavy engine roared angrily beyond the row of buildings in the next street, followed by the clunking of metal tracks crunching through masonry. It sounded like a tank to Mallory and as the leader broke into a trot the others responded likewise. The thunder of battle grew in intensity, a chorus of explosions, flying bullets, crackling fires and grinding machinery. Two Apache helicopter gunships roared overhead, nearly clipping the rooftops as they unleashed a torrent of heavy gunfire at some target a few streets away. Mallory prayed that the dense smoke was masking their group enough. As they ran on Mallory had the feeling that they were heading towards the outskirts of the city – which meant towards the front line of the fight and not away from it. He could only hope that the hostage was in a bunker somewhere and that the four of them would be left to fend for themselves.

The leader turned the corner at the end of the street, followed by his men. Mallory saw Stanza make the corner and when it was his turn he saw to his surprise that the line was filing in through the front door of a house. Mallory followed into the living room that was mostly taken up by a huge hole in the centre, its sides shored up by heavy pieces of timber as in the entrance to a mine. Fighters were climbing down into the hole that was lit from below – Mallory assumed this was the bunker he had been expecting.

A fighter came running in from outside, barging past Abdul who was a couple of fighters behind Mallory, shouting some kind of warning. The leader barked words of motivation that were repeated by his lieutenants. Mallory looked at the faces of the fighters packed around him, expecting to see signs of fear or panic. But there were neither. He looked at the demonic fighter carrying the money and watched as he pulled the bag off his shoulder and handed it to a young fighter, at the same time giving him what appeared to be instructions. Mallory watched as the bag was carried out of the house, thus bringing to an end his relationship with it. It was never meant to be, he mused.

The murderous-looking fighter was then handed a heavy cloth bundle which he thrust at Stanza who looked at it quizzically. The fighter displayed little patience with Stanza's lack of understanding and shouted a command as he shoved the bundle brutally against Stanza's chest. The journalist had no choice but to take hold of it, almost dropping it since it was heavier than it looked. Then he was unceremoniously pushed over to the hole and ordered to go down into it.

Mallory and Abdul had just been shoved into the line of fighters waiting to descend into the hole when a massive explosion outside brought down the front of the house, exposing the living room to the street. Several fighters fell under the cascading rubble and were either killed or seriously injured. The sound of falling masonry gave way to human screams and when the initial cloud of dust dissipated Mallory saw a fighter with a spear of window frame sticking through his chest.

The building across the road suddenly collapsed with a roar but this time it was not due to any explosion. A thundering Abrams tank punched through the walls as if it were a sandcastle, its gun barrel like a battering ram, and bore down on the house.

There followed an immediate scramble for the hole as the tank's tracks screeched painfully as it turned. When it stopped the business end of its gun barrel seemed to explode as a shell burst from it.

The shell was aimed along the street but the shock wave from the end of the barrel almost brought down the rest of the house. Everything went dark as dust completely filled the air, making it almost impossible to see or breathe. All Mallory was aware of after that was being shunted forward until the man in front of him dropped. He followed him into the hole, grasping for anything to hang on to.

The walls quickly closed in as the tunnel became narrower and Mallory had to release his handholds as quickly as he found them to avoid his fingers being stepped on by others descending from above. When he hit the bottom it was so abrupt that his knees collapsed under him and as he recovered the man above landed on him. As Mallory pushed himself to his feet, hands grabbed him and he was yanked in another direction. His face slammed into a dirt wall, breaking his nose, but the lower half of his body continued forward into a space and he dropped into a crouch as he entered a low tunnel.

He was given no time to recover as the man behind pushed him on with his boot and Mallory scurried on his hands and knees in the darkness until he bumped into the man in front of him. The dust was intolerable although it had improved a little from the hole entrance when he'd thought he was going to suffocate. The ground was rocky and quickly became unbearably painful, tearing the skin off his knees. Mallory squatted to put his weight on his feet, which meant shuffling along like a chimpanzee. His hands kept contact with the back of the man in front as he fought to keep going, his head occasionally hitting a jagged lump in the roof.

The shouting was constant, the man behind repeatedly pushing Mallory into the one in front who at one point stumbled, causing Mallory to fall onto him. A pile-up threatened and every effort was made to move on. When the man in front finally got going Mallory stepped on something lumpy that gave way in places and it was not until he reached the head that he realised he had been walking on a dead body.

The air suddenly became even thicker and almost too heavy to draw into his lungs. Mallory's mouth and throat were filled with so much dust that his saliva glands had given up and he wondered if he would ever reach the end of the bunker – wherever that was. He had never experienced anything like this before. The nearest thing to it had been the tunnels on the Royal Marine Commando endurance course on Woodbury Common but at Woodbury there was always light visible at either end and the air was at least breathable.

A loud thud above sent a shock wave through the earth that threatened a cave-in and for a moment Mallory's fear rocketed as it appeared that this was how it was going to end for him. He had never experienced claustrophobia before but he could sense the panic beginning to build and he concentrated on putting himself into a kind of trance as he moved on in order to deal with it, searching for a rhythm in the way he was advancing. As he fought to control his increasing anxiety the man in front came to an abrupt stop and Mallory was pressed into him by the combined weight of those behind. When the man moved again Mallory shuffled after him and saw that there was a distinct change in the light. Mallory's hopes rose that the tunnel was coming to an end.

The man in front paused again before shuffling a few feet forward. He did this several times and then abruptly disappeared. Mallory's outstretched hands found an earth wall and he reached higher to find that the ceiling had gone. He pushed himself upright, banging his back on the ceiling of the tunnel behind him and as he stood up hands from above grabbed him. He was pulled out of the hole and tossed aside onto a stone floor.

Mallory blew gobs of dust from his mouth and nostrils and wiped it from his eyes. Men were coughing and spluttering all around him and he blinked incessantly until his vision returned and he could make out where he was. They were surrounded by walls or parts of walls as if they were inside what had once been a building. But most of it, including the roof, was missing. A dozen fighters in varying states of recovery were hurriedly sorting themselves out, loading magazines into weapons after blowing and wiping dust from the working parts. The shouting had turned into heavy whispering as fighters continued to be dragged out of the hole. There was an intense sense of urgency. Mallory recognised the leader who was marshalling his men, ordering them to spread out behind a low wall.

A body suddenly landed beside Mallory like a sack of potatoes and he realised it was Abdul. The young man looked near to death and when Mallory got to his knees to see if he could help he saw Stanza too, lying in a semi-conscious state a few feet away. Abdul coughed and spluttered as he fought to breathe but Mallory was distracted by a sudden feeling that something ominous was about to happen.

The battle continued to rage with explosions, machine-gun fire, tanks crunching past and helicopters roaring overhead. Mallory initially assumed that they had been retreating as the front line of the assault rolled towards them. But if that was correct something was still not right. He shuffled to where he could look over a wall and saw an armoured troop carrier storm past with several US soldiers running behind it.

It was then that the penny dropped. The tunnel had not gone towards the centre of the town but towards the outskirts. It had been designed to pass beneath the enemy line of advance. The fighters were now behind the US Marines. The crafty bastards had timed it so that the assault would roll over them. But this wasn't an escape. Judging by the way the leader was forming up his men he was going to attack the rear of the assaulting line. The Marines had not pressed forward in depth and had chosen to extend themselves to present a broad front. If there was a second wave it was a substantial distance behind the first, something which the insurgents clearly planned to exploit.

As Mallory stretched up to see the backs of a line of Marines following a tank along a rubble-strewn street he was suddenly yanked around to face the insurgent leader. Abdul was standing beside the demonic fighter who looked even fiercer covered in a thick film of dust, his eyes like dark slits in a rock surface. Stanza was dragged over as the leader spoke and all three men were pushed towards a gap in a wall, an opening that had once been a doorway.

'We're free to go,' Abdul said, coughing.

The dark fighter shoved Stanza through the gap so hard that he sprawled on the ground and his bundle was thrown after him. Abdul did not need further convincing and followed as the fighter raised the barrel of his rifle to point it at Mallory's chest. 'Go,' he said, meaning it.

Mallory walked out through the gap, looking back, wondering if the man would pull the trigger.

A cry then went up from the insurgent leader – '*Allah akbar!*' – and all his men leaped over the wall with him and charged, shooting and screaming as they ran. The demonic fighter looked over his shoulder at his colleagues, back at Mallory, appeared to consider shooting him but then turned away and broke into a run, screaming his epithet as he disappeared into the dust and darkness. Seconds later the sound of gunfire and screams reached a crescendo and the muzzle-flash of discharging weapons became almost constant.

Stanza began to retch violently, crouched over and holding his stomach.

'You can throw up later, Stanza. We have to get going,' said Mallory.

Stanza sat back on his heels and looked up at Mallory, bile running down his chin and neck. 'Stanmore,' he said.

'It's over,' Mallory said. 'The money only bought us our freedom.'

'No,' Stanza said lowering his eyes. 'It bought us Stanmore too.'

Mallory followed Stanza's gaze to the bundle that had fallen open. Inside it was the severed head of a white man.

15

War Without Winners

Mallory, Stanza and Abdul stumbled on through rubble that had once been shops and houses on the edge of the town. The air was filled with the smell of cordite although the three were so used to it by now they hardly noticed. The bodies of dead Arabs had grown fewer as they approached the start line of the assault but Mallory remained alert to every sound and shadow. His two colleagues looked disconnected from the reality of what was going on around them as if numbed by it all, walking like automatons, Stanza carrying his bundle and Abdul following him like a blind man. Mallory had seen vehicles and troops moving on their flanks in the darkness but had chosen not to reveal themselves just yet. It was still dangerous out in the open and the Marines were likely to shoot first and investigate later.

The battle raged a good distance behind them now, although the occasional explosion went off nearby and ahead – probably mortars fired by insurgents in the town.

Mallory led them through a deserted building onto a main road and instantly pulled the others to cover when he saw several Hummvees parked a short distance away with a dozen or so troops gathered around. He told Abdul and Stanza to remain out of sight while he made contact. Then he stepped back onto the road, his hands raised in the air. The soldiers were cautious as he approached them but after he spoke, announcing his nationality, they could see he was a westerner and they relaxed, allowing him to join them. After a brief chat he returned with a sergeant and a couple of his men to collect Abdul and Stanza. Mallory had explained they were press who had got separated from their media pool and they showed their IDs as proof. The sergeant bought their story and allowed them to wait with the platoon. A couple of hours later a Hummvee arrived to take them to a checkpoint on the 10 motorway on the Baghdad side of Fallujah. A taxi was hanging around a few hundred metres from the checkpoint and the driver was happy to give them a ride back to the Sheraton Hotel.

Not a word was spoken during the journey and day had dawned by the time the taxi pulled up outside the first checkpoint. Mallory and Stanza climbed out. Abdul remained in the taxi and as Stanza walked away, carrying his bundle, Mallory stopped to look at Abdul who was staring at the floor. 'You going home?'

Abdul nodded.

Mallory wasn't quite sure what to say. 'I'll give you a call later. OK?'

Abdul didn't respond.

Mallory thought he understood and stepped back as the taxi turned around and drove away. He watched it as his thoughts turned to Tasneen and what he was going to say to her. He looked for Stanza, who was already halfway towards the US Army checkpoint, and then down at his grubby hands covered in cuts and abrasions. He felt his broken nose and attempted to clear his nostrils but they were too blocked with either dirt or dried blood.

As Mallory walked on deliberately slowly so as not to catch up with Stanza he contemplated his immediate future. There was nothing else for it but to head home, and as soon as he could. Tasneen was the only reason to hang about and frankly that looked more of a non-starter now than it had before he'd left for Fallujah. He couldn't go on with Tasneen without telling Abdul anyway, which she probably wouldn't want. As for Stanza, Mallory thought it best to avoid him too. The journalist was no doubt confused about one or two things, especially the sudden appearance of a million dollars, and Mallory wasn't sure if he should try and explain it to him. He decided ultimately to leave any decision-making until the following day and to sleep on it. Things might make more sense once he was cleaned up and rested. It had been a long day, to say the least, and at the end of it he was thankful to be alive.

Abdul sat in the taxi, staring into space as it cruised through the streets of his city that was already waking up. Since seeing Stanmore's severed head he had been trying to retrace every thread of the story from the night of the kidnapping to the point where his motivation became a quest to rescue the hostage in order to cleanse his soul. He had obviously drawn several wrong conclusions about his own role as well as those of various others and was still having difficulty interpreting Allah's overall plan. Allah must have disapproved of Hassan killing the American's Iraqi lover but that did not necessarily mean that He approved of Abdul executing Hassan. Abdul had obviously failed to see how he would have been no different from Hassan had he killed Mallory for the same reason. Fortunately for Abdul as well as for Mallory, Allah had intervened in time. And if Mallory was not meant to die then neither was Tasneen, something Abdul was hugely relieved about. He was going to need help sorting it all out and the first and only person who came to mind was Tasneen. She would figure it out with him. He would have to tell her everything, though, from the night Lamont had been kidnapped to the present. He thought it best not to tell her about his plans to kill her. He would have to tell her how he had nearly killed Mallory, but then, if he did that he would have to say why and then she would suspect that he had also planned to kill her. Honour killings for such reasons usually included both parties. Perhaps he could gloss over the attempted execution of Mallory. It might not affect the story all that much. The important part was about Lamont.

Abdul was feeling strangely better. Just the thought of having Tasneen to talk to again was a tonic. She was wonderful – although not entirely so, of course. Abdul would have to tell her that he knew about her and Mallory. That would put her on the spot but she deserved that much of a punishment. That was fair, he thought. She couldn't get off completely free.

Mallory closed his hotel room door, picked up his two backpacks and, looking clean and fresh despite a swollen nose and tiny scabs all over his face, marched down the landing towards the emergency stairs. He had not been to sleep but a long hot shower followed by a swift cold one and a change of clothes was almost as good. The salts in the water had revealed a dozen more cuts and abrasions, some of them requiring plasters, but apart from a few bruised ribs and the nasty bump on the back of his head he'd fared pretty well, considering everything he'd been through.

He noticed Stanza's door was open slightly and carried on past it, praying that the man would not come out at that moment. He suddenly thought of his relief who was going to turn up to find a most bizarre atmosphere indeed.

Stanza sat in his chair, staring at his desk where the bundle wrapped in its soiled cloth rested. He hadn't noticed until he put the bundle down and sat in the chair that fluids had been leaking from it and had dried into crusty scabs all over his hands and lap where it had rested throughout the taxi ride. He had been unable to bring himself to go into the bathroom and clean up. He felt drenched in despair, not only for Stanmore but for himself. The last twenty-four hours symbolised his life of partial achievements. He'd gone to Fallujah to bring back Stanmore and had returned with only a portion of him.

He tried to think of a single moment during the last month when he'd been in control of his destiny or his purpose on this earth and couldn't come up with one. He couldn't blame anyone else, either. When he thought of Mallory or Abdul nothing remotely flattering came to mind but he couldn't honestly reproach them. There were some questions he'd like answers to, though. Parts of his adventure had been so surreal that he wasn't sure if they had actually happened. If Stanmore's head hadn't been sitting there, leaking on his desk, he might have doubted whether that part of it too had been real.

He wondered what to do with it. It obviously had to end up back in Wisconsin but it wasn't really the sort of thing that one boxed up and took on a plane. Bureaucracy needed to be involved. The embassy was the obvious choice. He could look for that prick Asterman and give it to him.

Stanza sighed. This had to be the lowest point of his life.

There was a knock at the door which he thought he had imagined until a voice called out his name. 'Jeff? You in there? It's Aaron . . . Aaron Blant. The *Post*.'

'It's Jake, you prick,' Stanza wanted to say. But he didn't speak or move.

Blant stepped into the corridor, leaning forward until he saw Stanza sitting in his chair. Then he froze, momentarily horrified by Stanza's condition, caked in dirt and scabs. 'You OK, Jeff?'

Stanza raised his red-ringed eyes to look at him.

'I came by last night but you were out . . . I might have a fixer for you . . . You sent an e-mail.'

Stanza looked away without acknowledging the man's presence.

'You OK?' Blant asked again.

Stanza exhaled heavily.

Blant put his hand on Stanza's desk and into a puddle of viscous liquid. He quickly withdrew his fingers, unsure where to wipe them. 'I guess you heard about Lamont,' he said as he realised the offending liquid was leaking from the stained bundle.

Stanza blinked.

'Did you see the video? They released it yesterday. Cut the poor bastard's head off two or three days ago.'

Stanza rolled his eyes and sighed again.

Blant noticed Stanza's scabby hands and lap. 'You sure you're all right? You don't look so good.'

Stanza looked at his palms and thought he should wash them.

'OK, well, I'm gonna go,' Blant said, holding his sticky hand away from his clothes and looking forward to getting to a sink. 'If you need anything let me know.' Blant sniffed the traces of a foul smell in the air and his nose led him back to the bundle. He looked at Stanza, about to say something. Then he changed his mind and left the room.

Stanza got slowly to his feet, opened the balcony doors, walked outside and looked out onto the city. It might still be an interesting story, he thought. He'd clean up, make himself some coffee and start writing.

And he wouldn't tell Patterson until he'd filed it. *That* was a reaction he would look forward to. Stanza felt strangely confident – or, more to the point, fear-less. There was nothing anyone could do or say to him now. He had been through a test of fire and had emerged the other side cleansed in a way. But it would remain to be seen what he had become. He was different, though: he knew that much.

Then it stuck him. He wasn't going to write a news story. He'd write a book. That was his future. He'd tell the world the whole story from beginning to end – his story, his beginning – including all the characters and their roles in his life. Screw the *Herald*. He'd stay in Iraq on the *Herald*'s tab, researching all he needed. Then he'd fly to some remote island and write a goddamned book.

He felt better already.

Des pulled the car over to the kerb outside the depar-ture terminal of Baghdad International Airport where several sniffer dogs were playing with their handlers and took the engine out of gear. 'Well, me old cock. 'Ave a good flight.'

'Thanks for the lift.'

'No drama, me lad. You survived the BIAP for another day. Now all I 'ave to do is survive the trip back.'

'When are you home?'

'Another month. Might 'ave a couple more clients by then. Would yer be interested in working for me?'

'Same job?'

'Sure. Lookin' after media twats. Not brain surgery, is it? As long as we don't lose any. Trick is to scare 'em into not going out the 'otel. And when they're feelin' brave give 'em a bit o' food poisonin'. Yer know t'routine, lad.'

Mallory grinned as he held out his hand. Des took it in both of his and gave it a good shake. 'Mind yersel', yer mad bastard,' Des said.

'You too.'

Mallory opened the passenger door and was about to climb out when Des grabbed his arm. 'There 'e is, the bastard. At it again.'

Mallory glanced at Des and then in the direction he was looking. A short Arab in a smart, expensive suit was dragging a suitcase on wheels away from an immaculate black Mercedes sedan towards the departure lounge entrance, followed by two men who looked like bodyguards.

'That's Feisal, from the Ministry of whatever, the bloke in the 'otel I was tellin' yer about. The one who takes money to Dubai every coupla weeks. 'E's off again . . . Not a bad job, eh?'

They watched until the men had entered the terminal and exited from their thoughts. 'So long,' Mallory said.

'Be seein' yer, mate.'

Mallory took his bags off the back seat, closed the car doors and waved as Des drove away. He shouldered his bags and walked over to a couple of security guards and a sniffer dog.

A few minutes later Mallory walked into the

departure lounge, a large hall with a vast polished marble floor and vaulted ceiling. He looked over at the Iraqi security personnel guarding the entrance to the check-in hall, which was not yet open. A line of people had already formed in front of it, though, a mixture of Arabs and westerners. There were only a couple of flights that day: the others had been cancelled due to the battle that was still raging in Fallujah only thirty kilometres away.

Mallory could not be bothered to join the line and found a seat which he plonked himself down into tiredly. There were rumours that the flight might be cancelled anyway and if so he'd sleep in the airport until he could get a later one. There was no heading back into Baghdad for him, not until he had decided what to do with himself. He had two options as far as he could see. He could rejoin the Royal Marines and continue with his military career, or he could stay in Civvy Street and make as much money as he could doing the security-adviser malarkey.

When he considered returning to Baghdad he could not help but think about Tasneen. He'd spoken to her that morning but she'd whispered that she could not talk for long. Abdul had come home in a bit of a state, physically and mentally, and she needed to be with him. Mallory understood and told her he'd call her at work in a day or so. He didn't tell her he was leaving the country and that his next call would be from the UK. Abdul obviously had not yet told her about Fallujah and the money in the cemetery. Mallory decided to leave it all up to fate. Whoever was organising that show certainly had a good sense of humour.

The security guards at the gate seemed to be getting ready to open it. Mallory glanced around at the people converging on the line, suspecting there were more bums than available seats. Feisal appeared with his two burly bodyguards and joined the line. Mallory found it amusing that they had only one suitcase between them and the boss was carrying it. Life was unfair if nothing else. Mallory had gone through hell to acquire and then lose a million dollars and this guy simply walked into a vault once a fortnight and helped himself.

Mallory got to his feet and decided to take his chances with the flight. The opening of the security gate did not necessarily mean the flight was on but it was an indication that the airport still believed it was.

As Mallory joined the back of the line, Feisal and one of his bodyguards walked over to the ticket counter to talk with a member of the airline staff while the other minder remained in the line with the suitcase. The entrance doors to the concourse opened and a large group of men marched in with much bustle and fanfare. They were a mixture of Iraqi police officers and suited ministerial officials and they made a direct line for Feisal. As they surrounded him a boisterous row erupted. Feisal's accompanying bodyguard was dragged aside and the bodyguard who had remained in the line immediately went to the aid of his boss.

The shouting attracted the attention of everyone in the concourse, including airport security guards who unslung their weapons from their shoulders, wondering what was going on. Feisal clearly said something to one of the officials that was less than appreciated: the temperature of the fracas went up tenfold as Feisal's jacket lapel was grabbed. This provoked one of Feisal's minders to grab the grabber, which had a domino effect with everyone seemingly trying to grab a piece of Feisal and his minders. A punch was thrown and then a gun appeared, held high in the air in the centre of the mêlée while hands struggled to reach for it. Inevitably, a shot rang out and the hall erupted in screams as passengers dropped to the floor or ran for the doors. Security guards in various parts of the vast terminal converged on the hall and the pandemonium increased when they started aiming their weapons in a threatening manner, shouting warnings at anyone who looked remotely suspicious. A shot went off outside, fired by an overexcited guard, and was immediately followed by a dozen more that were fired by other guards infected by the excitement.

Mallory crouched behind a planter, just in case. His gaze fell on Feisal's suitcase where it stood in the middle of the hall alongside other luggage belonging to passengers who had been in the line.

Mallory was not sure what inspired him to get to his feet, pick up his backpacks and march through the chaos, stepping over prone passengers until he reached the suitcase, pick it up and walk away with it. Perhaps the dangers in the hall were minuscule compared with what he'd been through during the past twenty-four hours or perhaps it was nothing more than a moment of uncontrollable madness. Whatever the reason, Mallory continued on through the hall, fearing that he might be grabbed from behind at any moment. But as the cacophony continued behind him his confidence increased and, fighting the urge to look back, he walked past a food kiosk and into a public toilet.

The large noxious room was empty and Mallory continued on into one of the disgusting cubicles, closed the door and placed the suitcase on the rim of the foul seatless toilet. He realised that his heart was pounding in his chest and that adrenalin had been coursing through his veins: he fought to control his breathing so that he could listen to tell if anyone had entered behind him. There was no evidence he had been followed.

He reached for the latches on the side of the suitcase. Amazingly, they were not locked and he raised the lid to see rows of bundles of US banknotes wrapped in cling film. A random inspection of one bundle revealed it to be all one-hundred-dollar bills and Mallory fought to control himself. He was on the cusp of walking away with a fortune but also of spending a long time in an Iraq jail that he might not survive. The next few minutes would be crucial. He could not help doing a quick calculation and, experienced in such matters, came to the delightful conclusion that he was in possession of significantly more than one million dollars, probably closer to two.

It was time to speed up. Mallory opened his backpacks, emptied his clothes into the top half of the suitcase and placed the bundles of money into the packs. When he had got them all inside he could stuff only a couple of T-shirts back into the packs, which he strapped up. He opened the cubicle door a little, checked that no one had come in, grabbed his spare clothes out of the suitcase which he left on the pedestal, tossed the clothes into a broom cupboard, pulled a backpack onto each shoulder and walked out of the toilet.

A commotion was still going on in the hall, although it had calmed down a little when Feisal and his men were taken away. Mallory walked across to a stairwell that led down to the baggage-claim and arrivals hall. Once again he became uncomfortably nervous about being followed but as he left the bottom of the stairs and walked into the vast hall that was practically deserted everything seemed relatively quiet. His confidence increased as he headed through a set of double doors, strode past a couple of guards to whom he nodded hello and walked out into the bright sunlight. There was no traffic on the terminal road as Mallory crossed it. He entered the vast underground car park that was practically empty.

Mallory did a quick recce of the dark cavernous structure and found an even darker and more secluded corner beneath one of the massive ramps that led to the floor above. He put down his bags and took a series of deep breaths while he came to terms with what he had just accomplished. It was almost too much to believe and he had to open the top of one backpack and inspect one of the bundles to convince himself that it had really happened, pulling open a corner of cling film to feel the crisp new banknotes. The joke of it was that he was where he would have been had he successfully brought the money back from Fallujah. He now had to figure out how he was going to get it out of the country. It was a phase of the operation that he had resisted planning originally in case it jinxed everything but there were some potential pitfalls with this final leg that were obvious.

Flying the money out would be a problem since luggage searches could be quite thorough, not just in Baghdad but also in Amman. Mallory would never be able to explain away that amount of cash and there was every chance that it would be confiscated. Driving it over a border was probably the best option but not right then. It was far too dangerous and he would lose more than his money if he was stopped. It might end up being a case of finding a secure place to hide it and then getting it out when things calmed down. For the moment the best thing to do was head back into Baghdad, get a room at the Palestine or Sheraton Hotel and take his time coming up with a plan. A pleasant prospect that immediately came to mind was getting together with Tasneen again. Perhaps he could talk her into coming to England with him, or France or Italy or Spain, any of the places they had talked about. He could certainly afford the bribes for visas and so forth. A broad smile spread across his face as he thought how fortunes could change so quickly.

Mallory thought about calling Kareem but risking the BIAP with just one driver for security seemed like a pointless gamble. He told himself to start thinking minimum risk again, a basic rule of his profession that he seemed to have discarded somewhere on the road to Fallujah. As he pondered the problem several heavy engines gunned to life a few rows away and he walked out from under the ramp to investigate. The throaty noises were coming from several matt-black-painted muscular-looking vehicles belonging to the same *Mad Max* PSD team that had shot up Stanza. They were getting ready to move out and Mallory grabbed up his bags and headed towards them. He was certain they would give him a ride into Baghdad for a price. A few thousand dollars should buy him a seat.

The adventure was not yet over but Mallory had a good feeling about it. Perhaps Abdul would take part in it now since circumstances had changed. Mallory suddenly wondered what it would be like having him for a brother-in-law. Now *there* was something to think about.